Blood Dragon

Book Three of the Blood Trilogy

Katie Scarlet Edwards

Paperback ISBN: 979-8-9994871-5-5
EBook ISBN: 979-8-9994871-4-8

Dedication

To my friends and family, thank you for being there for me.

I would also like to thank anyone who picked this book to read. I hope you enjoyed it as much as I enjoyed writing it. Please leave a review on whichever platform you purchased or borrowed it from.

Did you know that very few readers leave a rating but for every new review (good or bad) an author squeals their delight? Reviews help your favorite authors gain visibility. Please do your part to help make them successful.

If you are interested in learning about upcoming books feel free to reach out to me at katiescarletedwards@gmail.com

Table of Contents

Prologue

A docile Nikolas waited beside his sister in the deep forest. Penelope shifted from foot to foot while Nikolas remained still. His face was devoid of emotion, and his jaw hung slack. A slight rustling had Penelope spinning to peer through the dense Norway spruce that covered this side of the Alps.

An impeccably dressed tall blonde man emerged from the trees. His pace was unhurried as he joined the trail Penelope and Nikolas had taken to reach this destination. Penelope watched the man closely, her father may trust the Fontaines, but she had her reservations. However, her father insisted she meet this vampire to acquire information, so that is what she is doing.

"What news do you bring?" She called out to the pale vampire.

Andre Fontaine leisurely approached the twins. Penelope showed her hand with her nervous fidgeting; clearly, she had heard of his family and believed the stories. Fantastique, he thought, it is always best to have the upper hand in these situations. Nikolas on the other hand had not even flinched on his arrival to the designated meeting location.

Andre gazed inquiringly at Nikolas. The man's features showed no acknowledgment that he had even noticed Andre's arrival. Slack jawed with eyes staring vacantly ahead as if he were seeing a different scene than the majestic beauty of the Alps. His hands hung loosely at his hips with the tiniest amount of tension showing.

"What is wrong with your brother, ma Cherie?" Andre asked. "He seems to be a bit out of sorts."

Penelope glanced at her brother and as if a command had been sent his jaw snapped shut. "Nothing is wrong, he is just tired. Isn't that correct Nikolas?"

"Yes, just tired." Nikolas' deep voice replied in a monotone lacking all emotion.

A sharp laugh burst from Andre. "It is true then. The rumors about the two of you, hmm, how fascinating." Andre watched Nikolas for a few more minutes then turned back to Penelope as if dismissing the beast of a man from his mind. "Tell your father that my brother has located the object we need. He shall be traveling to America soon to collect it."

"What is this object and how will it help my father's plans?" Penelope asked.

"That is of no concern to you at this time." Andre admonished her. "Once Marcel has returned with the object, we will send a communiqué through the usual channels." Penelope noticed a slight pause in Andre's patter when he referred to the object leading her to believe the object may in fact be a person rather than a thing.

"Of course." She responded. "Is there anything else you wish me to convey to my father?"

"Oui," Andre answered. "My sorciere wanted me to impart the following to your brother." Andre looked askance at the emotionless man standing beside Penelope. Impatiently she made a move along gesture with her hands. "La douleur du monde ouvrira votre esprit et votre cœur. Do you have any idea what she would be mean by this?"

Penelope thought for a moment but could not fathom what Andre's witch meant. "The pain of the world will open your mind and heart. I do not have a clue as to what that could mean in relation to my brother. However, I shall pass it on to my father as well; perhaps he knows something that I do not."

Chapter One

Cassandra

My day started out as any other day would. I woke early, refreshed from dreamless sleep, ate breakfast, did a little exercise then went to work for the Council. In my one hundred and thirty-two years, I'd never once dreamed. At least not one I remember. My mother said it was highly unusual for a witch not to dream. I don't know if the same could be said for vampire-witch hybrids, it's not like I had a handbook or anything.

Sadly, I also didn't have many friends that I could ask. Very few people took the time to talk to me let alone become friends with me. Most feared my power even though I had only used it purposely in service to the Council. A small shudder ran down my spine when an image of my mother's pained face popped up before I could quash it. I forced the image to the deepest regions of my mind then walked into my kitchen.

My kitchen was utilitarian to say the least. White walls, stainless steel refrigerator, which I regretted, I should've gone with the white one. Your average four burner stove, sparse counter and cupboard space and a small table with one chair. I was not the best cook except when it came to breakfast foods and usually ordered out for all other meals.

My breakfast was a hearty one, four eggs, eight slices of bacon, hashed browns and a tumbler of blood. My appetite was always a surprise to others considering how thin I am. My powers burn through my energy, so I learned many years ago to eat sizable portions before work. My superiors at the Council informed me the night before that two high profile shifters were brought in, and I would be interrogating the male this morning.

After an hour in the gym and pool I returned to my rooms to shower. I stood in front of my mirror debating on what to wear. I am tall for a woman, standing at five foot eight inches barefoot. Average breasts and a thin stomach tapered down to hips that had just barely enough curve to not be considered boy hips.

I pulled on jeans and a dark purple blouse, today felt like a purple day, then yanked on my favorite black leather boots. The mirror approved; silver hair, bright green eyes, rosy cheekbones that kept my pale skin from looking washed out. Good enough to interrogate a shifter, at least

My route to the cell block is mostly empty. The people that I do encounter either would not meet my eyes or in a few instances came to a complete stop and fled in the opposite direction. I sighed.

There were days I wished I didn't have my power. Or at least that Almerinda was here. She was one of the few amongst the Community who did not treat me like the plague. I always felt that she was a true friend; unfortunately, she was not always around for me to spend time with.

There were a few a few others who did not shy away from me. The vampire-shifter female, Aisling, always took the time to talk to me and make me feel like a normal person rather than just the Council's weapon. Jasmine, a witch who was always with Almerinda was another.

The guard noticed me before I noticed him. He immediately rose to attention. He gave me a quick summary of who was in the cell. A shifter of some sort, no one knows what type. He was under several spells that the Council had not been able to break yet. He was brought in with his sister who had been moved back out this morning.

The guard showed a little confusion about her immediate removal since the Council had instructed the night guard that she was to interrogate them both. I had not been told about the sister when I received my orders. The Council needed any information about who and what he was that I could extract from him.

I like this guard. Jeremy is a vampire and has been in the Elite Guard for almost four hundred years. He did not fear me, having worked with me since I came to the Council. He knew I would never use my powers on him or anyone else unless the Council required it. We had built a work friendship over the years, I always asked about his mate, another guard who worked in the field. He always tried to get me to come out to meet more people.

After a quick catch up with Jeremy, I stepped through the door he held for me. The interrogation room was grey, walls, floors, table and chairs, all grey. Not even different variations of grey, all the same shade.

Sitting at the, you guessed it; grey table was the largest man I had ever seen; he had to be at least seven feet tall. Each arm was the size of my whole body. He was such an impressive specimen that I felt a flush spread through my body from just looking at him. He had black hair, chiseled cheek bones, strong nose and cleft chin.

I took a hesitant step back; concern crossed my features. I needed to get my mind in the game. I could not allow his superb looks to distract me from my job. When he lifted his head and opened his eyes, I felt a peculiar tingling in my stomach.

I stared into the eyes of the man I was sent to abstract information from. Deep brown like fresh soil flecked with green that swirled as he watched me. I've never seen eyes like his before. He sat with his expansive hands clasped in front of him, mutely meeting my gaze with startled eyes. His unfocused sight suddenly became clear, and an abrupt clarity filled it.

I noticed the change in his lucidity a second too late. I could feel his consciousness take control of my mind. I was being drawn down a dark path into what felt like the depths of his soul.

One moment I was staring into his swirling eyes. The next – cold stone crunched under my boots, a scent of minerals hung thick in the air. Bright colors of light swam in front of my half-closed eyes. My vision cleared, I stood in a cavern. A pool of pink water in the middle and him, shirtless, water sluicing over scars and muscles that made my throat go dry.

The beast of a man with raven black hair sat in the pool, the water lapping at his bare abdomen. The same man who, just moments ago, was fully dressed and whose head was bowed in defeat, mind you, I thought. An arm the size of a tree trunk lifted from the pool, beckoning me to join him.

Unable to stop my traitorous feet I walked to the edge of the water. Just as I reached the rocky border of the underground pool, I gained a modicum of control. With great effort, I halted my forward progress.

"Who are you?" I whispered.

The man came to his feet, water running down his tapered muscles revealing a very prominent staff. Once again heat suffused my body as my gaze caught and held on his naked form. As he moved toward me, I saw a flash of purple and green on his back. My feet skittered backwards from the rim of pink water.

"What are you?" I couldn't have seen what I thought. Shimmering, unnatural, like a lizard's skin, but beautiful.

The man walked closer to the water's edge. "I am yours and you are mine. You have released me from darkness. I am now in the light."

His hand lifted once more beckoning me to join him. My feet began moving of their own volition, carrying me into the cool waters and his fiery embrace. Our lips met in a scorching kiss and my mind opened to him fully.

One hand crept to the nape of my neck and the other snaked around my waist. He pulled me tight against his hard chest as he broke our sealed lips apart. Anchored to his rock-hard body, he stared deep into my surprised eyes.

"Are you real?" His deep voice sent shivers down my spine. His eyes held mine captive. "Tell me, are you real?" He demanded gruffly.

I was unsure of his meaning, but I knew I was real, although I wasn't sure if what was happening was real. I held his gaze firmly, slowly nodding yes. Fire smoldered in his unusual eyes as his lips descended upon mine again.

A swirling sensation engulfed me, and I felt the water turn turbulent. When I opened my eyes, the cavern walls were spinning around me. Snapping my eyes closed again, I allowed my senses to be overwhelmed by the man currently plundering my mouth with his tongue.

This felt like what dreams were supposed to be, not that I had anything to compare to. The imposing man in the pool of water had my ideal looks for a man, so clearly this was just a wonderful and highly sensual dream.

The air changed around me. No longer steamy and humid, it was now clear and cool with a slight breeze. I opened my eyes just as the man broke the kiss once more. Shock rippled through me as I looked at my new surroundings. Yep, this definitely had to be a dream.

The landscape rising all around me was out of a hallucination. Trees the size of skyscrapers rose out of the ground, at least I believed they were trees. The bark was black and what looked like leaves were purple and blue instead of the greens I was used to.

The sky was a blue so dark it almost looked like night, but an orange sun was hanging brightly in the middle. Another planet with three crisscrossing rings also shined in the sky to the right of the sun. I stood on a cliff edge with the man and stared in awe at a body of rose-colored water below. Pathways crisscrossed through the dense trees that rose higher than the cliff edge.

A rumbling bass voice spoke into my left ear. "You are not dreaming. We are in my world now. You opened my magic and freed me from my sister's control."

I whirled in his arms, taking a step back. Confusion swamped my features; the man was fully clothed again and was standing entirely too close for comfort.

"We're what?" I squawked. My eyes darted at the unusual scene around me. I shut them firmly, trying to block the weird colored trees from my mind.

I rubbed my eyes then opened them to see the same vista with the odd colored trees, sky and water. Gigantic birds or something birdlike flew off in the distance too far for me to clearly make out their size and species. The sun glinted off their bodies in sparkling brightness.

Stepping closer, his deep voice rumbled right next to my ear, causing a shiver of want and desire to run down my back. "I said we are in my world now. Who are you?" The dangerous man asked me.

"I'm Cassandra. I was sent by the Council to get information out of you." I explained quickly then asked. "How did we get here?"

"You work for the Council?" A threatening tone entered his voice. I considered felling him with my power but had no desire to make an enemy of the one person who may be able to get me back to reality. Although I still wasn't entirely convinced this wasn't a dream. I eyed the towering beast of a man with trepidation.

"I would never hurt you." He attempted to reassure me. "I could never injure my mate."

"You're what?" I screeched again. What in the hell was wrong with me? Since when do I screech like a freaking banshee?

"Surely you feel it." He insisted. "The minute you entered the grey room I felt the pull. I knew with all certainty as soon as my sister's control slipped from my mind."

I stared around in disbelief, a wave of dizziness washed over me. When I swayed on my feet, the man reached out to steady me. Misinterpreting his intentions, I shied away causing my high heel to catch on a protruding rock.

I felt myself falling backward and heard a loud bellow of no from the man. The edge of the cliff was much closer than I had realized, and the trajectory of my fall propelled me right over the edge. The wind rushed by me and the last image I saw before everything went black was a beautiful emerald and amethyst dragon soaring over the cliff after me.

Chapter Two

Arianna

Over a thousand years and I still had nothing to show for all my efforts. Gods, a thousand years, and what did I have? A mate who snarled more than he spoke, children who'd slipped into his shadow, and a bond that felt like a chain.

My mate was a vicious asshole that I spent as little time with as my bond would allow. The only bright spot had been my children. The birth of Penelope and Nikolas had been a celebratory day for all dragonkind. The females had such high hopes that they would finally find a mate. Once Nikolas had reached maturity every known female had been presented to him. Unfortunately, not one of them had mated with him.

I took it in stride though, knowing that the true strength of the dragons came when they mated with other species, such as me and Fraxinus. My mind wanders back to that fateful day on the field of battle. I woke early that morning to join my coven in the dubious task of closing two portals. I wholeheartedly agreed with closing the door to the fae realm, but I had misgivings regarding sealing off the dragons.

I had been rushing to meet my coven when a sudden pounding had erupted in my head. The throbbing abated if I followed the direction, I felt my feet being pulled. Any attempt to deviate and continue to the coven meeting caused an unbearable stabbing through my brain.

With no recourse available, I found I was unable to go anywhere but along the path of least resistance. I arrived on the edge of a great battle between a few hundred fae and about twenty dragons. It appeared the dragons were gaining the upper hand as more fae fell to the ground unmoving.

A beautiful sleek bluish green dragon swooped low to attack a fae. It had not seen the three other fae lying in wait. I called out a warning, but it was too late. The three hidden fae rose up and, using their magic, hurled jagged boulders into the dragon's exposed soft underbelly.

A roar of pain and fury erupted from the dragon's mouth followed by the earth shooting up through the fae. The fae writhed in pain impaled by the spikes created by the earth dragon. Screaming with hate, their deaths were not easy. Sadly, the injuries the dragon had sustained appeared to be death blows. I stared in horror as I watched the dragon crash to the ground.

I turned to leave and felt the stabbing pain in my head again. The draw I had been feeling pulled my body towards the fallen dragon. A large man entered the field a little off to the left of me. I watched his approach warily but held my ground. He paid me no attention as he walked past me to stand over the fallen dragon.

The man sighed forlornly as he stared down at the form on the ground. I gasped as the dragon changed into the spitting image of the man standing over top of it. The man asked me for assistance in getting the body from the field. I could still feel a faint spark of life coming from the fallen dragon; however, something told me to remain quiet. We pulled the body off the field. The huge man advised me he was Hawthorne, the fallen man's brother and had hoped to return him to their realm.

A loud crack erupted from the sky causing us both to jump. The coven had completed the spell to close the portals. Hawthorne wailed in anger and despair then turned and spat on his brother's inert form. He leaned over and checked for a pulse, finding none he spoke harshly to me.

"Leave him or bury him, I care not. His selfish actions have trapped me in this world."

With his final pronouncement, Hawthorne strode away, not looking back. I watched his plodding gait for several minutes before I thought to leave as well. The instant I tried to move away from the man on the ground I felt the stabbing pains again. Clearly, the Fates required I do something with him.

Bending over, I placed a hand on his forehead and recited a levitating spell. The man's body lifted into the air and followed me as I returned to my home to decide what to do with him. Upon entering my house, I placed his massive body on my diminutive bed, his legs falling over the bottom edge, his feet resting on the floor.

An hour later, I still sat by the bedside, unable to move away due to the pain I would feel if I tried to leave his side. My gaze returned again and again to his hawk-like nose and sculpted cheek bones. My hand jerked back from his cheek when his eyes snapped open, brown flecked with jade and utterly aware. The bond settled over me like a wave, a tranquil clarity settled my racing mind. I had found my mate, and it was a dragon.

Centuries had dulled that first spark. Now all that remained was the ash of his temper. Our years together weren't all horrible. Fraxinus could show kindness and the first couple of hundred years together was quite blissful. On rare nights, his laughter would shake the cliffs and for a fleeting moment, I'd forget the monster he became.

But as time passed and we failed to produce offspring, the seething rage I always sensed just below the surface boiled over more frequently. We began spending fewer days together, often not seeing each other for months or years at a time. Then a little over four hundred years ago, Fraxinus came to me with news. He had found the solution to our fertility problem.

Davina, the head of our hidden society, knew what ritual needed to be performed if dragons hoped to have children. I was ecstatic and agreed to visit the island where Davina was living. Our arrival on the island was met with hope from its inhabitants. If we were able to successfully produce offspring, then there was a chance for the rest of the dragons too. Davina had two talismans from the dragon's home realm and combined with the ritual we should be able to have children.

No matter how many attempts we made, we were only able to produce one pregnancy. Fortunately, twins were common in Fraxinus' family, and I happily gave birth to Penelope and Nikolas a year after our arrival on the island. We remained together until Nikolas came of age. Fraxinus had placed so many expectations on our son and when they failed to occur, he became more sullen and angrier. Fraxinus dragged Penelope into his madness. She did her best to pull Nikolas into their schemes as well. Once again, I was alone, losing my children to my mate's devious plans.

Now, I had to tell my mate the news that had reached me just this morning. There was no telling how he would take it. Ever since his twin brother had been captured by the Council and Alistair's experiments had failed, he spent most days moping around the island in his dragon form, refusing to communicate with anyone. Penelope was the only one who could usually get him to shift back to human form. Now, if the news was correct, she was gone and who knew how Fraxinus would react.

The scent of moss dragged me back to the present. I found him, as usual, in his dragon form on the western side of our little island. When I entered the lush green clearing, he barely lifted his head in acknowledgment of my presence.

"Fraxinus, I have news, and I need you to shift so we can speak since you have closed your mind to me."

Fraxinus lifted his mammoth scaled head a minuscule amount from the moss-covered ground. His green flecked eyes gave me a baleful glare before sliding closed again as he lowered his head back to the ground. I grit my teeth in consternation. He was such a stubborn asshole.

"Fine, if you're going to ignore me, I won't tell you the news I received of your children."

I pivoted on my heel to leave the clearing. A loud growl emanated from Fraxinus' throat. I peeked over my shoulder. A green smoky shimmer had enveloped Fraxinus' dragon form and now a giant of a man stood in its place.

"What news?" His growl was just as menacing sounding in his human form as it was in his dragon form.

I took a small step back before steeling myself against his intense glare. I dug my nails into my palms, prodding my body to not flee from him. Now that I had his attention, I almost wished he had refused to change.

"Frax, I have received news that Nikolas has disappeared out of the Council's headquarters with a vampire-witch shifter. The informer was only able to say that she went in to interrogate him and several hours later they were both gone from the room and no one had seen them leave."

Fraxinus' joyful bellow shocked me to silence. "Good." A grin split his face, all teeth, at my confused look he explained. "Nikolas must have mated with the woman. The boy has finally served a purpose."

I bristled at his reference to our son in such a way but knowing the rest of my news decided to remain silent. "I have news of Penelope too. She is also missing from the Council's captivity." Fraxinus perked up even more at this statement, but I held him in check with a raised finger. "However, I fear that she may not be safe. The report I received indicated that she was being taken to Luis."

Fraxinus roared with displeasure at this news. "I expect you to find her immediately." He paced angrily toward me, fists clenched at his side. "Drag her back by her hair if you must." He growled, glaring down his nose at me, his brown and jade flecked eyes swirling madly.

His glare hit me like a physical blow. I forced my feet to root to the earth, even as my pulse screamed to run. "I am not the one who sent her on this foolhardy mission, Frax. Plus, even if I did find her, she would never return under my orders, she only listens to you."

Stiffening my shoulders, I stalked away from my mate. Turning my back on him was difficult, his temper was unpredictable, and I never knew what could come my way. Not once in our centuries together had he struck me, however uprooted trees from his temper tantrums had come close.

I muttered a protection shield as I continued my trek across the clearing. "Find her yourself." I yelled over my shoulder. The moss swallowed my footsteps as I fled – from him, from Penelope's recklessness, from the weight of a thousand years of mistakes.

Chapter Three

Cassandra

My eyes slowly opened as my mind came back into focus. Never in my life had I had such a vivid dream, or any dream for that matter. I stretched my body and relished the feel of the soft blankets cuddling me. I inhaled deeply, the air crisp and clean. The sound of birds chirruped outside my window. A feeling of peace had me burrowing deeper into the mattress.

Wait a minute, I thought as my eyes sprung open. Where was the smell of the city? Birds outside my window? When has that ever happened? My inner peace was replaced by a touch of nerves.

As my eyes came into focus my surroundings began to make less sense to me. Above me were purple and blue leaves, a dark sky and worried brown eyes peered down at me. A squeak escaped my lips as I tried to move away from the face looming above me.

"Don't be afraid." The man's deep voice begged me. "I won't hurt you."

I held my body still as my mind filled with memories that were apparently not a really interesting first dream. "What happened?" I asked in a voice barely above a whisper.

"You freed me." He answered with a shrug and a smile.

"I think I need more information than that." I replied with a little more steel in my voice. His simple answer aggravating me more than I expected.

"Of course." His gentle smile, melting my irritation. "I am not entirely sure which part you are inquiring about, but I will do my best to answer what I know."

As if unable to stop himself, he reached his brawny hand to touch my cheek. When I didn't flinch away a sly smile spread across his face. Heat spread along my jaw bringing a blush to my cheeks. I pulled my face away from his hand, needing the separation to refocus my mind.

"My name is Nikolas, up until yesterday I was under my sister's control. My memories of the last fifty or so years are very fuzzy and jumbled. I do know that you released her hold on me and for the first time in a very long time I feel like my mind is my own."

"Why would your sister need to control you?" I asked. Probably not the most important question I should be asking but it was the first one to pop into my head.

"Because I did not agree with her tactics and as her twin, we were stronger together, so she needed my strength to bolster hers."

"For now, I suppose that answer will have to be enough. We shall revisit your sister's motives at another time." I moved away from Nikolas and sat up.

I stared incredulously at my surroundings. The two of us were lying on a four-poster bed plopped down in the middle of a field of purple grass. Consternation crossed my features as I tried to make sense of the view before me. Rising out of the purple grass were more of the monumental black trees I had noticed from atop the cliff. A pink lake lay off in the distance, and I still couldn't fathom why a bed was sitting in the middle of a field.

Nikolas cleared his throat; he watched my face turn from awe to confusion. "Perhaps I should start further back than just yesterday?" My baleful glare prompted him to add, "There is much you do not know about our world."

I shifted my body further up in bed and rested my back on the headboard. My neck was getting stiff from sitting in bed. I turned my attention back to Nikolas. "How about you start with what you are and move forward from there?"

His grin softened his fierce features causing a ripple of desire to pulse through my private parts. Gods, was it hot here? I squirmed on the bed, 'get yourself under control,' I berated myself.

Nikolas' grin grew wider as he felt my desire for him through our mate link. "Of course, my heart, I shall do my best to answer any and all questions you have." His rugged hand clasped my tiny one it. "I am one of the last male dragons in the human realm. Until yesterday I was the only unmated one on the other side of the portal."

I gaped at him. "How can that be? The dragons were closed off centuries ago."

"Just because the portal was sealed does not mean there were no dragons left on the other side of it. My father mated with a witch just as the portal was sealed. It took them many years, but they eventually found what was needed to produce

16

offspring. Unfortunately, they were only able to have one successful pregnancy. My sister and I are twins, which are very common in my family. And as is also common amongst the twins in my family, we are often at odds with each other. My father was also a twin and from the stories he has shared, he and his brother did not bond either."

Nikolas drew small circles on the inside of my hand as he continued speaking. "You are high in the Council, correct?"

"I was not Council, but I worked for them." Pulling my hand from his, I tucked it underneath my buttocks. "I knew many of the secrets because I was the one who extracted them from those trying to keep them. However, I was not a Council member and did not have any part in the decisions made."

"Having knowledge of many of the secrets than, you must have known of Hawthorne?" I gave a slight nod in answer. "Hawthorne is my uncle. He and my father had a falling out many centuries ago. My father was the cause of that rift."

As Nikolas spoke, I felt his muscles tense the more he talked about his family, especially his father. While he spoke, I continued to marvel at my surroundings. On first look, I had thought the tree's bark was black, on closer perusal I noticed there was variations of black and dark grey within the bark. The leaves and grass were beautiful shades of blues and purples, some dark violet, some as pale as periwinkle. The best part of this world, though, was the aromas from the forest. Everything smelled so clean, no pollution from gas engines or garbage. Just the scent of the forest around us, a mix of juniper, lilac and the tang of citrus.

"My father hates his brother out of jealousy. Hawthorne was first born and would have ruled our home world if he had not been trapped in the human world. When my father learned of the plan to close the portals, he tried to trap Hawthorne within the human world and return to our world and lay claim to the kingdom. His plan failed when he was brought down in battle by several fae as he was trying to get through the portal."

"That was over a thousand years ago though." I stammered, his words bringing me back from my awe of the scene around me. How long did dragons live? I asked myself.

"Centuries." Nikolas answered as if I had asked that question aloud.

"Apparently private thoughts were negotiable now." I mumbled. Nikolas' sly grin was the only answer he gave me.

"Are you saying Hawthorne was a dragon king?" I twisted my fingers together, what could this mean for me? Was I mated to a dragon prince? "The same man that has been held captive by the Council for over two hundred years, that Hawthorne?"

"Yes, he was. My father and sister have been trying to free him for almost fifty years." Nikolas advised me. "As much as I would like my uncle to be free, he cannot be given into their clutches. My father believes that if two sets of twins were to unite their powers than he could open the portal to this realm again." Nikolas spread his arms wide, indicating the strange land around us. "Normally mating releases the power to open portals but for whatever reason, his mating with my mother did not give him that power. I think that is why he despises her so much. However, when our souls combined in that grey room, I felt a surge of new powers open inside me. If you look inside yourself, you will probably discover something new too."

I turned my mind's eye inward and found that he was correct. I could sense a strengthening within me that was not there before. I would have to spend some time investigating these changes once Nikolas finished his tale. With a small smile I requested for him to continue.

"I am not against the portal being reopened. I just fear that my father's reason for doing so is not as altruistic as he claims."

"Why does he say he wants the portal opened?"

"He says it is so dragons can be reunited with their loved ones on the other side. But like I said, my father only ever looks out for himself, so that public reason is bogus." Nikolas relaxed back onto the headboard beside me.

While we sat there, the bed groaned under us, then morphed into a comfortable plush couch. "Sorry," he apologized when I let out a small squeak of surprise. "I conjured the bed for our rest, but it was becoming too uncomfortable to sit on. I felt this would be better."

I bent my head in acquiescence. "It is, that hard headboard was beginning to chafe. Thank you." Nikolas smiled again, sending my heart stuttering in my chest.

My Gods, if only his smile does that, I can't wait to actually feel his lips on mine again. Now where did that thought come from? "Please continue." I requested dragging my mind back to the matter at hand.

"My father only wants power and will do anything to get it." Nikolas added with a sly grin, obviously he had picked up on my inappropriate thoughts. "Fortunately, he mated with a woman who does not seek power just to have it. My mother is a kind and caring witch who has thwarted many of my father's plans over the centuries. He has no idea she has worked against him though."

"My father is also the reason my sister turned out the way she did. She is cruel, sadistic and single-minded when it comes to reaching her goals. I believe if they had successfully opened a portal they would have killed me, and my father would have tried to rule through her. She has not found a mate yet so would be allowed to rule while searching for him." Nikolas stared into his lap as he added, "He tried to make me like him too, but fortunately my mother's influence was stronger for me."

"Wait, how is your mother alive? Witches don't live centuries." I interrupted again.

Nikolas shifted closer to me as he answered. "When a dragon mates with someone their longevity is shared with their mate. The only drawback to this is if a dragon's mate is not a dragon, such as you are to me, then the mate will also die if the dragon dies. I tell you this for two reasons. One because we are mated and you need to know should something happen to me; you would also perish. Two because I believe this intertwining of life forces is why my mother has never tried to kill my father."

I leaned my head on the back of the couch and closed my eyes in silent contemplation. Nikolas' story was quite compelling. It would seem I had mated into some type of Shakespearean tragedy. Mother hates power hungry father and the princess was a psychopath leaving the poor prince sad and lonely. A soft chuckle pulsed from Nikolas' tightly sealed lips. I glanced at him to see him struggling not to laugh.

"What?" I demanded.

"I am not a sad and lonely prince." Nikolas tsked then made an oomph sound when I jabbed him in the ribs with my very pointy elbow. "Careful, love. Mated minds are terrible at keeping secrets. Also, I doubt I would be considered a prince any longer. My father has been missing from this realm for over a thousand years."

"Who rules this land now?" I asked. A loud rustling noise erupted from the trees to their left, almost in answer to my question.

19

"I have a feeling we're about to find out." Nikolas raised one eyebrow then beckoned for me to stand up. The couch disappeared once we were on our feet. A few moments passed and I had just started to let my guard down when several men and women entered the clearing from all sides, effectively surrounding us.

Chapter Four

Aisling

Breaking into Council headquarters was not exactly on my bucket list of things to do before I die, and yet here I am. As a vampire-shifter hybrid, I have worked for the Council, mostly alongside Almerinda, for almost a hundred years.

Until recently I was content to follow the commands I received without question. Right up until my oldest brother, Cillian, uncovered information that led him to believe things weren't exactly as they should be within the Council.

Cillian was killed and my brother Evan started investigating why. My fists clench and my breaths come in jagged gasps; I need to get myself under control. We caught his killer, but that just led to more questions. I take a few calming breaths then focus on the foul-smelling sewer system I am currently traversing.

My feet have brought me to the grate that opens into the lower levels of headquarters. Taking another moment to center myself I think about all the lies we were told. Over two hundred years we believed Hawthorne was the monster behind the experiments. Turns out he was just the assistant, and one of the last male dragons. The Council's lies ran deeper than we thought.

The man who led the experiments was killed a few years ago by Penelope (I'll get to her in a bit). The story told by the Council is that the dragons were forced back into their realm over a thousand years ago and no living dragons remained in our realm. This is false; there is a community of mostly female dragons living on an island near Greece and in Central America.

One other thing Hawthorne imparted was that hybrids are not a new species and existed up until the Fae Dragon wars occurred. After the wars ended and the portals were all sealed between this realm and the Fae and Dragon realms, the majority of the remaining species began to isolate themselves from each other. When that happened, interspecies mating came to an end, therefore no more hybrids.

Our foray into the mountains of New Mexico didn't exactly end the way we had hoped. Hawthorne was free and we had found all the objects our dear departed brother had hidden. Now we needed to return those objects to a group of people run by a woman who may have spawned the devil herself.

I am now speaking of Penelope, newly dead, but knowing all the atrocities she had committed over the years didn't make me want to speak well of her just because she was dead. Penelope and her twin brother Nikolas are dragons, and according to Hawthorne most likely his niece and nephew.

They are also the ones who held and tortured my brother, Evan. We believe Nikolas was under several controlling spells cast by his sister, so my judgment of him is still out. Penelope on the other hand proved many times over that she deserved the end she received at the hands of my younger brother Cormac.

I grab the grate and pull my body up to it. Bracing my feet on notches along the tunnel, I poke my head into the grate's opening. I don't sense anyone on the other side, so I slip the grate open, and move it to the side. I climb into the hallway and replace the grate. I look down and notice I'm leaving wet, sludgy footprints. I need to hurry this little break-in along.

Evan, my older (and favorite) brother, decided to take some time to be alone with his new mate. Alessandra or Ali as she preferred, rolling her eyes when Evan used her full name. I liked her immediately, anyone who could put my brother in his place was okay with me. They met after Evan had disappeared for several months. She was a nurse who worked at the local hospital. He was dumped by someone, to this day we still don't know who, in the ambulance bay of the hospital.

Ali helped get him cleaned up just before he escaped from the hospital. He then tracked her back to her apartment and like a crazy stalker broke into her place and somehow convinced her that not only was he her mate but that the supernatural world was real. I got to witness some of this so-called courtship and even I am amazed at how he was able to get Ali to fall in love with him.

Happily, two of my brothers recently mated. Cormac, our youngest sibling, and Jasmine returned to the family homestead in Oregon to share their happy news as well. I wish Jasmine was at my side here at headquarters rather than at home with my brother.

Jasmine is a formidable witch. Her reputation keeps many people at bay and would make sneaking around the Council offices much easier. However, she and my brother deserve some time to cement their mating before we all have to jump back into a possible fight with the Council, the fae, the dragons or all of the above.

22

I just wish our eldest brother Cillian had been alive to witness all this. On this unhappy thought, I need to get my mind back on the task Almerinda set for me. Fortunately, Almerinda is on our side. She is now probably the oldest vampire on earth. Her maker, Luis, was killed by a vampire named Elodie.

There is something different about Elodie but only a few people seem to know what and those that do (my brother Evan being one of them) have been sworn to secrecy by Elodie. When she killed Luis, Almerinda inherited Luis' holdings. Due to a spell, he had placed many years ago, she also gained control of his progeny.

Enough reminiscing. Right now, I need to focus on not getting caught. I peek around the corner taking a quick glance down the hallway that leads to the holding cells. I am still surprised that I have made it this far into Council headquarters without being caught. No guards? Thank the gods, maybe I'll actually get out of here undetected.

I'm here looking for clues as to what happened to Nikolas and Cassandra when she went to interrogate him. Since I am supposed to be on the other side of the country right now, enjoying some much-needed downtime with the family, I have to sneak around like a thief in the night. Almerinda thought it best that we not alert the Council of my arrival or why I am here.

I slinked down the hall, clutching the walls as if that would hide me from anyone in this place. Reaching the interrogation room without incident, I slip inside. The room is bare except for two chairs and a table, all of which are grey metal. Gods, what is it about governmental type agencies and grey furniture?

I walk to the center of the room and place a small object in the center of the grey steel table. Sending a quick text message to Jasmine; I sit down on the floor and wait.

After almost five minutes I'm about to text her again when a sudden flash of blue light emits from the object. I open my camera on my phone and begin recording. My wide eyes track the activity in the flickering light in front of me. The clear images became fuzzy about half-way through.

About twenty minutes pass and the light fades. The object on the table has disappeared. I can't say for sure what I saw, hopefully someone else can see past the blurriness. Maybe my sister Saoirse can dig into it on her computer, she is better at new technology than I am.

I close my camera app and pocket my phone. Moving to the door, I cracked it just enough to look down the still empty hallway. Good, my path is clear, no one has noticed my intrusion. I steal into the hall, letting the door snick noiselessly closed. Now, I need to make it back out of the building without getting caught. Wish me luck.

Chapter Five

Arianna

The moment Fraxinus' wings disappeared over the horizon; I summoned my coven. We had perhaps hours before his return. Six people arrived within thirty minutes of my call. Over the centuries, I have worked alongside these six people to thwart as many of Fraxinus' despicable plans as I could. Once our twins were born, he let his guard down around me again and I saw what he planned to do with them. I knew I could never allow him to succeed so I recruited this group to help me.

A month after the birth of Penelope and Nikolas, Fraxinus and I were lying in bed together. For the first time in almost five hundred years, I could hear his mind. I listened without letting him know I was aware of his thoughts. Gods, how his thoughts horrified me.

When he woke and saw me watching him, he mistook my look for one of lust. His mind remained open to me as he kissed his way along my jaw line and slowly pulled me into his arms. I probed deep into his thoughts all while faking pleasure in his arms. As his cock penetrated me, my moan was not of pleasure but disgust.

His lust quenched, he withdrew his member, believing I had enjoyed the act. As usual, not one for cuddling, he rose from our bed and went to get a shower. I lay in bed, my hands gripping the sheets, forcing the bile back down. If his mind was open to me then my mind was also open to him. I was going to have to be extremely careful with my thoughts any time he was near.

The memory still scorched my mind, that afternoon, four centuries ago when his thoughts spilled into mine. Our bed had become a shrine of deception, his touch no longer appealing to me. As his plans unfolded in my mind, I knew I would do anything to stop him.

"Thank you all for coming, I have news." I announced as soon as everyone was settled. We convened in my small living room. The windows were open to allow a fresh breeze in, and the balmy air curtailed the goosebumps that had formed after my chilling meeting with my mate.

Fraxinus thought we were just friends, never believing I would work against him. My coven of seven, twelve would have been better, but I only trusted this select few, all came to attention as they awaited my news.

My coven included three witches, two vampires and one dragon. The witches were daughters of the first three witches I approached after hearing my mate's plans. Their mothers had imparted the knowledge of his plans to them before they died almost a hundred years ago. Malina, Temperence and Diana had listened to their mother's stories and immediately agreed to continue their work with me. The three had been raised together and were the best of friends.

The two vampires and the dragon have been by my side since I approached them four hundred years ago. Matthew and Annie Pappas are mated vampires who live on one of the sister islands. We became close friends and later confidants, when I learned of Fraxinus' plans they were the first people I told.

They agreed that he needed to be stopped and suggested that I also include Davina in our group. I worried about bringing her into the fold due to her position as leader of the dragons. Matthew and Annie assured me that Davina would be on my side. Their assurances were well founded, and we have worked for years to curtail as much of Fraxinus' plans as we could.

What I heard and saw that fateful morning was his intention to use my children, especially Nikolas, to reopen the portal to the dragon realm. If that were all, I would have endeavored to help him achieve his goals. It was what he wanted to do once he got the portal open that caused my revulsion. I always knew Fraxinus had a cruel side, I just never realized how truly evil it was.

His plan was to return to his home realm, not as a savior but as a conqueror. He had been working with Luis, one of the first vampires, and a family of psychopathic vampires out of France; to not only open the portal to the dragon realm but also to the fae realm.

By unleashing the fae on the dragon realm, he intended to enslave any dragons who opposed his rule. Dragons and fae have been enemies for as long as anyone can remember. Dragons are usually stronger and able to fend off any attacks from the fae. However, a sneak attack such as what Fraxinus was planning would cost many lives and possibly allow the fae to overwhelm the dragons.

Fraxinus only cared about one thing and that is having power over others, especially those he believed had wronged him. His grudge list read like a

Shakespearean tragedy; his brother for being born first, his parents for refusing to upend tradition, an entire realm for failing to bow.

Hawthorne and his mate came through the portal to try to bring Fraxinus back to the dragon realm before the portals were closed. When they all became trapped on this side, Fraxinus began plotting to kill Hawthorne and his mate. He joined with the Fontaine family and Luis and eventually they managed to catch Hawthorne unawares.

Unfortunately, Hawthorne's mate was killed. I wasn't sure if Hawthorne had survived the attack until about two hundred years ago when Fraxinus let it slip that he was working with Alistair Reynolds, creating hybrids. I expected he would try to kill him again, but he did not.

I learned from my daughter, Penelope, why he let him live. Penelope was much like her father; Nikolas was more like me. She followed Fraxinus everywhere and hung on his every word. She craved power and had a cruel streak just like him.

One night, after years of silence, she finally condescended to eat dinner with me, she told me about Hawthorne. I believe she only shared their plans because I was not showing enough awe over how impressive she thought she was. Fraxinus had heard a tale from one of the older dragons in our community that told of twins being able to open sealed portals.

The storyteller insisted that two sets of twins from the same blood line could amass the same power that a mated pair did and then they would be able to open the portal. According to Penelope, when the time was right, she and Nikolas would bind with Fraxinus and Hawthorne to open the portal again. They just needed to find a witch strong enough to perform the spell.

A cough from Davina brought my mind back to the present. My coven, my friends, all looked at me expectantly. They must have seen Fraxinus' departure. A sight none of us had seen for over a hundred years. I began the meeting by conveying the news I had recently shared with my mate as well as his reaction.

I scrubbed my hands down my arms, warming them again. Every time I encountered my mate, I left feeling entirely too unsettled. "I believe that Nikolas must have mated with Cassandra. His mating must have allowed him to open a portal. Whether that portal was to the dragon realm or just somewhere else on earth, I cannot say."

"What about Penelope?" Diana: the petite, barely reaching five feet and plump as a butterball, witch questioned. Her dark brown almost black eyes and pitch-black hair giving her the look more of a modern vampire depiction than a witch.

"As you may have noticed, Fraxinus recently departed our island." I glanced out of the window currently flanked by Matthew and Annie. "I may have led him to believe that our daughter was in trouble and could be saved if he acted quickly. At this moment he is rushing to try to get her back from Luis. What I failed to impart to my dear mate," a derisive laugh escapes my throat, "is that Penelope was killed by one of the children of the O'Brien clan."

"How could a vampire-shifter of their lineage kill a dragon?" Temperence rose to stand to her five feet seven height, confusion showing in her sea foam green eyes. Her long bright red hair swished in the breeze from the window. Her muscled arms twitching with the nerves she was trying to suppress.

"I only know that the youngest O'Brien somehow managed to overpower her." I answered, a pensive frown on my face. I too wondered how he was able to kill my daughter.

"Perhaps he had some assistance your informant was unaware of." Davina supplied, always the pragmatist. One of the reasons is she had been a close confidant for so many years.

"Be that as it may, if he had not killed her, I believe that Luis would have as she fell into a trap he had laid for her." My voice hitched, and I cleared my throat before continuing. "By the by, Luis is also dead, although I am unable to determine how. My informant was not present for his death and only knows that he has been dealt with accordingly."

Annie, a tall impatient woman with flowing black hair and deep bronze skin spoke up. "Does this mean Almerinda commands his progeny?" Her mate, Matthew, stood to her side staring through the window. Their resemblance was so alike that people often thought they were siblings rather than lovers.

"I believe it does. I am sure that old fool never revised his spell, probably believed she would never truly turn on him." I replied.

Malina giggled in a rather girlish way for such a tall woman, standing just shy of six feet. Her short cropped blonde hair vibrated with the motion and bright blue eyes twinkled. "Men, no offense Matthew, but how many centuries must we watch men underestimate us?"

28

Matthew shrugged, after seven hundred years with Annie, he knew better than to argue. Matthew hailed from the Americas before they became America. Annie had been one of the original vampires and had met him on a walkabout around seven hundred years ago. When they met, he was called Lalawethika. After they mated and he joined her here, he changed his name to Matthew and adopted her surname

He gave his mate a sardonic grin. "I was one of those idiots at one time until I met my Annie. She set me straight on the power of women."

Annie stretched up to place a quick kiss on his cheek. "It did take you a few years to fully learn though." She bestowed an adoring smile on her mate before bringing her attention back to our group. "I am sorry about Penelope, Arianna, you have my deepest condolences."

I gave a curt nod to the group as everyone murmured words of sympathy. "While I appreciate your words, I lost Penelope years ago when she fell too far under Fraxinus' influence. Honestly, I am not sure I ever really had her. She was always so much like her father, hungry for power no matter who she hurt to get it. Including her own twin." We fell into silence for a moment, each of us lost in our own thoughts.

"So, Davina, any thoughts?" I asked, jarring the silence. "With what I described, do you believe my son may have met his mate in Cassandra?"

"If as you say, they disappeared from a locked room and no one saw them exit, I do." Davina answered after a few minutes of careful consideration. "Only a mate would be able to break the spells his sister had used on him. Also, he never had the power to open portals before. If there was some way for me to see the portal he opened, I could tell you where he opened it to."

"I unfortunately do not have any way to show you." I answered unhappily. "I think it may be time to reach out to Almerinda and the O'Brien's. The reports that have gotten back to me say that they have freed Hawthorne, killed Penelope and Luis, and rid the world of Dimitri and Desiree. We need more allies if we hope to stand against Fraxinus, the Fontaines and whoever else he may work with to try to complete his goal."

"I agree." Davina stood and walked to stand in front of me. "Albeit I do not think you should be the one to reach out to them. They have probably discovered that Hawthorne is not the father of your twins. They may not feel comfortable talking to the mother of the people who held and tortured one of their own."

"As usual, Davina, your wise council is correct." I answered with a rueful smile. "So, who should we send as emissary?"

Chapter Six

Aisling

"The Council headquarters heist went smoothly." I spoke quietly into my phone. "I have video for review and will be on the next plane home in about..." My voice trailed off as a sudden shift in the air, followed by an airport announcement that made me pause.

"What's happening, sis?" Evan grumbled through the phone line.

"Shush, I need to listen." I retorted. The announcement repeated itself. *Due to unforeseen weather circumstances, all flights are grounded. Please remain calm, we will update as soon as we have more information.* Well, fuck! Unforeseen weather circumstances could only mean one thing; a witch is causing problems and that means I need to get out of here ASAP.

"Listen, Evan, I have to get out of here. I believe a witch has tracked me here. I'll call when I've lost them." I abruptly ended the call in the middle of whatever he was saying.

I scanned my immediate area for anyone either watching me or purposely trying to look like they weren't watching me. Seeing neither of the two, I followed a large group of men and women towards the counter.

I looked out the floor to ceiling windows of Philadelphia International Airport onto the tarmac. A heavy and thick fog had rolled in on what was supposed to be a clear and sunny day. People were pressed against the windows staring in awe at the sudden appearance of the fog.

The fog was clearly the work of a witch with a strong affinity for weather. I wracked my brains trying to think who in the Council had this type of power. After a few minutes of thought, it came to me. Aubrey, she was a young witch who had been recruited a couple years ago. Hmm, what does she look like?

Yes, I thought, an image of her popped into my mind. She was short, a little on the heavy side, brown hair, and always wore the same damn converse sneakers. Those bright blue and green ones that if I remember correctly, I had seen not too long ago on a woman wearing a nun's habit. Now what concourse did I see her in?

I snuck up behind Aubrey. I had found her three gates away from my departure gate. I had to stop her spell, when the fog that came in out of nowhere suddenly lifted there would be pandemonium in the airport. Hopefully, I would be able to escape much easier in the chaos.

She sat in a row of seats with two other women also wearing nun's habits. One clearly a vampire, with their translucent skin, the other I was unsure, some type of shifter maybe. Not another witch though. Well, damn, there was no way for me to reach her without having to deal with her friends. So, I guess, onto plan B.

I searched my surroundings, weighing all options when an idea came to me. I looked around the sitting area until I found the perfect patsy. Armed with a small amount of guilt and a vast amount of hope that my idea would work, I approached my tool. The young woman sat with her head bowed, reading a book, seeming unconcerned with the delay of her flight.

"Excuse me." I nudged her shoulder causing her to look up sharply. I put on my best scared face and leaned over. "Could you help me, they won't let me go."

Her face hardened for a moment before smoothing out. "What are you talking about?" She asked quietly, matching my low tone.

"My parents sent me to a school to straighten me out." I used air quotes around straighten me out. "I escaped and now they found me." I pointed at the three fake nuns. I stuttered my words in the best simulation of a scared girl that I could muster. "They hate that I am a lesbian. I begged my parents to let me come home. The school is more like a cult. They beat us to make us repent our wicked ways." I finished.

Anger flashed in the woman's eyes as she took in my counterfeit fear. "Do you need money or something?"

"No, I have money. My parents are rich and didn't notice that I stole a bunch of money from my father's safe before they shipped me to the school." I shuddered as if the idea of either stealing from my parents or the school caused fear in me. "I just need a distraction so I can get out of here. They must have found me when I bought my ticket. I'm so stupid; I should've known my father's reach would have found me." I gave her my best scared innocence look I could.

"I can cause a distraction for you." She gave me a slightly evil looking smile before standing up. "Leave it to me."

32

I smiled in thanks and slowly backed away from her. Her pins on her backpack are what drew me to her. 'God is Dead' 'My Body, My Choice" and a rainbow pin with LGBTQ Pride on it. But the best was her shirt that proclaimed, 'I survived the cult of DJT". I don't follow human news close enough so I am not sure what the cult of DJT is but figured she was not a fan of cults so my fake story would rile her up.

My wingman, or girl, wing-girl? oh whatever, approached the three fictitious nuns and immediately began haranguing them about how evil they were.

"You have no right to imprison people for who they love!" Her voice rang loudly through the terminal. Murmurs washed over the crowd as everyone turned to see what the commotion was. Cell phone cameras were opened as people readied to record whatever new incident was happening.

Her tirade continued about how wrong they were to try to control other innocent people just because they didn't agree with their choices in life. She was on a roll, that's for sure. More people rose from their seats to see what was happening; a few even looked like they wanted to join her in yelling. Security was called; and the young woman converged on my three foes.

The smell of burnt coffee was beginning to override the sandalwood scent of magic. I glanced over my shoulder to see the witch flanked by the two Elite Guards become surrounded by the growing crowd. Essentially, I got the chaos I needed to make a hasty retreat.

My legs were itching to run, but I walked through the airport with an unhurried gait. I didn't want to draw any attention to myself. Keeping pace with the slower moving humans around me went against my instincts to race as quickly as I could away from the three who were sent to capture me. However, I didn't know if they were the only ones looking for me.

I ducked into a Hudson News and quickly grabbed a baseball cap, hoodie and sunglasses. Paying with cash, I sped out of the store and put my new purchases on. The sunglasses rested on top of my hat, wearing sunglasses inside was a quick way to draw attention to someone trying not to be recognized, but I wanted to appear like a tourist.

My eyes darted left and right, my fingers beat a constant choppy rhythm on my legs. Thank gods, I could see the exit ahead of me. With one last look over my shoulder, I escaped the airport onto the departures sidewalk. I lucked out on a taxi just emptying its occupants. I walked up to the driver just as he set down the last piece of luggage from his trunk.

"Are you available?" I asked while my eyes continued to sweep for Elite Guards.

"Yes, ma'am, just as soon as I pass these bags off to their owners." He tilted his head to the open back seat door. "Go ahead and get in, I'll be there in just a sec."

I gave him a smile of gratitude then climbed in the backseat. I slouched low in the seat while waiting for him to get in. He finished his business then came around to climb in the driver's seat. "Where to?"

There was only one safe place in Philadelphia, and I dreaded going there. "Um, I guess, the Bellevue Hotel."

The taxi smelled of falafel which set my stomach to grumbling. As we pulled away from the airport, the unforeseen fog dissolved like cotton candy in the rain. Either my activist friend had broken the witch's concentration, or they realized their prey had escaped. Someone would be answering for that failed ambush today, just not me.

I opened my phone and called my brother back. He answered before the first ring even finished. "What happened?"

"Unexpected complications, I'm in a taxi heading to the Bellevue. I'll call back when I get to my room." I ended the call, not wanting to say much more in front of a random taxi driver.

The taxi's vinyl seats squeaked under me with every bump in the road. We veered east toward 95, the taxi driver hollered through the plexiglass divider. "Somethin' goin' on at the Logan, gotta shoot out to 95 to avoid the mess."

I nodded with a smile and rested my head onto the taxi's headrest. The stench of sweat wafting off the cushion had me lifting my head back up immediately. About twenty-five minutes, and many potholes later, later we pulled up in front of the Bellevue. I paid the taxi driver, giving him a generous tip and slid across the cracked vinyl to get out of the car.

A Bellevue Hotel porter opened the back door. "Good afternoon, Miss O'Brien."

I gave him a small smile. It would seem Evan had called ahead for me.

"Hello, John, how are you today?" I gave him a cheeky smile.

Per usual, John's jaw worked like he was chewing on words he'd never say as he settled for a nod that barely moved his chin. He was always a man of few words. One of these days I would get him to smile. Goals, gotta have goals.

The Bellevue Hotel was built over a century ago by a family of wolf shifters. The hotel had predominantly human customers, but the top two floors were always held for supernaturals passing through that needed a place to lay low. The Council was aware of this location but would never trespass or cause issues with the owners.

The Collier Pack was not one anyone, including the Council, would ever want to anger. With over five hundred pack members spread up and down the entire eastern coast of the North American continent, they were the largest and most disciplined pack of shifters in the world. Coming here would make me safe from the Council, although once I stepped foot off the property, I would be fair game again.

John handed me off to Silas, a much more talkative wolf shifter, and returned to his post out front. We bypassed the front desk and headed straight to the elevators. Sometimes it was nice when your brother called ahead for you.

"Hello, Miss O'Brien. We have readied the blue suite for you. Currently there are two others seeking refuge here. We would appreciate if you would refrain from entering the top floor while you are staying here unless invited by its occupants."

I agreed as we entered the elevator to take us to my floor. Silas placed his thumb on a scanner inside a small door he then motioned for me to do the same.

"Please place your thumb on the scanner so we can key your floor and room to your DNA." His request sounded more like an order.

I placed my thumb on the scanner. A light glowed for a moment then a sharp prick took a small sample of my blood. Sticking my thumb in my mouth, I sucked the blood from the end.

"Good, now only you will be able to access your room." Silas informed me as the doors slid shut cutting off the quiet jazz that had been playing in the lobby.

We arrived at my floor and Silas preceded me out of the elevator. This floor only had four doors to four different suites. Red, blue, green and yellow doors greeted me. I stepped up to the blue door and placed my thumb on its scanner. The door snicked open, and I entered with Silas following behind me.

"I will send Emily to your rooms in a few hours. She can help you obtain anything you may need while you are here. Please take some time to compile a list.

35

Also, Evan has requested you call him once you are settled. Room service is available twenty-four hours, and the kitchen is well stocked if you choose to cook as well as with fresh blood. Is there anything else you have need of, Miss O'Brien?"

"Is Michael in residence?" I asked hesitantly.

Michael Collier is the leader of the Collier Pack. Many years ago, we had a hot and wild fling that ended amicably. He met his true mate a couple years ago. We remained friends, but his mate was not as friendly. She was always at his side, as a mate would be expected.

When Michael and I had been together, we both knew it was temporary until one or both of us found out mates. We enjoyed our time and had no hard feelings when it ended. Blair, his mate, did not see it the same way. She always viewed me as competition and could not understand how he and I could remain friends after the years we spent together. She was a young human, only twenty-two when they met. She still had many of a human's sensibilities having only been a shifter for about ten years.

"He is not in residence at this time." Silas answered, interrupting my memories. "I believe he is in Toronto at the moment and won't return for several months."

"Good, I would hate to upset Blair by being here." I answered impishly. "Perhaps you could send him a message though?" I asked hopefully.

"It would depend on the message." Silas answered with a cautious tone.

"I promise I am not trying to start problems." My defensive tone caught his attention. "There are issues brewing within the Council. We do not know who all is involved. It would be to his benefit if he were to contact my brother Evan. As I am sure you are aware, with Cillian's death, he is now head of our family. We may need assistance from the Collier Pack."

"Of course, I will pass that on to Mr. Collier when I call in my daily report to him. Will there be anything else, Miss O'Brien?" I told him no and Silas showed himself out. The door closed quietly behind him.

Alone, I wandered the hotel room, performing a quick search. Then, I pulled my phone from my pocket and dialed Evan again. "Hey brother, I made it to my room in one piece. I asked Silas to have Michael call you. If he's not already aware, it might be a good idea to clue him in."

"I agree, however I already asked Brian to apprise his brother of everything that has happened since my abduction." Evan responded. I could hear my family in the background and for a short moment allowed myself to miss them. Evan continued, "Michael has always tried to remain neutral to interspecies politics. Unfortunately, that may not be feasible anymore if the prophecy Damian shared with us is true then his pack will be affected as well."

The prophecy a witch seer told him about a little over ten years ago seemed to point to Cassandra and Nikolas. 'Our savior sprung from the root of a sickened tree, with pain at his side they will stave off the impending hordes.'

"You're right, it's probably better for him to hear all this from Brian. So, what about me? I can't stay hidden in this hotel indefinitely. I have video of Nikolas and Cassandra's disappearance." I paced around the opulent room already feeling penned in.

"You won't be there for long. I need to confirm something first but if what I have heard is correct than the person you need to show that video to is staying in the Bellevue right now."

"Really, Almerinda or Jasmine is here?" I asked dubiously, a tinge of hope in my voice.

"No, they're both still out here on the west coast. We've heard that an emissary from the dragon stronghold arrived at Dulles Airport and rented a car. We have Saoirse working on tracking down information right now. She tracked the car to Philadelphia but is still trying to determine exactly where the person went once they arrived in the city. We expect it was there since it is neutral territory for supernaturals, but she hasn't confirmed yet. Once we know, I will call you. For now, rest up and be ready."

Chapter Seven

Cassandra

The people surrounding us did not look happy to find strangers in their woods. Every muscle in my body coiled tight, vampire instincts screaming at the circle of hostile faces. Nikolas' warmth beside me, our bond, kept me from bolting or attacking. That was something I was going to have to get used to. I never thought I would mate with one of the Council's prisoners. Yet here I was mated and accepting it like it was nothing to be concerned about.

My focus reverted to the men and women around us. Nikolas grasped my hand in his, strengthening our connection. *Say nothing and most especially do not use your powers.* I heard his voice in my mind as if he was speaking out loud.

I acknowledged his I'll call it a recommendation not a command even if it did sound like a command with a slight nod. A faint chuckle echoed through my head, my lips quirked. Damn mate bonds. Apparently, sarcasm translated perfectly. We'll have to discuss that later too.

A man almost as towering as Nikolas stepped forward. His intimidating scowl rested first on me then on Nikolas where it remained. "Who are you and how did you come to be here?" A voice like a grizzly bear rumbled out of the man's clenched jaw.

Nikolas brought his free hand to his forehead then to his heart and sunk to his left knee pulling me down with him. A look of surprise rushed across the man's face before quickly being replaced with his scowl again. "Answer me." He growled, breath hot against Nikolas' face.

Keeping his head bowed Nikolas answered. "I am Nikolas, son of Fraxinus, nephew of Hawthorne and grandson of Magna Quercus." The men and women around us erupted into a loud roar of denials at Nikolas' declaration.

"You lie." The bear sounding man condemned. He pulled Nikolas roughly to his feet. A woman, not much smaller than the leader, grabbed me and pulled me up as well. "We shall take you to Profitis Magda. She will find the truth."

Ropes were produced from bags and quickly secured around our wrists. I tested the strength of them and found that even my vampire side could not stretch them. For a moment I wondered what they were made of but the jab in my back prodding me forward broke my inspection.

I stared around in awe as we were marched to see whoever this Profitis Magda was. The Profitis part sounded more like a title than a first name. I watched my captors out of the corner of my eyes for a bit. I couldn't find any weaknesses that I could manipulate for our benefit. Other than using my power of pain, I really had no way of attacking. Since I had already agreed not to use that power, I turned my scrutiny to the scenery around me.

The captivating views kept my attention on what I was seeing rather than the possibility that Magda would be just as welcoming as our captors had been. The black and grey bark on the trees was smooth on most of the trees, every now and then I would notice markings that looked as if they were carved by a horn. I really wanted to rub my hands on it to see if it was as smooth as it looked but being bound made that impossible.

We were following a well-worn dirt road. The air was crisp; the citrusy scent I had noticed earlier overpowering everything else. I could still pick up the faint lilac and juniper smells as well, but the citrus was stronger. I inhaled deeply, if nothing else went right today, at least there was no pollution here.

As we trudged along in silence, I noticed several animals pacing us on the other side of the trees. One of the more inquisitive animals crept closer until I could make out some of its features. It was about the size of a raccoon; tawny fur covered with two dark brown ringed tails and grey eyes like saucers in an alien shaped face.

"Do not stare in their eyes too long, they can be exceedingly hypnotic. They are carnivores and lull their prey with their eyes before slowly devouring it." The woman guarding me spoke this quietly into my ear causing me to jump.

I shook myself, unsure if what she said was true or if she was trying to scare me. Either way, from that point on I kept my eyes centered on the road in front of me.

After several hours of tromping along the dirt road, the trees finally gave way to a sweeping open field. Our captors came to a halt at the edge of the field. My guard moved me to stand beside Nikolas. He moved to stand behind me, and I felt his hand touch my back. *I am here.* Nikolas reassured me through our bond.

Just feeling his hand on my back and hearing his voice in my head sent ripples of awareness through my body. My jangled nerves settled and a sense of peace

39

fell over my mind. The warmth from his hand on my back started a churning of anticipation that pulsed through my synapses in a wave of heat.

My head swirled, as my body leaned into his. The image of us back in the cavern rushed through my mind. Nikolas' naked form with me plastered to his chest caught in the searing kiss that had awakened my body to his. Nikolas' hand clamped hard on mine, letting me know he was envisioning the same scene.

A loud growl followed by a strange musical keening snapped our minds back to our present situation. Embarrassment stained my cheeks red as I distanced myself from Nikolas. With a low cough, Nikolas also adjusted his body too. Thank Gods for the weird noise that Arlien had made, otherwise who knows what we would have done in front of everyone.

Bringing my full attention to the field in front of us, I noticed a form moving towards us. As it came closer, I was able to pick out more features. It was an older woman with silver and red hair, deep lined skin and sharp amber eyes. She was hunched over a cane, however even hunched she still stood at least six foot tall. Within a few minutes she greeted the leader with a strong clear voice.

"Arlien, what brings you to my land?" The woman intoned imperiously. Arlien bowed his head in deference, the rest of his crew except my jailer went to one knee repeating the same gestures Nikolas had made.

So, our bear man was named Arlien. I would file that name away. It was always good to know the name of a possible enemy, just in case you needed to curse them later.

"We found these two intruders." The grizzly bear named Arlien answered. "The male proclaims to be grandson to Magna Quercus. I brought him to you, Profitis Magda, to ascertain his truths and falsehoods."

Profitis Magda craned her neck to look at the two of us over Arlien's shoulder. "Wise decision, if he is who he says it would not be in your best interests to handle him inappropriately."

Magda came to stand in front of me. Her gaze ran up and down my body as if inspecting me for defects. When her eyes met mine, I felt a probing in my skull. Memories I had kept buried rushed through my mind. A scream tore from my throat as Magda clawed her way through my memories. My mother's face twisted in pain came unbidden to the forefront of my thoughts.

"Stop!" Nikolas roared behind me, thrashing at his bound hands. "You may interrogate me any way you wish but do not torment my mate so."

A merciless grin spread across the lined face of Magda. She moved closer to him, breaking our connection. My mind was my own again and I fought the shudders her invasion into it had caused.

"Ah, a dragon mated to a chimera. Newly mated it would seem." She placed a gnarled finger on his forehead for a mere second. "Arlien," she barked over her shoulder. "I shall find your answers. Bring them to my house at once."

With a flourish of her hands the empty field was replaced with a small town. One moment, there were endless trees. The next, the forest melted away to be replaced by orange and yellow brick buildings. The dirt road widened and became a hard black surface. Several people moved along the edge of the road going in and out of the buildings. Smoke curled from chimneys, and the scent of cooking meat set my stomach to growling.

We were led down the center of the road to an immense house at the end. The house was made of what appeared to be silver bricks and stood two stories tall. No windows graced the front, simply a thickset black door with a small door cut into it to allow anyone to look through to see who was knocking. Magda approached the door and with a flick of her wrist it opened to allow us entry.

Don't fight them, Nikolas sent into my mind. *Please,* he added as if an afterthought. Clearly, he was picking up on my hesitation. I did not want to go into this woman's house. Having my mind plumbed like that was, to say the least, not pleasant. A quick glance at our captors told me escaping would not be easy. After a second more contemplation I followed Magda into her house.

The interior matched the exterior in its lack of charm. The black wood furniture was functional and practical with no adornments of any color or consideration for comfort. Whitewashed walls carried no decorations.

In the center of the room sat a circular fire pit with a blazing fire. No smoke rose from the fire, and I could not tell whether the fire was real or perhaps the wood here did not burn the same as wood in my own realm.

"Sit!" Magda ordered.

Nikolas and I walked to two of the black wood chairs. I moved to sit down but was stopped by Nikolas' hand on my shoulder. *Hold.* He spoke into my head.

41

Speaking out loud, Nikolas announced to the room. "Remove the bindings." When no one moved to do his bidding, he spoke again. "Profitis Magda, you have already looked into my mate's mind as well as my own. You know we do not intend any harm or mischief. Therefore, as a gesture of fairness, remove the bindings so we can meet in comfort and friendship."

Magda held his gaze for several minutes before a small smile slipped across her face. "Well, my boy, you may or may not be who you claim, but you certainly have the silver tongue of Magna Quercus."

The smile was replaced almost immediately with a haughty glare. She turned to Arlien and with a flick of her wrist indicating our bindings, ordered him to remove them, for now.

Once the ropes were off our wrists we took our seats. Magda marched around the room, pulling items out of thin air and tossing them into the fire. As each item hit the flames, sparks of different colors erupted.

As I watched her move from place to place, I realized the white walls and black furniture were an illusion. Each time her hand would grasp an object, I could see splashes of color behind the object. It would seem she kept her true home hidden from visitors. Magda finally finished grabbing things then went to stand on the opposite side of the fire from where we sat.

She raised her hands in the air and began chanting. "Apollo heed my call. Athena harken my voice." The flames rose higher and began shifting through all the colors of the rainbow. "Your lowly servant has need of guidance to learn truths and gain wisdom."

The flames leaped and dipped then suddenly shot out and encircled Magda. Ah, so not true fire at all but magical fire, no wonder there wasn't any smoke. Magda opened her mouth and sucked the flame inside her body. Her eyes grew wider, and I could see the flames swirling in her eyes. One eye focused on me and the other turned to Nikolas. I tried to block her probing, but she was too strong. Her mind pushed deep past my fore mind and dove into my memories.

Nikolas gripped my hand tightly in his and I could feel him shield parts of me while leaving his mind open completely to her probing. *Thank you.* I was not ready to face those memories again, to be honest, I am not sure I ever will be ready.

Magda roamed around in our minds for what felt like hours but was in truth only about five minutes. My body began to relax as I felt her consciousness withdraw

42

from my own. My hand still clutched Nikolas' hand; I had no intention of letting go any time soon either.

Magda lifted her arms in the air again as the flames began to leech from her body. "I thank you great Apollo and wondrous Athena for your assistance today. May blessings always be on your house." Once again, the flame rested in the fire pit and Magda turned a critical eye upon the two of us. She cocked her head at Arlien and pronounced. "He tells the truth. He must be taken to the king immediately."

Chapter Eight

Aisling

Three damn hours. That's how long I'd been pacing this gilded cage. Sitting still was not in my skill set. My hobbies didn't lend themselves to sedentary moments.

If I wasn't working for the Council or tracking rogues with my family, I tended to spend most of my time outdoors doing outdoorsy things. Although this room was well appointed and the furniture was comfortable, I would have rather been running around in the forest.

The young shifter, Emily, had come and gone. She arrived at my door about an hour after I finished my conversation with Evan. I gave her a small list of items I would need while I waited, nothing too exciting, just bare essentials.

Until I knew my next move I couldn't request any of the more interesting items the Collier pack kept available to anyone in residence. For a cost, of course. Emily had returned with the things I asked for and said she would be available if anything else was needed.

I flopped down on the plush blue couch and snapped the TV remote off the coffee table. The TV turned on to a rerun of a show called Supernatural. I love this show even if it isn't very accurate. I snorted at the screen, I mean really, vampires don't have that many teeth. Plus, ghosts don't exist as far as I have seen.

Although, I wouldn't mind Dean Winchester trying to stake me. Once again Crowley, the king of hell, was betraying the brothers and the episode was just getting into a good fight scene when I heard a loud rap on my hotel door.

I snapped the TV off with the remote, plunging the room into silence. No one was supposed to be able to access this floor without my express permission. My body went still, every sense straining. Should I answer, pretend I wasn't here or just attack whoever happened to be out there? My phone vibrated, jarring me out of my indecision.

Caller ID told me who it was as I swung the phone up to my ear. "Saoirse." I whispered into the receiver. My ears twitched as I tried to listen for movement in the hallway.

"Aisling." My younger sister, and the computer genius in our family, spoke rapidly. "Answer the door. The woman on the other side is Davina. She used to be head of the dragons on this side of the portal. She was sent by Arianna, as far as I can tell she is on our side. But keep your guard up all the same." Saoirse hung up before I could say anything in return. She had taken less than ten seconds to deliver her information.

Forewarned as to who stood on the other side of my door, I swung it open just as the woman was raising her fist to rap again. A tall blonde woman stood with her hand in the air. She lowered her hand to her side and opened her mouth to speak. Before she had a chance to say anything I reached out and grabbed her, dragging her into my room and shutting the door with a kick of my foot.

"Davina, why are you lurking outside my door?" I asked, my back leaning on the door with a nonchalance I didn't feel.

If she was surprised that I knew her name, she hid it well. Her nostrils flared slightly, probably scenting my glass of unfinished blood or the remnants of the steak dinner I had eaten. I looked the woman in front of me up and down. She was five foot eight or nine, thin but not skinny, sharp facial features and the brightest green eyes flecked with silver.

Hawthorne had explained that dragons had flecks of color within the main color of their eyes that denoted what type of dragon they were. The six types of dragons are earth, air, wind, fire, blood and spirit. Based on Hawthorne's information, Davina must be a spirit dragon since she has silver in her eyes.

A small uplifting of her lips was the only indication Davina gave of my unusual welcome. Davina glanced around my messy hotel room then returned her attention to me. "Arianna Konstantin sent me. She believes our goals are aligned and hopes we can assist each other."

I let out a small humph and raised one eyebrow, giving my uninvited guest a look of mistrust. Our information indicated that Arianna was mated to Hawthorne's brother Fraxinus. From what we could determine, Fraxinus was not exactly a good guy. We had no reason to believe that his mate would be any better.

Plus, she is the mother of the twin dragons who had kidnapped and tortured my brother. However, since we were in neutral territory, I was willing to give Davina the opportunity to change my mind.

"Let me get this straight, you want me to trust the mate of our enemy?" I spat more vehemently than I intended. My hands partially transformed, and I took a moment to calm myself, retracting my claws before continuing. "She's the mother of Evan's torturers for Fates' sake."

The silver in Davina's eyes flickered brightly for a second before reverting to their bright green with silver flecks. "You are correct; you have no true reason to trust her, or me. I can only do my best to earn your trust."

Davina strode to the center of the room and placed a small orange ball on the ground. The ball was something like what I had used in the Council's holding cells.

Witches used these types of devices to record scenes they needed to preserve or recreate scenes thought lost. They could also be used to send messages that need to be kept private. The message can't be hacked like modern technology as the device is usually coded to someone's blood. Davina pulled a small knife from her pocket and pricked her finger, dropping three small beads of blood onto the top of the orange ball.

An image of who I assumed was Arianna Konstantin began to form. Once the woman appeared to be fully there the message began to play.

"Hello, Aisling, as you may suspect, I am Arianna Konstantin. I sent this message through my friend and coven member in hopes that we may be able to form an alliance. I wish I could have come to you myself, but I am unable to leave our island without raising my mate's suspicions. I, alongside Davina and a few others, have worked for centuries to thwart Fraxinus' plans. A witch within my inner circle foresaw your stay at the Bellevue. Davina volunteered to meet with you to share as much information as she knows. I also would like to extend my condolences on the loss of your brother, Cillian. I did not know him personally but his reputation within the dragon community was well respected. Finally, please accept my sincerest apologies for the pain inflicted by my children on your brother, Evan. There is no excuse for Penelope's behavior, and I hold no animosity against your family for their role in her demise. As for my son, Nikolas, he is innocent in his actions. For almost a century he has been controlled by his sister with the use of several spells. Please take this information into consideration as you search for him." The image of Arianna bowed her head and the message blinked off.

"As nice as that was," I waved in the direction of the now defunct orb, "that does not prove anything." I snorted, allowing disdain to coat my words.

Davina glared at me before wiping it away to revert to her normal placid look. "I agree. Pretty words and flowery speech will not change the information you undoubtedly have uncovered about Arianna and the role her children have played in recent circumstances. I do not have any further proof of our sincerity." She moved to sit on the edge of the couch, her movements dainty and precise. "If you would sit with me, I will tell you all I know and then you can decide whether to accept our help or just take the information I share and send me on my way."

I watched her for several moments. My fingers drummed on the velvety arm of the couch. Davina didn't fidget, she didn't blink, she just waited like stone. Damn dragon patience. I on the other hand could not sit still. I stood up again and tromped across the room. By the time I left here, the cream-colored carpet was going to have a bare spot from all my pacing.

I spun back to face Davina, who still sat unmoving on the edge of the couch. Damn, she was good. I really didn't think I had much choice. We needed answers and she may be the only one who could get them to me right now. I opted to at least hear her out. "Fine, tell me what you know."

Davina gave me a thin smile, crossed her legs at the ankles and relaxed her shoulders almost imperceptibly. "A witch within our coven saw that you would be here and that you had obtained information that would allow me to determine whether a portal had been opened by Nikolas. If one has been, I am one of the few who would recognize the dragon realm if that is where they, he and Cassandra whom we believe he has mated with, disappeared to."

"Why you?" I asked snappily.

"I am one of the only dragons that remain in this realm who once lived in the dragon realm. A dragon must have dwelt in Fabeldyrverden to see its true nature."

"Fabeldyrverden?" I asked, horribly mangling the word she had spouted.

"That is the name of the dragon's realm." Davina explained.

"We have Hawthorne, he could confirm for us." I retorted. "So, what do I need you for?"

The thin smile that seemed to be one of the few emotions she allowed returned to her face as she glanced around the room. "I do not see Hawthorne here.

It is my understanding that the Council is looking for you and therefore the safest place for you at this moment is within the four walls of this hotel. He cannot come here, and you are unable to go to him. I am an unknown to the Council having not left my island for over five hundred years. My forged identity allowed me to pass right under the Council's henchmen undetected. So, unless you want to wait for who knows how long to find out where Nikolas and Cassandra have disappeared to, it would be in your best interest to accept my assistance."

I rose from the couch and began pacing again. I still didn't know if I could trust Davina, Arianna, or whoever else was in their coven. Unfortunately, she did have a point, for the foreseeable future I was trapped in this hotel. There was no doubt in my mind that the Council was watching the exits just waiting for me to leave so they could scoop me up. Coming to a decision, I walked back to the couch and sat back down.

"For now, we will share information. If at any time I have reason to suspect a double cross by you, Arianna or your coven, I promise you will regret it." I growled.

"Understood." She nodded at me, completely at ease as if my threat meant nothing to her. "We have no wish to anger the O'Brien family. We genuinely hope to form an alliance."

I met her tranquil gaze and saw the truth in her face. To this day, I don't know what I saw in her features, but whatever it was, it led me to believe her intentions were true.

"Will you show me the recording?" her quiet request had a pleading sound to it.

After a second of hesitation, I pulled my phone from my back pocket and opened the gallery to play the video. Davina sat forward in her seat and watched with rapt attention. She was seeing more than I had been able to. At the halfway point when my video only showed blurriness to me, her mouth popped open forming an O. Her silver flecks jumped madly about her eyes. Her hand reached out to grab mine in a death grip.

A whispered "Fabeldyrverden" escaped her lips.

Chapter Nine

Cassandra

My feet ached and my body was drained, even my vampire side was begging for a bed. Our trek through more trees and along narrow and wide paths seemed unending. We hiked for five days before finally reaching the outskirts of an expansive city. Up and down hills, through the strange black barked trees.

After Magda had made her pronouncement, Arlien and the rest of our captors had turned much more conciliatory toward us. Arlien even almost apologized for his initial treatment of us. Mind you he didn't say he was sorry, not sure the bear sized man knew that word. However, his churlishness receded and while most of the guards kept their distance, they no longer treated us like the enemy.

Nikolas had offered to change into his dragon form, something I really wanted to see, to save time. Arlien insisted that it was safest if we traveled by foot and would hear no further discussion of it. I think he was just afraid we would escape and then he would have an awful lot of explaining to do to whoever the current king was.

Speaking of the current king, I wondered what was going to happen now. If what Nikolas had said was true, then he was probably the rightful king. Would there now be a power struggle or outright fighting for the throne? Also, what does that make me? If I am mated to the proper king does that mean I have to be queen? Too many things to worry about on top of how was I going to get back to my own world?

A muscular hand clasped mine in his and I felt a sense of calm descend upon my rambling questions. I stole a peek at Nikolas' profile then found my eyes caught in his as he turned his face to meet my glance.

Do not fret. Nikolas spoke into my mind. *All will be well, I promise.* Peace enveloped my body, and I felt myself relax into the steady rhythm of putting one foot in front of the other. *You need not worry about a power struggle. After more than ten centuries since my father or uncle stepped foot in this realm, I have no claim to the throne. Nor do I want it.*

Well, that was a little unexpected. Surprisingly, his pronouncement seemed to regenerate my aching muscles. My racing brain reassured, I squeezed his hand in acknowledgment and gratitude. I can cross those worries off my list. I need only worry about how to get home now.

Nikolas chuckled quietly and pulled my body closer to his. "I will get you home safely when the time is right." His deep voice sent shivers down my spine and deep into my groin. Would I ever get used to his effect on me? I sure as hell hope not, reverberated loudly through my skull in his gravelly purr.

Now that we were no longer bound like prisoners, the female guard that had pushed and pulled me to Magda's home was less menacing. Leilei still looked fierce, but her tone had become less antagonistic. She regaled us with stories of the world around us and took the time to point out interesting, if sometimes terrifying, things around us.

We encountered several different animals, most of which I ignored due to the warnings of Leilei. For instance, the animals that look like alien raccoons were quite deadly. When she warned me not to stare at them, she had been truly protecting me from their powers.

On the other hand, unicorns are real. At least in this realm, although they are not exactly as we described them in our mythology. While they are horse-like in appearance they are gargantuan compared to a typical horse. If you can imagine a Clydesdale horse then multiply its size by about two, you have the size of a unicorn. They are pale gold in color and have different colored horns depending on the type of powers they wield.

On our third day of travel, we came across a herd of them. Arlien called everyone to a halt as they thundered by in a field to our right. The ground shook from the force of their hooves causing my teeth to rattle in my mouth and my bones to tremble. A heady musky scent wafted off the herd. For the first time in days the aroma of citrus was not the strongest smell in the forest.

A lone blue horned unicorn approached Arlien. They had what looked like a staring contest for several minutes then the unicorn blew out a breath ruffling Arlien's hair. The unicorn twisted away and struck off after the rest of the herd. Arlien announced we would camp there for the night to give the herd time to finish their business.

Leilei guffawed, startling me. "Their business?" she laughed even more and waggled her eyebrows suggestively. "There'll be some babies come spring, I would think."

I snorted as the meaning behind her words caught up to my sleep deprived brain. Our days of travel had allowed us a lot of time to become acquainted. While I didn't necessarily see her as a friend, I also didn't view her as an enemy any longer. Plus, she was the only one willing to speak with either of us.

The talkative Leilei was also very informative when it came to dragons. Which was great since I knew next to nothing about them, believing that they were either extinct or myth. I was thankful for her instruction as I needed to learn as much as possible about my new mate.

Six types," Leilei counted on her fingers, "earth, air, fire, water, spirit and blood."

"So, no mineral or vitamin dragons?" I asked with a cheeky grin.

Leilei just rolled her eyes then continued my education. "So, earth dragons have a hunter green underbelly with emerald and mint green scales. Their eyes are a deep walnut flecked with jade prisms. Air dragons have a midnight blue underbelly with pearl and sapphire scales. Their eyes are mahogany with topaz flecks. Fire dragons have black underbellies with yellow, orange and red scales. They have yellow or orange irises flecked with crimson prisms."

"Are the air dragons so dark since your sky is darker than my world?" I stared at the indigo sky above me, still trying to come to terms with how dark it was during daylight.

"I suppose. But I have never been to Gaia so I cannot compare." Leilei shrugged her shoulders, a wistful look in her eyes. "Now, water dragons have a magenta purple underbelly with fuscia and rose-colored scales."

"Wait a second, why are water dragons purplish pink?" I interrupted once again, my brows drawn down in concentration. We were sitting on the edge of a field full of large green and yellow flowers. They looked similar to zinnias, but each bloom was the size of a cantaloupe. They had a sweet-smelling aroma that blended well with the musk from the unicorns.

Leilei pointed to the stream at the edge of the field. I noticed the water had a pinkish hue to it, then I remembered the body of water I had seen on my first day. Of course, I thought, the waters in this realm were different shades of pink.

She resumed speaking, a small grin on her face. "Water dragon eyes are a deep purple with rose quartz flecks. Spirit dragons have a slate-colored underbelly with pale multihued iridescent scales. Their irises are either bright green or pale blue with flecks of shiny silver. Blood dragons have maroon underbellies with crimson and gold scales. Their eyes are completely black with ruby flecks sparkling across the surface."

"Okay." I replied as she finished her descriptions. I wondered why she became a guard when she seemed to really love teaching people. I didn't feel close enough to her yet so instead asked. "So, what are their powers?"

"Each dragon has powers tied to their type." Leilei straightened her shoulders, and I knew this was going to be a long lecture. "Air, earth, fire and water are easy to understand. Their type denotes what they have the greatest power and control over. Spirit and blood are a little more complicated. Spirit dragons can commune with the dead; they can stop another from succumbing to death, and with the proper training pull the spirit from someone's body and hold it within their own. Holding the spirit can be used to help heal someone or kill them quickly. They truly have the power over life and death.

"How does holding the spirit allow the person to heal?" A small shiver ran down my back as I considered the kind of power that would allow someone to be able to do this. My power of inflicting pain seemed minor in comparison.

"If someone is close to death, they can pull their spirit out until a healer can be found to fix their body. Then their spirit can be returned to their body." Leilei said this as if it were a simple little thing. "Now, if the intent was to kill, they just release the spirit into the void."

My eyes grew large at the enormity of this power. If any of the types of dragons were to be feared, I feel as if this type was it. To have the power over life and death like that was astounding, as well as rather terrifying. I hope I never have to fight a spirit dragon.

"As scary as that is," I ran my fingers through the thick purple grass, the blades were soft, and I saw what looked like tiny hairs on each one. "What about blood dragons? What are their powers?" Blood dragons were the most interesting to me being as they are how vampires were created.

"A blood dragon's powers are rooted in the blood of living things. They can increase or decrease the strength of another by adding or removing components

52

of the blood." A sly grin came over Leilei's face. "They also have the power over life and death just in a different way than spirit dragons."

"Are you serious?" a loud gasp sprung from my mouth. Blood dragons are killers too? This just gets better and better, doesn't it. I should have expected this though; they did create vampires. It's not as if vampires are sweet, innocent and cuddly creatures. "Go on," I gestured to Leilei to finish.

She gave me a funny look, as she scrutinized my face. It is almost as if she didn't expect my reaction. Then again, maybe she didn't. I am part vampire, part witch.

"One power they can bestow upon another is immortality." She explained. "Dragons have very long lifespans, and a blood dragon can share the power of long life through a blood exchange."

"The first vampire was a human that caught the attention of a blood dragon, right?" I had heard that snippet somewhere over the years. Although until recently I hadn't given it much credence.

She nodded. "He fell in love and did not want to lose her. With the intent of keeping her by his side forever he drained her body while replacing her blood with his own. The drawback was that she now needed fresh influxes of blood to survive. Others learned of this and began performing the blood exchange with other humans thus creating a new species."

I learned that vampires inherited other attributes from their dragon makers other than immortality. The vampires created by dragons also gained some of the powers of their maker. When vampires began creating other vampires the dragon traits began to diminish. They did not lose their long lifespans however they were no longer completely immortal. Vampires made by other vampires do age, just significantly slower than humans and other species such as witches and shifters. One particularity that transferred to vampires, whether they were spawned from a dragon or another vampire, is the Blood Affinity.

As Leilei explained it, dragons find their path in life through a drawing to another's blood. Much like vampires they may have an affinity for someone that is not their true mate. Most often though their blood will call to their mate's blood. There are occasional instances when their blood draws them to a different source. When this occurs, it is predominantly guided by the hands of fate. Fate always searches for ways to maintain balance in the realms and has on occasion usurped a dragon's Blood Affinity for its own purposes.

"Wait," I interrupted her again. "You speak about fate as if it is a person."

Leilei took a long moment before she answered. For a second I believed she wouldn't explain at all. "Clotho, Lachesis and Atropos are fate. They are not people, although they can appear as such if they choose to unveil themselves to someone. Now, do you want to learn more about dragons and vampires or Fate?" she asked with an exasperated huff.

I contemplated my options for a few minutes. I really wanted to know about dragons and vampires but learning there were three beings that guided the realms was intriguing as well. After going back and forth in my mind I decided. "Dragons and vampires for now. Perhaps we could revisit Fate at another time?"

"Dragons it is." Leilei rolled her eyes. "But don't whine to me when Clotho spins you off in a direction you don't like." She said this with a shameless smirk.

She was a fount of information about both species. When fate interfered with a dragon or vampire's affinity it left that being unable to mate. Many of those affected in this way found ways to end their lives.

A dragon is stronger with their mate, only finding their true powers when their mate joins them. An unmated dragon, especially one that had their affinity stolen for fates use, will never reach their full potential and their powers remain weaker. Vampires have similarities with their affinities, although most vampires do not have extra powers, those that do will find a strengthening of their powers when they meet their mate.

"After the vampires began creating other vampires, most dragons stopped creating more vampires." Leilei explained. "An edict was set forth many centuries ago that forbade the creation of more vampires by dragons except in the instance of finding one's mate. Our world was becoming overcrowded due to the extra species. The edict was announced, and we were able to slow the drain on our resources. When the portals to Gaia were closed our realm was able to flourish again. We no longer worry about outsiders causing problems within our realm. We have had peace for over a thousand human years. Now, the old king's grandson has returned and brought a chimera with him. I worry that complications will arise once again."

I glanced at Nikolas out of the corner of my eye to see how her statement affected him. Only the white-knuckled grip on my hand betrayed him, his face carved

54

from marble. I opened my mouth to respond; a slight shake of his head stopped my words. Resting my head back on his shoulder, I kept our secret.

The morning after our unicorn encounter, we started walking just after dawn. For the next two days we hiked in silence. Even the verbose Leilei concentrated on putting one foot in front of the other. Our speed had increased. Arlien was acting as if we were late.

The city appeared on the afternoon of the fifth day. We stopped long enough to get a drink then continued down the path leading to the city in silence. From this distance the city looked like any large city I would see in my own realm. Missing were electric wires, cars zooming by, and other signs of the modern world. If I had doubted, I was no longer in my world, this was a jarring reminder that I wasn't.

I estimated we had walked another two miles by the time we reached a wide pink river. Arlien held his hand up, bringing his troop and us to a halt. One of the younger guards stepped forward and raised his hands to his mouth. A loud bellow erupted from his wide mouth that sounded like a cross between a crocodile's growl and a loon's screech. The hair on the nape of my neck stood on end at the unusual sound.

A herculean man appeared on the opposite bank flanked by two dragons. Judging by their coloring, one was a fire dragon, and the other was a water dragon. The man stared at each of us one by one before he bent his head toward the water dragon.

Slowly the water began to churn. As the churning got faster what appeared to be a bridge of water began to form. Once the water's shape fully looked like a bridge it hardened into solid ice. Arlien led our group onto the bridge of ice and toward the city.

The instant Nikolas stepped from the bridge; the two dragons flanked him. I made to move between him and the water dragon on his left. Leilei held my arm. "Do not interfere." She whispered. "They will not harm him. He is the grandson of the Magna Quercus; they are duty bound to protect him."

"How do they know who he is?" I murmured back.

"The minute we left old Magda she would have sent a message to the palace." Leilei advised me. "I am sure that is why Arlien forbid flying even though it would have taken us half a day to get here. He wanted to allow the current king time to prepare for the true king's arrival."

I absorbed this information in silence and followed the procession into the city. Nikolas had stopped me from telling them he had no designs on the throne. I am not sure why and he did not see fit to share his reasons with me. I would keep quiet for now and see how this played out. Hopefully the current king was more welcoming than Arlien and his crew had been at first.

Chapter Ten

Arianna

Fraxinus had still not returned from wherever it is he had absconded to. Every hour Fraxinus stayed away was a gift. My shoulders hadn't unclenched in centuries but now I could almost breathe easily. Although not knowing how much he had learned was a tad bit stressful, having him absent from the islands was a boon.

Davina reported in last evening to let me know she had arrived in the United States and was working on contacting one of the O'Brien siblings. Hopefully the vision Malina had foreseen was accurate and Davina would find Aisling O'Brien at the hotel in Philadelphia. For now, we all sat impatiently waiting for further information from Davina.

Matthew stood and began pacing the room in agitation. We were all on edge, not knowing what was happening in the world outside our secluded islands. Annie rose to block Matthew's path, drawing him into her arms to provide some comfort.

Suddenly, Malina's body became rigid, and her eyes turned white as she found herself dragged into a vision. We all watched her concernedly as we worried what her vision would tell us. Her body sat ramrod straight on the couch as she stared out of her unfocused eyes. Fists bunched at her side; her lips pulled back in a rictus of pain.

This was going to be a bad one, I held my breath in anticipation of what she was seeing. My breath rushed from me when her body collapsed onto the chair. Her eyes remained milky white but whatever she was seeing no longer caused her anguish. Long moments passed before her pale lilac eyes cleared and returned to focus on us.

"Fraxinus will return in the morning. We must leave the island before then. He knows we have worked against him all these years." Malina's pronouncement was met with a flurry of activity as everyone in the room, except me, panicked. This eventuality was something I had planned for. Each year we worked undetected against him was always a surprise to me.

"Calm down, everyone!" I bellowed at the room. All eyes turned to me as their frantic actions ceased. "All of you gather any belongings you need and meet me at the docks in one hour. All will be well." I assured them. When no one moved to do my bidding, I ordered. "Now!"

The three young witches and two vampires scattered to their lodgings. I walked around my home, grabbing items I knew I would need and stuffing them hastily into bags. After four hundred years, I would leave these islands and never return. So many times, over the years I had expected Fraxinus to learn of my betrayal. Knowing it was only a matter of time I had made sure to always have an escape plan in place.

Mating with a dragon had increased my powers and I had used those increases wisely over the centuries. One thing Fraxinus never understood is why he could not open a portal home after we had mated.

Initially I had used my powers to keep his portals from opening since I was unsure if it would be wise to immediately open a portal after my sister witches had worked so hard to close them. Over the centuries, most especially after my children were born, I knew allowing Fraxinus back into the Dragon Realm would be a horrible mistake.

Fraxinus always believed there was something wrong with our mating that kept him from attaining all his powers. When in all actuality it was simply me holding him back. He blamed me, saying I was weak when the reverse was true. I had been a formidable witch before we mated, once my powers grew after our mating, I was next to unstoppable.

I always sensed a darkness churning in Fraxinus and never fully trusted his ambitions. I used a simple spell that bound his portal opening powers. When I first placed the spell, I had every intention of removing it after the times of unrest died down.

Unfortunately, Fraxinus proved to be too volatile to consider allowing him to return to Fabeldyrverden. I tempered the guilt and remorse I felt over keeping the female dragons from their home world with the knowledge that I was protecting them and the other dragons from a madman.

We would have a long journey ahead of us. Many years ago, I had set up a safe house of sorts on one of the small islands near what is now Alaska. At the time there were many native tribes that hunted and fished in the area but none of them made the island home.

I spelled the island to appear smaller and less bounteous of fish and game causing the tribes to not venture to the island anymore. Matthew and Diana had made several trips across the world to equip the island with modern conveniences. So, we would at least not be arriving on a primitive island with no amenities. I did not have proper travel documents so therefore we could not fly. Even with the aid of witchcraft we would be stuck on a boat for a little over a week.

I made one last trip through my home ensuring I had gathered everything of consequence from within. The last thing we wanted was for Fraxinus to return home to find any clue as to our plans or where we had disappeared to. Once I exited my home for my final time I turned to stare at the building for a moment. Malina came to stand beside me. "Did you remove everything you will need?" She asked me.

"Yes, I have. You can burn it down now." As I turned to walk away Malina spoke the spell that would incinerate my home while not touching any of the trees nearby.

After centering herself and giving thanks to all the elements Malina recited. "I call on the fire elemental to remove this building from this island. I call on the water elemental to protect the land surrounding this building. I call on the air elemental to remain calm so as not to spread the flames. I call on the earth elemental to swallow the ashes so as to replenish the field."

Once her recitation was complete, she pulled her athame from her pocket, slashed it across her palm allowing blood to well up. Flinging her blood into the air, a rush of heat enveloped the two of us as the elements responded to her pleas.

The fire burned hot and fast, within minutes my home was a smoldering pile of ash. Rain pelted the land surrounding my old home while the wind held still. When there were no longer any flames the rain doused the ashes to ensure the fire was out completely. Just as the rain subsided the earth below churned the ash swallowing it up. Where once a small three-room house sat was now a clear field of fresh green grass.

Malina and I strode down the pathway toward the docks. We joined the rest of our coven, minus Davina, and boarded the small boat that would take us out to sea. We would meet up with a merchant friend of Matthew's in five hours. Tygus had agreed to take us to our new home near Alaska.

The boat was loaded with our remaining belongings. Temperence and Diana assured me that each of their homes had met the same fate as my own. The three witches had lived together for many years. Temperence had dealt with their home and Diana had removed Matthew and Annie's home. We would never be able to return to this island while Fraxinus was still out there.

Our trip was quiet and fortunately uneventful. We made excellent time and passed Crete almost an hour ahead of schedule. Having a witch with a strong proclivity for all the elements helped. Malina was rare in that she could command all four elements with equal strength. Using her authority over water, she propelled our boat faster than the engine would have done so. She also had a seer's ability which had helped us tremendously over the years in anticipating Fraxinus' plans.

Diana had great command over the fire element only. However, she was also able to pinpoint exactly where a person was anywhere in the world if she had an object belonging to them. With this power she could also guide us to any destination if it appeared on a map. Essentially, she was a human GPS. When we thought, we may have to abandon the island, Matthew had obtained an old shirt from Tygus that Diana was currently using to guide us to his ship.

Temperence, while seeming like the sweetest and kindest of the three, was the deadliest. She is what is considered a warlock. Over the centuries, humans have bastardized the word to mean a male witch but that was not the true meaning of it. A warlock is a witch, whether male or female, whose powers lends themselves to war and fighting.

Temperence has the ability to wield magical weapons that she is able to conjure out of nothing. Depending on the situation, she may pull a flaming sword from the aether, or an ice pick made of ice. The weapons she furnishes herself with are always perfect for the situation at hand. She is also well trained, as all within her line has been, in how to use any weapon she can conjure. On top of all that she instinctually knows how to use any weapon used against her, even if she has never laid eyes on it before.

"We're early." Matthew announced. A low fog clung to our boat as we sat immobile in the Mediterranean Sea.

"Do not worry." Diana answered. "We are in his path. Tygus will come this way within an hour. We simply need to wait here. Going to him would be out of our way."

"This is a good place to wait." Malina announced. "We will be safe here until Tygus arrives." We exchanged glances. Malina's visions had saved us from Fraxinus' rage more times than we could count. If she said to wait, we waited. We relaxed our tense postures and settled in to wait for the larger ship to meet up with our small boat.

Less than forty minutes later, we heard the sound of a ship's engine coming entirely too close to our location. Matthew hit our horn sending two quick bleats of noise into the open sea. Malina lifted the fog enshrouding our small boat. Once we were able to see across the water again, we spied a jumbo freighter bearing down on us.

I could hear the engines churn in protest as the freighter attempted to stop before hitting us. A muttered spell from Malina pushed our boat back while bringing the freighter to a sudden halt. The sound of heavy items crashing onto the ship's deck was followed by an angry yelling.

"What the feckin' shite was that?" Tygus bellowed. At least I assumed the tall scraggly bearded blonde man standing at the railing was Tygus.

"Sorry," Malina called back, craning her neck to look at the not so happy captain. "I didn't want to be run over."

"Perhaps, ye coulda warned me ye were sittin' in the midst of a fog bank. Yer closer than ye should be." Tygus thundered as he stomped away from the railing. A couple of seconds later a rope ladder came flying over the side of the ship. "Hurry yer arses up and get on up here."

None of us needed to be told twice as we hurriedly scrambled up the side of the ship. This was not the best way to meet Tygus. Once we had all clambered over the rail, Tygus called out to another bearded fellow.

"Jacky me boy, fetch their belongings to their rooms. Quickly now."

Jacky looked as if he could be blown over with a strong wind, so I had my concerns that he would be able to gather our belongings without dropping them into the sea. Jacky scrambled to peer over the side of the ship. He scrutinized the bags and boxes of our belongings for almost five minutes.

Without warning, our entire boat lifted from the sea, bumped along the choppy waves of the water then began to rise straight up. The wooden boat groaned as it crested the railing, saltwater dripping from its hull to pool on the deck. Jacky's face flushed scarlet with effort, the veins standing out on his forehead. Our boat hovered for a moment before shifting sideways, coming to a gentle landing on the ship's deck in front of us.

A small smile of relief spread across Jacky's face. He walked to stand next to the boat and after smelling the objects, splayed his hands out to his side and sent our bags and boxes careening out of the boat heading down a hallway. Our items split off into different rooms as we watched.

"Now, if ye didnae notice your things went into the rooms assigned to each of ye." Tygus announced. "I'll be askin that ye not wander the ship too much. Wouldna want any of ye stumbling into somewhere ye don't belong."

"Of course." Matthew replied. "We'll do our best to stay out of the way."

"Grand." Tygus ran his gaze up and down each of us as if he were assessing our value at auction. "Now which of ye is Diana?"

Diana moved forward to stand in front of Tygus. She handed his shirt back to him.

"As I ken it, ye will be guiding us to the final destination." Towering over her, Tygus looked down at the short witch. Diana nodded. "Ye follow me so we can get this shite straightened out." Tygus turned on his heels not waiting to see if she would follow or not. Diana threw a nervous glance at me then trod along behind him.

The rest of us followed Jacky to the hallway. We each found our rooms by finding our belongings. At the end of the hallway was an open area that held a table and chairs. We agreed to clean ourselves up then meet back at the table to await Diana's return.

After quickly washing up at the sink in my room, I returned to the central meeting area to find Matthew and Annie already waiting. A large teak table was bolted to the middle of the floor. Ten chairs surrounded the table, all also made of teak, but each had a thin orange cushion tied onto it for comfort. I looked around the rest of the room and noticed all the furniture, except the chairs, was bolted down.

Less than five minutes passed before the rest of my coven including Diana arrived. Thank the Gods, the silence was grating, and I fully expected Annie or Matthew to start giving me inane facts about something or other. I loved them dearly, but their idea of small talk was quite different than what most people would discuss. Once they gave me a tiny lecture all about honeybees.

"We are on course. Tygus expects our trip to take eight days even with the aid of spells." Diana explained as she took her seat. "Our trip, out of necessity will skirt around the bottom of South America. We cannot risk going near the Panama Canal to reach Alaska's coastline since it cuts too close to our sanctuary."

"Malina, please keep an eye out for any snags we may encounter." I requested of our seer. A quick nod of her head told me she heard me. She sat with her arms folded on the table, her shoulders dropped slightly. Based on her posture, I felt we were safe for now. "We should rest until we either hear from Davina or get to Alaska."

Tygus and Jacky entered the open room, Jacky bearing a tray laden with fresh fruits, vegetables, cheese and diced meat.

"Yer arrival was after dinner; this is the best we have at this time o' night." Tygus stood at the head of the table like a general, his feet spread and hands behind his back. "We keep to tight mealtimes so as to keep the ship running smoothly." We each agreed to not interfere with his ship's operation. "Now, some ground rules. Ye cannae use magic unless necessary. This ship is shrouded in many spells letting us slink through the cracks of the modern world. Can ye agree to that?"

When we all nodded, Tygus continued. "Ye can have supervised visits up to the deck twice a day. I repeat my earlier rule, ye cannae wander about me ship alone. Yer, not me only guests on board. They have secrets just as important to them as yers are to ye, do ye ken?" Once again, we all agreed. "I will leave ye to yer dinner then. Jacky will be with ye just down the hall if ye have need of anything."

Jacky pointed out which room was his before he followed Tygus to the end of the hall. They conducted a hushed conversation, with a few glances in our direction. I tried to hear what was being said but they were talking too low for me to pick up more than a couple words. I looked at Malina who still seemed at ease so figured whatever they were discussing must not be anything bad towards us.

I turned my attention to the food before us. The tray had a good variety of options to choose from; however, I noticed the lack of blood for my vampire friends though. All but Matthew and Annie began to eat. I looked back to see Tygus disappear around the corner with Jacky close behind, before I had a chance to ask if they had anything for my vampires.

Loading my palate with an assortment from the tray, I asked my two vampire friends, "How long since either of you fed?"

"It has only been two days." Matthew assured me. He held Annie's hand in his and showed no outward signs of distress.

As my belly filled, the creaking of the ship rocking on the waves began to lull my mind. The salty air left a welcome tang on my tongue. For the first time in centuries, I was away from the island and Fraxinus. Even though our future was uncertain, calmness settled over me.

"We will be fine to last the entire journey if necessary." Annie added her assurances as well.

"Perfect." I smiled around a mouthful of cold ham. Swallowing, I added, "However, if the opportunity arises to feed before then, it may be in your best interests to do so. I need everyone in fighting shape. I don't know what to expect when we arrive at our destination."

Chapter Eleven

Aisling

"Davina confirmed that Nikolas and Cassandra went to the Dragon Realm." I spoke into the phone when Evan answered.

"Hello, Aisling. It is wonderful to hear from you too." Evan replied, his voice roiling with sarcasm.

"Hi Evan!" I rolled my eyes hard enough to strain a muscle. "Is that better?"

"Sure. Much." I could hear the smirk in his voice. "I'm putting you on speaker phone so everyone can hear." Shuffling noises and furniture scraping could be heard through my phone speaker, but no one spoke.

"I will too." I pushed the button to turn my speaker on and placed the phone on the ornate coffee table in front of me and Davina. "Davina is here with me. Who is with you right now?"

"Our family, Almerinda, Damian and Hawthorne." Evan responded. "We'll bring Jace and his brood up to speed once we know what we are dealing with. I would like to leave them out of everything if possible, however different events lead me to believe we will need as many allies as we can get before this is all done."

"What about Almerinda's team, where are they?" I asked.

"They are out hunting rogues at the moment." Almerinda's voice came through the phone. "We will keep them apprised of any new developments."

"There are more rogues?"

"Yes, we believe they are being changed and let loose in our region to distract us." Cormac growled, I could picture Cormac grinding a fist into his palm. "Davina, is there any chance you know of the Fontaine family?"

"I do." Davina gasped. "How do you know of them? They have always been a European problem."

"I have known of them for centuries. I have also avoided them as much as possible." Almerinda advised us. "My interactions with them stopped when I came to the New World many years ago. My maker, Luis, was well acquainted with them. He worked with the family on several different projects over the years."

"A little over a year ago, Marcel came to the U.S. searching for his sister as well as attempting to overthrow the Community for his brother Andre." Evan interjected. "He was spurred on by a vampire named Amanda. They were using each other; her to get revenge on her maker, him to find his sister. Jaxson, her maker, allowed Amanda to live, however his brother, Jace, did not as she had used his newly found mate as bait. Jace killed Amanda and Elodie, Marcel's sister, allowed the Community to take Marcel into custody. Elodie also helped us rid the world of Luis a few weeks ago. Each time she shows up when she is needed then disappears again."

Davina stood from the couch and began pacing around the room. Lost in thought, she mumbled to herself occasionally. While Davina ruminated on whatever had caused her pacing I added. "So, if Marcel is in custody and Amanda is dead, why bring them up?"

"Marcel is not in the custody of the Community. Per agreement with the Tribunal in Europe, we turned him over to them." Almerinda explained. "Since he did not break any of their laws, they more than likely released him."

"So, he could be back in the states causing problems?" I shouted, causing Davina to stop pacing and stare at me. I ground my teeth, punching my fist. Gods dammit.

Jasmine's silky laughter filled the room. "Absolutely not. I may not have been able to spell him, but I was able to put a tracker on him before he left the country. If he had entered the U.S., I would have been alerted immediately."

"If you couldn't spell him, how did you track him?" I asked, my gut bubbling with unease. This was the first time I was hearing that Marcel was impervious to spells. I tucked that bit of knowledge into my brain just in case I needed it someday.

"Before he was turned over to the Tribunal, he was held at the Council headquarters for almost a month. While in our custody he had all his belongings taken. I put the tracker in that gaudy ring he wore on his pinky finger. It looked old and I figured he probably never took it off." Jasmine crowed proudly. "I was unsure if magic would work on his belongings once he put them back on, so I used good old modern electronics." I could picture the self-satisfied grin she was wearing right now as she expounded on her scheme. "I have watched him travel all over Europe for the past year. Not once has he journeyed more than two hundred miles from his home."

"So, Marcel is unable to sneak around. However, there are more Fontaine siblings as well as all their guards." Davina added as she came back to sit beside me.

"That may well be," Almerinda commented. "However, Amelie and Laurent have sought asylum with the Community. They are currently residing in one of my homes. Andre or any of the guards could come here, but why?"

"I may know." Davina answered quietly. "Andre and Marcel have been working for many years with Fraxinus to reopen the pathways to Fabeldyrverden and Alfheimer. They need Elodie to unseal the fae realm and they believe that the combination of two sets of dragon twins could break through to the dragon realm."

"I understand why Fraxinus would want to return to Fabeldyrverden," Hawthorne blurted. "But why would they want to reopen the path to Alfheimer?"

"Simple," Davina's lips curled. "Fraxinus means to rule Fabeldyrverden by any means possible. He would burn the world to rule its ashes."

"We get that part." Ali, my brother's new mate spoke up, always direct and to the point. "But what does the fae have to do with it?"

"Marcel has fae blood and foolishly believes he can control them so he can use them to help defeat the dragons." Davina's sneer pulled her lips further back, "Fraxinus has promised Gaia, the human realm, to Andre and Marcel in exchange for their assistance taking control of the dragon realm. They are all idiots." She spat angrily. "Marcel does not have enough fae in him to open a portal, there is no way he could even attempt to control one of them, let alone an entire army. I suspect that if he were to open a portal, the fae would help only as long as they needed them. Once the dragons were overrun, I am sure the fae would slaughter Fraxinus and the Fontaines immediately."

"Why do the fae hate the dragons so much?" I asked.

"I wouldn't say it was hatred that fueled the constant fighting between the two realms." Davina turned to face me on the couch. "Those of us who lived during the times when the portals were all open had many interactions with the fae. They are not all vicious murdering fiends. Once upon a time, there was much intermingling between all the species that called Gaia and the other realms home. When the first vampire was created by a blood dragon, the problems began to arise."

Davina continued her tale, and oh what a tale it was. The blood dragon who created the first vampire was a second son of the reigning king and queen named Braedon. He fell in love with a mortal woman and changed her into a vampire.

No dragon had ever performed this transformation before. When he found that the woman possessed many of his traits he shared his knowledge with other dragons. He believed that the information he shared would be used wisely. Unfortunately, not everyone changed humans for love as he had done. Many changed them to be servants or playthings.

Over time, the king proclaimed that no more vampires could be made by dragons unless the human was the dragon's mate. At that time, mates were found in different species more frequently than in modern times. What is called hybrids now were once very commonplace and were called chimera. To be two or three natured was not uncommon.

I sat back on the soft couch, stretching my arms out along the back. Davina took the chair beside the couch, relaxing into her story. It seemed that everyone on the other side of the phone was also settling in for story time.

Many years passed, and peace reigned amongst all species. At the time, the fae seldom came to Gaia and almost never traveled to Fabeldyrverden. The vampire population remained small, most choosing to live within the dragon realm with their makers.

A delegation of fae was meeting with a delegation from the dragon realm led by the king's second son. Braedon brought his mate; the vampire he had created with him.

Casius, the leader of the fae delegation felt an unyielding draw to the woman. He stalked her and eventually managed to get her alone. The scent of her blood drove him to distraction. He killed her and devoured her body, his strength increased, and he felt an extreme surge of energy after consuming her flesh.

When Braedon sensed his mate was in danger, he rushed to save her but was too late. Braedon and Casius fought to the death, each striking the death blow on the other at the same instance.

"The Dragon Fae Wars began with their deaths." Davina sat forward in her chair, her foot tapping a slow rhythm on the floor. "Dragons have always been protectors and often were called upon to settle any disputes between different species. The fae, for the most part, had held themselves separate from the rest of us. Once they learned that a vampire's blood and body would increase their strength and energy, more of them began to hunt vampires. The dragons fought to protect the vampires from the fae.

"I believe if the vampires had not figured out how to create their own progeny, the wars would have died down." Davina concluded.

"Really?" Almerinda's voice sounded unsure. "The fae don't strike me as the type to just stop fighting."

"I suppose that's true." Davina replied. She rose from her perch on the edge of her chair and walked around the living space. "However, most of the vampires created by a dragon choose to live in the dragon realm. They were able to survive on their maker's blood. When the few vampires that lived in Gaia began creating their own offspring the fae was able to find them easier. The fae could not resist the allure of a vampire's blood and hunted them for sport, much like humans hunt deer and other wild game. After the fae began killing vampires, the dragons and the fae became mortal enemies."

"If Fraxinus wants to rule the dragon realm, why doesn't he just open a portal?" Cormac interrupted. "From what I understand, he is mated, and his portal powers should be working."

Davina grinned at me before answering. "Because his mate has been working against him since the beginning. Arianna is one of the most powerful witches ever born. On the day the portals were sealed she mated with Fraxinus. Initially she held him back from returning home to allow the fallout from the wars to subside. Over time she continued to block his portal opening powers because she sensed he was not a good man. After the twins were born, she learned just how evil he was. She brought a few of us into her confidence and for several hundred years we have worked toward one goal. Keeping Fraxinus out of Fabeldyrverden!"

Davina was panting by the time she finished her tirade. She bent at the hips, lowering her head between her knees. Low mumbling came from her, and I suspected she was working to calm herself.

"I understand now." Hawthorne added. "She was the witch who pulled him from the field of battle when I believed he was dying. When the portal sealed, I was so angry at him that I didn't take the time to fully confirm whether he lived or not. How is she able to block his powers?"

Davina took a final calming breath then stood back up. "She cast a spell on him before he regained his strength. He convalesced for several months before his wounds healed fully. The spear the fae had gouged him with was laden with poison. Arianna was able to pull most of the toxin from his body allowing his dragon form to finish the healing process." Davina explained before adding, "She was supposed to be one of the witches helping seal the portals when Fate intervened and sent her to him instead. Why is it that you never returned? You were mated to Marlena so you should have been able to open a portal."

Silence descended on the other end of the call. I looked at Davina then at my phone to confirm we still had a connection. Everyone was interested in Hawthorne's answer. Minutes passed and a slight cough emanated from my phone and still no answer from Hawthorne.

Just as I was about to say something, we all heard him speak in a forlorn tone.

"Because I was forbidden." Davina's sharp intake of breath was all I needed to know this was serious. "The king and queen, my father and mother, sent me to this realm to bring back their child and I failed. I do not know if the banning was intentional or accidental. My powers would open a portal, but it was sealed from the other side. My mother's last words to me before I stepped through the portal to this realm were 'do not come back unless you have your brother.' As I said I don't know if she purposely meant to block my return or if her powers did it unintentionally."

The hotel heater sounded overly loud in the silence that followed Hawthorne's confession. Even Davina's pacing had stilled, her boots scuffing the plush carpet. No wonder Hawthorne always seemed so lost. Cut off from his home world by his mother, left in this world where he lost his mate and the only family he has left hates him.

"All I do know is that I tried many times before I lost my Marlena to return to Fabeldyrverden and I was never able to get around the seal." Hawthorne's gruff voice whispered into the phone. "I could see my home world and not touch it or walk in it. When my Marlena was killed, I lost even the power to open a portal. I have not seen my home in over seven hundred years."

My throat tightened and tears prickled the back of my eyes. I swiped them away before the traitorous bastards could fall. While truly heartrending what Hawthorne had endured, this was not the time for sadness. I stiffened my back, placed my feet firmly on the floor in front of the couch, and rose to pace the room.

"I understand even more why you worked with Alistair." I commiserated across the phone line with Hawthorne. "But now, we need to come up with a plan. I am stuck in this fancy hotel room, hiding from the Council. You are all on the other side of the country. Arianna and the rest of her coven are on the other side of the world and apparently Cassandra and Nikolas are in the dragon realm. Somehow, we need to get us all in one place. Any ideas?"

Chapter Twelve

Cassandra

Entering the city, I gaped at the unexpected sight. The guards who had herded us here wore muted blacks and purples, camouflage, I'd assumed, considering the forest's color palette. The colors of Magda's town were also quite subtle. The people had worn browns and silver clothing with very little colors, and the red and orange brick had been faded yet sturdy looking. Magda's house of silver brick was the most impressive building in the town.

The capital city, on the other hand, was a plethora of every color imaginable. The city was a vibrant rainbow of beautiful fabrics and masonry. Many of the women wore dresses and gowns befitting a debutante's ball during the heyday of the English Ton. Not all the women wore dresses, quite a few wore pants and shirts, but all wore the brilliant shades of color.

The men were slightly more subdued than the women wearing a great amount of black but even they had splashes of color in their shirts and pants. The buildings were made of stone, wood or brick but each was a bright bold color.

As the gate completed its journey to full open, the sounds of voices raised in happiness and anger, and every emotion in between came to an abrupt halt. Clearly, we were expected and each and every inhabitant of the city had come to the streets to greet us. The two guards flanking Nikolas began walking, keeping their eyes forward they marched down the center of the main brightly colored thoroughfare. Everyone jumped to move quickly out of their path. The rest of us followed behind the guards keeping close pace with them.

I craned my neck to look over my shoulder and noticed the crowd filling in behind our rear guards as we passed. As we advanced further down the street, I noticed that the noise of conversations stopped as we got closer then resumed once we had gone by.

I gawked at my surroundings trying to take in every new sight I could. When I peered down some of the side streets, I noticed stalls set up with people selling items as if they were making a fair day out of our arrival. A few times my eyes met another's eyes, most often showing either confusion or happiness. Occasionally I would meet hostile eyes too. It would seem not everyone was happy to see the return of Nikolas.

The main road was about three miles long and our progress was hindered by people not moving quickly enough out of the way. A few of them even went so far as to try to stop the guards with questions. Each one was politely but firmly rebuffed by the guards and then our walk would resume.

The aroma of savory meat and sweet pastries met my nostrils, and my stomach grumbled. We had not eaten since we broke camp this morning and I was getting peckish. I could see our destination crawling closer. I really hope there's food inside that castle. At this pace it was going to take forever to get there. Okay, so maybe not forever, more like a bit more than an hour. Our walk ended abruptly at the base of an enormous set of multi-colored steps. This place loved its colors.

I stood at the bottom of the castle steps, my head thrown back, my mouth open in awe. The building itself was made of the same silver bricks as Magda's house. It was squared off having a turret at the corners of each square. I counted ten windows vertically on each turret leading me to believe there were ten floors in each one. The windows were spaced further apart than a human's building would be, which made a kind of sense to me since even in their human forms, most of the dragons of this realm were seven feet tall and above. More color met my eyes as I glanced at the stairs leading up to the castle entrance.

Each stair was a different color starting with hunter green followed in order by midnight blue, black, magenta, slate, maroon, emerald, sapphire, yellow, fuscia, iridescent and finally crimson. I realized that these colors represented each type of dragon.

When we came to the top of the stairs, we stood on a spacious platform of red, orange and yellow. Leilei, who had remained at my side, whispered to me telling me that the color of the platform denotes the current ruler. That must mean the current king is a fire dragon.

As soon as Nikolas stepped onto the platform, the colors, red, yellow and orange, swirled like liquid fire, veins of green and purple bleeding through. Nikolas turned his head, his arm muscles rippled as his hands bunched at his side. Relief settled over his features when our eyes met.

I refuse. His words pounded through my head. The crowd erupted in gasps as the colors snapped back to their original blaze. The castle's platform had

73

responded to his fervent avowal in my head. My jaw, which I hadn't noticed was clenched until it released, fell open.

"That was unexpected." Leilei murmured beside me. "Perhaps old Magda was correct."

"About what?" I hissed out of the side of my mouth.

Surprise spread across her face, "I didn't mean to say that." She stammered.

"But you did, so what was Magda correct about?" I hissed again.

"She said he did not come here to claim a throne but to lend assistance in a coming war." She whispered. "Now hush, things are about to get interesting."

Get interesting, I thought. For me this entire day had been entirely too interesting for my liking. I had a routine that I lived by and ever since I was sent to interrogate Nikolas my routine had been upended.

I like order and regularity. Keeping to my routine helps me keep my powers in check so no accidents happen. Although, I have had several instances that should have caused me to unleash my power on some unsuspecting individual yet had been able to reel it in without any problems. I wonder if mating had somehow dulled my powers in some way.

That is not it. Nikolas' voice reassured me. *Our mating has strengthened your powers, including your control over them. Emotions should have less sway over your control.*

Well, if nothing else about our mating turned out to be good, at least there was that. A sudden image of me wrapped in Nikolas' arms, kissing him passionately jumped into my head. I could feel his strong calloused hands running down the smooth skin of my bare back. *Stop it,* I admonished Nikolas. A deep husky laugh reverberated through my mind.

I truly hope that you will find more good about our mating. A low growl formed in my throat; I was unsure if it was a laugh or a snarl as I glared at the back of my mate's head.

I tore my eyes from the silky black hair of my self-satisfied mate. The enormous silver doors began to open, causing many of those who had followed us to fall back. Nikolas and his two guards remained where they were, so I did too.

Due to the size and heaviness of the doors they did not swing open quickly. As we waited, I edged a little closer to Nikolas. Leilei didn't try to pull me back, so I moved closer still until I was able to reach out and touch his arm. At my touch he stretched his arm to me, clasping my hand in his. We stood that way until a resounding thunk made the two of us jump.

A man not much taller than me stepped through the door. I was truly beginning to believe everyone here was giants. White, blonde hair and silver flecked blue eyes told me he was a spirit dragon. I sent a silent thank you to Leilei for the history lesson on the way to the palace. He wore light grey loose-fitting shirt and pants that put me in mind of the gi worn for karate training.

He stared at Nikolas for several minutes before bringing his dour gaze to rest upon me. I squirmed a little under his scrutiny and was very thankful when he turned his eyes back to Nikolas.

"Greetings, grandson of the Magna Quercus. We are honored to meet you and to offer welcome to our kingdom. King Lucian requests that we adjourn to the main hall where he awaits." His deep voice boomed across the crowd that had formed. "Please follow me." He stated in a more moderate tone. Those that had been watching began to disperse as we walked through the heavy door.

Nikolas pulled me to walk beside him. No one attempted to stop me this time. *When I refused the crown, they no longer felt the need to protect me.* Nikolas explained while we walked down the hallway heavily decorated in gold, red, orange and yellow. Paintings of battles against what I assumed were fae and portraits of different kings and queens hung every few feet. Nikolas came to a stop in front of a portrait of a man who looked as if he were the twin to Nikolas.

Arlien noticed we had stopped and came to stand on Nikolas' other side. "Magna Quercus, the Mighty Oak, your grandfather. He was a compassionate and fair ruler but after your father and uncle were sealed away in Gaia, he and your grandmother renounced the throne."

"Why didn't they try to have more children?" I asked, I assumed dragon fertility was longer than your average witch, shifter or human.

"The queen withdrew into a melancholy no one was able to penetrate, including the king." Arlien responded with a glance at the portrait next to Magna Quercus. The woman was stunning, thick black hair, soulful brown eyes and a more feminine version of Nikolas' hawk-like nose. "They moved to the southern chalet and seldom venture from their self-imposed exile."

Nikolas frowned in concentration at their portraits, as if he were memorizing their faces. Maybe he was, when I tried to speak to him through our

75

bond, I felt a resistance that hadn't been there before. He squeezed my hand lightly, a slight tremor in his own.

"Many attempts were made to reopen the portal, however after several years it was determined to be a lost cause." Arlien's speech interrupted my focus on Nikolas' remoteness. "Since our rules require the ruler to have a mate and be capable of producing an heir a new line was started. His brother Pinus Fortis ruled for a thousand years. King Pinus was a strong and fair ruler who produced two children. Lucian Griffin, our strong lord of light and his sister, Serafina, our fiery angel. We must move along; Orson is getting impatient to present you to the king."

Nikolas and I looked down the long corridor at Orson. The man was obviously anxious to move along, what with his toe tapping and fidgeting. He must have been told to allow us to feel comfortable otherwise I believe he would have dragged us down the hall by our hair if necessary. "One question," Nikolas held Arlien back. "How long has King Lucian ruled?"

"Our king ascended to the throne thirty years ago." Arlien replied.

He pulled his arm free from Nikolas to stride down the hall giving us no choice but to follow. The sudden reopening of his mind to me had me stepping back from Nikolas. I forced my feet to move back to his side, just as his words penetrated my psyche.

That means Lucian has twenty years to find a mate or he will have to forfeit the throne. Nikolas informed me. I wondered what would happen if he didn't find his mate. *He would have to give up the throne and either his sister or someone else would have to rule.*

Nikolas wasn't kidding before when he said he could read my mind. This could come in handy, allowing us to communicate with no one else being the wiser. A quick squeeze of my hand told me he agreed with me. Would they try to make him accept the throne?

That is a possibility, but I will not accept. I guess it would be in our best interest then to make sure Lucian meets his mate.

We entered a cavernous room while we continued our conversation in our heads. Red, orange and yellow silks hung from the ceiling. Banquet tables lined the walls on both sides. Approximately one hundred people sat at the tables watching us in earnest as we marched down the center of the room. At the head of the room, two imposing silver thrones sat, one occupied and the other empty.

A rather tall man with a mane of dark auburn hair and close cropped slightly lighter red beard, reclined in the throne on the left. His long legs extended out in front of his body as if he were ready to take a nap rather than meet his long-lost cousin. As we got closer to the throne, he slowly pulled himself to a more appropriate position.

A young woman with hair the same shade of red as his beard sat in a smaller throne like chair to the left and slightly behind Lucian. She kept her eyes downcast; her hands twisted in her lap. This must be the sister

Nikolas came to a halt about five feet from the throne and repeated the salute he had given to the guard when they accosted us in the forest. Right hand to his forehead then brought to rest on his heart as he kneeled on his left knee. I kneeled along with him with my hand on my heart, but I had not done the whole motion.

King Lucian abruptly vaulted to his feet. We looked up to find him grinning happily at us. Lucian reached out his hand to clasp Nikolas' hand in his. Pulling him to stand he embraced Nikolas as if they were long lost friends instead of having just met. Over his shoulder, Lucian blared, "Serafina, come, meet your cousin."

The woman moved in a less excited manner than her brother. When she stood beside her brother, she gave us a timid smile and lowered her head. "I am happy to make your acquaintance." Her voice was soft and like honey. "I hope your journey was not too arduous."

I reassured her that our trip to the palace was not too strenuous and thanked her for asking. Other than the red hair, Serafina and her brother were complete opposites.

Lucian was tall, at least six feet eight or nine. He had a muscular build, but unlike Nikolas who was all bulk he was more streamlined. His auburn hair came just below his shoulders and was currently held back with a leather tie. His eyes seemed to shift color from yellow to orange while having a constant shimmer of crimson flecks swirling. Lucian was also louder and more gregarious with his speech and mannerism.

Serafina was close in height to me, maybe an inch or two shorter. Her long hair reached almost to the floor. Her eyes, when she lifted them to allow you to view them were orange with red flecks. It was hard to tell what shape she had under the flowing red gown she was wearing. The only thing I could tell for sure about her body was that she didn't have very large breasts as the rest was hidden in the many layers of her gown.

The contrasts between the two were fascinating. Lucian seemed to revel in the spotlight, while Serafina did everything she could to shrink behind her brother. Where he was imposing and bold, she was soft and unobtrusive. I suppose living in the shadow of Lucian; one could expect his sister to be more reserved and quieter.

"Come, we can go to our chambers behind the great hall where we can have some privacy from all the gossip mongers hoping to catch some exciting trivia to share with the rest of the city." Lucian bellowed.

Clearly, he wanted all the people at the tables to hear, and possibly those still out on the steps. A faint giggle escaped Serafina's lips as she followed her brother out of the throne room. With no other choice, Nikolas and I proceeded behind her while Orson and Arlien brought up the rear.

The room we entered was smaller but no less lavish. A fire burned in three of the six fireplaces along the walls. Scattered around the room were different groupings of chairs and sofas. Lucian led us to a group of four gold chairs and a red velvet sofa. Once Lucian sat in one of the gold chairs, Nikolas pulled me to sit next to him on the sofa. The other three took the remaining chairs.

"Now, cousin," Lucian began. "What brings you to Fabeldyrverden?" Confusion must have been splashed across my face because he added. "That is what our realm is called."

"There is a war coming. I do not know for sure when, but I do know my father will be what causes it to start." Nikolas announced. "I have been held captive by my sister through the use of spells for many years. I finally met my mate which broke my sister's hold on me and allowed me to open a portal to here. Although, I was bespelled, I do remember many of the things said in my presence when my sister and father believed I was not paying attention."

"What purposes did your sister and father use you for?" Lucian inquired.

"Most often just to siphon my powers, sometimes I was used to torture people they wanted information from, but mostly just my powers." Nikolas replied, his hand clamped down on my thigh.

I shuddered when I thought of Evan O'Brien and what I had heard was done to him by my mate. Thank the gods he had met me, and his sister's spells were broken. I could feel the anguish he felt over his actions even if they were directed by someone else. I pulled his hand from my thigh, lacing our fingers together.

"Penelope was my twin. She is no longer alive." A small note of sadness entered his voice to be quickly cut off, replaced with a more unyielding inflection "I felt her loss not long after Cassandra freed me from her spells."

I had no idea that she had died or that he could feel her death when it occurred. How unfortunate that he could not have been there when she died. I know she was not a good person, but she was still his twin sister. *Do not bother with feeling sorry for me. I lost my twin years ago; it just took some time for her to die.* Oh, I guess that kind of makes sense considering how horribly she had treated him, still my heart hurt for his loss, regardless of when he had experienced it.

"And what exactly do you expect this realm to do for you?" Lucian's imperious tone caused a ripple of unease to slide down my spine. Gone was the jocular playful cousin from the great hall. "We have been shut away from Gaia and the other realms for more than a millennium. What concern could we ever have with a war in Gaia?" Lucian flicked his wrist in a dismissive gesture as if he were brushing Gaia, my home world, off his lap like an insect.

"I believe my father intends to open the gates to Alfheimer and release the fae." Nikolas's jaw clenched, his voice raw as gravel. "If he were to,' He broke off, his fingers on his free hand digging into his thigh. He started again, "If he were to accomplish that, I expect he'll continue his plan to try to overthrow this world with their aid."

"First," I spoke up from his side, pulling his hand away from his thigh, I held both hands in mine, "you have no reason to blame yourself for your father's actions." Reaching one hand up, I forced his face to meet mine as I reassured him through our bond as well. "And second, how does he think he can open a portal to the fae world if he couldn't open one to here?"

"There are those in Gaia that carry fae blood. My father plans to use one of them to gain access to a small faction of fae who wish to rule Gaia." Nikolas explained to me. "He has promised them Gaia in exchange for their aid in taking Fabeldyrverden." Giving his attention back to King Lucian, he added, "I did not come here expecting you to help in a war in Gaia. I came here to escape the Council, which has grown corrupt, and warn you of the impending war should my father manage to open paths to either realm."

I stiffened at his insinuation that the Council was corrupt. I worked for them, well at least up until I disappeared through a portal with Nikolas. Granted some of them could be assholes and not very kind to those they deemed the help. But corrupt? The only one I would ever suspect was Luis, the old vampire, but not many trusted his intentions in joining the Community. We were going to have to have a serious discussion about his accusations. I dragged my focus back to the conversation, hoping I hadn't missed anything important.

"When do you plan to leave?" King Lucian was asking when I started listening again.

"Once we have rested and I can figure out how?" An abashed Nikolas replied.

Serafina spoke up for the first time, her voice was low and demure, "Do you truly not know how you opened the pathway?"

"I do not." Nikolas replied. "My father was unable to open portals so was never able to teach me."

"How could he not?" Lucian exclaimed. "Every mated pair can open portals. Who was your mother, the woman he mated with?"

Nikolas looked at me in confusion for a moment. Apparently, he had never thought too in depth about the fact that his father could not open a portal to his home world. "Her name is Arianna Konstantin. She is a witch."

King Lucian and Serafina shared a knowing glance before their eyes returned to us. "What is it that we are missing?" I demanded.

"Please describe your mother to me?" Serafina asked quietly. "How long ago did they mate with each other?"

"My mother is tall and thin with black hair like mine, violet eyes, a sharp nose and full mouth. She has a very imposing look to her, although she is very kind and caring unless you cross her." A soft smile spread across Nikolas' face as he thought of his mother. "She is a very strong witch. She was a member of the coven that was sealing the portals. She met my father as she was on her way to the ceremony. He fell in battle, and she pulled his mostly dead body from the field and nursed him back to life. Why?"

Another look of acknowledgment passed between Serafina and Lucian. "I see." Serafina replied before rising from her seat. "Follow me." We looked at each other for a moment before standing as well. Lucian, Arlien and Orson remained in their seats. Apparently whatever Serafina wanted to show us they either already knew or didn't care to know.

We walked through a door opposite the one we had entered. Stepping through the doorway we were greeted with more paintings depicting battle scenes, posed portraits and scenes of what looked like historical events.

Serafina walked about halfway down the long hallway before coming to a stop in front of a woman with flowing black hair and violet eyes with arms raised in a gesture I knew all too well. Arms stretched in front of her with hands and fingers steepled together. This was the classic stance of a witch performing a defensive spell.

The being opposite her had a human look to it but was much taller with extremely pale skin, pale blonde hair, pointed ears, and black eyes that burned with hatred for the woman facing it. The fierce concentration on the woman's face decried the amount of power she was wielding against the other creature.

Nikolas gasped loudly as he stared at the woman as if seeing a ghost. His knees buckled and he fell to one knee, dragging me down with him. *Mother?* He spoke into my mind. I looked at the woman depicted with renewed interest. This was his mother? Why was she in a battle scene painting hanging in a place of honor in the halls of the dragon realm's palace?

"Just as I expected." Serafina's soft voice spoke from above us. "That is Arianna of the Danu line. Your mother hails from the most prestigious witch family to have walked Gaia. Her ancestor is considered the mother of gods having spawned An Daghdha and the Mor-rioghan. The scene in front of you is when she defeated Morbicus, a fae general who had killed thousands of casters, striga, and dragons. She argued against closing the portal to our realm saying that to close us off would be tantamount to surrendering to the fae when they returned."

Serafina knelt in front of us. She placed her hand on Nikolas' chin to raise his face to hers. "She was a great friend to the dragons. It heartens me to know she found her mate and produced someone as kind and strong as you. I just wish Fate had not intervened and gave her a mate such as your father." Standing quickly, she indicated the door we had entered this hall through. "We need to return to my brother; he is tolerant of my whims but does worry when I am left unattended for too long."

Nikolas and I rose to our feet, but I did not move to return to King Lucian just yet. Staring at the painting, I studied the woman who gave the world Nikolas on one side and Penelope on the other.

As powerful as I could be, especially with my ability to inflict horrendous pain on a body without touching it, I believe this woman would in truth be stronger than me. There was not a hint of fear on her face as she stared down an enemy revered to be next to invincible.

Serafina stood next to me for a moment before I heard her quiet whisper. "She was the best friend I ever had."

Her words caused me to turn to stare at her. "Yes, she and I were great friends. She wanted to stay in Fabeldyrverden, but my vision changed her mind." Serafina supplied in answer to my questioning gaze.

"Your vision?" I asked.

"I was blessed, or cursed depending on how you look at things, with the prophecy gene." A wry grin twisted her mouth as she continued, "I am often more protected than Lucian and held apart from most due to my seer abilities. They do not want to lose their advantage, their, what do witches call it, hmm, yes, their crystal ball." Sadness crept into her eyes, "Arianna treated me as a friend not a tool. If I had not foreseen her future in Gaia, she would have stayed here with me."

Serafina hooked her arm through mine and pulled me away from the painting. I grabbed Nikolas' hand and dragged him with us. "Now, come, we must return before they worry."

Just as she finished her sentence, the door opened, and Arlien stepped into the hall. "Sera, darling, you know how anxious Orson can get." Arlien stepped closer and took her hand in his, bringing her hand to his lips, he kissed her palm in what was clearly much more than a subject to his king's sister.

"You are right, my life," Serafina pouted becomingly at the stern looking guard. "I notice you don't seem too anxious about my absence."

"Perhaps, because I know you are made of sturdier stuff than Orson and quite often your brother gives you credit for." The smile he gave her was so full of love and gentleness that it made his normally harsh features handsome and boyish.

Nikolas pulled me closer to his side as we advanced down the hall to re-enter the chambers where King Lucian and Orson awaited us. *They may seem mismatched, but they are true mates as in they bonded as well as fell in love.* Nikolas told me then added with a seductive note to his voice in my mind. *I hope that we find that too.*

Gods, I hoped that too. His words sent electric jolts through my body. I felt an intense physical reaction to my mate but did not know him well enough to determine if it was more than physical. After seeing the way Serafina and Arlien looked at each other, I yearned for the same feeling for my mate.

We passed through the doorway to find a remarkable site unfolding in front of us. Serafina had stopped walking approximately four feet inside the room and was now hovering about five inches off the ground. Her body levitated and spun slowly in a circle.

As she faced us in one of her rotations, I saw that her eyes had turned a brilliant crimson, filling the entire eye red. Her lips parted as if in speech, but no sound emerged. Arlien stood in front of her, walking in a circle, keeping his eyes locked on her bright red ones. His mouth also moved as if in speech although a faint whisper could be heard from him.

Without knowing what to do, Nikolas and I came to a stop. Serafina and Arlien continued their strange dance for about ten minutes. As if the strings were cut, Serafina's body suddenly slumped forward to be caught in Arlien's strong arms. He lowered her gently to the floor then sat beside her on the thick cream-colored carpet. She clung to his chest, sobbing.

King Lucian and Orson came to stand beside the couple on the floor. Lucian knelt beside his sister. "Sera, are you well?" His voice shook with worry. "What did you see?"

Orson handed a dampened cloth to Arlien who then used it to cool Serafina's forehead. Arlien made a small shooing gesture at Lucian and Orson. Lucian moved back with a small glare. Orson, if possible, turned even haughtier and looked as if he were going to reprimand Arlien for his impudence toward the king. If it weren't for the fact that Serafina was crying, I would have found it funny.

Nikolas pulled me into his arms with my back formed to his hard chest. We stood that way while Serafina brought her emotions under control. While we waited patiently, Arlien soothed his mate, Lucian paced like a caged tiger and Orson fretted around like a mother hen. Occasionally Orson would hand things to Arlien, who would take them then put it to the side. By the time Serafina was able to stand all manner of detritus had piled on the floor beside her.

83

"I have seen your mate." Serafina pronounced once she had gained her feet. Being the only unmated two in the room, Lucian and Orson looked at each other than back at Serafina for confirmation. "You, brother. I have seen your mate, and she is a spitfire." Serafina grinned mischievously at her brother.

"If, as you say sister, you have seen my mate," Lucian countered, "then why were you crying? This should be cause for celebration, should it not?"

"You must travel to Gaia with Nikolas and Cassandra. You must travel alone, not even with your guard." Serafina frowned slightly. "Not even I can travel with you at this time. Your mate awaits you in a place called America. This is happy news, but I do not see what happens after you meet her. That is why I was crying. I do not know if you will return from your journey to Gaia and the land of America."

Lucian and Orson looked at Arlien as if to verify her story. With that one look I realized that while Serafina had the visions, it was Arlien who helped her interpret them. The comforting was not only to provide succor. They had been speaking with each other in their minds as they sorted out the scenes she had seen. Arlien confirmed her statements were true.

King Lucian stomped away from his sister muttering to himself for a minute. He looked at me and Nikolas. "Do you know of this land called America?"

I almost giggled but knew this was not the time or place for humor. I had to remind myself that these people had been closed off from our world for over a thousand years; America had not even been 'discovered' by that time. And, yes, I used air quotes even in my head, since it was not uninhabited land when the Europeans arrived on its shores. "We do, King Lucian." I answered. "I actually live in America."

"That is good; you will be my guide then." King Lucian advised me as if I were one of his subjects. Nikolas nudged my side as if he knew where my thoughts were heading and possibly that those thoughts might burst from my mouth. *I'll be good*, I thought loudly at him.

"We must make arrangements for the kingdom." King Lucian stated as he dismissed us from his mind, turning to speak with Orson. "If there is a chance I will not return, Serafina must rule in my stead. I have no choice but to go if my mate is in Gaia. Our rules would not allow me to continue as king."

"Yes, sire." Orson answered solemnly. "I shall begin the preparations to make Serafina your proxy. If you have not returned by your fiftieth year of rule, she will automatically become queen with Arlien, her mate, as consort. Until then she will rule as your vice-regent."

Lucian pivoted back to us, "Now I expect things have changed quite a bit since I last visited Gaia. I need a history lesson, and you need to learn how to harness your portal powers if we are to claim my mate."

"Might I make a suggestion, King Lucian?" Nikolas asked. Lucian waved his hand in the imperious motion he was so fond of again. "Your clothes are too fancy for America and while I realize claiming your mate is important, chances are she will be involved in some way in defending the world from the fae. If you hope to succeed in wooing her properly it may be beneficial if you thought a little longer on giving aid to our cause."

"I will think on it but not because I need to woo anyone, if she is my mate she will have no choice but to accept me." With this final declaration, King Lucian swept from the room to begin preparing for his journey to Gaia. Nikolas and I shared a knowing look. If his mate was a spitfire as Serafina stated, then she may not be as willing to just fall into the arms of a man who only cares about securing his throne.

Chapter Thirteen

Aisling

The clock ticked toward midnight when two calls shattered our waiting game. Davina received a call from someone named Annie just as I received a phone call from Evan.

Annie and Davina spoke for several minutes before Davina hung up. She turned to tell me something, but Evan was updating me on current family issues. "She's done on her call." I told Evan. I put Evan on speaker phone again and indicated to Davina to speak.

"Arianna and the rest of the coven are on their way to our island near Alaska." She announced.

"Wait a sec, you have a secret island in Alaska?" I asked shocked.

"We do. Arianna set it up many years ago as an escape if we ever needed it." Davina explained. "It would seem Fraxinus has learned of her duplicity over the years. They were forced to flee our home. They are currently on a ship somewhere near the southern tip of South America."

"Well, that is both good and bad news." Evan's voice groused through the phone. "Good since they will be closer to us here in Oregon but bad because now her mate knows she's worked against him."

"Way to state the obvious, brother." I smirked at Davina. "So that helps get them closer to you, but we're still stuck here hiding out from the Council."

"That's why I called. Michael Collier should be arriving there any moment." Evan stated. "He has promised to help the two of you get out of the hotel."

"That is great news indeed." Davina commented. A shiver of unease crept up my spine. I wasn't worried about Michael, his mate on the other hand didn't always make things go smoothly for me.

"So now we will all be closer together except Nikolas and Cassandra." I quipped. If only we had another pair of mated dragons that could open a portal. I appraised Davina out of the corner of my eye. "Has anyone thought of a way to get in touch with them?"

"No, we're still all coming up empty on that matter." Evan griped. "Hopefully we can figure something out by the time we are all in one place. Davina, do you know how to reach this island?"

"Of course." She answered. "I can guide us in once Arianna lets me know they are there. Until Arianna is on the island entry is blocked to everyone but her, Matthew and Annie. She placed a spell hiding it from the world centuries ago. Matthew and Annie are the only two the spell allows in since they have been updating it over the years to make it more livable as well as making sure it has kept up with new technology."

"Great." Evan actually sounded optimistic for once. Since Cillian's death the only thing that had lifted his spirits had been meeting Ali. "Call me back when you are safely away from the Bellevue." Evan ended the call, and we resumed our waiting.

We made ourselves comfortable on the elegant yet comfy furniture. After a few minutes of silence, and a ton of hemming and hawing on my part, I decided to just ask Davina out right. "Could you open a portal to the Faberdyl place if you met your mate?" I still couldn't seem to say its name properly.

Her head swiveled in my direction. A mask of concentration, hope, and maybe a little fear coated her expression. For a moment I wasn't sure she would answer me, then she replied, "Yes and no." At my look of irritation she added, "What I mean is that yes, I will gain that power but no, it wouldn't be immediate. I sincerely don't know how Nikolas was able to do it with no training.

We reverted to silence, both of us considering our options. My stomach let me know it was hungry, loudly. Wandering into the kitchen I asked Davina if she was hungry too. At her nod I whipped up some dinner. After a dinner of grilled chicken, baked potatoes and asparagus we returned to the living room. I clicked on the TV for noise, since it seemed she was all talked out for the time being.

I found HBO, and funny enough, Game of Thrones was playing. I left it on and watched Davina's reactions to the show more than the actual show. If her laughter and disbelief were anything to go by, Game of Thrones was not based on fact.

The episode was just ending when a knock sounded at my door. I waved Davina to one of the bedrooms and went to answer the door. So far no one has seen her in my rooms. We wanted to limit the number of outside people who knew of our connection, even if Davina was an unknown with the Community.

Once the door closed behind Davina, I opened the door to find Michael Collier and his mate, Blair, standing in the hallway. His wolf-shifter energy filled the doorway, all woodsy scent and barely leashed power. A slight sneer raised Blair's lips when she saw who answered the door. She quickly smoothed her face back to a neutral look before Michael could see it.

"Mr. Collier, thank you so much for your help." I kept my voice formal sounding for Blair's benefit. Throwing the door open, I swept my arm wide, allowing them to enter.

Michael raised one eyebrow at my calling him Mr. Collier before striding into my room like he owned the place, which of course he did. "Hello, Aisling, what have you done this time?" He chuckled softening the admonishment into a joke.

"Nothing that was not sanctioned by the head of my family." I replied, indignation stiffening my spine.

"I wouldn't expect you of all people to break the rules, maybe bend them a little." A small smile cracked his lips. "However, I also know you quite well, and you don't always stay within the lines of the assignment."

Blair bristled at his reference to how well he knew me. Gods, when would she ever get over our past? One-time humans can be so, well, human sometimes.

"All jokes aside, Michael, did Evan fill you in on what is happening?" I asked, trying to turn the conversation back to the business at hand rather than the past that could wind up setting his mate off. I really didn't have time to defend myself against an angry shifter. Especially when that shifter was the alpha's mate.

"He did. Seems as if you have gotten yourself into a bit of a mess." He scratched his fingers through his thick brown beard. "Where is the dragon?" He asked as he looked around the room as if expecting an actual dragon to be sitting on the couch.

Davina stepped out of the bedroom she had hidden in. "Hello, Mr. Collier. Thank you for your assistance getting to America as well as in introducing me to Aisling."

"You are welcome." Michael answered while Blair continued to glare daggers at me when he wasn't paying attention to her. "So, Evan has requested that

I help the two of you get out of Philadelphia without the Council knowing you have escaped their evil clutches."

"He did lead us to believe you had a way out for us." I responded.

"Oh, darling, I do. I just don't think you're going to like it very much." Looking at his mate, he laughed. "Although I am pretty sure my mate is going to love it." He walked to take her hand in his before whispering to her. "I wish you would accept that Aisling and I are in the past."

Before things could get more awkward, I interrupted their sickening gushing at each other. "Ahem, so what is this plan?"

"Tomorrow is garbage pick-up. I have requested two trucks due to the extra trash we have from a party. The two of you will be the extra trash in the second truck. Two of my men will get you to the garbage truck and then escort you to Jace McFadden and his group. They will get the two of you to Oregon." Blair's snicker told me she very much enjoyed me being referred to as trash.

"You are certain the Council will not suspect anything?" Davina asked from her position by the bedroom door.

"Quite." Michael answered. "It is not uncommon for my hotel to request more than one truck. We often have extra things that need to be removed, most times it is just trash but on occasion it is someone like you two that need to leave more secretly."

"So, you've done this before?" I asked. At his nod I added, "Is there any way that someone on the Council would be aware that you do this?"

"Doubtful. However, as time is tight this is the best option to get you both out with none being the wiser." As far as reassurance went, that was probably the best I was going to get.

"I guess we have no choice. Let's hope that no one that is looking for us has knowledge of your tactics." I flounced down on the couch, indicating to Davina to do the same. "What time do we need to become garbage?"

"You have about four hours." Michael checked his watch to confirm.

"Do I know the men that will be helping us?" I asked.

"You know one of them, James agreed to return from hunting rogues with Brian and the rest of his team. I told him with everything going on I needed at least one of my lieutenants on this side of the country." Michael's face darkened for a moment before he added. "The other is new to my pack and is earnestly trying to prove himself. I am hoping that James can bring him to heel better than I have been able to."

"Do we need to worry he'll cause problems?" Davina asked the question I was thinking.

"No, he is just young, not only as a new shifter but as a human he was only seventeen when he went through the transformation." The surprise I was unable to hide impelled Michael to explain more. "He is Blair's younger brother."

Well, that explains why someone was changed so young. Most born shifters don't even experience their first shift until they are twenty so under normal rules he would not have been allowed to be bitten until at least that age.

I was curious about the back story on why he was changed so young but didn't ask. Judging by the looks of remorse on Blair's face and the stony looks of anger on Michael's it is probably best to let sleeping dogs lie.

"Well, then it is good that James came back to help." I stated with true sincerity. "If anyone can help him get some control it would be James."

We discussed several more things unrelated to the plan of escape before Michael and Blair said their goodbyes. By the end of the evening, perhaps this was wishful thinking on my part; I believe Blair was starting to lose some of her animosity towards me.

"What did you ever do to his mate?" Davina blurted as soon as the door was closed behind them.

Apparently, it was wishful thinking; I thought before answering, "Michael and I had a fling several years ago. We knew it would never go anywhere since we knew we were not mated. When I went to congratulate them, she didn't respond well to my presence. Blair was human and still has a human's sensibilities about sex and relationships. I tried to be friendly but the more I tried the more she hated me. It probably doesn't help that my family and the Colliers are old friends, so she can't keep me away completely."

"Do you think her brother will cause any problems for us, knowing her animosity towards you?" Davina asked.

I thought about that for a minute. I didn't trust Blair not to hurt me, but I trusted Michael to keep her in check. "I don't know the answer to that. I never met the brother. I don't know if he would turn against his alpha to help his sister exact some misguided kind of revenge on me."

My mind wandered for a moment to my time with Michael. It had been over for years and was never anything more than fun had between two consenting adults. As soon as I heard he had mated, all I felt was happiness for him. I wasn't holding any hopes of more from him. I wanted to meet my own mate not lust after someone else's.

"We really have no choice though. Tomorrow morning, we get to be taken out like the trash."

Davina laughed at my little pun then said, "I'm going to lie down for a couple hours." She went to the bedroom, closing the door behind her. I paced the room, my nerves too wound up worrying about anything and everything that could go wrong tomorrow.

Chapter Fourteen

Cassandra

After King Lucian left his private chambers with Orson, we were shown to a suite of rooms fit for royalty, composed of a sitting room, small dining area, bedroom and a luxurious bathroom. Soft plush carpets greeted our tired feet as we stepped into the sitting room.

We both removed our shoes, not wanting to dirty the lustrous carpet. Sumptuous comfortable chairs covered in purple velvet like material sat in a half circle facing an enormous fireplace. A low fire was smoldering in it when we entered giving off just enough heat to make the room comfortable without being stuffy.

Through a wide archway I could see a black wood table with six chairs. At either end of the table, elaborate place settings sat made ready for a meal to be served. I truly hoped that meant we would be fed soon, as we had not eaten since this morning. I spied a substantial bathroom through an open door to the right of the sitting area; the sunken bathtub looked deep and wide enough to hold ten people. Once we ate, I planned to take a nice swim in that tub to wash the grime of traveling from my body.

There was one other door which I assume led to the bedroom. We could visit that room later. Just the thought of climbing into bed brought mixed feelings. Our hosts expected Nikolas and me, as mates, to share the bed but I was unsure if I was ready for that. For now, I would focus on hopefully getting something to eat and then using that beautiful tub.

The young female dragon who escorted us to our rooms stole furtive glances at the two of us. Our arrival from Gaia was quite a surprise to the populace of this realm. Over a thousand years have passed since any outsiders had arrived from Gaia. Fortunately, the looks she threw our way were merely inquisitive and showed no hostility as I had seen in the crowds on our way to the palace.

"Milord and lady, I am Trista; I will be your servant while you are here." She actually curtsied, causing me to giggle. Mortification colored her cheeks pink as she lowered herself further.

"Stop." I leaned down to pull her up from her almost prostrate form on the floor. "I apologize for laughing. In Gaia we are not a lord or a lady, and no one bows to us." I explained trying to soothe her hurt feelings. "I am just not used to someone calling me lady or bowing."

Trista gave me a tremulous smile. "I believe I understand. You must know that here many people will bow to you. You are the mate to the true king, even if he has refused the throne he is still of the royal family."

"I understand. I am sorry if I upset you."

"Do not concern yourself, I will be fine." Trista straightened her spine and put a little more steel in her voice. "Now, my room is across the hall. You can ring for me using this." She pointed at a pull rope that fed into the ceiling. "Dinner will be delivered in about an hour. Might I suggest a bath before dinner?"

"A bath sounds lovely." This woman must be a mind reader. Trista walked into the bathroom and held the door for me to follow her. "I should be able to manage on my own." Once again, I had apparently committed some kind of faux pas as her face took on a decidedly unhappy look. "I am not used to having someone help me bathe." I explained.

"I see." Trista replied tersely. "I shall at least draw your bath, and then I will leave you to undress and bathe on your own."

With jerky movements she twisted the taps causing light pink water to begin filling the tub. Placing her hand under the flow of water, she tested the temperature. Finding it acceptable to her she stepped back from the tub and with a quick bow left the room.

A crackling fire was going in here as well, filling the air with a calming juniper scent. The floor beneath my feet was warm to the touch and I found myself rooted to the spot. The tub had a strange fascination for me. I stood staring at the pink water filling the tub, my mind wandering to another pool of pink colored water and the inhabitant of that pool.

My cheeks flushed with heat and a tingling spread throughout my body centering in my groin. Lifting my fingers, I traced along the curve of my lips, memories of that perfect first kiss circling in my head. Strong hands landed lightly on my shoulders, causing my heart to leap into my throat. I could not determine if it was fear or desire that caused my reaction.

His chest pressed against my back, warmth seeping through my shirt as his arms encircled me. Once the surprise of him being in the bathroom with me passed, I leaned into his hard chest. A feeling of rightness enveloped me. Nikolas seemed content to just hold me in his arms allowing me time to become comfortable with his nearness. With my head tucked into his chin, I watched the pink water fill the mammoth tub.

Once the tub was filled, Nikolas released me. Turning off the taps he turned to face me. The heat in his eyes had my toes curling and fire spreading through my body. Everywhere his eyes settled burst into flame. Gods, if just a look from him seemed to ignite me, what would it feel like to have his hands on me?

As if he had heard my thoughts, which he probably did considering our mate bond, he stepped closer to me. He lifted a lock of my hair and twirled it around his finger, pulling me closer to him. He raised his other hand and cupped my chin with it as he leaned in to brush his lips across mine. Lust rushed through my veins at the slightest touch from his lips propelling me into his waiting arms.

Nervousness fled my mind to be replaced by a burning passion when Nikolas deepened our kiss. His hands released my chin and hair, traveling down my body to pull at the bottom of my shirt. He held still as if he were awaiting my permission. Decision made, I placed my hands over his and pulled them away. Stepping back from him, I saw disappointment flash across his face to be quickly smoothed away.

I held his gaze with mine as I pulled my shirt up over my lace bra then slowly dragged my jeans down my hips. Standing in front of him in a lacy bra and panties was a little unnerving until I met his eyes and saw the yearning in them. He moved toward me, but I held my hand up.

"Undress." I ordered. A small quirk of his lips told me he quite enjoyed being bossed around by me, at least in this context. My eyes feasted on the hard muscles of his chest when he removed his tight t-shirt. I wanted to run my hands over the firm planes of his chest and abdomen but held myself back, wanting to see all of him.

Nikolas stared with desire at my scantily clad body while he lowered his dark pants over his hips and to the floor. His cock stood at attention beckoning me closer. Nikolas yanked me into his arms again and our lips met in a clash of desire. I

94

ran my hands up his chest to wrap them around his neck; my tongue darted out, probing for entry into his mouth.

A low moan rumbled through Nikolas' chest as he pulled me closer still, thrusting his tongue into my mouth. His rigid shaft pulsed against my abdomen, and I reached down between us with one hand to grasp it firmly. Slowly, I massaged his stiff member from base to tip feeling his cock buck in my hand. The rumble of desire grew in his throat when he lifted me into the air. I wrapped my legs around his body and felt the tip of his hardened staff rub against my damp center.

Nikolas lowered our bodies to the warm tiled floor. He pulled my hand from between our bodies, holding it with my other hand above my head. His slow onslaught of my body started at my mouth as his experienced tongue jousted with mine.

Leaving my mouth, he ran his lips along my jaw line and down my neck. His free hand trailed along my hip, up my side to cup my straining mound in his hand. Suddenly both breasts sprang free, and my destroyed bra fell away to lie beneath me. His hand returned to massage one breast while his tongue flicked across my nipple on my other breast eliciting a moan of desire from me as heat shot from my breasts into my core.

Nikolas lathed first my right then my left breast with his tongue as he slowly ran his hand down my tense abdomen. Shudders of pleasure shook my body when his hand slipped into my panties to cup my moist center. I nearly came off the floor when his finger slowly entered me fluttering over my clit sending jolts of pleasure through my body.

Gods you are amazing. Nikolas' deep timbre resonated through my mind as wave after wave of sultry heat swept my body.

Nikolas released my hands from above my head, moving his mouth down my body away from my breasts. With one hand continuing its assault of my clit, the other pulled my panties down my leg, revealing all of me to him. Tongue skimmed across my stomach then slowly probed through my already damp curls to replace his finger.

Electric spasms of delight racked my body with each thrust of his tongue into my wet opening. My hands clenched his hair, guiding his tongue to my most sensitive spot. All thought left my brain as I felt my climax nearing. My hips rose to meet each spearing from his tongue with wild abandon.

95

"Gods, Nikolas, oh Gods." I yelled out as my climax took me over the edge.

Nikolas did not give me a moment to recover before moving to cover my body with his. I reached between us grasping his cock in my hands. Moving up and down his long shaft, I felt him tremble in excitement. His member pulsed as a small amount of pre-cum formed on the tip. Running my finger over the tip, I swirled the moisture around the tip, pulling another deep moan from my mate.

Unable to hold back any longer, Nikolas pulled my hands from his member. Positioning himself at my still quivering entrance, he caught my eyes with his.

Look at me, my heart. Our eyes held as he eased into me, allowing my body to accommodate his massive size. When I started to move his hands gripped my hips holding me still. His cock jerked inside of me, sending a ripple of heat to my core. He slowly withdrew then rammed back into me.

"Gods, Cass, you're so tight." Nikolas panted as his shaft speared me again pushing me closer to the edge once again. I could feel my body tightening and readying for release when he slowed his rhythm.

"Not yet." Nikolas said before his lips met mine in a searing kiss. He held himself immobile above me, cock hard and pulsing within me. His tongue plundered my mouth, pulling more moans of lust from me. Nikolas began moving his hips in a slow sensual circle, my sheath contracted and convulsed with each stabbing of his tongue. Just when I began to believe he meant to torture me forever with carnal pleasure, he slowed his movement.

"Cass" his growl brought my eyes up to meet his. "Gods, you're perfect." A satisfied smirk crossed his face as he drove his cock into me. His thrusting came faster and harder.

My breathing sped until I was panting with need. A rumble began low in his chest, building into a deep growl of satisfaction. I felt myself start to climax as my wet pussy clamped on his thrusting cock forcing wave after wave of fiery heat and desire shuddering through my body. Nikolas roared with satisfaction as he spilled his seed within me.

Our bodies lay entangled together on the hard tile floor while our breathing gradually returned to normal. Nikolas rolled off me, pulling me close to his side while he drew a lazy circle on my backside. He placed a chaste kiss on my temple. I looked up to his face to find a contented smile gazing down at me with love.

After a few more minutes getting our bodies under control Nikolas murmured, "Would you like your bath now, milady?"

I giggled at his use of the word milady but nodded as I did really want that bath. Nikolas rose from the floor then helped me up. I expected to feel a little self-conscious over my state of undress and the acts we had just performed. However, I experienced none of the normal after sex jitters worrying about whether he'd call or enjoyed it.

As I placed my hand in his to allow him to pull me up, the feeling of rightness enveloped me again. Nikolas lifted me in his arms and carried me to the bathtub. I expected him to set me down so I could step in, but Nikolas had other ideas.

Stepping over the side of the tub, he carried me into the water. He sat down, placing me between his legs. The water had cooled a little while we had enjoyed each other on the floor. I mumbled a quick spell under my breath, reheating the water.

A sigh of pleasure slipped past his lips as I leaned back into his chest. Hmm, I wonder if that sigh was due to the spell or me.

You, always you.

Happiness flowed through my body at his words. Nikolas chuckled contentedly behind me. He picked up a sponge from the side of the tub, lathered it up with a citrus scented soap and began to wash my back. Everywhere his hands touched me, heat flared. I could feel my body responding to each touch. It took a lot of willpower to keep my hands to myself so we could finish our bath.

Smelling fresh and clean, our skin pink and shiny, we rinsed off then grabbed the thick towels to dry. Neither of us wanted to put our filthy clothes back on, so we wandered out of the bathroom in hopes of finding something to wear in the bedroom.

As tempting as the enormous four poster bed was, we both veered away from it. In a closet I found a couple of sumptuous light green robes. Passing one to him, I donned mine while peeking at his naked form when he dropped his towel. A satisfied grin appeared on his face when he caught me looking.

With one last wistful look at the bed, I walked out of the room heading into the dining area. It would seem someone had entered our rooms while we were occupied in the bathroom with each other. The table was laden with meats, vegetables and cheeses I didn't recognize but smelled divine. Nikolas had followed me from the bedroom and spying the food, pulled me into the room. Like a perfect gentleman, he walked me to my seat and held it for me before taking his own seat.

"I don't know what any of this is. Do you think it's safe for us to eat?" I asked, my mouth watering with hunger.

"I am sure it is fine." He replied. "As hungry as I am, I don't care what it is."

We both piled our plates high with different items from the table and began to eat. The food was amazing. The dark meat I tried tasted like beef while another lighter meat had a distinct taste of chicken. The vegetables also reminded me of different vegetables from Gaia. One was like corn, and was probably a relative to our corn, although its kernels were a dark orange rather than the yellow, I was used to. We ate with gusto until our bellies felt ready to burst.

Nikolas sat back with a look of content on his face. However, his question took me a little off guard. "When is the last time you fed?"

I dropped my fork, not expecting him to ask that when he looked so relaxed. "The morning, I was sent to interrogate you."

Just the thought of consuming blood had my mouth watering. Until he brought it up, I hadn't thought much about not having blood. Now I couldn't think of anything else.

I was old enough that I could go several weeks to a month without feeding if I didn't overexert myself with my magic. It had only been a little over a week, and I hadn't really used much magic, but I had a gnawing feeling in my chest now that Nikolas had mentioned feeding.

"You need to feed then." He advised me as he rose to stand beside me.

"I can go a month without feeding." I replied petulantly.

I don't know why but I was embarrassed about needing blood. Nikolas was a dragon, not a vampire. Even though vampires were created by dragons, he was not a blood dragon. Based on the color of scales I had seen on him he was an earth dragon, although he also had purple scales so maybe I was missing something.

"You must feed more often until you grow accustomed to the energy expended during our mating." Nikolas held my gaze watching for a sign that I understood.

My cheeks flushed with color as I realized that the energy he was referring to was from our sexual exploits. "Gods, I love your blushes." He murmured quietly.

In a louder voice he added, "You must feed and since I do not believe my dragon would like it much if you fed from another, you will need to feed from me."

Unbidden my eyes darted to the pulse at his neck. Just the thought of slicing my teeth through his skin had me becoming aroused. I could almost taste his blood, my mouth watered with the thought of taking even the tiniest sips from him. He held his hand out to me. When I placed my hand in his he pulled me to stand next to him.

"Come, my heart." His deep voice sent shivers down my spine.

He led me into the bedroom, closing the door behind us. Releasing my hand, he stepped to the side of the bed and disrobed. I stared hungrily at his naked form, first at his neck with yearning then at his already hard cock with a different kind of want. Nikolas lay in the middle of the bed, shaft rigid and upright. He beckoned to me with one hand and grasped his staff with the other. "Take from me anything you need."

I ripped my robe from my heated body and flung myself on the bed. I crawled to his side, my eyes feasting on his hand clasped around his firm shaft. You would think I would be sated and not need him as badly as I did right now. My body trembled with just the thought of mounting him. Gods, I needed him so much right now. The knowledge that he would also allow me to feed from him caused throbbing throughout my entire body.

I don't allow you to feed from me, I crave it. I want to feel you wet with need and wrapped around me while you take my blood.

Needing no further encouragement, I pulled his hand from his cock, pushing it and his other hand above his head. I ran my tongue along his lips, probing for entry. His mouth opened and I plunged my tongue into the depths of his mouth. A low moan rumbled in his chest when I grasped his manhood with my hand, stroking him firmly from base to tip.

His tip became moist as I rose above him to lower myself on him. With his staff seated fully to the hilt, I brought my mouth to his neck. Moving slowly up and down on his cock, my teeth bit through his skin sending warm blood into my mouth. I swallowed greedily as my motions sped up. Having drunk my fill, I rose from his neck to ride him like a bucking stallion. Nikolas watched me through hooded eyes as I took my pleasure from him. I lifted my hips, slamming them back down over and over again.

I arched against him, my body tightening as his thick length filled me. Every thrust sent me closer to the edge. In a quick motion, Nikolas flipped our positions throwing me on my back. His hips moved faster, pushing into me harder and harder. I cried out as waves of lust enveloped me.

I bit into his neck once again gorging on his blood. His roar of pleasure echoed around the room as he rammed into me one last time, spilling his hot seed into me while I sucked his blood from his neck. My body shuddered with my release.

Nikolas fell to my side, dragging me against his sweat slicked body. My mind and body filled with a satisfied contentment as we fell asleep wrapped in each other's arms.

My rest was its typical dreamless blackness. The light shining in my eyes from the open window woke me from sleep. Tangled in each other, legs and arms twisted up together, even asleep, we had clung to each other. Nikolas shifted behind me, a deep inhale followed by his hand coming to rest on my hip. I knew he was fully awake when his hand slipped from my hip to grasp my firm buttocks in his hand.

Gods, this was the best way to wake up. A contented chuckle rumbled behind me telling me he had heard my thoughts. I imagined all the things I wanted him to do to my body. His shaft stiffened and I knew he had seen that thought as well.

Putting action to my thoughts, he pulled me closer. spreading my legs with his strong hands his hard shaft speared me from behind. Tremors cascaded through my body as he quickly took me to the precipice. Nikolas roared his release behind me as we reached our climax together.

We lay panting in each other's arms, neither of us able to or wanting to move. Our breathing slowly returned to normal, yet neither of us moved to escape the other's body. Content, I sighed deep. With a smile, I grabbed his hand and pulled his arm tight around me.

"I've never felt like this with anyone before." I whispered, a little nervous how he would respond.

"Of course not. Neither have I." I could sense the grin on his face even without looking at him.

When he smiled, he looked so open and handsome. I decided then and there I would do whatever I could to make him smile more. His fierce countenance would be a thing of the past.

"I will hold you to that, my heart." Nikolas spoke into my ear.

"We need to get up." I stated reluctantly. I really didn't want to leave our bed and his arms, but I knew we needed to meet with the king this morning to start preparing for our return to Gaia.

"Just a few more minutes." Nikolas pleaded as he pulled me firmer against his chest.

I snuggled into him and figured a few more minutes wouldn't hurt. We lay there for a lot longer than a few more minutes. For a moment I felt like I was part of just a normal couple, not one trapped in a different realm with who knows how many people searching for us. It was nice, at a slight ahem from Nikolas I amended that thought, okay it was great, wonderful, amazing. He shook with laughter, and oh what a beautiful sound it was. Deep and full of mirth.

My eyes were getting heavy, and I felt like I could take a nap when the bedroom door banged open. King Lucian and Orson strode into the room, uncaring that we were lying naked on the bed with nothing covering us. Nikolas shielded my body with his and a low growl rumbled in the back of his throat.

"Calm yourself." Orson admonished.

"You are late." King Lucian announced. "I do not like to be kept waiting, even by you." He barely looked at us as he harangued us about punctuality.

"We apologize, your highness." Nikolas stated although his tone of voice did not sound appropriately apologetic. "If you would be so kind as to allow us to dress, we will join you at once."

Lucian's gaze finally alighted on our unclad bodies. His cheeks turned crimson when he noticed our state of undress as his eyes settled on the much larger form of Nikolas. I yanked the sheet further up, glaring at Lucian's audacity. With no apology, Lucian and Orson swept from the room, giving us privacy to get dressed. Our clothes, unfortunately, were a filthy mess on the bathroom floor. Nikolas opened one of the closet doors and found a broad assortment of clothing that looked as if it would fit him.

I checked the other closet and happily found clothing in my size too. When Magda forewarned them of our arrival, she must have also given them our sizes. We dressed quickly, Nikolas in black pants that looked like a type of leather and an emerald, green tight-fitting shirt that molded to his form like a glove.

101

I dressed similarly in black loose fitting harem style pants and an emerald, green shirt. With my bra destroyed, I worried I would look too wanton with my breasts hanging free. Luckily the shirt I chose had a bodice sewn into it that provided the support I needed. My choice of colors was not in solidarity with Nikolas, although I had no reason to not want that, but because all the available bottoms were black and all the tops emerald green.

Once we were suitably dressed, we left the bedroom to find Lucian and Orson sitting on the purple velvet chairs. "Trista is arranging breakfast. Until it is here, sit, we will start my lessons on the changes of Gaia." Lucian commanded, a muscle twitched in his jaw.

I really wanted to tell him off for just barging in but my more sensible self prevailed. Much to Nikolas' joy, I chose to bite my tongue. We were currently treated as honored guests, but we didn't know the king. It was safest if we did as we were asked until we either learned to trust he wouldn't just behead us or how to portal out of here, whichever came first.

We sat together on a loveseat and looked at each other to see who would start. Deciding it was to be me, I began, "Well, first, they do not call that realm Gaia. It is called Earth and is predominantly made up of humans. Most races that are not human, such as shifters, vampires and witches live in hiding. We do not share the knowledge or our existence with any human that is not our mate."

"Why are the humans in charge, we used to rule the world together as equals?" King Lucian looked completely perplexed by my statements.

"After the portals were sealed, the different species met and decided that due to the damage the fae dragon wars had caused all non-human species would recede into hiding." Nikolas explained. "It was determined to trick the humans into believing they had not witnessed all that they had. Back then it was easy to fool people into thinking what they saw with their own eyes was not real. Humans were very superstitious then and passing the events off as shared hysteria seemed the best idea at the time."

"Now humans have advanced in technology that if they were to learn of all the different species that walk the earth, they could cause harm to many of them. If not all of us, what with their bombs and guns." I continued.

"What are bombs and guns?" Orson asked.

"Weapons that can cause injury and death." Nikolas responded. Our history lesson continued in this manner for several hours. Each new revelation invoked countless questions from Lucian and Orson. Breakfast came and went, followed by lunch then dinner. We talked; they listened. They questioned, we answered. Hours passed and we had barely scratched the surface of all that had changed in Gaia since Lucian had walked on its surface.

Finally, night fell, and Lucian determined we would rest then resume our talks in the morning. He also wanted to practice portal opening with Nikolas. Now that the seal had been broken from Gaia's side, any mated dragons would be able to open portals. King Lucian had announced an edict forbidding it until more could be learned. He would be the first and only dragon to step through a portal to Gaia until he deemed it was safe for others to travel there.

Exhausted from talking all day, Nikolas and I bathed but had no energy to do more than that. With robes wrapped around our bodies we dragged our tired selves into our bedroom. "Gods, Cass that was draining." Nikolas complained as we fell into bed together.

"And we get to do it all again tomorrow." I grumbled. I reached out and pulled his arm around me. We were fast asleep within moments of our heads hitting the pillows.

Chapter Fifteen

Arianna

We made excellent time with no issues with Tygus, his crew or our fellow stowaways. What we expected to be at least eight days was shortened to only six. With the combined aid of Malina and Tygus we sailed faster than we had hoped. We arrived off the coast of Unimak Island. Jacky lowered our boat and belongings into the sea. Our destination was a bit further on, but this was the closest Tygus would get to the Alaskan coastline.

Magic was able to hide his ship, but he felt safest when he didn't tempt fate by messing with human technology. We said our goodbyes, and he promised to come to our aid if needed again. The heated looks he sent Diana's way had me imagining we would be seeing him sooner rather than later.

They enjoyed each other's company many times on our journey. While I would never begrudge any of my friends their happiness, I worried that one of them would get hurt when the other found their mate. Diana assured me he was not her mate and therefore was just a passing fancy.

Matthew steered our small boat toward our hidden island in silence. A thrill of excitement ran up my spine at the thought of returning to this island. I was curious what changes Matthew and Annie had made over the years.

Due to my mating with Fraxinus, I had not been able to come here often, and it has been almost three hundred years since I was able to last visit. I had hoped to visit it more frequently, but when Fraxinus had stopped leaving our home near Greece I could no longer sneak away.

On our approach, I told Annie to call Davina so she would know we were on the island. Annie frowned when her call went straight to voicemail. This was the third missed call. Annie left a simple message stating that we are here but did not elaborate further. I hoped their escape had gone as planned rather than the alternative.

Hopefully, whatever plans the O'Briens had come up with worked to get Davina and the O'Brien hybrid out of Philadelphia had worked. Now that we had all agreed to work together, forgiving past grievances, we all needed to be somewhere we could not easily be found. Once we were all together, our next plan would need to be to find a way to get my son and his mate out of Fabeldyrverden safely.

We arrived at the edge of the shield surrounding the island. Matthew looked at me to confirm I was ready. The whale-like rocks loomed ahead, jutting up from the ocean floor. Salt spray stung my face as we neared the barrier. With me in the boat, we had nothing to worry about.

One wrong move for someone else and they could be lost in my maze of spells. Attempt to come in from any other point and one could end up wandering the seas for eternity, trapped between the past, present and future. However, none of the traps at this distance would cause any harm, they only caused disorientation or redirection.

Every coven member knew the safe passage through. They would need to guide our allies through safely and carefully. My spells would remain in place to keep our enemies out.

We reached the dock within minutes of crossing the spell's barrier. My eyes lit up at all the changes Matthew and Diana had made over the years. My heart sped up when I took my first step onto the dock. Gods, it had been too many years. Anger at Fraxinus for, well for everything he had done welled up in me. After a few calming breaths I looked around at the improvements my friends had made.

On my last visit this island held little more than a one room shack and a small dock. Now, three ample two-story houses are situated about a quarter mile from the expanded dock. The dock was solid enough that several small boats or a few larger vessels could tie up and not ram each other.

Magic guarded our borders, but Matthew and Annie had embraced human ingenuity for our comfort. Three identical stone houses stood at the top of the hill. Each house was identical in size; however, the first house had a panoramic porch that ran along the entire front and down one side. The other two houses had simple stoops leading to their front doors.

"We were unable to finish the second and third house." Annie explained when she saw where my gaze had ventured. "The front house is completely furnished but the other two have the bare minimum inside. We thought we would have more time." She gave me a half-hearted smile with a shrug of her shoulders.

"Do not concern yourself," I reassured her with a small pat on her arm. "I am sure those who are coming to join us will be grateful just to have a roof over their head, electricity and running water. Although, we should probably warn them to bring items such as blankets and such to help them be more comfortable."

"Of course," Annie agreed her smile lighting up some. "When Davina returns my call, I will let her know what the living situation is so everyone can bring the necessary items."

"Good, now how about we unload our possessions and get settled in to wait."

Each of us grabbed whatever we could carry and began the short trip from the dock to the main house. Matthew pointed out all the improvements they had made. A considerably sized water tower sat off to the right of the island, which Matthew stated was full of rainwater.

The water tower had a satellite antenna that would allow us to continue to have cell phone service as well as connect to the internet. Solar panels covered every roof, as well as generators sturdy enough to run all the electricity for several days if necessary. All in all, Matthew and Diana surpassed my hopes of what would await our arrival here. I let them know how happy I was with all they had accomplished.

The house was cool upon entering it; Malina quickly lit a fire with the logs that were resting in the fireplace as we set about unloading our items. The house had four bedrooms on the second floor and wonderfully, each bedroom had its own bathroom. There were also two other houses that could be used if we didn't all want to live together.

For now, my coven would remain together in this house. With the extra groups coming, many would probably need to bunk in rooms together. Matthew and Annie would share one room, the witches; Temperence, Diana and Malina would share a room, when Davina arrived, she would have her own room, and I would have my own room.

I offered to have one of the witches bunk with me but they said they preferred to share a room. Something about always being together unless one of them was carnally engaged was mentioned at which point I stopped listening and just agreed they should stay in the same room if that is what they wanted.

Everything was put away and we all gathered around the large ornate dining room table. I noticed that Annie and Matthew had goblets in their hands and surmised that they had ensured a well-stocked blood supply for their feeding. The rest of us tucked into a tray of meats and cheeses that Temperence had set out for

106

our dinner. Now all we could do was wait for word from Davina and the eminent arrival of our allies.

Chapter Sixteen

Aisling

The moment of our escape had arrived. A loud knock sounded on the door to our fancy cage; I mean suite of well-appointed rooms. Davina and I shared a nervous glance.

Michael's plan should work but there was always the chance something could go wrong. Neither of us relished the idea of being captured by the Council. Although, since Cassandra was MIA in the dragon realm, I wasn't even going to try to pronounce its real name, at least we wouldn't be tortured by her if we were caught.

With one final glance at Davina, I grasped the handle and pulled open the door to confront my fate. I know, I know, a little dramatic, right. On the other side of the door stood a young shifter I didn't recognize but behind him stood the tall lithe form of James Collier. His stern features broke into a lopsided grin when he saw me.

"Aisling, you little runt, Michael didn't tell me it was you I was throwing in the trash." Only someone as tall as James would call me a little runt. I am about five and a half feet but next to James' six-foot six frame I looked like a little runt. James gave me a quick hug then stepped back to survey Davina.

I light breeze could have knocked me over when I saw the way James and Davina stared at each other. James' eyes roved up and down Davina's body like he was going to eat her up. The look she was giving him said pretty much the same thing. What the hell was going on? I thought. Suddenly, everyone is mating. Gods, when was I going to be lucky enough to meet mine?

"Hey, I hate to break up the eye-fucking party, but aren't we on a schedule here?" I interrupted their staring contest with a jab to James' belly and a flick of my finger to Davina's nose.

James recovered first, glancing quickly at me only to have his eyes return to gaze longingly at Davina. "I wasn't expecting this." He sort of apologized. "This changes things." He murmured quietly. "I'll need to tell Michael. First, let's get you two to safety."

All business, well almost all business, since he latched onto Davina's hand like it was a life preserver, James led us from the room to a wall at the end of the hall. I looked around confused for a minute until James reached out and pressed his palm in the middle of the wall.

Our heads all spun when we heard the elevator ding behind us. "No one should have access to this floor." James growled as he pushed firmer on the palm reader.

A loud snick followed by a low rumble sounded as the wall slid in about two inches then moved up into the ceiling. An elevator door opened on the other side of the false wall. We all stepped inside, and the doors snapped shut behind us. Thankfully, we hadn't seen anyone exit the other elevator.

James looked at all three of us when he said, "No one is to ever learn that this elevator exists, do you understand."

We all nodded our heads yes. Then my stomach jumped into my throat as we dropped twenty stories in about five seconds. The doors opened into the underground service garage, and we followed James out into the garage bay. A deep look of reluctance crossed his face when he had to release Davina's hand. He lifted me into the back of a garbage truck then turned to Davina to lift her in beside me. James lowered the back of the truck, enclosing us within it.

Gods, this truck reeked. I heard the doors close and the engine start. We were jarred when the truck began to move and even with our reflexes, we both landed on our asses on the slime covered floor. This was going to be a long disgusting ride. James had left a small electric lantern lit for us so we would not be in total darkness. When I looked at the filth covering the walls and floor, I almost wished he hadn't.

I glanced at Davina to see how she was handling this only to find a bemused look on her face. "Are you alright?" I asked, nudging her when she seemed to barely notice my question.

"What, oh, uh, yes." Davina stammered. "I'm fine. I just never believed I would ever meet him. Well not exactly him as in James Collier but him as in my mate. I've been here in Gaia for over a thousand years. I can't believe I've finally found him. And gods he is stunning." A very satisfied look came upon her face. "I mean, you've seen him, he's just so handsome, and tall, I was so afraid my mate would be short." She gushed more about how amazing James looked. Then suddenly she stopped and looked at me shrewdly. "You haven't slept with him too, have you?"

109

I sputtered in surprise at her line of questioning. Humans were normally the prudish ones, not other supernatural species. "No, I haven't. Would it really matter if I had? Mating trumps everything."

"No, of course not, it wouldn't matter a bit." Davina reassured me. "I was just curious if you knew how he was, well, I mean, how well he performed, gods do I really have to spell it out for you?"

I laughed, having not seen this side of Davina in our short time together. Seeing her flustered made me like her just a bit more.

"I wish I could answer you bumbled question, but I know nothing of his sexual prowess or lack thereof. James has always been a very private person, I am sure he has had sex, but he never boasts about it like others like to. If his cousin, Michael was more circumspect, I probably wouldn't have the issues I have had with his mate."

"I suppose that is good news." She commented ruefully. "However, I wouldn't have minded if you had said he had many women who all raved about how great he wielded his sword."

We both doubled over with laughter. Tears were streaming down my cheeks before I got myself under control again. Gods, this side of Davina was so much more fun than the resolute dragon that had arrived at my hotel door a couple days ago.

"Serious question," I announced once we had stopped laughing. "Now that you have mated, you can learn how to open a portal to the dragon realm?"

Davina considered my question for so long, I wasn't sure she would answer. "Hmm, we'll have to start training immediately. But he won't reach the full power of a dragon's mate until we have consummated our mating as well as performed the rites. We need a dragon or very powerful witch to perform the rites. I could ask Arianna, but I suspect she'll have her hands full trying to find her son."

"How about Hawthorne?" I asked hopefully. "Could he perform the rites that you're talking about?"

"I believe he could." She answered hesitantly. "Let us hope the loss of his mate does not affect his power to command the talisman."

"Yes, let's hope." We both fell silent, lost in our own thoughts.

I don't know why all of a sudden everyone seemed to be finding their mates. Once, years ago, my mother had told me about the Fates, and how they liked to play with people's lives. Sometimes causing havoc and other times aligning things just so.

With all the recent pairings, especially vampires like Jace, Almerinda, and Gabriel who had each spent several centuries alone, I wondered if the Fates were somehow controlling all the recent matings. If the Fates are involved, are they working for our benefit or not?

Either my nose was broken, or I had become immune to the stench. Being part shifter usually made smells more potent however I had never been the best at scenting things. For once I was grateful my sense of smell was wonky for a shifter, especially since Davina continued to scrunch up her nose in revulsion. We traveled in silence for almost two hours before she broached a subject I had been worrying about.

"Do you think that perhaps your mate is a dragon and that is why you haven't met them yet?"

I chuckled ruefully, "Until a few months ago, I didn't even know dragons still existed in our world. Plus, I am a hybrid; I could have more than one mate out there. Is there a chance one is a dragon, I suppose that could be the case." I thought about her question a little longer then added, "I hope I only have one mate. I really don't care what species he is as long as he is not a dick."

"Hmm, that is something to consider, I guess." She responded thoughtfully. "I would hate to end up with someone like Fraxinus. If ever the Fates had intervened, that mating was a definite one of their worst decisions."

"You have stories of the Fates too?" I asked. "My mother used to talk about them as if they were actual people just sitting around fucking with everyone's lives."

"I don't know that I would say they, as you put it, fuck with everyone's lives." Davina pointed out. "I do believe that they intercede when a course correction needs to happen. There are many instances in history when a being has been mated with another being that they absolutely abhorred. The mating, in those instances, has nothing to do with love, sex or procreation, and everything to do with rectifying a bad situation."

"Really, that must have sucked for the ones involved." I retorted. "I mean could you imagine meeting your mate, thinking everything was going to be great and amazing, only to learn you hated them and the whole reason for finding them was to kill them or something almost as dire?"

"I can't imagine the feeling that person would have." She uttered in a voice so low and forlorn sounding. "I know that Arianna has faced something like that. She did at one time believe that Fraxinus was redeemable. She hoped that providing him with a child would change him. When she came to my island many years ago, I could see the hope on her face. Fraxinus did seem to change when they learned she was pregnant. When she learned how truly treacherous, he was, I also saw that hope fade. Her only happiness was gained from her children, and he even managed to steal that from her. He corrupted Penelope who in turn tried to corrupt Nikolas. When Penelope was unable to sway her brother to her side, she turned to a Fontaine witch to gain control of him. That was when Arianna lost all and yet she continued to fight in hopes to get her son back as well as defeat Fraxinus."

"I don't understand one thing though." I watched Davina closely to detect if she lied when she answered my next question. "Why didn't Arianna just kill Fraxinus?"

"She can't," sadness coated her words. "If he dies, she will die too. When a non-dragon mates with a dragon, they gain the immortality of a dragon. Dragons and fae are the only truly immortal beings. Vampires age, albeit slowly, they age. Shifters and witches live for about the same life spans. But, if a shifter, witch or vampire were to mate with a dragon they become immortal if their mate lives. Kill their mate and they die."

"What if one of us mates with a fae?" I asked more out of curiosity than anything.

"I wouldn't know, to my knowledge, the fae have never mated with any other species than their own kind." She explained. "Fae are nothing like any of us even if they look similar to humans, extremely tall and thin humans, but humanoid in appearance. To a fae, a vampire is food that increases their strength and energy. A shifter is a dirty animal that is beneath their notice. Witches are held a bit higher than shifters and vampires but not by much. They are viewed as neither food nor animal and seen as harmless playthings."

"They sound like real assholes." Aisling commented ruefully.

"Fae have been known to steal humans, take them to their realm, do something to change them, and then return them to Gaia. They return years later to

112

see if whatever they did to them affected the human. If the human has fae qualities sometimes the fae take them back to their realm. No one knows what happens to them when the humans are stolen away, only that they never come back if taken a second time."

Wow, I thought, there was so much I needed to learn about dragons. I had already studied all the species I could possibly mate with, now I need to learn as much as I could about dragons. Who knew what species my mate would be? Gods, I just hope he's not a giant bag of dicks like Fraxinus. I peppered Davina with questions about dragons and after a while an idea formed as to what a dragon mate would be like.

From her descriptions, it sounded very similar to a vampire's Blood Affinity. A dragon mated with someone whose blood called to them. Once they met that person, they would do anything to bind that person to them. Not every mating was about sex and procreation though.

The only dragons who hoped for a mate to further their line were those of the ruling classes. The dragon realm was ruled by a king or queen, and they had a set amount of time to find their mate, or they would have to give up their throne to the next in line. If they found their mate, then they were expected to produce an heir within yet another set amount of time. If they mated and produced an heir, they could rule for a thousand years.

At that time, their heir would take over the throne and the whole process would start again. Dragons, not of the royal family, did not have to worry about having children, and according to Davina, frequently waited years before having children, while some never did.

With as many questions as I could think of answered, we fell silent again. We had been in the back of this smelly truck for almost four hours now, so we should be close to Jace's home. He and his new mate had settled into her house in Altoona. The drive should have taken about four hours, barring any issues or crazy traffic.

Gods, I wished we could teleport like all the TV shows and movies show us doing. It would make things so much easier. I suppose once James learns how he and Davina should be able to teleport when they open portals. How cool would that be?

The truck came to a stop, and we heard the doors open. The back of the truck was wrenched open by James. Without waiting for permission, he pulled

Davina from the back and kissed her. Me and the young shifter who I assumed was Blair's brother looked everywhere but at the two wrapped in a passionate embrace.

He met my eyes and rolled his at me as if to say, 'What are you going to do?' I chuckled then cleared my throat loudly. When that failed to break the two sucking face apart, I tapped James on his shoulder. Then I punched him in the back when the tapping failed to get his attention.

James reluctantly pulled his mouth away from Davina's kiss swollen lips. Panting heavily, they stared at each other as if they had found their savior. In a manner of speaking, I suppose that must be how it felt to them. Blair's brother coughed then stepped closer to the back of the truck.

"Sorry, I need the horrible smell to drown out their scent." He looked embarrassed as he continued to explain. "I am young and new, my sister changed me without permission. So now I fight urges most shifters already know how to deal with." He nodded his head at the two lovers in front of us. "For example, his lust has driven me crazy this whole drive, but I was able to ignore it until her lust combined with his. Now I have an overwhelming urge to rut with just about anything that moves."

Incredulously, I stared at him in shock at all he had shared with me. "That must have sucked for you."

"You don't know the half of it." His rueful smirk had a tinge of anger and sadness laced through it. "I love my sister, but I wish she had left me human or at least waited until I was of the proper age to be changed. Christ, I was still going through human puberty when she bit me. My hormones are so out of whack that sometimes I go into a rage that I can't control. James was supposed to help me, now, I don't know that he can. His mating has really amped things up, I could barely tolerate being around other shifters who weren't newly mated."

He looked so forlorn that I almost reached out to hug him. His words flashed across my mind causing me to reconsider. If he was that amped up over the scents floating around from James and Davina, having my body so close may not be the best idea.

Rustling in the trees on the side of the road got all our attention. A tall black-haired vampire stepped onto the road holding the hand of a curvy red-haired vampire. Jace and Cat had arrived.

"Christ, are you fucking kidding me!" The young shifter blurted. I looked at him in confusion then I saw where he was looking. Jace and Cat had only been mated for a few months, and judging by the condition of her hair had probably just had sex not too long before joining us.

"James," I hollered, "you need to do something about Blair's brother. He's about to lose it."

It took James two seconds to see what was happening before he rushed the young shifter. Slamming into him, James tossed him inside the garbage truck and slammed the hatch closed. Cat looked between me and James in confusion. Jace leaned over and whispered something in her ear that must have answered her unspoken question as a look of understanding came over her features.

A loud howl erupted from inside the truck, causing the hairs on the nape of my neck to stand on end. We could hear his body ram into the sides of the truck. "Gods, I forgot." A mollified look came over James. "I should have been better prepared. I wasn't thinking."

"Obviously." I spat, poking him in the chest. "That poor kid is in there suffering because you couldn't control yourself. You were supposed to be helping him." I yelled angrily. I don't know why I was so angry about this. I didn't even know the kid's name but for some reason I was super pissed about this.

James pulled out his phone and dialed a number from memory. The call was answered on the second ring, and I could hear Michael's voice coming through from the other end. "Yes?"

"We have a problem." James answered. "Tommy is not going to be able to remain with me and I can't return right now." Silence from Michael met his comments. James strode toward the back of the truck, guilt sagging his shoulders. "I've met my mate." His low voice carried to the rest of us easily. "Tommy has gone into a bloodlust. I believe his senses were overwhelmed from being exposed to me and my mate as well as Jace and Catriona's arrival."

"I see." Michael's anger was palpable even through a phone call. "Where exactly can I find my brother-in-law?" James passed on the coordinates for the truck's location. "I will send someone to collect him. Is he secure for now?" When James assured him, he was, Michael stated. "Good, go with your mate. Once we have Tommy under control, I will let you know when you can return. Oh, and

115

congratulations on your mating." Michael ended the call before James could say anything further.

Turning to those of us not locked in a garbage truck, James stated, "Well I guess, we'll all be going together."

Jace gave a small nod then turned to walk back into the trees. "Our ride is waiting about three miles from here. We thought it best not to meet you in a car on the off chance you were followed."

Our trek through the trees was a quiet one. James and Davina could barely keep their hands to themselves. Jace and Cat weren't much better but at least they kept their hands above their clothing. Being the only unmated person here was quite annoying. Choosing to look anywhere but in front of me, I stared at the newly full moon above me.

Newly mated couples were all like this, most of them had the decency to find a private place away from others until their initial urges wore off some. This is why Jace and Cat were less handsy than James and Davina. At one point I believed James was about to drag Davina off into the trees. We managed to make it to the waiting SUV without incident.

The SUV's engine hummed as we sped away, but my nerves didn't settle. What if the Council had tracked us? Who was the person coming uninvited to my hotel floor? Would Michael get to Tommy before he hurt himself? And for Gods' sake, the damned smell of desire permeated the inside of the SUV so much that I had to roll the window down and hang my head out of it. The ride to Cat's house felt like forever even though it was only ten minutes.

The instant the vehicle came to a stop I pushed the door open and jumped out at a run. Gabriel and a tall good looking but brightly clothed man of what appeared to be Latin descent came out to meet them. I had met Gabriel not too long after Evan was found. The man with him must be his mate, Robert. Great, just what I needed, another pair of mates to deal with.

"Hello, Aisling. It is good to see you again." Gabriel's smooth voice with a hint of French accent greeted me. "This is Robert, my mate."

Robert took my hand in his. "It is a pleasure to meet you." His smile was infectious, and I found myself returning it. "I expect you are hungry; I have prepared a fine meal for everyone." Surprise lit my face causing Robert to explain further.

"Although I am a vampire now, I still love to cook; we also have a few humans and witches living in our home, so I still get to flex my muscles in the kitchen."

The intense Gabriel I had dealt with in the caves was gone, standing before me was a relaxed and smiling Gabriel. The love he had for Robert was evident as he laced his arm through Robert's arm leading us into the house. I almost laughed out loud when Gabriel reached his hand down and pinched his mate's ass affectionately.

We entered Cat's house to what sounded like a raucous party. Cat caught up with me and spoke quietly in my ear, "Don't worry, once we've all eaten most of the noise will go down the street to Robert and Gabriel's house." She pointed to a beautiful Victorian style house about a half mile away. "Only Jace and I live here but everyone wanted to meet the dragon."

Gabriel released Robert's arm, watching him walk to the kitchen with lust in his eyes. Thank goodness we didn't have Tommy with us any longer. He really would have gone berserk with all the hormones and pheromones floating around in the air. Gods, I could barely tolerate it, and I wasn't even a fledgling.

We entered the dining room to find a grandiose table with seating for eight. Along one wall was a solid red oak sideboard with a chair sitting on either side of it. The laughter and frivolity of the three people standing around the table cut off on our entrance.

"So, introductions." Jace started as he walked into the room behind me. "You met Gabriel and Robert out front; this is Tina a witch and her human mate Harri." The two women gave us a little wave. "Beside them is Derik a vampire, he is in town visiting and will report back anything necessary to our friends in Cleveland. Should the need arise, I believe Jonesie, and his crew would happily join in our fight."

Cat moved to stand next to Jace and everyone looked at me expectantly. I realized after a few seconds that they were waiting for me to introduce us. "Uh, well, I am Aisling, I do know some of you but for those who don't know me, I am a vampire shifter hybrid. Behind me is James, wolf-shifter and Davina, dragon." A loud ahh came from all assembled as they all stared intently at Davina.

Cat danced up to Davina, keen interest on her face. "What kind of dragon are you?" She looked at her expectantly. Davina looked a little surprised to be asked that question prompting Cat to add, "Hawthorne and Elodie explained quite a bit to us about dragons and the different types."

Davina gave her a quick nod before saying, "I am a spirit dragon." Perplexed looks met her pronouncement. "We're rare, only one in every thousand or so inherits life and death magic." Cat took a hesitant step back. "Do not worry, I would never use my powers of death on a friend, I would however use my powers of life for one."

"Well, then I plan to be your friend." Cat stated decidedly.

Harri wandered behind Davina, then poked her in the back. Davina spun around, shock on her face. Before she could say or do anything, James had moved in front of her to glare down at the foolhardy human.

"Harri!" Cat screamed as she jumped between her human friend and the angry wolf shifter. Davina just looked bemused and not the least bit put out.

"What?" Harri giggled, her blonde hair with a streak of pink in it shaking with her laughter. "I just wanted to shock her into changing onto a dragon."

Davina pulled James back to stand beside her, covering her mouth to keep the laughter in.

"Did you think she had an on/off switch on her back?" My eyes met Davina's, and I could see she was barely keeping it together.

"Not exactly," Harri held her head low trying to look innocent. I saw the mischievous glint in her eyes though. "But with all I've seen in the past year, I wouldn't be surprised."

Robert burst through the kitchen door, effectively changing the subject with yummy smelling food. His arms laden down with a heavy tray brimming with some kind of pasta dish. My stomach grumbled when the delicious aroma hit my nostrils.

Thoughts of Harri's antics disappeared with the smell of food. Davina and James sat to my right, Tina and Harri took seats across the table from us. The vampires in the room slowly sat down in the remaining available chairs in the room. Cat tapped her friend in the back of her head and wagged her finger at her. This must not be unusual behavior for Harri.

Robert walked back into the kitchen, returning almost immediately with a large pitcher and a bottle of wine. The smell of blood hit my senses making my mouth water a little bit more. I had not consumed blood for over a month, and I was beginning to feel the effects of it. My reflexes were a little slower and my strength was not at its usual level. I was still faster and stronger than the average human but without the regular consumption of blood I was weaker.

Walking around the table, Robert poured either wine or blood into each person's goblet. When he came to my side, he raised an eyebrow in question as to which I would prefer. I smiled and indicated that I would take a goblet of blood.

Gods, if I had fangs, I think they would have descended when the smell of the blood hit me fully in the face. After meeting Ali, I read a few of the books she used to read. They were quite entertaining with how wrong the authors described a vampire and a shifter. Vampires did not have fangs for one, and most shifters preferred to eat their food with a knife and fork.

The sounds of silverware clinking were all that could be heard as we all dug into our food. Davina, James and I all complimented Robert on the meal. It was one of the best meals I had ever had. Robert preened in his seat next to Gabriel, apparently becoming a vampire, had not stolen his skills as a cook nor did it remove his enjoyment for receiving compliments.

Once dinner was complete, we withdrew to the living room to discuss our current circumstances. After Davina and I recounted all we knew to the room. Derik excused himself saying he needed to call Jonesie. I asked Jace who was Jonesie.

"He is an old friend and someone you would want as an ally." Jace answered. "From all you have told us, it sounds as if we should be expecting some kind of fight. Especially if this Fraxinus dragon can open a portal to the fae world." He looked at Davina then asked. "Is the island where your coven has gone big enough to house several more people?"

"I think so." Davina glanced at me before adding. "I have never been to the island. I would also need to confer with Arianna to ensure she would allow more to come."

"Perhaps you should do that." Jace advised with a touch of steel in his voice, his fingers drummed on the arm of the couch. "Considering her mate plans to unleash the fae on our world just so he can take over a different world, I would think she would welcome any help she can get."

Davina yanked her phone out of her jacket pocket. "Damn, three missed calls. I forgot to take it off silent mode."

While she fumbled with her phone, I pulled my phone out and called my family too. Ali answered and I explained that we were with Jace and Catriona, safe for now. She called everyone at my home to come and listen to the call just as Davina's phone was answered.

"Davina? Are you alright?" A male voice came through the speaker. James bristled at hearing the male voice but said nothing. Davina placed her hand on his thigh, calming him. I guess James has an on/off switch. I shook my head, to clear my mind. Gods, why was I so focused on all the mated couples?

"Yes, Matthew, we made it out of Philadelphia safely." She placed the phone on the coffee table next to mine. With both phones' speakers turned on, everyone was able to hear all that was said. Derik returned from the hallway, ending his call with Jonesie. "We are with the O'Brien's friends in a small town about four hours from the city."

"That is great to hear." Arianna chimed in. "We were worried when we had not heard from you. Did you encounter any issues?"

Davina gazed with longing at James before answering. "We had a few unexpected situations arise but no issues. We are safe and I will tell you everything when we arrive on the island. Are you prepared for us to come?"

"In a manner of speaking." Matthew explained that they were only able to fully furnish one house; two had sparse furnishings with no beds. He described the other amenities they were able to complete.

"That will have to be acceptable. We will be leaving here soon to rendezvous with Aisling's family in Oregon. Once we meet with them, I will guide them in through the traps you have set." Davina replied and then added. "However, there is another matter I need to discuss." She glanced around the room quickly. "Jace McFadden and his brood have indicated their desire to join in our fight. He also states that he has allies that he believes could be helpful to our cause."

Silence from both phones greeted this statement. After a few minutes, Evan's voice spoke from my phone. "Jace, do you refer to Jonesie and his group?"

"I do. My brother also intends to join us in the morning." Jace answered.

"Arianna," Evan called out, "I know the people he speaks of. I can assure you they would be very beneficial to our fight."

"All may come to the island, but I would caution anyone whose intentions are not pure." Arianna announced in a stern voice. "The traps I have laid around the island will only permit someone who intends no harm against me or my loved ones to enter. Be sure your friends aspire to be my friends, or they will not enjoy the consequences of being false allies."

"I will be sure to convey that to any who wish to come." Jace replied. I noticed a slight tensing of Derik's lips at Arianna's statement. Hmm, I wonder if he is truly a friend or not. I suppose we will find out if he opts to join our trip to this mysterious island of Arianna's.

Chapter Seventeen

Cassandra

King Lucian was a major pain in the ass. Every day for the past five days all we had done was teach Lucian about Gaia and learn how to use Nikolas' portal opening ability. Each night we collapsed into bed, only to drag ourselves up at dawn to repeat the grueling routine. The more time I spent with Nikolas, the more I realized how intelligent and caring he was. Each new discovery made me hate his sister a little more.

Her control of him had turned him into a monster and I could feel the regret and shame he felt even though his actions were directed by her. On nights after we returned from educating Lucian we often spoke about his conflicted feelings while we scarfed down food. I tried to reassure him that since he was not in control he could not be held accountable for anything he did. However, we both worried that when we returned to Gaia, the others would not be quite as forgiving.

The morning of the sixth day arrived. We awoke and for the first time since we got here there was no one rushing us to meet King Lucian. "Morning." I smiled into the eyes of a man I was pretty sure I was falling in love with. Having heard my thoughts, a satisfied grin stretched across his face. Nikolas leaned in closer and gave me a quick kiss. Unhappy with such a chaste kiss, I wrapped my arms around his neck and pulled his mouth back to mine.

Exhaustion be damned, we hadn't had the energy to make love since the first night. This morning, I was determined to revisit the hard planes of his muscled body. I ran my hands down his back while deepening our kiss. I felt his response nudge me between my thighs as he pulled my hips against him. This was a much better way to wake up than our previous mornings.

Almost an hour later, we emerged from our bedroom to find the dining table laden with breakfast. With our plates piled high with food, we sat down to eat. Just as I was about to take my first bite of food a loud rap sounded on the hall door. Nikolas called out for whoever it was to enter. Orson walked into our suite of rooms followed by Trista and another man each carrying a large bundle of fabric.

"Good morning." Orson greeted us with a more severe look than normal. "I hope you enjoyed your uninterrupted morning." We gave each other a look of longing before returning our attention back to Orson. "Trista and Niall will need to help you dress this morning." We must have both looked as if we were going to argue about needing help getting dressed since he added. "Today you must officially abdicate the throne to Lucian. The ceremonial dress is quite cumbersome and can be difficult to get into without assistance."

That must be the bundles each of the servants were carrying. "What is all involved in this whole abdicating the throne ceremony?" I continued eating my breakfast while Orson explained.

Apparently, just refusing the throne upon entrance into the castle was not enough. Nikolas and I, as his mate, would need to take part in a rather lengthy ceremony that would officially have Nikolas give up his place in line for the throne. Orson told us it needed to be done before we could return to Gaia. Especially since Lucian would be returning with us to find his mate. Lucian needed to have full authority of Fabeldyrverden to leave his sister in charge.

We finished eating and I left Nikolas with Niall to get ready in the sitting area. Trista and I withdrew into the bedroom to start the long process of preparing me for the abdication ceremony. Trista removed the gown from the outer wrapping and hung it on a peg near the door. The gown was a masterpiece, pale green bodice spilling into emerald skirts, all edged with amethysts that caught the light like dragon scales.

"My Gods, that is beautiful." I gasped, causing Trista to reward me with a small smile. "I'm curious though," Trista looked at me expectantly, waiting for me to continue. "What do the colors signify? I've noticed most of our clothing is green or at least has green in it."

"I forget that you are from a world where dragons are not commonplace." Trista replied kindly. "Each dragon wears variations of their dragon coloring. Nikolas is an earth dragon; therefore, all of his clothing is required to have emerald, mint green or brown."

"I see." I answered then I thought of the purple scales I had seen on him. "But he also has purple scales when he changes. What does that mean?"

"We honor his witch side with the amethysts. His mother is a spellcaster, or witch, and when they mate with dragons their offspring have purple scales

123

intermixed with their regular colors." Trista answered. "Now, any offspring you have with Nikolas will be a very intriguing mixture since you are chimera. You'll have to complete the ceremony but once you do, combining dragon, witch and vampire will be very interesting indeed."

Well, that is something for me to think about. Trista and I fell quiet. My mind wandered as I thought about the possibility of children with Nikolas. Trista only interrupted my thoughts when she needed to direct my movements while she did my hair, make-up and helped me dress.

Would they be more like him or me? Or better yet, a combination of our best traits while weeding out any of our bad traits. I always worry about passing on my power of pain to another innocent child. My mother's face rose to my mind before I could stop it.

I tried to tamp it back down, but her features swam in front of my eyes. The pain etched across her face had me sucking in a sharp breath. I tried pushing the memory from my mind, but it wouldn't leave. Hurt and despair felt like a crushing weight on my body. She cried and begged for me to release her; I tried. I really did try. I just didn't know how. The bedroom door slammed open, jerking me from my memory and causing Trista to jump letting out a small squeak of fear.

"What is wrong?" His strong arms wrapped around my shuddering body. "I felt your fear and agony." While holding me close, he spun to glare at Trista. "What did you do to her?" He roared.

"Nik, it wasn't her." I gulped loudly, trying to bring my feeling back under my tight control. "It was me; I couldn't stop it." I sobbed.

"Leave us." Nikolas ordered Trista from the room. Once she was gone, with the door shut tightly behind her, Nikolas held me away from him so he could look at me. "What do you mean?" his voice softening as he took in my smeared make-up.

"These two weeks have been a little disordered for me." I hiccuped as another sob tore through me. "I can usually keep them blocked. Trista and I were talking about children, and I didn't mean to think about her, but I couldn't stop it from happening."

Confusion crossed his features. "I am not totally following you." Nikolas pulled me back into his arms. "Who is her?"

124

Another shudder of pain and revulsion wracked my body. "My mother." I whispered.

Nikolas squeezed me tightly. "I have not pressed you on your past. Gods know I have no right to judge someone." His hands rubbed up and down my back, soothing me. "But I think I need to know more. If whatever happened causes this much grief in you, I need to know how to combat that grief."

I stepped out of his arms and walked to sit on the edge of the bed. He is my mate; he deserves to know. Keeping my head down, I told him my most horrendous secret. My nails dug rivulets into my palms, blood trickling to pool in my hands.

"When I was five, my mother caught me lighting fires with my mind. My mother was a witch too, but we lived in the human world, not within a coven. She had married a human man, and he didn't feel comfortable living amongst her coven. If I hadn't been showing off my powers to human children," my breath hitched, remembering the fear on her face when she caught me lighting pieces of paper on fire with several other children watching. "My mother was so angry but also scared. Her coven had warned her that raising a witch from such a mighty line amongst humans would be dangerous."

Nikolas sat on the bed beside me, taking my hands in his he wiped the blood away. I could feel his love for me through our bond. Gods, I hoped this story didn't change his mind. *Never!* reverberated through my head. "Let me finish before you say that."

He grabbed my body and turned me to face him. "I would never hold anything from your past against you. You are my mate; you are my life. I will always honor our bond with love and trust." His lips met mine with a searing kiss that almost made me forget the pain on my mother's face.

I twisted out of his embrace. "I must finish telling you what happened." Standing, I put some distance between us. I needed space so I could get it all out in what telling.

He sat back on the bed and gave me an assessing look. "Fine, but know this, it doesn't matter. It will change nothing."

My heart lifted with his declaration, and I truly hoped he was right. "My mother pulled me from the yard of my friend's house and rushed us home. She gave no explanation to my friend's parents or me for that matter. When we arrived at our

125

house, she sent me to my room. She locked me inside while she went to find my father."

My voice broke again, Nikolas must have sensed where my tale was leading. He remained silent though, allowing me to continue.

"I was scared and mad and really didn't understand what I had done wrong. My mother lit fires all the time with her powers. She used her powers all the time at our house. When she came back to let me out, my father was not with her. She yelled at me about how bad I was. I started to cry and yelled back. 'But you do it all the time'. I was so confused and the more she yelled at me for being bad the more scared and upset I got."

I turned to stare out the window; I couldn't face Nikolas for this part. "My power manifested that day and I had no idea how to control it, or what it even was. I just wanted my mother to stop screaming at me and making me feel bad. The power shot out of me and into her. I didn't know what I was doing. Her face twisted in pain and fear, and I didn't know how to make it stop."

I covered my eyes as the memory once again flooded my mind. "My father returned home to find me crying on the floor beside my mother's body. She was not dead, but she may as well have been. I inflicted so much pain on her body that I drove her insane. I couldn't pull it back." I sobbed as tears rolled down my cheeks.

Nikolas had risen from the bed, standing behind me. He pulled me into his arms, soothing me he caressed my arms. "My father took us to the coven. When no one could reverse the damage, he told them he didn't want me. Almerinda came and took me away to be raised by the Council. I never saw my mother or father again. He died when I was around forty. My mother is alive, but her mind never returned from whatever insanity I drove her to."

Nikolas carried me back to the bed and held me in his lap, rocking me while I poured out my deepest shame. "If I had been raised in modern times, we never would have been able to hide me. Too many cameras that capture everything, but more than one hundred years ago our biggest worry was that someone would accuse me of being a witch and capture me before the Council could get me to safety. I have lived in service to the Council for as long as I can remember. They tend to my mother for me, and I pry secrets from unwilling prisoners for them."

I sobbed loudly in my mate's arms. His reassuring murmurs the only other noise in the room. After several minutes I finally pulled my head from where he cocooned it against his chest to meet his eyes. I worried as I raised my face to his that I would see disgust or hatred, or worst of all fear. His loving walnut hued eyes met my frightened blue ones.

"We have both done things we regret." Nikolas whispered as his eyes met mine with only love and understanding reflecting back at me. "You did not know better when you were a child. As for your work for the Council, I am sure you believed you were aiding a just cause. I could never hate you or feel revulsion or fear. Gods, Cass, you are my mate, and I love you for the woman you are now and the woman you were before. I love all of you, without your past you would not be the amazing creature I hold in my arms today."

Gods, could he be any more perfect. "Nik, I love you too. We are a perfectly imperfect pair of lost souls bound together forever." His arms wrapped around my body, holding me tight against his chest. Once I felt my tears were under better control, I pulled away to look up at his chiseled face. "I've only ever shared that story with one other person. Thank you for being as understanding as she was."

"As I stated before, I would never hold your past against you, especially not the actions of a scared five-year-old little girl. Your father should have done better by you." He rubbed his firm hands up and down my back soothing me further. "But if your father was a human, how are you a hybrid?"

"The man who turned his back on me was human. He was not my biological father though." Silent tears ran down my cheeks again. "A vampire got my mother pregnant. She did not know she was carrying me until long after the vampire she had slept with had left. She was almost five months along when she met the man who helped raise me until I was five. I never knew my real father."

"Who is the other person you shared your story with?" He asked, curiosity and possibly a bit of jealousy tingeing his voice.

"When I was taken to the Council, I told Almerinda what had happened. She told me I was not at fault but convincing myself of that fact has been very difficult. The Council had warned my mother that living openly amongst humans was not a good idea. My parents loved each other but my father insisted that my mother and I pretend that we were human and powerless. She loved him so much that she walked away from the world she knew. I shut my memories of my parents away in a dark recessed area of my brain."

I rose to pace around the bedroom with my head lowered. "I hate my power. Not all my powers but the one that drove my mother insane. I wish I never had to use it again. All these years working for the Council and using my power has left me feeling dirty and used." I raised my eyes to meet him, unsure what I would see in them.

Love and acceptance shone back at me from his walnut hued eyes. He stood from the bed and walked to stand in front of me. Placing a finger under my chin, he tilted my head up. "You never have to use that power again. When we return to Gaia, you do not have to return to work for the Council. We will forge our own path forward."

A light knocking sounded on the door and Trista poked her head into the room. "I apologize, milady, milord. Orson has stopped by twice now and he is becoming exceedingly impatient with the delay."

I motioned for her to enter. We could not keep the king's man waiting any longer.

"Come in Trista. I am better now. Although, I suspect you're going to have to reapply my makeup." I gave her a tremulous smile with a shrug as if to say, what are you going to do?

Trista came fully into the room, shooing Nikolas out the door. My hands still trembled as Trista reapplied my make-up, Nikolas' presence outside the door grounded me. By the time she fastened the last clasp on my gown, I could almost pretend the cracks in my armor weren't still bleeding. In no time, she had repaired the damage from my mental meltdown.

I stepped from the room to find Nikolas staring at me as if he had never seen me before. I twirled in place, causing the gown to whirl outward. He marched to my side and lifted my hand to his lips.

"You are absolutely stunning." He whispered just before his lips caressed the back of my hand. Shivers and tingles raced throughout my body when his mouth touched my skin. A giggle sprung from Trista's mouth at our steamy display.

With great fortitude, I stepped back from Nikolas. I gazed appreciatively at the picture he presented. His black hair and green flecked eyes shined brightly. The clothing he wore fit him like a glove.

A hunter green silk shirt that clung to his pecs was tucked into tight black pants that tapered down into a pair of leather knee boots. The crowning touch was

128

the black cloak fastened at his throat with an amethyst dragon clasp. All he needed was long flowing tresses blowing in the wind to look like a romance novel cover. I am almost certain that a little bit of drool formed at the corner of my mouth as I stared at him.

Orson chose that moment to rap loudly on the outer door. Entering without waiting for a welcoming call, he scowled at each of us. "Perhaps, where you come from kings are kept waiting by their subjects, but here it is considered unacceptable behavior."

"We did not intend to cause any problems." I snapped, my nerves were already frayed enough, I didn't need lord high and mighty bothering me more. "And if you must know, in America there are no kings anymore. Perhaps, it would benefit King Lucian to remember that. If he intends to go there to find his mate, he might want to keep that in mind. A lot has changed in the thousand years since he was in Gaia."

Orson simply harrumphed, then turned on his heel and stalked through the open door. "Follow me; we need to get the ceremony completed."

Nikolas and I followed Orson down the hallway and found ourselves back at the entrance to the main hall where we had initially met Lucian and Serafina. Orson instructed us to remain outside the door until we heard our names announced. We would be expected to present ourselves to the king and Nikolas would need to officially renounce his claim to the throne. Apparently, refusing the throne on the outer steps was not enough to formally abdicate.

Almost an hour had passed when we finally heard our names called. Nikolas had begun tromping around the room, irritation rolling off him in waves. The thoughts I picked out of his brain were all centered on Orson. I didn't blame my mate; the smaller man was a lot to deal with. Rushing us just to have us sit out here for an hour was only the latest infraction.

At the sound of the doors opening, we came to stand together. The ornate doors swung open to reveal a hall filled with at least five hundred people. I stared around the hall, noticing that each type of dragon was represented. The different types were also grouped together, blood dragons standing with blood dragons and so forth. Gods, I hope I don't trip walking down this aisle. Nikolas clasped my hand in his and gave me a quick squeeze of reassurance.

129

We made it to the front of the hall without incident. Once again, King Lucian was sitting on the throne with the empty throne beside him. Serafina and Arlien sat in smaller chairs behind him. However, gone was the laid-back king from our first meeting, although to be honest, we hadn't seen much of that side of him in days.

This man sat stiffly upright, holding a scepter in one hand. On his head was a crown made of rubies and diamonds, denoting his fire dragon status. His clothing was form fitting just as Nikolas's was, but his shirt, pants and boots were all black and he wore a crimson cloak lined with white fur.

Nikolas repeated the hand to head then heart gesture before pulling us both down to our left knees. Keeping his head bowed, he intoned loudly. "I, Nikolas, son of Fraxinus and grandson of the Magnus Quercus do hereby renounce any and all claims I have to the throne of Fabeldyrverden. In doing so, I proclaim my fealty to King Lucian for ever more. If King Lucian is unable to fulfill the requirements of his office I will honor his choice for successor."

Orson stepped in front of us and placed his hand on the top of Nikolas' head. A strange sensation enveloped our bodies; a feeling of something being pulled from within caused me to glance quickly at Nikolas. The rubies and diamonds in Lucian's crown shimmered to green and purple before settling back to their original colors.

It is only the mantel of rule being taken from me and given to Lucian. You feel it because of our bond.

I watched as Orson took two steps backward then turned and faced King Lucian. He placed his hands on either side of Lucian's head below the crown. A faint hazy shimmer settled over Lucian's body, and I noticed the hand holding the scepter trembled slightly. As if reaffirming their acceptance, the rubies glowed brighter, casting a crimson shroud over Lucian's face. Once Orson moved away from Lucian, the red glow faded, and a resounding roar erupted from the dragons in attendance.

With the official acts completed, the ceremony turned more into a celebration. Nikolas and I mingled amongst the dragons of Fabeldyrverden. I felt freer now that I had shared my secret with Nikolas. The loss of the weight of a possible rule seemed to lift Nikolas' spirits as well. The two of us danced late into the night, although neither of us was anywhere near as elegant on the dance floor as

Serafina and Arlien were together. For such a mountainous man he could spin and twirl better than anyone I had seen back in Gaia.

King Lucian stopped us as we were trying to slip away, fatigue evident on his face. "Might I have a word with the two of you before you retire?"

While it was worded as a request, we knew as king he could command us. "Of course, King Lucian." Nikolas replied at the same moment I nodded.

We followed him down a passageway that I had not seen before. There were very few lanterns to light the way causing me to realize this area must not be used often. We took so many turns I feared we would be lost. A small shiver of worry worked its way up my spine. *Do not worry; I don't believe he intends any harm.* Nikolas reassured me with a squeeze of my hand. About ten minutes and several more turns led us to a solid and rather heavy looking door.

King Lucian approached the door, drew a symbol down the middle of it then stepped back. As soon as he stood next to Nikolas, the massive door cracked open then slowly swung to reveal an unlit room. Once King Lucian stepped over the threshold lanterns flickered to flame.

The lanterns revealed a barren room with a shallow pool of water in the center. The floors were made of the same silver stone that Magda's home had been constructed from. The walls were covered with old, faded tapestries. Lanterns hung evenly spaced along the walls, emitting just enough light to see where we were walking. Lucian beckoned the two of us forward.

Off to the left a small door I had not noticed sprung open and in walked Profitis Magda. Her flowing silver and red hair hung loosely around her shoulders and down her back. Her plain robe from when we met was replaced with a red and silver gown that clung to her tall form. She still walked with a slight hunch over her cane but now had a more regal bearing while standing in the presence of the king.

"Your highness," She gave a diminutive bow of her head to the king then turned her attention to me and Nikolas. "Gather round, I need to show all of you something."

The three of us moved to stand beside her on the side of the pool of water. For once the water was not pink. The crystal-clear clarity of the water surprised me. I had grown used to the pink tinge to all the water in Fabeldyrverden. Magda must have noticed my confusion as she explained. "This water resides in Gaia. It is one of two pools that transcend the borders between our two realms. They can only be used to see not travel."

"Where is the other pool located?" Nikolas asked, I was curious too. I had never heard of pools of water that could see into other realms.

"It is buried deep in a cave under the highest peak in Tobbat." Magda replied, I was still confused as I had never heard of that place "It is of no consequence where it lies. I can see everywhere with the pathways open."

"What is it you needed to show us that required me to leave the celebration?" King Lucian impatiently interrupted our discussion. He strode to the side of the pool, gazing at its clear surface.

Magda stepped closer to the water, allowing her bare toes to sink into the water along the edge. A low murmur came from her. A ripple began to run along the surface of the clear water. Magda must be invoking a spell, the longer she spoke I realized she was repeating the same words. I had never heard the language she used and assumed it was the language of the dragons. A small nudge from Nikolas led me to believe I was correct.

Slowly a scene began to form on the surface of the water. A woman that I recognized as Arianna Konstantin, Nikolas' mother was conversing with four other women and a man. With no sound coming through we could only guess at their conversation. None of them looked upset or angry so I felt safe in guessing they were in no immediate danger.

"That is Arianna of the Danu line, do you know the people with her?" Magda asked Nikolas.

"Yes, that is my mother and five of the people she called her coven." Nikolas answered then went on to describe the group. "There is one person missing, Davina, the only other dragon in her group. The three women standing closer together are witches. The man and woman who look like they could be siblings are a mated vampire pair. They have been my mother's most trusted allies and friends for many years. I do not recognize the room they are standing in though. None of their homes have that kind of furniture."

"Since you and your mate arrived on my doorstep, I have been using the sister pool to this one that is in my home to try to locate your mother. Nine days ago, I saw her and her coven on what I can only describe as some form of watercraft. They were picked up by a much larger vessel and taken to an island that was not there until it suddenly was there. Since they arrived on the island they have done nothing but talk, sometimes while holding some type of black object near their faces. This morning, they became more active as if they were preparing for something then they went back to sitting around occasionally holding those black things to their mouth and ears but mostly just speaking to each other. Unfortunately, these pools can only be used to view, not hear, therefore I am unable to tell you what is being said."

"So, what we are seeing is what is happening at this moment?" I asked.

"Yes, they have been sitting at that table for quite some time now." Magda responded. "This is where you need to go when you return to Gaia."

"No," King Lucian insisted. "We must find my mate, not go traipsing off looking for his mother."

"My apologies, my king, I should have led with that." Magda bowed her head a little lower than when she had first addressed him. "Your mate will be there. Serafina has confirmed that there is a beach outside this house where you will first see your mate. She has been here several times watching with me."

Lucian looked at the scene with renewed interest. Perhaps he hoped that one of the women he could see was his mate. He showed no reaction to any of the women, and his irritation at being interrupted resurfaced.

"How am I supposed to portal to a place I have never been to or even knew existed until today?" Nikolas spurted.

"Starting tomorrow we will work harder on teaching you how to open a portal. You have seen where we must emerge, that is where your focus will be from now on." King Lucian advised him then swept out of the room leaving us staring at Nikolas' mother and her coven of five.

Magda cleared her throat, interrupting our gazing at Nikolas' family. "Have you completed the ritual yet?"

We turned as one in confusion. "What ritual?" We asked at the same time.

"You must complete the Sanguis Draconis ceremony." Magda gave us a hard glare as if we should have known this.

In my defense I was a vampire witch hybrid and just recently learned about dragons. Nikolas on the other hand, maybe should have known but who knows what his father actually taught him.

133

"If you do not complete the proper steps of the ceremony, you will never gain your full powers as a mated pair." Magda pronounced. "For one thing without it, you'll never master portaling."

"I do not know of this ceremony." Nikolas admitted, anger in his voice and a flash of scales across his skin. I moved to his side and placed a restraining hand on his arm. My touch calmed him, and he turned back to Magda with less vigor. "Everyone here seems to forget that I was not raised in this realm. My father was not concerned with teaching me all I needed to know. He was more focused on using me to increase his own powers."

I could feel his anger ratcheting up again as he began to pace around the room. When he turned back toward me, I stepped into his path. I placed my hands on his cheeks and brought his face into line with mine. "Nikolas, all will be well. I am sure Magda," I inclined my head in her direction, "can help us with all that is necessary for us to complete the Sanguis Draconis."

Meeting Magda's hard stare, Nikolas asked. "Is she correct, will you help us?"

"Absolutely, I want nothing more than to help my king." Before Nikolas could correct her on who was king, Magda added, "If you do not have your full powers at your disposal then I fear King Lucian will not prevail in obtaining his mate. Without his mate, he will never reach his, er, his full potential."

"What do we need in order to complete the ritual?" I questioned. I chose to ignore how she had stumbled over her words when mentioning Lucian reaching his full potential.

"Do not worry; I will gather all that is necessary. We shall meet here again tomorrow night. It is the perfect night as Vesuvius and our moon will be in alignment."

At my look of confusion, she explained that Vesuvius was the ringed giant that circled their planet. According to Magda, Vesuvius and the moon came into alignment four times each year. Most Sanguis Draconis ceremonies were completed on one of those four dates as the dragons believed that they received extra gifts from the gods and the Fates on these days.

We agreed to return the following night. Magda advised that there would only be the two of us and her present for the ritual as it is a very private affair. She handed me a bottle of oil. She informed us that we should bathe together using the

134

oil mixed in our bath water. The oil would open our minds and bodies fully to each other. I had thought that had already happened, but Magda assured me that the oil would burn away any lie, even ones we told ourselves.

"Tomorrow before coming here you must soak in the oiled water for an hour. Do not dry off after you soak. Allow the oiled water to remain on your skin. Return here together at the appointed time."

With her final instructions given to us, Magda shooed us from the room. We returned to our living quarters to find Trista and Niall waiting to aid us in disrobing from the intricate ceremonial clothing. Once our clothes had been packed away, the two left us.

Our night had been a long one and neither one of us were in the mood for anything but sleep at the time. Crawling into bed, our heads barely touched the pillows before sleep took us. My last thought before sleep pulled me under, was focused on Magda's hesitation about Lucian's future. Something in her demeaner had set off alarm bells in my head.

Chapter Eighteen

Aisling

We woke early the next morning to begin preparing for our trip to the west coast then on to Arianna's hidden island. Jace and Catriona left at first light to meet with Jonesie and his crew in Cleveland, Ohio. They said they would return to the house later tonight and left a to-do list for the rest of us to work on. I volunteered for the supply run, anything to escape the newly mated couples' constant pheromone fog.

I wandered around the big box store for a few hours, mostly wasting time but also grabbing items we would need. Last night we had decided that the best option was to drive even if it would take longer. We needed to keep a low profile so the Council couldn't find us. Once we reached my home then we would take a boat to the island near Alaska. I stocked up on lots of ready-to-eat packs of food and several cases of bottled water.

So much has happened over the past few months. In all honesty, ever since Cillian had been killed. All the new mates popping up, the Fates must have some reason for bringing everyone together. My mum had a devout belief in prophecies and the Fates controlling everything.

I was not entirely sold on the idea that someone many years ago could say what was going to happen. Although, recent events were starting to open my eyes to the idea. Mum once said to me, 'when you meet your mate, you'll face your greatest foe, and that foe will be you.' To this day, I still didn't understand what she meant. How could I be my own foe? One thing I knew for certain, something was pulling me westward. We just needed to get to Arianna's island.

I snapped out of my revelry noticing a man was following me around the store, time to check out. He was human, he must have thought I was going to steal something. I must admit my hours of wandering around probably did seem a little suspicious. I dragged my two overflowing carts to the register. Once my order was rung up and I had paid, the man moved onto someone else to stalk. I loaded up the back of Cat's SUV and headed back to her house.

On my arrival back at Cat's place, there were several more vehicles in the driveway than when I left. Gods' this better be Jonesie's crew and not someone else. My eyes scanned the front yard and surrounding forest. Other than the heady scent of pheromones in the air, nothing jumped out at me. Gods, I had just got my sinuses cleaned out.

A loud booming voice roared from the open front door, followed by an incredibly large ebony-skinned vampire. Based on descriptions I had heard this must be the infamous Jonesie. The man had to be at least six and a half feet if not more but moved with the grace of a ballerina. He bound down the porch steps and skipped to stand in front of me.

"And who might you be little lady?" His deep voice pounded my ear drums with how loud he spoke.

Cat came out of the front door, coming to stand next to him. "Jonesie, what have I told you, the entire town doesn't need to hear you?" She smiled at me and added. "Aisling, I trust your shopping was uneventful?"

"Hey, Cat," I answered. "Other than a security guard tailing me for a bit to make sure I wasn't going to steal the twelve cases of water I had." I gave her a cheeky smile then focused on the colossal vampire eyeing me up from beside her. "I'm Aisling O'Brien." I held my hand out to shake but was swept up into the behemoth of a man's arms in a fierce bear hug.

"We don't stand on ceremony in my family. I knew your brother Cillian. He was a great friend of mine." Jonesie intoned into my right ear. Was there anyone out there that Cillian hadn't known? "Jace and Cat informed me that he was trying to help these dragon shifters, so I felt it was my duty to lend my arm to the cause."

"Well, we're glad to have your arm. I hope the rest of your body comes with it, though." I joked causing Jonesie to boom out a raucous laugh as he finally returned me to my feet.

"I have no intention of parting ways with it so you will have all of me for the fight that is coming." While we were talking a group of vampires came to stand on the front porch. "You also have my family." He waved his arms to encompass the people standing on the porch. Every one of them nodded along with Jonesie's words, Derik being the only one who looked unsure. I was going to have to dig out the cause of his discomfort before we made it to my home in Oregon.

The sound of a loud truck backfiring had us all looking down the road. Cat's smile grew wider when she saw who was approaching her house. The driver was a petite brunette with big brown eyes. The passenger seat was occupied by a man that looked eerily like Jace, although his hair was a bit lighter.

I was happy to see Jaxson. He was a legend in the Guard. His fighting prowess would be very welcome if Fraxinus was able to open a portal to the fae world. The woman must be Tanya, his mate. I never met her as she is one of the main reasons that Jaxson left the Guard.

The old truck came to a stop behind Cat's SUV and the two vampires got out. Jaxson gave me a nod then moved past me to speak with Jonesie. Tanya gave Cat a tight hug then turned to look at me. "Hello, I don't believe we've met." She held her hand out for a quick shake.

"We haven't, I'm Aisling O'Brien." I shook her hand back and nodded at her mate. "Jaxson and I worked in the Guard together for a short time before he quit."

"Ah, yes, he mentioned your family to me." Tanya released my hand. "It's very nice to meet you." Tanya glanced back at Jaxson then wrapped her arm through Cat's. "They'll be talking forever about stuff I don't care about. Shall we go inside? Is there anything else that needs done before we leave?" Just when I thought I was essentially being dismissed, Tanya reached a hand behind her, grasping mine and dragged me along.

After hours of organizing and reorganizing the many vehicles we were finally ready to leave. Since the time had gotten close to eight at night we decided to have one final meal at Cat's house, get some rest and get an early start in the morning. We updated my family as to our expected arrival date and all headed off to our respective sleeping areas.

The next morning dawned gloomy and rainy. We all piled into the different automobiles we had packed the day before. I found myself wedged between Jonesie and Derik on the bench seat of Jonesie's 1974 Chevy pickup. Good, just where I wanted to be, I needed to grill Derik on why he seemed so pained about traveling to Arianna's island.

Our trip started out quiet, the early morning dreariness seeming to drag down everyone's mood. Derik dosed off in the seat beside me with his head propped against the window. Occasionally Jonesie would hum along to whatever song was playing on the radio. As we followed the highway, I found myself being lulled by the music and the sound of the tires on the road and soon I was also asleep.

Derik nudged me, jarring me awake. We had reached our first pit stop. We all took turns in the restrooms and filled up our vehicles. Then we got back on the road, this time with Derik driving. Deciding this was as good a time as any to try to learn more about Derik, I asked him to tell me about himself.

Derik had been with Jonesie's group for a few hundred years. They were family first, lovers on occasion when the mood struck them. While Jonesie was one hundred percent homosexual, Derik liked to play with both men and women. Before he was turned into a vampire, he had been married and arrived in the American colonies in the early 1600's. His wife died from typhoid fever not long after their arrival.

"How did you end up living with Jonesie and his group?" I asked.

"Hmm," Derik murmured. "I met Gabriel." A sly smile crossed his face.

"Gabriel, as in Robert and Gabriel?" I prodded, could this be the reason for his not so happy expressions.

"The one and the same." Derik chuckled. "Before I met him, I had been strictly hetero. There had been a couple times before that I had felt a mild interest in a man but nothing like what I felt when I first met him. Back then, homosexuality was hidden, and I did my best to fit in. Even as a vampire my Puritan upbringing held me back. Right up until Gabriel came storming into my life."

I pictured Gabriel. He was a difficult vampire to figure out. When we met at Ali's apartment, he was so serious and on task. Now, surrounded by his mate and their friends, he was carefree and kind of sparkling.

"He was a Guard at the time and very open about his sexual appetites." Derik chuckled at his memory. "He sensed my interest and before I knew what was happening, we were in bed together. When he left the Guard, I followed. We knew we weren't mated but the sex was so damn good. Fortunately, we found a home with Jonesie. His family, as he calls us, changes as people come and go. Jonesie likes variety when it comes to his many lovers, I like that too, but I also enjoy the closeness we have as a family."

"Oh, wow, I had no idea you and Gabriel were a thing before." I wonder if this is why he sometimes looks upset.

"We were a thing of sorts," Derik replied cheekily. "Like I said, I like variety, and up until he met his mate so did Gabriel. We enjoyed each other many times over the years but we also enjoyed the company of many, many others too."

Well, damn, I was really hoping that would explain my edginess about him. We lapsed into silence again; both lost in our own thoughts listening to Jonesie snoring loudly. Derik fiddled with the radio dial until he found a radio station playing classic rock. Our next pit stop came up and we once again filled up our gas, and shuffled drivers. This time I was behind the driver's wheel.

We leapfrogged across states, only regrouping at predetermined checkpoints to avoid drawing attention. The human world may not notice twelve vehicles in a caravan, but we knew there were witches in the Council who tracked those types of anomalies.

We had a close call in Iowa. I think the Elite Guard came across us by accident. But he recognized me and tried to take me into custody. I took care of him and Jonesie disposed of his partner in the restroom. We got away clean, but we felt it was best to deviate a little from our direct route.

Google maps had estimated forty hours driving time, however with gas stops and a few detours, our total trip took closer to forty-eight hours. When we reached Oregon, we all regrouped at a Wal-Mart in Eugene, Oregon. From here, they would have to follow me into my family's encampment.

Supernatural species used spells to hide their homes. Especially for large families or tribes. Our home was hidden behind a cloaking and shrinking spell. Humans would totally freak out if they knew there was a settlement of vampires, shifters, witches and hybrids living just outside Eugene, Oregon in the Willamette National Forest.

Jasmine and Cormac were waiting on the human side of the barrier when we pulled up. The wards held, shimmering like a mirage and visible only to supernaturals. To a human, this road looked like a dead end. Little did they know the road continued into a small town that had stood here for two centuries.

"Is everything alright?" I got out of Jonesie's truck, dread settled heavily over my shoulders. The forest air smelled wrong, the crisp pine of home had an underlying odor of decay. Cormac's downturned mouth and drooping eyes had me rushing to his side.

"Yes and no." Cormac responded solemnly, his head sunk into his shoulders. "Nothing has happened from the Council, the rogues, the fae or any other enemies we may have out there."

I opened my mouth to ask why the long faces then, when Jasmine pulled me into a tight embrace. My legs buckled at his next words.

"Mum's not doing well." Cormac continued while Jasmine squeezed me tighter. "She won't be coming to the island. Da's about to lose it and we're all a bit on edge right now."

"What do you mean, Mum's not well?" I stammered as tears began to leak down my cheeks.

"Ash, you know she's getting up there in years. Most shifters only live at most three hundred years. Mum's pretty damn close to that age now." Cormac's deep voice was laced with sorrow as he added. "The loss of Cillian," his voice trailed off. He squared his shoulders and added, "She hid it well, but the last few weeks, well, she's fading. Da keeps begging her to fight but she's weak, we can all see it."

I sunk to the pavement, pulling Jasmine down with me. Cormac scooped us both into his large arms. He set Jasmine, his mate, down but kept me, his older sister held tight to his chest, sensing I was the one who needed the most comfort right now. I heard Jasmine approach the rest of my party to explain what was going on. I couldn't focus on that though.

"I need to see her, Cormac." My voice barely above a whisper, I burrowed my face into his neck.

Cormac gave me a brief nod then walked through the barrier, leaving the others to follow Jasmine in. Once we were through, I pulled myself from his arms and ran to my mum's home. I found her in her bed, pale and withdrawn, my da standing guard. My heart snapped in two when I saw her weakened state. My da gave a slight shake of his head at my questioning glance.

"Mum." I cried falling beside her bed; I clutched her hand with my trembling fingers. The shades were drawn, blocking all light from the outside world. A lone candle sat on the bedside table, the only illumination in the room. My da reassured me that was her preference, she wanted the warm glow rather than harsh electric lights.

"Aisling, dear. I am so glad you made it home in time." My once vibrant mother whimpered. Her hair, no longer full and thick, spread flat and lifeless on the pillow.

"Mum, please." My body convulsed, feeling as if I were being torn apart. It was too much, too soon. I wasn't ready to lose her.

"Gods, it is wonderful to see you." Tears spilled from my eyes, as she wiped her hand across my moistened cheeks. "I need to tell you something before I leave this world."

"No, Mum, you can't go yet." I wailed.

"I am sorry, honey, but it is almost my time. I have felt it coming for a while now. Your siblings and da don't want to accept it any more than you do, but it is a part of life. Death comes to us all one day. My day is just coming sooner than any of you want to reconcile yourselves to."

She patted my cheek then lowered her shaking hand back to mine. "Now listen closely," She commanded, steel returning to her voice. "Many moons ago, a seer told me of your fate. I didn't want to believe her at the time because I know how hard this will be for you." She pulled me close with a strength I did not expect from her frail body. "He comes soon, he will be your mate in every sense of the word, however, he will also infuriate you to the point of wanting to kill him. No matter what you do or what he does, you must accept him."

"Why?" I mewled like a baby.

"The fates of all worlds rely on your mate standing with you in battle. It is imperative that he fights at your side, or all will be lost." Her grip became painful as she squeezed my hand almost as if she thought to brand me with her words. "Promise me that no matter how angry you become you will not let your temper push him away." When I didn't answer quickly enough, she squeezed even harder, drawing blood with her nails. "Promise me Aisling Sinead O'Brien, on your blood, promise me!"

"Yes, mum, I promise, on my blood. I will honor your final request." My vow seemed to break her strength. She collapsed back onto the bed, her eyes closed, and her hands fell to her side. Her face took on a serene, almost peaceful look, no longer etched with pain and determination.

Tears streaked down my face and my da howled in agony as my mother took her last breath. Our mournful wails brought our family to her room. My da

142

pulled the sheet over her, his hands shaking as he covered his mate's body. Evan led us from the room, his face a mask of remorse.

We clung to each other in sadness throughout the night. Future mates and wars would have to wait. Mourning trumped all else.

Chapter Nineteen

Cassandra

It is finally time to return to Gaia. The Sanguis Draconis ritual with Magda fused our powers, amplifying them far beyond what either of us could achieve alone. Magda insisted that had we not performed the rites that Nikolas may never have truly perfected his portal opening. Now Nikolas and I have practiced opening portals so much that he can now hit the intended target within an inch.

It has taken an additional two weeks of nearly constant training to get to this point, but we are finally ready to go home. Part of that training was for me as well. I had no idea how much portal opening relied on both mate's powers. Our minds had to merge, focusing on the exact destination. The further we wanted to travel the more power that was needed to make the distance.

When Nikolas dragged us into the dragon realm, he had used our connection to cross the distance. He also had a heavy helping of fear of my powers to cause pain as well as the sudden inrush of his own powers being released from his sister's spells to aid in boosting our jump.

He'd confessed weeks ago that his escape was blind panic. The portal had been fueled by desperation rather than direction. Fabeldyrverden had been described to him so many times by his father that he was able to picture it quite clearly. His mind only sought a place that would be completely safe from the Council.

We have educated Lucian as much as possible about the world as it is now. He has even gone so far as to tell us to just call him Lucian, rather than King Lucian. When Orson is absent, he even relaxes enough that the imperious ass he can be is not as present as usual. Serafina and Arlien bring out a more boyish side to the king. Lucian seems to love teasing his sister, she gives as good as she gets too.

Lucian can be entertaining and kind but there is always an air of superiority around him. He is trying though; he no longer issues commands and has even stopped just barging into our rooms when he needs something. I am sure being raised to be a king has shaped most of his personality. I just hope he cannot be quite as overbearing when we are in Gaia.

Each night before bed we all gather in the room with the viewing pool to observe the activity at Nikolas' mother's location. More people have arrived, many of whom I recognized. With each new person viewed, I gave background information to Nikolas and Lucian for the ones I knew.

The entire O'Brien family, minus their mother and father were there plus a new female attached to Evan's side. Almerinda and her personal Guard arrived the day after the O'Briens. There was a dark-haired vampire holding her hand that I did not recognize, Almerinda must have finally met her mate. There was also a witch in Almerinda's group that I did not know who had a familial look to Jasmine.

The next group to arrive looked to be a large contingent of Collier shifters, although I did not see Michael or his mate amongst them. And finally, Jace McFadden, his mate Catriona, Gabriel previously of the Fontaines, and a man I assumed was his mate, arrived with an assortment of vampires, witches and shifters.

It would seem as if they were preparing for a war to come to the island. Let us hope that it is not us that they are preparing to fight. I know from Nikolas' thoughts that he worried constantly that he would be met with hostility from everyone but his mother, and sometimes he even worried she would turn her back on him.

I am not a seer and have never had the power to look into the future. I believe my lack of dreams is the reason I could never harness that power. However, if I did have the sight, I would place bets that Lucian's mate arrived on the island already as there has been one woman that his eyes track anytime she is within view.

Gods help them, because if I am correct, their mating is going to be full of fireworks. If it weren't for the chance my mate will be attacked upon our arrival, I would be much more excited to go there just so I could witness Lucian being brought down a peg or two. Thank Gods Nikolas is nothing like his cousin.

Tomorrow we will make the trip to Gaia. Nikolas and I returned to our rooms after watching the island for the final time tonight. Niall had already lit the fires, and we were greeted with wonderful warmth upon entering the sitting room. The seasons were changing here, and frost was forming on the windows. The hallways were always cold and drafty.

The aroma of roasted pig and potatoes permeated our suite of rooms. My stomach grumbled with hunger as I headed to the dining room. We ate a scrumptious meal that had been prepared by Trista in readiness for our return from training. Trista and Niall had taken great care of us while we were here, even if we had started off a little shaky.

With our bellies full, we took a relaxing soak in the massive tub. The citrus scented soap calmed my nerves and my aching muscles. Forcing thoughts of tomorrow from my mind, I climbed from the tub. Nikolas followed me out. Wrapping a thick towel around me, he grabbed a separate towel for himself.

I drew Nikolas to our bed where we made love; desperation seemed to envelop both of us as we clung tightly to each other. Our rhythm was slow and deliberate, our voices hushed. When our climax came, our bodies were in perfect harmony.

I lay beside my mate, the afterglow of our lovemaking fading. Nikolas stared at the ceiling, his hands bunching the sheets at this side. A slow shuddering breath escaped him, his eyes slitted and a flicker of scales pulsed across his arms. I pulled his hand free from the bedding, unfurling his fingers to clasp them in my own.

"I will be by your side no matter what tomorrow brings." I assured Nikolas. His concerns about facing those he had harmed were at the forefront of his mind. An image of Evan O'Brien stood out but, more importantly, his mother's face staring at him with disapproval.

"I know you understand how I feel. Knowing your past, would you not worry if you were going to have to see your mother or father again?" A stab of pain pierced my heart at his words. "I don't say this to hurt you, merely to acknowledge that I know you fully comprehend what I am going through at this moment." He pulled me closer, caressing my back in a soothing motion.

He was right, I did understand why he feared returning to Gaia. His actions may not have been his own, but he was still the person who enacted them. I knew Evan having worked with him for many years at the Council. Most of the time he was a levelheaded hybrid but there were stories about when he would lose it, usually in battle, and then all bets were off. Hopefully we will encounter the levelheaded Evan and not the hotheaded one. Perhaps he had mellowed some when he met his mate.

"I do understand." I pushed a sense of calm through our bond. "I know you worry and have good reason to. I am sure that your mother was aware you were under your sister's control. She will welcome you back with open arms. Happy to have her son back. As for Evan, we will face him together and if he is not aware that you were being controlled, we will do our best to explain it to him. If he can't accept your apology and move on, then we will return here and to hell with whatever war your crazy father plans to bring to Gaia."

A small chuckle rumbled through his chest. "Gods, woman I love you." He punctuated his statement with a searing kiss that led to a few more rounds of lovemaking. When we resurfaced again, he added. "We will make him understand and then we will stop my father too. Although, I would not be against returning here, that tub is amazing."

We fell into a deep sleep, wrapped in each other's arms. The next morning, we were woken by Orson once again walking into our bedroom unannounced. Nikolas pulled the blankets up to cover our naked bodies while I glared balefully at the king's right-hand man.

I will not miss him though. I informed Nikolas. Out loud, my breath seething through my lips, I berated Orson, "How many times do we need to tell you to knock?"

"I knock when there is not a pressing matter." Orson replied nonchalantly. "At this moment, there is a small issue we need to resolve before your trip. As you are leaving soon, I needed to have this discussion before you left and without the presence of King Lucian."

Interesting, I thought, Orson was talking behind the king's back. Nikolas arched an eyebrow at me. That got both of our attention. "Fine, we can talk but not in here. Go out to the sitting room and let us get dressed." I responded, with electric sparks skimming across my hands. I stared at my hands with wonder, that was new.

With an apprehensive glance at my hands, Orson left the room without having to be told twice. That binding ceremony must have unlocked this new power. Nikolas reached for my sparking hands, I pulled them away, worried what they would do to him. Undeterred, he grabbed my hands, the electricity fizzed and seemed to be absorbed by Nikolas' hands.

"What was that?" my voice trembling at a higher octave than normal.

"It's as you thought," he reassured me with a small kiss to my forehead. "The ceremony unlocked something. Our powers are growing, your irritation at Orson coalesced into the sparks on your hands. If you had less control, you probably would have zapped him."

147

An image of me shooting him in the ass with a lightning bolt jumped into my head. I was unsure if I thought of that or if Nikolas had, either way it broke the tension I was feeling. Laughter bubbled up in the back of my throat, spilling out when Nikolas waggled his eyebrows at me.

We had just gotten our laughter under control when three loud raps pounded on our bedroom door. Whatever it is he wishes to discuss it must be extremely important, even his concern about my new powers couldn't stop his impatience.

Nikolas and I hurriedly finished dressing then went to speak with Orson. Surprise washed over both our faces when we walked into the living space to find Serafina waiting for us. We had not been alone with her since the first day. We shared many meals with her, but her brother and Arlien were always present. Finding her anxiously pacing near the couch was unexpected to say the least.

"Oh, thank gods; I could see you before you left." Serafina surged towards us. "I need to warn you of something."

"Come, sit down." I said taking her hand in mine and drawing her to the couch. "What is it?" My tone calm, I held her hands in mine.

"Lucian must not be told of this until he has met his mate." Her eyes pleaded with both of us. She stared forlornly at the door as if she expected him to burst through it at any moment. "You must promise before I tell you."

We looked at each other for half a second before turning back to face her. "We promise." We stated at the same time. However, our silent communication remained unsure if we would honor that promise.

Satisfied with our response, Serafina began speaking. "I have had another vision. Arlien was not there, and I have thus far been able to shield him from seeing it too." She yanked her hands from mine; she stood and began pacing the room.

Her nervous energy was infecting me too. I rose from the couch as well. Following her around the room, I asked, "What have you seen?"

"Lucian will not return to Fabeldyrverden. At least, not from what I have seen. I cannot see if he lives or dies." Her stare took on a faraway look, as if she were experiencing the vision again. Her eyes remained their normal orange, red flecked irises, so I knew she was not caught in another vision.

"A battle will occur in a snow-covered landscape, when this event happens, Lucian and his mate will be surrounded. They are surrounded by a contingent of fae. I see them fall to the ground with no allies around to help."

Serafina's words were like a slap to the face. My head spun to my mate, his eyes met mine, worry and fear matching my own.

"Why must this be kept from Lucian?" Nikolas asked. "It would seem like important information."

"Because, I have searched the future, in every instance that he is told before he meets his mate, he remains in Fabeldyrverden to protect her. Each time he sacrifices their future the war breaks through to our world, and we all die. He must go to Gaia and meet her for the war to be stopped in the cold barren landscape I have seen him fall in." A shudder ran down her body, and she fell back despondent on the couch. Speaking low with deep sadness, Serafina added, "I may never see my brother alive again once he steps through that portal, but he must meet his fate if all our worlds are to be saved from your father and the fae."

I sat beside her on the couch. I pulled her hand into mine and reached my other hand to her chin. Tilting her face up to mine, I promised, "We will honor your request. We will also do everything in our power to ensure he and his mate survives." I whispered fiercely to her.

All business, Orson cleared his throat. "Now that she has conveyed her vision upon you, I must return her to her rooms. Arlien and the king have been meeting with several of the king's advisors this morning. I expect they are close to concluding their business and Arlien will be heading back to your quarters." Orson looked speculatively at Serafina. "You must make yourself presentable for your mate and brother otherwise they will suspect something."

Rubbing her hands down her arms, Serafina made an effort to pull herself together. A couple of minutes passed then, her composure returned. She got to her feet and pulled me into a quick hug. "I wish we had more time to become closer. I fear I may never see you again either." Catching Nikolas' eyes she said, "Please send my love to your mother. She was a great friend, and I have missed her for so long." At his nod, Serafina released me and stood from the couch. "I shall see both of you in the viewing room before you leave."

Once Serafina and Orson had left our rooms we grabbed each other in a tight embrace. *Gods, how are we going to save Lucian and Aisling?*

Nikolas pulled me away from him. "What do you mean? Who is Aisling?"

"If I am correct, she is his mate. Have you not noticed that he follows her with his eyes any time she is within view?" I smiled at his look of confusion.

"No, I haven't noticed anything of the sort. To be honest though, I also have no idea which one is Aisling is either." He dragged me back to the couch. We sat beside each other while I explained who Aisling was and why I believed she was Lucian's mate. Once I finished my description Nikolas conceded I may have a point then stated, "I suppose we'll find out soon enough since we'll be traveling there today."

Chapter Twenty

Arianna

Our small coven of seven had expanded to a few hundred. Davina and her new mate James had arrived a week after she had escaped from the Collier-run hotel in Philadelphia. She'd travelled across the United States with our allies. She broke away in Oregon for some privacy with her mate and to introduce him to us as well.

James is a wolf shifter from the Collier pack. His cousin, Michael, is the head of the pack. I believe that his mating with Davina is probably why Michael pledged fifty wolves to our cause. If things turned out even half as bad as I worried, they would, the fifty wolves would be more than needed.

The day after Davina and James arrived; the rest of our guests began arriving. One of us would meet the boats and guide them in past the wards. We had decided to avoid attracting the attention of humans, we would stagger arrivals over several days. Having a large group of boats suddenly set out from the Alaskan coastline then disappear in the sea seemed a bad idea.

The first to arrive would be the O'Briens. The family came through my safeguards without difficulty. They did, however, look rather dejected, and I learned not long after they had settled in that their mother had passed recently. That explained why the entire O'Brien clan arrived, children, mates, even grandchildren.

Evan, now head of the family with the death of Cillian over a year ago, assured me that one house would be plenty. Their father remained on the mainland to direct any more recruits our way. He would also continue to provide shelter to anyone needing a safe haven at the O'Brien's hidden compound. A small group of witches, shifters and vampires remained at their compound as well.

Evan had also come bearing gifts. His deceased brother had managed to collect several relics from the dragon realm. Relics that could be used in our fertility rituals. If we could get a few more mated pairs, we could begin to restart the dragon lines on this side of the portal. Davina and James would also be able to perform the rites that would give James the power to transform into dragon form.

Aisling had come to see me on the day Jonesie and his crew were to arrive. She was worried about one of the vampires named Derik. When I asked her what specifically bothered her, she could only say that she was getting weird vibes, like when someone's facial expressions didn't match their words. He just felt off to her. I reassured her that my wards should stop him, however I made it a point to meet him.

Jonesie dragged a feeble looking vampire up the dock to meet us. "He has an aversion to boats." The deep timbered vampire explained. "Before he became a vampire he almost drowned on one. I am sure once he has been back on land for a bit he will improve."

"Perhaps a small helping from the blood we have brought will speed along his recovery." I offered, hoping the explanation was correct. I would have to speak with Jasmine, from what everyone says she is quite powerful. My skills did not bend towards truth-seeking. According to Almerinda, that was an ability that Jasmine had.

By week's end, my island was filled, brimming and humming with activity. Training drills, strategy debates, and the occasional drunken songs from Jonesie's crew. Amazingly there was no fighting amongst the different groups. Having a shared enemy sure could do wonders to unify different species

The de facto leaders of each group met twice a day, morning and evening. Our meetings stayed mainly on the topic of my mate and his plans. We also danced around the subject of my son. The biggest question was how to get him and Cassandra back, followed by whether we should want them back. I knew where I stood on that matter.

I have not outright asked Evan and or the rest of the O'Brien clan whether they hold a grudge against him for his actions, mostly because I fear their answer. I miss my Nikolas, not the one controlled by his sister, but the kind and caring Nikolas I knew before. However, I worry that his return will not be entirely welcome amongst the community living on my island.

I awoke the morning after the final group arrived with a sense of hopeful anticipation. Gods willing today would be the day my son finally found a way back to me. Although there was the greatest of chances that if he did find a way back from Fabeldyrverden it would not be under the best of circumstances.

He could either end up back on the island near Greece and into his father's hands or here to face a very angry O'Brien family, or anywhere for that matter. I suppose I can't postpone it any longer. Today I would need to speak with Evan regarding his feelings toward my son.

With a renewed sense of determination, I set out to find Evan. I found him walking along the beach with his mate Alessandra. They looked so happy and relaxed together that I almost turned away from my mission. Ali spotted me first and called out a greeting.

"You look serious." Ali stated bluntly. "Has something happened?"

"No, nothing has happened." My voice trailed off. When I looked at Evan, I forced the words out, "I need to speak with you."

Understanding flashed across his face. His jaw clenched, "I wondered when you would bring this up." Ali pulled her hand from his and started to move apart from us. Evan yanked her back to his side. "Stay, you are part of this too."

I stiffened my back, readying myself for whatever answer he would give. "I need to know what you plan to do to my son if and when he arrives here."

"That will depend on which version of your son shows up." Evan answered, his stance relaxed other than a tightening around his eyes.

I am not sure what look he saw on my face whether it was fear or hope as I was feeling both those emotions at the moment. Minutes passed with the only sound between us, the crashing surf and screeching gulls in the air.

He added more insight. "If the man you have described comes here then I will discuss the past with him calmly, but on the flip side if the man who tortured me," his voice lowered and his eyes darkened, "shows up then he will not have only me to contend with. My family still harbors some resentment."

"To say the least," Ali grumbled, her eyes blazing with fury, flashing steel grey. I could see she was struggling to control her animal side.

"Right," Evan took a slow breath, he gripped his mate's hand, restraining her. Slowly, she inhaled then let out a long exhale. Her eyes shifted back to their normal amethyst color. With a silent apology, she nodded at Evan to continue.

"They believe, as do I that Nikolas was being controlled by his sister. Her death by my brother resolves their urge for vengeance but they will not be so forgiving if he shows up here with the intent to harm me or any of us." I saw another flash of the anger Evan was working hard to suppress. "We've already lost one brother to your family's machinations. Giving you our trust has been difficult considering it was your mate and offspring that took him from us. But we have it on good authority,"

"Jasmine," Ali interjected again.

"That you are on our side and had nothing to do with his death." Evan finished as if Ali's word was part of his speech. "I promise you, as head of my family, that if Nikolas arrives with no intent to harm then we will forgive his actions as not his own."

The pent-up tension that had been holding my spine stiff, dissipated from my body at his proclamation. Hands, that I hadn't even realized were clenched, released to hang loose by my side. "Your words have assuaged my mind." I smiled at the two hybrids before me. "Thank you."

I left them to finish their afternoon stroll along the beach. As they moved further down the rocky coastline, Ali's laughter carried over the breeze to me. Their affection for each other infected the world around them with a lightness in the air.

My thoughts turned back to my son. I had to believe that when his sister died, the spells were lifted and the Nikolas I knew and loved was returned to himself. I sent a silent prayer to the Gods and Fates that his mate would also give him the love I had just witnessed between the hybrids. Hopefully I will soon find out.

Chapter Twenty-One

Aisling

We have been on Arianna's island for five days. We'd arrived battle ready, only to stagnate in restless waiting. Then nothing happened. We'd been prepared and then sat around twiddling our thumbs.

Reports came in often from my Da and Michael Collier regarding different events out in the world but nothing regarding Fraxinus or the fae. Twyla, a witch on Almerinda's guard checked in with her family as well. They reported no activity in the Canadian tundra where they lived.

Fraxinus had to know we were all working against him. We had killed his daughter; stolen his brother and he may even think we stole his son from him. Plus, his mate and her coven had escaped before he could capture them.

If what we have heard from Arianna is correct, he is working with the Fontaine family but according to Jasmine, Marcel is still in Europe. I suppose Andre could have left Europe but that seems doubtful as he has always ruled from a distance and sent others to do his dirty work.

The one person I wish had shown up was Elodie. She is a Fontaine but left the family centuries ago and has no love for her siblings. No one, including her progeny Jaxson, has heard or seen her since she helped us dispose of Luis a couple months ago. She has a little fae blood, but we don't hold that against her. She has always used it to help us.

A loud shout from the front of Arianna's house pulled me out the front door of my house. I rushed down the steps, yanking my knives from the sheaths on my hips. I rounded the corner to see everyone staring at a shimmering orb that hovered about head high in the air. Davina jumped in front of one of the wolves who was about to touch the shiny orb.

"Don't touch it, you idiot." She hollered. "That is a portal beginning to open. Everyone step back but be on guard." She yelled louder.

I saw Arianna move closer to the orb with a look of hope and fear on her face. This could be her son coming through, but which Nikolas would it be? The orb began to spread wider and soon we could see vibrant colors, blues, purples, greens and pinks, all swirling around. Occasionally a form like a tree or that of a person's body would appear, then it would mash together and churn and gyrate together.

Just when I thought it was never going to solidify into a doorway or opening the edges stabilized into a complete circle which expanded to the size of the front of a city bus. The circle turned a brilliant silver then out of the silver Cassandra appeared holding the hand of an enormous man with black hair. Arianna rushed forward, throwing herself at the dark-haired man, embracing him and sort of shielding him from the rest of us.

Everyone was watching Nikolas and Cassandra so no one else seemed to notice the tall auburn-haired god that followed behind them. My heart stopped beating for a full minute then thundered in my chest in a staccato of rapid beats. I could not tear my eyes from the man. Tall, broad shoulders, tapering down to narrow hips with long muscled legs encased in black leather. Gods, how I wish I was that leather. His eyes scanned the faces around us as if he was looking for someone specific.

When his eyes met mine, recognition seemed to flair in them. I had never seen this man before, clearly my libido would have remembered him if I had. Stepping from behind Cassandra and Nikolas, tall dark and handsome headed in my direction. I glanced at Cassandra and saw a knowing look on her face as she watched him walk directly up to me.

Gulping, I raised my eyes to meet his as he came to a stop in front of me. A frisson of desire spiked through my stomach. I wonder if this is how Evan felt when he first saw Ali. After all this time, I think I have met my mate.

"I knew it the minute I saw you." The man's deep voice sent shivers down my spine. The air crackled between us, half a second of electric recognition before his demand shattered the moment. "You are my mate and must return to Fabeldyrverden with me immediately." With that pronouncement he turned to walk back to the portal.

Amusement spread across Cassandra's face as she watched our interaction. The man finally noticed that I was not beside him and looked back at me with a raised eyebrow in question. His imperial tone and high-handed attitude did nothing to endear him.

"Excuse me?" I growled.

Without returning to my side, he answered. "I said you are my mate and must come with me now."

Cassandra gave Nikolas a sly look, which told me she completely expected this to happen. I noticed our audience was more interested in our interplay then the fact that a man who tortured my brother had returned. I walked to stand in front of the man claiming to be my mate. Maybe he was, maybe he wasn't, but I'd be damned if he was going to bark orders at me like I was his servant.

"Listen, bub, I don't know who you think you are, but I don't just bow down to any man who claims to be my mate." I poked him in the chest and realized how hard his muscles were. I will admit I salivated a little at the thought of touching him in a less pokey way. "So, let's try this again. Who the fuck are you?"

Shock erupted on his face as he stared down at me like I was an alien or something. His composure recovered quickly, and he announced, "I am King Lucian Griffin, ruler of Fabeldyrverden. And I am your mate so you would do well to listen to me."

A startled guffaw burst from my lips at his royalness pronouncing to all and sunder who he was and how I should just bow down at his feet and follow his commands. His imperious look was replaced by confusion at my response.

"Here's the thing, your highness, we don't exactly do kings here. Plus, even if you are my mate, I don't follow orders from overbearing jerks." I turned on my heels and stomped away.

Walking away from the man I could sense was my mate was one of the hardest things I had ever done. I know what my mother said about accepting him once I had met him but there was no way I was going to let him order me around like that.

Plus, I needed to remain here to fight the fae and, also, according to my mum he needed to be here for us to win. I hoped my gambit would pay off and he chose to remain in our realm. My mother was correct about one thing though I really did want to kill him, if only a little bit.

If I didn't have shifter and vampire hearing I may not have caught Cassandra's happy giggle and comment to Nikolas. "Told you so." To which Nikolas replied, "I never doubted you for a minute, love."

Clearly their mating had panned out better than mine was starting. I truly believe the Gods must hate me. Sending a man like the almighty King Lucian as my mate. Other than the fact that he was entirely too gorgeous for words, he was a pompous ass. Ignoring the niggling in my head of my mother's voice I continued my angry stomping across the yard to enter my house. I would check in later to find out whether Nikolas was redeemed or killed.

I was just opening the door to my bedroom when I heard the front door slam open. Feet thundered up the stairs and pounded down the hallway, coming to a stop at the threshold. I knew exactly who it was but refused to turn around and look at him.

Our mate bond had recognized his nearness the moment the front door banged onto the wall. Call it stubbornness, which I was famous for, or cowardice which I felt a little unsettled about, but I could not turn to face this man yet.

His angry breathing began to slow, and I felt his gaze rake up and down my backside. I stiffened in response; a mixture of indignation and arousal coursed through my veins. My traitorous skin burned everywhere his gaze touched. How dare he just stand there ogling me, I needed the anger to keep my resolve in place.

"You need not fear me, young one." His aristocratic snobbish tone dampened my desire quicker than a cold shower.

I spun on my heels, anger lacing my words. "I don't fear you." I spat vehemently. "I do however find it quite unacceptable for you to be in my bedchamber." I mimicked his accent allowing condescension to drip from my voice.

Once again that annoying eyebrow shot up while he looked down his nose at me. "Serafina said you would be a spitfire." He mumbled. A satisfied grin spread across his face as his eyes swept up and down my body scorching me with his ownership.

He stepped closer to me, fully entering my bedroom. I was determined to hold my ground even though his movement forced me to crane my neck to keep eye contact. Perhaps he wasn't actually looking down his nose at me, he was rather tall.

"Who is Serafina?" I asked before I could help myself, unable to hide the tinge of jealousy in my voice.

I didn't think it was possible, but his look of satisfaction seemed to grow with my question. "There is no need to worry, she is my sister and has the sight." A possessive glint in his gaze. "She saw you in Gaia and bade me come to collect you."

He was now standing so close that I either had to give ground, which I could not do, or remain so close our chests were almost touching. I inhaled and a heady feeling encompassed me at his scent; woodsy and clean but with the underlying aroma of burnt sage.

My body betrayed me again and I felt myself swaying into his body. I caught myself before I did something as silly as swooning into his arms. Those books of Ali's always had the heroine swooning into the arms of the hero, and I was determined not to fall into that old trope.

I stiffened my spine with resolve. "I am not just some trinket that needs collecting." I replied with exasperation. Feeling I had held my ground long enough, I stepped around him. I kept my back to him while I tried to regain some control over the tremor his nearness had evoked.

"I fear I have not handled this properly." Lucian replied, sounding almost apologetic. A glance over my shoulder revealed a stony face and flashing of red and black scales along his arms up to his neck. They were there and gone in the blink of an eye, but I had seen them. I turned back to glare out the window. He was not apologizing, merely stating a fact.

"Cassandra and Nikolas tried explaining as much about Gaia as they could but much of it made little to no sense to me." I jumped a little when his hands clamped down on my shoulders. His movements were so quiet that even my cat ears hadn't detected him. "Will you give me another chance?"

Of course I would give him another chance. He was my mate; I knew it the minute our eyes met. I was also going to make him wait for an answer. If I just threw myself into his arms, as my body was begging me to do, I would lose any chance of being on equal footing with him in the future.

I swear the Gods really love to toy with me. Just a few short weeks ago I was whining about not having met my mate. Now I have and he is a dragon king from another realm with a superiority complex. Just my luck.

"I need time to think." I answered, trying to hide the desire I felt with each caress of his hands on my shoulders.

I knew our mate bond was informing him of every flutter of my heart just the same that I could feel his longing for me. I shrugged away from his hands, stepping away from him again. I really needed to stop giving up ground to him. Turning around, I crossed my arms over my chest.

"I need space; you need to leave my room." I moved my hands to my hips, forcing them into fists.

A look of chagrin showed on his face, but he seemed to accept that if he wanted a happy mating with me, he would need to win me over. His desire to drag me into his realm seemed to be at war with his wish for a happy future. His internal struggle melted into me through the mate bond that was already growing stronger.

"I will give you some time to think." Shaking his head, he stepped back and with a stiff bow walked to the door. At the doorway he paused and with burning need in his eyes, his possessive growl seared my heart. "Mark my words, you are my mate and will be mine."

He spun on his heels and stamped down the hallway. I rushed to my door and kicked it shut. Gods, I needed that barrier to keep me from chasing him down the hall. I threw myself on my bedding, hugging my trembling body tightly.

"Gods, I asked for a mate who was not an ass. Clearly you didn't get the memo."

Chapter Twenty-two

Cassandra

Their first meeting went about how I expected it to. Knowing Aisling the way I do, Lucian has his work cut out for him. She'll inevitably yield to the mate bond, but not before teaching the great King Lucian he's no longer royalty here.

After she stormed off with him following, all eyes turned back to land on me and Nikolas. Well, I suppose it could be worse. There was a lot of distrust in the eyes of those encircling us but so far no one had attacked. Nikolas' mother stood at his side now, challenging everyone with her stance. I heard Nikolas murmur to her to stand down, and she relaxed her pose.

Almerinda was the first to move forward. I received an unexpected welcoming hug; we had never been much for displays of affection. I knew she had always considered me a friend, but this was unusual for her to be so open.

"Cassandra, my dear, I worried we would never see you again." She spoke quietly in my ear before releasing me. She stepped back then spoke louder so all would hear. "I see you have brought someone with you." She shouted as if these people had no idea who the man next to me was. "Care to do the introductions?"

Before I could speak, Nikolas stepped forward. "If Evan O'Brien is here, I would like to apologize for my actions."

Evan moved around his brother Cormac who had apparently been standing guard. His new mate held his hand as they stepped forward.

"I am here. What do you have to say to me?" His posture stayed casual, but steel threaded through his words.

His mate was unable to hide her nervousness as she bounced from foot to foot. She cocked her head slightly reminding me of an animal when it was listening to something no one else could hear. Her posture unwound, and she came off the tips of her toes. So, he was not as amped up as she was. Awesome, that meant we were dealing with the less savage side of Evan.

Nikolas took a small step closer to Evan but when Cormac growled low in his throat he retreated to my side. "I have much to atone for," Nikolas began, his voice rang loud across the gathered crowd. "I regret my actions every single day. I would like the chance to make amends for my transgressions against you and your family."

"The way I hear it, you were being controlled by your sister. So, it would seem she needs to make amends not you." Evan responded with an even cadence. His mate slipped her hand in his. His partially shifted hand informed that his outward calm was something he was working to maintain.

"As I understand it, your brother there," Nikolas pointed to Cormac, "has actually already taken care of Penelope."

"How could you know that?" Evan's mate gasped, accusation clear in her voice.

"My sister controlled me with many spells; one of them linked our minds." Nikolas explained.

I gave him a sharp look. Why had he never told me of this spell? *I am sorry. I should have told you.*

"The subjugation spell requires the master to join their mind with the subdued. This spell allows the master to have complete control over the other person. It also opens a doorway into the master's mind. I had no control over my actions as my sister was in command of them, but I was in her mind just as much as she was in mine."

"Oh, Nikolas," Arianna's distraught face crumpled at this revelation.

Nikolas kept his gaze on the O'Brien family, refusing to allow his mother to distract him. His skin shimmered, glimpses of his green and purple scales flitting seen then unseen. "The day you killed her I felt her death as the last of our connection was severed. Had I not already mated with Cassandra; you may not have prevailed over Penelope. Our connection was tenuous, but she still tried to draw from my powers. When I felt her in my mind again, I used my bond with Cassandra to force her out."

Arianna sobbed as she listened to her son describe one of the many ways his sister had harmed him. "Nikolas, I wish I could have saved you from her." She swiped at the tears coursing down her cheeks.

"Mother, you could not have done anything." Nikolas reassured her. "She caught me unawares. Her and father. Remember when I left many years ago and refused to come home?" Arianna nodded. "They threatened to hurt you if I did not return. I came home to save you, but they were at the docks with Martine. Before I could run, Martine spelled me. The next memory I have that I know is mine and mine alone was seeing Cassandra sitting across from me ready to interrogate me."

Gods, if his sister wasn't already dead, I would use my powers on her to avenge him. A feeling of warmth washed over me, *I love that you would do that for me.* I squeezed his hand in response then focused back on the crowd around us.

"As you have all heard, he is not responsible for the actions his body performed against you." I made sure to meet the gaze of everyone watching for any sign that they would respond negatively.

"Cormac," Nikolas stated, "I believe I owe a debt to you and your mate, Jasmine, for helping to release me from the final threads of my sister's spell. I don't know if meeting my mate would have completely broken her hold on me or if she would have still retained some control. Her death leaves me no doubt that her control is totally gone."

"You're, ah, welcome." Cormac's response sounded more like a question than acknowledgment. The large man shifted on his feet seeming at a loss for more words.

Evan chuckled at his brother's unusual response. After sharing a long look with his mate, they stepped forward, Evan reaching his hand out to Nikolas.

"I will accept that you are telling the truth. However, I will caution you that we will be watching you." Evan gripped Nikolas' hand in his.

"As you should." Nikolas agreed, returning Evan's steely gaze with one of open invitation.

"Almerinda says I can trust Cassandra's judgment implicitly. But I also trusted another once as a friend and fellow guard member. His mating changed him," Evan's voice cracked as he released my mate's hand. "Well, let's just say he no longer had total control of himself. For now, we will welcome both of you and if you prove true to our cause we will forgive old transgressions."

The tension I had not realized I was holding in my body rushed out of me. My muscles suddenly felt like jelly, and I nearly collapsed with relief. Thankfully, Nikolas sensed my weakening and wrapped his arm around my waist, securing my body to his side. I had no urge to fall over in front of everyone.

I will always support you, whether it is emotional support or just keeping you from falling flat on your face.

163

I giggled quietly and then laughed out loud when I saw Lucian emerge from the house, he and Aisling had entered a few minutes before. He looked unsure of himself and much like a lost little boy.

I received a few startled and curious looks at my laughter. "I am sorry; I am not laughing at any of you." I lifted my chin in Lucian's direction. "He has a lot to learn about how things are here."

Arianna snickered. "Lucian always was a bit full of himself. Why is he here?"

"Who is he?" Almerinda asked me then turned to Arianna, "And how do you know him?"

"There is much we need to share with you." I answered. "Is there any chance we could do it in a less 'you're surrounded' way and maybe in more of 'have a cup of tea' way?"

Silence stretched between us, long enough for seabirds to cry overhead, long enough for a tendril of discomfort to wind up my back. When everyone realized there was no danger, most of them wandered off, going back to whatever they had been doing before our arrival.

Ali stepped forward and took my hand in hers. "Since Evan isn't going to kill your mate, I suppose tea sounds nice, though I'm more of a vodka and cranberry drinker myself."

Her comment shocked laughter out of me. I was not expecting such a direct acknowledgment of how tense the situation had been. I allowed Ali to lead me up the hillside.

"I'm Ali, by the way. I have heard much about you, but we've never met." The young woman babbled at me, not giving me an opportunity to answer. "Is it true you can hurt people with your mind? That's kinda crazy, right?

Ali continued her diatribe as she guided us to the house she shared with the rest of the O'Brien clan. Her non-stop chatter seemed like a nervous tick. Rather than leading us inside, she toured us around the corner. Placed around the back of the house were several outdoor chairs and tables.

"There are only three houses on the island." Ali explained. "Most of us find it better to be outside except when we wish to have private moments." A light flush colored her cheeks reminding me she was human not too long ago.

Evan pulled Ali onto his lap and placed a quick kiss on her lips. Her rambling cut off, "Sorry," she said, shifting on his lap, getting comfortable. "I tend to babble when I'm nervous."

"Don't we know it." Cormac ducked as a rock flew out of her hand, aimed at his forehead. Their banter was refreshing.

The seats filled up. Arianna sat in a canvas chair and indicated the two seats beside her for us to sit in. Nikolas and I sat beside his mother and the rest who had stayed spread out on the other available chairs and ground.

Lucian meandered over to stand near our group, looking lost at sea. Arianna noticed him and motioned for him to join us. I had never seen him look so unsure of himself. I think he expected to show up, claim his mate and step back through the portal Nikolas had created. With Serafina's vision fresh in our mind, we had agreed that we would not open a portal for him.

For now, Lucian was stuck in Gaia until he and Aisling could come together and learn to open a portal back to Fabeldyrverden. Lucian looked around and saw no chairs left. He inspected the ground as if it might be contagious before he flopped onto the ground beside Arianna's seat.

Chapter Twenty-three

Arianna

"So, where to start?" Cassandra glanced at everyone, then her eyes settled on Lucian. Apparently deciding that Lucian was probably who they were most curious about, she stated. "So, this is King Lucian, but we have told him there are no kings here so he shall go by Lucian. Oh, Arianna, I almost forgot, Serafina sends her love."

Serafina's name sent warmth flooding through me, after all these centuries the friendship burned bright. "Is she well?" I asked.

Lucian answered before Cassandra, "She is very well. She has mated with Arlien, they have not had children yet, but you know how it is in Fabeldyrverden. Children are only required when one needs an heir. Arlien helps her with her visions, and they are devoted to each other and the crown."

"What of the crown?" I inquired. "Cassandra said you are King Lucian?"

"I am, yes." Lucian replied. "Magna Quercus stepped down after both his sons were trapped on this side of the seal. My father ruled for a thousand years, as is tradition, then stepped aside. My rule began thirty years ago. My sister, Serafina, your dearest friend, stands as my proxy until I return with my mate."

The large form of Hawthorne rushed from the direction of the trees where the wolves had taken up residence. The resemblance between him and Fraxinus still caught me off guard sometimes. Nikolas saw him and flinched back. "That is your uncle, not your father. Rest easy, son." I comforted him as best I could, but I believe he gained more reassurance from his mate's presence.

Lucian noticed Hawthorne just as he reached the edge of our group. "Uncle? Thorne, is that you?" Lucian rose from his position on the ground and the two men embraced. "It is so good to see another friendly face." Lucian espoused.

"Have the seals been broken?" Hope laced Hawthorne's voice.

"Only mated pairs can travel at this time." Cassandra answered. "We do not know how to break the seal the witches placed over a thousand years ago. And even if we did know how, we wouldn't until Nikolas' father is stopped."

"So, what's stopping mated dragons from coming here?" I asked the three of them.

"Lucian gave a royal edict prior to leaving prohibiting travel between the realms until he returns." Nikolas explained. "We had no idea what we would be facing when we came here and felt it best for now to keep the rest of the dragons safe."

"While I agree with wanting to keep them safe," Almerinda interrupted, "we may need them if war comes."

"Why should my people die in a war that is not of their making?" Lucian asked coldly.

"But it is of a dragon's making." Almerinda replied with more ice in her voice than his. "It is your uncle who wishes to start this war. Perhaps I should have Cassandra open a portal and shove him through it. Then he would be your problem and not ours."

"She would never." Indignation resounded through Lucian's voice as he stepped toward Almerinda menacingly.

Damian, a tall black-haired vampire and Almerinda's mate, placed himself between Almerinda and Lucian. "You may be a dragon," he growled, "but I am pretty sure you've never messed with a former Navy Seal turned vampire."

Lucian paused, a look of confusion appeared on his face. "Since I have no idea what a Navy Seal is, you may be correct." As the two men were about the same height, he glared at Almerinda around Damian's body. "You cannot send Fraxinus to Fabeldyrverden. He would cause much harm and damage."

"Hence you see our dilemma." Almerinda's haughty tone matched Lucian's: clearly both were used to leading. "Although, I am sure you will soon see reason. If your mate is the woman you chased into the house, I can guarantee she will not scurry off to your realm."

"We shall see." Lucian retorted. "While she has proven a little difficult thus far, I am sure I can get her to comply with my wishes."

As one, all that knew Aisling laughed uproariously at his statement. I chuckled as well; I did not know the hybrid female well but even I could sense she would not be so easily tamed. While I was closer to Serafina, I always had a soft spot for Lucian. I hope that his mating was not the Fates intervening as they did with mine. Yet, if this was a true love match then perhaps it would do him some good to have a mate that would not just roll over for him.

Lucian gaped at those who were laughing for a moment. His regal manner slumped back to sit on the ground. "Perhaps, I need to learn a bit more about the woman I have mated with." He grumbled quietly under his breath. His hands yanked on the hardy tufted hairgrass that grew all over the island.

Sympathy welled inside me; Lucian was a proud young dragon when I last saw him and didn't seem to have changed much. Underneath that imposing exterior, there was also Serafina's brother. I can still picture the younger Lucian playing games with Sera and I at their country estate. That person just needed to come back out of wherever he had stashed him.

"Hell, yeah you do." Evan spit out from my left. "I may be able to help you." Lucian lifted his head, hope shining in his eyes. "Aisling is my sister, and my best friend. I want nothing more than for her to have a loving and happy mating such as my own. We'll talk later after we have finished our discussion here."

Lucian nodded with optimism finally breaking through his slumped shoulders. "Thank you, I look forward to it."

"Now," Evan returned his attention to the entire group that had gathered. "We need more information from you two." He pointed at Cassandra and Nikolas. "Did the seer who saw Lucian's mate see anything else?"

Cassandra and Nikolas shared a look that told me there was something else, but they answered no anyway. Hmm, another mystery to solve. I still hadn't spoken with Jasmine about Derik, now I needed to also find out what my son and his mate were hiding.

"We did learn one thing that seems quite important in Fabeldyrverden." Cassandra announced. "Did you all know that Arianna comes from the Danu line of witches?"

All eyes locked on me, I sighed, after a thousand years, the truth would finally be told. Well, Cassandra really knows how to deflect attention from her secrets. She gave me a knowing smile as if she had read my thoughts. I smirked back; I would ferret out their secrets soon enough.

"She is correct. I once lived with the dragons. About fifty years before the portals were sealed, I left Fabeldyrverden and travelled to Gaia. Serafina, Lucian's sister, had seen that I would meet my mate in Gaia." My hands formed into fists as

I suppressed the anger I was feeling for my mate so I could finish speaking. "She could not tell me everything, but she did warn me that I needed to keep him from reaching his full potential. When I asked her why, she told me that the reason was blocked from her."

Hawthorne shifted slightly from foot to foot before adding. "Sera probably did not tell you what she suspected of Fraxinus because she knew how important it was for you to meet your mate. If she had told you all she knew you may have refused to meet him."

"What exactly do you know about all this?" I rounded on Hawthorne, the air whipped around my body, my magic was attempting to lash out at him. I needed answers, not a dead dragon.

"Not long before I left my world to come here and try to bring Fraxinus home, Sera searched me out." Hawthorne explained, meeting my stare with guilt in his eyes. "She never told me the name of your mate only that she had foreseen it. She knew if you did not meet him, he would survive the fae attack, even without your healing skills. His survival, without you blocking his powers, would lead him to bringing the fae back sooner. A future without your children being born always ended with the fae overtaking this world and the dragon realm."

"Why didn't she tell me?" I moaned. "She had to know I would never do anything to allow the fae to win." My heart beat erratically in my chest. I chanted quietly to myself to calm my racing thoughts.

"I only know what she told me." Hawthorne reassured me. "She said you could not be told until after your female child was dead. She had seen many futures and the only ones that did not end in destruction had you mated with two children, with the female child dying."

Oh Sera, I thought, all the futures she has seen, and not all of them good. She must have known she would probably never see me again and yet she still sent me here. Gods, how I would hate to have the sight.

"I did as she requested. From the moment Fraxinus began to regain strength I forced our shared powers down. He always believed it was because I was a weak witch." A derisive laugh burst from my throat. "Thankfully, he and I had never crossed paths when I was in Fabeldyrverden."

"How is that possible?" Cassandra arched her eyebrow, much the same was my son always did when he was upset and confused at the same time. "We've seen the tapestry at the palace." A small spark jumped from the end of her finger.

"What tapestry?" I implored; I was not enjoying the feeling of cross-examination from my son's mate. I truly had no idea what she was talking about.

"Mother." Nikolas intervened with Cassandra and me. He placed his hand on her arm, holding her back. She was clearly upset, what with the sparks on her hands and now her eyes had begun to swirl like a dragon's does when they are agitated. "We need honesty from you, and everyone," his hard stare scanned us all, "we've both been lied to by people we trusted for so many years."

I had never lied to him, and I wasn't sure who had lied to Cassandra, but I understood why they would be frustrated and angry. Neither one of them had been treated fairly by much of anyone. Nikolas, used by his sister and father, much like Cassandra being used by the Council. Both used for their power.

"I apologize." I reached my hand out, taking both of theirs in mine. The electrical energy faded, as I pulled it into my body. "I honestly do not know what you are talking about."

"There is a picture of you in the hall behind the audience chamber." Lucian informed us from his unhappy seat on the ground. "It depicts your battle against Morbicus."

"Oh." My mouth had dropped open with this revelation. I snapped it shut and said, "I lived with Sera's family in the country. By the time I left to come to Gaia, Fraxinus had already come to this world. So, he had no idea that I was a Danu witch. Thank gods for that, I believe if he had known, I never would have succeeded in fooling him as long as I did."

"How could he not have known?" Evan questioned. "If there's a picture of you at the castle?

"That tapestry was hung after the portals were sealed." Lucian supplied, sitting straighter when everyone looked his way again. "When my father assumed the throne, he commissioned many new tapestries for the castle. One of them was the defeat of Morbicus, the Great Fae General by Arianna of the Danu line."

"Plus, Fraxinus was never interested in history." Hawthorne moved to stand closer to Lucian. "The battle you speak of happened almost sixty years before the portals were sealed. If I am correct, you were quite young in that battle." He looked at me, waiting for my answer.

"Yes, I was only twenty when I faced him. I left for Gaia not long after that battle." I couldn't hold back the trembling I felt at my memory of that battle. "Had I not been a Danu witch, I doubt I would have survived let alone defeated him."

"Okay, for us dumb people," Ali growled from Evan's side. "Maybe someone could explain what the hell the Danu line is."

Lucian stood, brushing off the grass and sand from his tailored pants. "The Danu line is the most powerful line of casters to ever walk Gaia. Many of the beings believed to be gods in this world were Danu casters, what you call witches. They are called the Tuatha De Danann or the folk of the goddess Danu. Centuries ago, there were many different tribes of casters, however many of them had ceased to exist by the time the portals were sealed. The Danu line was down to only two or three casters, one of which was Arianna."

"I've read about the Tuatha De Danann, but they're not real." Ali admitted. "Folktales and old lore, but not real." Her hand waved in a dismissive gesture.

"Are you not a chimera?" Lucian's tone brought a low rumble from her mate. At Ali's look of confusion to the word he used he amended his words. "A shifter and a striga? Two species combined into one?" She nodded slowly. "Then if you believe you are real why would the Tuatha De Danann not be?"

Cassandra kicked Lucian in the ankle, glaring at his imperious tone. "I apologize for sounding so condescending. I am not used to engaging in conversations with new people." He raised his eyebrow in question at Cassandra. She smiled back at him all while shaking her head slowly.

"I think I should tell my history." I motioned for Lucian to sit back down. "My grandmother was the fabled Mor-rioghan. She had many children, one of which was my mother. My grandfather was human and had no magic. He ruled over a large area of land in the northern wilds of Ireland. My mother said it was a love match, and Grandmother even pretended to be human. She aged as he did, then on his death, she reverted to her young form and left my mother and her brother behind. My mother never saw her again."

Nikolas took my hand in his. He knew some of the story but not all. "We heard that she had died but it was never confirmed. The older ones of the Danann had much longer lives than average witches do. My mother lived for eight hundred years before she passed."

"Wow!" Ali gasped. "I had no idea that some of the gods of myths were real."

"All of the gods of myths are real." I smiled; her inquisitive mind was refreshing. "My father was from a different line of the gods. What humans call the Olympians. His great grandmother was the caster known as Eris; she was the Greek's goddess of chaos. My father only lived for about six hundred years. We believe that as the lines mingled with humans and other species more, their life spans diminished."

I glanced around to see if anyone looked confused with my telling. No one seemed lost so I continued. "Many believe the Danu line is more powerful than all other lines, but I am not so sure. Danu magic flows like water, but Olympian power strikes like lightning. I met Eris after I returned to Gaia. I can assure you she was quite powerful. Whether any of the Gods of old still walk amongst us, I couldn't say. I have not seen any of them since I saw Eris close to a thousand years ago."

"Mating with Fraxinus, gave me the longevity of a dragon otherwise I would probably have died many years ago too." My hands formed into fists. For centuries I had held my emotions in check, now I was struggling again. "Being as powerful as I am, I was able to suppress my mate's powers, so he was unable to open a portal back to his home realm. That's what also kept me from becoming a full dragon's mate. Davina helped us conceive the twins when she performed a fertility ritual for us. We did not complete the Sanguis Draconis ritual though, so I have never completely ascended to full dragon."

Cassandra and James stared at me, her with anxiety and him with confusion. "With proper training and undergoing the ceremonial rites of mating you will be able to transform into a dragon."

James looked excited but if his hand wringing was any indication, also a little nervous. He was a wolf shifter so the idea of changing forms may not be as daunting for him as it would for Cassandra. Davina and Nikolas had their work cut out for them.

Lucian and Evan both glanced at the window where Aisling now stood watching us. Her face was a mask; whatever emotions she was feeling, she was hiding them well. Her eyes locked on Lucian; I could see her struggle right before she whipped her head to the side. I look at Lucian, a small, satisfied smile had developed on his face.

"If she accepts Lucian," I nodded at her window, placing extra emphasis on the 'if', "she can also complete the rites to become a full dragon's mate." I quickly glance at Lucian again and see his smile has been replaced with a frown, his eyes hooded.

Chapter Twenty-four

Aisling

I stewed in my bedroom far longer than necessary. But knowing what I should do and actually doing it? Yeah, that was the problem. I needed to meet this Lucian head on not hiding away from him and our mating.

I watch Lucian from my window as he interacts with the group gathered around the fire pit. Warmth spreads through me with every move he makes, graceful, deliberate, like he knows I'm watching.

His large hands are currently digging then smoothing the sand around him. I imagine those same hands on me, with each stroke across the sand my body becomes more flushed. As if he sensed me watching him, his eyes rise to my window. Our eyes meet and a jolt of electricity shoots straight through me.

It takes every bit of strength that I have to wrench my eyes away from him. A knowing smirk crosses his face as he turns his attention back to whoever is speaking. I rush from the window and throw myself onto my bedding on the floor. Gods, grant me the strength to withstand that magnetism I feel from him. I can't let him consume me if I have any hope of being happy with him.

I give myself five more minutes to wallow then force myself up from my pile of blankets and pillows. Well, time to face the music. I glanced out the window on my way past and noticed that Lucian is nowhere to be seen. A sliver of panic runs down my back. I'm about to rush from my room to search for him when I feel calm settle over me. He must be nearby.

I slowly creep down the stairs, like a thief in my own home. Pausing at the kitchen door, I hear Evan and Lucian's voices through the door. Traitor, I think, when I overhear Evan telling Lucian all about me. Currently he is explaining to my mate that I have a bit of a temper and how best to manage me. I am about to burst through the door but stop myself before I do. That would just be reinforce the whole 'she has a bit of a temper' comment.

I listen for a minute longer, then slip quietly down the hall to the front door. I tug at the door, hoping they don't hear me. The door swings open, and I go in search of Cassandra. She should be able to give me some information about Lucian.

Plus, I want to know more about the happy torturer known as Nikolas. Evan may say all is forgiven, but I'll form my own opinion.

The meeting area is the other way, but that is also where the kitchen window is. I want to avoid being seen, so I turn in the opposite direction. I want to find Cassandra without encountering Lucian. Just as I turn the corner, Cassandra barrels into me.

"Oh, there you are." Cassandra blurts. "I was looking for you."

"That's funny," I retort. "I was looking for you too."

"I sent Nikolas to spend some time with his mother and to get to know his uncle." Cassandra smiles shyly. "I am sure you have misgivings about him, and I will answer all your questions. And," she gives me a knowing look, "we need to talk about Lucian. Let's go walk down on the beach so no one can interrupt us."

She grabs my hand and pulls me away from the house. We walk in silence for a few minutes before I blurt, "By the way, I really am glad you're okay. I know we weren't best friends or anything like that, but I always liked you."

"Thank you." Cassandra gives me a shy smile. "I always liked you too. You were one of the few who treated me like a person instead of just the Council's torture machine."

"Glad you noticed." I grin back. "Maybe we can become good friends then, you know, as long as your mate doesn't turn out to be a bad guy and all."

Cassandra laughed happily, "Well then, we shall be the best of friends. Since I've seen inside his mind, I know that Nikolas is not a bad guy. His sister, on the other hand, was a truly horrible person."

Our trek brought us to the sand and pebbled beach. The cold dark water lapped on the ground with very little surf. The ocean was calm today, unlike my nerves which were a complete wreck. Cassandra seemed different from the girl who worked for the Council. If nothing else, mating seems to have relaxed her some. She had always been so tense and sometimes even a bit scared. This more carefree side I was witnessing was a very welcome change. Our feet made a swishing path through the high grass.

Our shoes crunched along the beach trail, and we came to the edge of the water. We sat down on the rocky beach. The quiet was broken only by the sound of the gentle waves crashing on the ground near our feet. I leaned back, tilting my face to meet the afternoon sun. I peaked at Cassandra; she had also raised her face to bask in the sun.

Our minutes of peace together came to an end when Cassandra pronounced, "You need to know that Nikolas is very conflicted about how to go forward after what his sister did to him. Not just him, obviously, but to so many others too."

She glanced at me as if gauging my reaction. I kept my expression neutral and motioned for her to continue. I suspected that she needed to get everything off her chest about Nikolas before we could discuss anything else.

With a small smile, Cassandra continued, "Having control of your own body and mind taken over by somebody else is horrible. Now imagine that person is your twin sister, the person who is supposed to be closest to you over everyone. She used his body and his powers for her own gain. She used his strength and size to intimidate and torture people. He was trapped in his body and had to witness every atrocity she made him perform all the while being unable to stop it. I understand that Evan has forgiven him. I don't know if Nikolas has forgiven himself."

Tears ran down her cheeks. I sat up and grabbed her hands in mine. I pulled her into a hug, slowly patting her back. "Don't cry." I pleaded. "I am sure he will come to terms with everything. Like Evan said, he is forgiven since he was not in control." I continued to pat her back while I waited for her silent sobs to subside.

With one last hiccough, Cassandra pulled away from my embrace. She wiped the tears from her face. "Eventually, I suspect he will too. It's just hard watching him beat himself up." She gave me a sheepish grin before adding, "I don't think I've ever received a hug from a friend before. I do really hope we can be friends."

"I think we can." I replied, leaning back on my hands. "Now tell me all about the dragon world." I demanded, hoping to learn something about my mate and where he came from.

Cassandra described the dragon realm to me. Her descriptions were so detailed, I felt like I could see the pink waters and dark blue skies. After hearing about many of the different animals that lived there, she then told me about the ceremony where Nikolas officially refused the throne. A large lump settled in my stomach, and my lack of excitement must have shown on my face. Cassandra stopped her tale to ask if I was okay.

"I really don't know." I answered, my voice catching on the last word. "He really is the king of that world, isn't he?" She nodded yes to my question. "Oh Gods, what am I going to do? If he's the king and he's my mate, then what does that make me?"

"I suppose you'll be his queen." Cassandra nudged my foot with hers. "It won't be as bad as you seem to think, if your face is any indication."

"I can't be a queen." I blurted. "I hate fancy gowns with a passion. Have you ever seen me in a dress?"

"So, you won't wear fancy gowns." Her helpful tone was a little grating.

"It's not just dresses. Do I look like a queen?" I pointed out my current choice of clothing. Holey jeans, and a t-shirt that had a rip in it from my last training session with the wolves. My boots were scuffed and worn looking. Shit, even my hair was a mess, I'm not sure I combed it this morning since I planned to train, not meet my mate.

Cassandra laughed, nudging my arm. "I don't think he cares what you're wearing."

I gave her a light shove back, smiling while I did it to show I was kidding around. "He's also a bit of a dick." I grumbled under my breath.

Cassandra's laugh burst from her startling a few birds that had been edging closer to us. "You're right, he has a lot to learn. There's more to Lucian than just arrogance. You must understand something about him. He was quite young for a dragon when he was told he was going to have to rule. Most of the ruling class have their children quickly after mating, especially ones in line for kingdoms. The earlier they are born the longer they can live normal lives before having to learn how to rule a kingdom."

Cassandra went on to explain how the dragon realm was ruled. A king or queen rules for a thousand years. At the end of their rule their eldest child inherits the throne. In a perfect situation that child has already mated and produced an heir.

Occasionally, such as in Lucian's situation, the previous line of heirs is wiped out. Lucian and his sister should never have been in line for the throne. If the proper line of succession had been followed Hawthorne would have inherited. He and his mate had not produced offspring, but they would have if not for being trapped in Gaia. If Hawthorne did not produce an heir, the throne would have passed to Fraxinus and then to Nikolas.

177

"When the portal was sealed, trapping Hawthorne and Fraxinus in our world, their parents had to step down, and a new line of succession started." Cassandra turned from the water to face me. "Magna Quercus turned the throne over to his brother Pinus. Lucian was around one hundred and fifty when the portal was closed, a mere juvenile for a dragon. King Pinus forced Lucian to start his training at that time too. The carefree youth his sister described turned into the somber and severe man you have met."

"So, what you're saying is that he comes by his arrogance naturally?" I inquire while keeping my eye on the calm waters around us. I worry that my mate is only an arrogant ass and nothing else.

"In a manner of speaking, yes." Cassandra intones. "I met King Pinus once while we were in Fabeldyrverden. He no longer lived at the palace and only visited one time. He was described to me as a strong and fair ruler. I can attest to the strong part. His visit was quite stressful for Lucian and his sister. I could not confirm anything for sure, but I suspect that their father was very strict and not prone to showing much affection. Their mother was not much better from what I witnessed."

"What is his sister like?" I asked, worry tinting my voice. What if she was just as daunting as he seemed? In his defense, I really haven't spent much time around him, he could be a fun-loving guy but so far all I had observed was the overbearing man.

"Serafina is more laid back than Lucian. Sera likes to laugh and have fun. Although, she does have a serious side. I believe her visions haunt her, so she tries to find happiness anywhere she can. Her mate is much like Lucian, somewhat stern and a little overprotective of her. When Lucian is around her, he tends to let his guard down more and can be a little less dour. I do believe you and Lucian are well matched."

I snorted my disbelief, biting my tongue so I wouldn't say anything I might regret later. My eyes wandered over the surrounding sea. The waters were calm today, unlike my nerves. As I stared at the horizon a herd, or was it pod, of whales swam by, their blow holes spouting plumes of water in the air.

Cassandra touched my arm, prodding me to face her. "I know it seems like a lot. Believe me, I know. I met Nikolas under not so optimal circumstances, too. I got ripped from my world and thrust into a new world with him. I only knew that the man I mated to was being held prisoner by the Council for torturing Evan. At least, you have friends and family to help you while you assimilate to your new circumstances. I had no one that I could fully trust."

"I suppose you have a point." I conceded less gracefully than I probably should have. "I just need to get to know him better. You say he has a softer side?"

Cassandra described more about Lucian to me. He was raised as the heir apparent by a man who took everything too seriously. His mother wasn't much better than his father when it came to affection either. On the plus side, his sister sounded like a counterbalance to his parent's sternness.

Lucian was used to having everyone jump to do his bidding and as king he would expect everything to go exactly the way he ordered. My initial reaction to his command probably threw him a little off balance. Cassandra also described events when he did not seem to have a stick up his ass. I wanted to meet the man from those stories.

One such story stuck with me, reminding me of my brother Evan. Cassandra giggled as she told the short tale. "One night, after dinner, Sera, Arlien, me and Nikolas were walking back to our rooms. Lucian had disappeared immediately after the final course. We came to the hall that would lead to Sera and Arlien's rooms. Carnival-like music was coming from her hall. Nik and I followed them down their hall. The sight we saw was unbelievable. Lucian had set up a mini street fair in their hallway. He yelled happy birthday to Sera as soon as he saw her."

I was trying to picture the snooty Lucian I had seen compared to what Cassandra was describing. It was difficult to see it though.

"That's not the half of it. Lucian was wearing a jester's outfit, and he was juggling. Plus, he had brought in some animals as a petting zoo. Sera really loves animals." Cassandra's smile was infectious, although mine was more from picturing him in a jester's outfit. "The best part is it wasn't even her birthday. She told me later that he knew he wasn't going to be there on her birthday so set it up before we left."

"Thank you for sharing all this with me." I grabbed her hand in mine and pulled her into another hug. She stiffened for a few seconds before relaxing in my arms. "If we're going to be friends, you are going to have to get used to hugs. The O'Briens are a pretty affectionate family, we don't hold back with people we care about."

Cassandra's mouth spread into a dazzling smile. "That is why I think you will be just what Lucian needs. His sister always tried to pull him out of his imperious shell. I feel like you'll bring out his playful side. I promise you; he does have one."

I kept hold of her hand as we walked off the beach to return to the houses. It was time for me to face the music. I needed to get to know my mate. Hopefully he would be more than just a controlling king from another world. For both our sakes, I really need him to be more than that.

Chapter Twenty-Five

Cassandra

Aisling and I wrapped up our chat about Nikolas and Lucian. Judging by her smirk, I'd say she's at least resigned to Nikolas, now. Good. Now I get to watch her and Lucian dance around each other like two marionettes tangled together.

I knew if I was correct that she was his mate that it was not going to be as easy as he expected. Lucian was used to everyone jumping to his commands, so having a mate like Aisling was going to be an eye-opening experience for him, or possibly ego shattering. Either way, I'd pay to watch.

Everything I knew about her made me believe she was the perfect mate for him. She was fierce and strong, something she would need to keep him from walking all over her. He needs a mate that will not bow down to his every whim.

My wandering feet brought me to the large crackling bonfire. Nikolas, Hawthorne and Arianna were gathered around the fire. Nikolas just finished asking his mother if she knew where his father could be when he saw my approach. He gestured to the spot beside him on the bench and I sat down next to him.

"I don't know for certain." Arianna shrugged. "But if he were close, I'd feel him through our mate bond."

"Well, that's a relief." I held my hands to the fire. The sun was setting and without its warmth, the air was growing chilly. "What kind of powers does his father have?"

Arianna's smile rested on us, she seemed happy with how close we were sitting. "Fraxinus has the basic powers of a dragon. Without being able to reach his full powers, he can change into a dragon, has superior strength and speed, and of course his long life. However, he has no access to the extra powers of a mated dragon."

"So, no shooting flames from his eyes or anything like that?" I halfway joked, considering I really hadn't had much time to research what all a dragon was capable of.

Arianna laughed while shaking her head no. "No dragon can shoot fire from their eyes. A fire dragon can from their throat, though."

"Good to know." I rested back, leaning into Nikolas. The smoke from the fire had blown in my face when the wind changed direction. I had a small coughing fit, Nikolas looking on with a mixture of amusement and concern.

I got my coughing under control and took a sip of water Arianna provided. "So, everyone keeps mentioning extra powers," I leaned forward holding Arianna's gaze with mine, "but no one seems to want to share what they actually are."

"Well, as you know," Arianna supplied, "there is the power to portal. Other powers depend on the dragon and who his mate is. The one constant is that their powers are increased. Have you noticed any changes in your abilities?"

Nikolas and I glanced at each other then turned back to his mother. "We have," Nikolas answered for us. "I, for one, have been able to feel the life in the earth more than I did before I mated." I gave him a questioning look causing him to elaborate. "As an earth dragon, I have always felt the life of the soil and plants around me. In small doses I could even help them grow stronger. Now, with our mating, I feel a stronger connection, almost feel like its talking to me."

"Have you tried to do more than you could before?" Arianna asked him.

"No." He shook his head, annoyance suffusing his tone. "Most of our time in the dragon realm was spent teaching Lucian about Earth or learning how to properly open a portal."

"What about you, Cassandra?" Arianna focused her steely gaze on me.

"Maybe, I'm not sure." I responded quickly. "Like he said, our time was not our own in Fabeldyrverden. I feel like maybe I have more control. Before I met Nikolas, I had a set routine to keep myself grounded. In the past I have had a few accidents with my power to inflict pain. But now, I feel like I control that power instead of it controlling me."

"Did the two of you complete the Sanguis Draconis ceremony?" Hawthorne's gruff voice spoke up for the first time since I joined them.

"We did." Nikolas and I answered at the same time.

The memory of the preparation before and the ceremony itself, our skin soaked in oil, whispered vows, - nope. Stop, I need to focus. Nikolas squeezed my hand tightly in his, as he remembered the rather erotic ritual too. I shook my head, clearing the image with a silent reprimand to my mate to get his mind back in the moment. I rueful chuckle snuck up his throat.

With my mind back in the present, I dug my free hand into the bag I had carried from Fabeldyrverden. I pulled a couple of glass vials from the bag. Magda had given me the bottles after our ceremony was complete with instructions to bring them to Gaia.

"Profitis Magda sent these," I handed the bottles to Arianna. "One is to be used for Lucian and Aisling when they are ready to complete the ceremony. The other two are for anyone else that would like to perform the ritual. She believed there would be at least one more dragon here that would find its mate."

Arianna's eyes shone with remorse as she took the bottles from me. After a lingering look she placed them in a backpack at her feet. "Magda was correct," her voice held a note of guilt or sorrow, it was hard to pinpoint what exactly. "Davina mated with a wolf shifter when she was on her way to this island. I am sure she would appreciate being able to complete the Sanguis Draconis with him."

"Well, if you completed the ritual," Hawthorne stoked the fire, sending more smoke and a few sparks into the air, "then you and Nikolas should be able to access each other's powers as full mated dragons are able to. Also, with practice, you, Cassandra, should be able to shift into dragon form."

"I can do what now?" I sputtered, jumping in my seat causing Nikolas to reach out to steady me so I didn't fall off the back of the bench. This had been mentioned before but until now it hadn't fully sunk in what they meant.

"The true power of mated dragons is the sharing of their gifts. With time and practice, you will both learn how to harness each other's powers." Hawthorne expounded as if he were speaking to a class of students rather than just the two of us. "You will need to teach each other how you access your own powers."

"And how exactly do we do that?" I asked, scuffing my foot against a stone in the firepit.

"With practice." Arianna tossed a small stick onto the fire. "It won't happen overnight, but I believe you can do it"

"She's right," Hawthorne added. "Work with each other to become stronger. The two of you now have a combination of dragon, witch and vampire. As the old saying goes, 'what's mine is yours, what's yours is mine.' You will need to work together to master your newfound skills."

183

My hands trembled as Nikolas pulled me closer to him. Do I really have the power somewhere within me to become a dragon? I am sure my excitement also shone through on my face. How amazing it would be to be able to fly alongside my mate. *I cannot wait to see you in dragon form.* Nikolas' voice intonated in my head. We were going to have to start practicing immediately, I thought. A low chuckle rose out of Nikolas's throat as he pulled me closer to his side, wrapping an arm around me.

"What else do we need to know about being mates?" I asked his mother and uncle.

"Other than having new abilities, the rest is much like any other relationship." Hawthorne's voice cracked, his eyes seemed focused on a different time. "My Marlena and I promised that we would always be honest and true to each other. No matter how difficult life became, we never broke that promise. When I lost her, I…well. Some days the only thing that kept me breathing was knowing Sera's message needed to reach Arianna. Now, I have only the defeat of my brother to look forward to."

"Do not speak like that." Nikolas admonished his uncle. "You have family here, even if we are not your mate or a child, we are your family."

"I will keep that in mind." Emotion choked Hawthorne's voice causing it to shake. "I promise I have no intention of going anywhere until Fraxinus has been dealt with."

Chapter Twenty-Six

Arianna

My heart damn near exploded watching Nikolas and Cassandra, actual smiles, linked fingers, the whole deal. After everything, my son finally looked happy. I had worried for so many years; his sister and father had made his life hell for so long.

I did have some concerns when I first heard who he had mated with. Many of us have heard of Cassandra and her powers, although the stories of her being a vicious witch were a little unfounded. Plus, having someone with her strengths on our side would be highly beneficial.

Listening to Hawthorne, Cassandra and Nikolas talk, I glanced around at all that had assembled on my little island. The numbers alone were astounding. Davina informed me this morning that with the last group to arrive we were at over two hundred.

When we left our hidden Greek island for this cold one near Alaska, I never expected so many people to rally to our cause. Granted, our cause was also their cause. Keeping the fae and my mate from taking control of this realm was of utmost importance to all species.

My mind came back to the people near me just as Davina and James joined our little group around the fire. "Good news, Davina." I announced as she came to rest in the chair to my left. Inquisitiveness crawled across her face. "Cassandra and Nikolas brought alsklingberry oil from Fabeldyrverden."

Davina jerked, swinging her eyes to stare hopefully at my son and his mate. James, having no idea what this meant, looked to his mate then me for an explanation. "Really?" She blurted happily. "Can I see it?"

I handed one of the bottles of oil from my bag to Davina. "Courtesy of Profitis Magda by way of Cassandra."

Davina practically ripped the vial from my grip. Her grin could've powered the sun. She turned to James with tears in her eyes. "We can be properly mated now."

"That sounds great." James answered her smile with one of his own. "Care to explain what that little bottle of liquid has to do with our mating?" Davina and I

185

described the Sanguis Draconis ceremony and what it means for a dragon and their mate.

"When did you complete the ceremony?" I asked Nikolas.

"Two weeks ago." He answered after a moment of calculations in his head.

"We'll have to determine when Vesuvius and the moon are in alignment so the ritual can be performed at the proper time." Davina's hopeful smile spread to James' face as well. "If you'll excuse us, I must get started." She bounced to her feet, pulling James with her and they rushed off to our shared house.

I smiled to myself, seeing Davina happy was almost as good as seeing my son happy. I glanced at him; Cassandra curled into his side. The fire continued its slow burn, sparks jumping into the sky. The spicy scent of the smoldering hemlock filled the air.

I didn't want to interrupt our idyllic time, but as the old saying goes, time waits for no one'. I was starting to feel the pressure of time building. Since it was just the four of us again, I decided it was time to get some answers from my son and his mate.

"Well, I think it's time for you to reveal whatever secret you're keeping from me." I gave them each a pointed stare. They locked eyes for a minute, telling me they were having silent communication that mates can perform.

When no answer was forthcoming, I repeated my request. "Listen, I am sure you think it is best to keep this private, but something tells me this will affect us all. So, spill it." Nikolas squirmed at my use of my best mother tone and yet he and Cassandra continued their internal conversation. I started to doubt they would answer me.

Finally, Cassandra opened her mouth to speak. She snapped it shut as she responded to Nikolas once again through their bond. After a few more seconds and a sharp shake of her head, she breathed a loud sigh then jumped straight into the secret. Her nails dug into Nikolas' wrists, "Serafina saw them die." She spat, like the words burned her tongue.

"Now, that's not exactly what she said." Nikolas corrected her. "She said she saw her brother and his mate surrounded by fae."

Cassandra eyed Nikolas warily. "True, but she also said her vision showed them falling with no allies to help them and that her brother would not return to Fabeldyrverden."

"She never said they die." Nikolas argued. "Merely that she could not see Lucian returning to their home world. Maybe, he chooses to remain here with Aisling."

"Do you truly believe the great domineering King Lucian would actually decide to give up his throne for his mate?" Cassandra retorted with a wry twist of her lips.

"Stranger things have happened." Nikolas muttered. "You put up with my snoring."

"Touche." She gave him a quick kiss on the cheek then sat back down beside him.

She held his hand in hers, caressing the back of it with her thumb. Small flickers of energy tingled at her touch. I did not think they were even aware of how in tune their bodies were becoming. Her gaze met mine, then looked down to see what I was staring at. Seeing the energy pulse across their arms, her eyes lit up, and she turned a bright smile my way.

Nikolas, seeming unaware of our quiet delight, resumed his argument on behalf of Lucian. "I know him as well as you do. You and I both saw many facets to Lucian. True, he could be overbearing as the king, but we also witnessed a playful and more caring side, especially around Sera. Perhaps, Aisling will be able to tame the more dictatorial side of him."

"The Lucian I knew before I came to Gaia was nothing like the Lucian who walked through the portal this morning." I broke into their diatribe. "His current demeanor reminds me much of his father."

"Pinus was always a power-hungry fool." Hawthorne's loud snort sent a nearby gull shooting into the air. "He was quite adept at making people believe he was only looking out for everyone else. But I do not sense that type of thirst for power in Lucian."

"He was never cruel, just imperious." Nikolas added after another speechless conversation with Cassandra. "He was always welcoming to us."

"But he always had a stick up his ass when Orson was around." Cassandra added.

"Ahh, there is your answer then." Hawthorne and I shared a look of our own, as he spelled it out for them. "Orson was an advisor to Pinus before I came to Gaia."

"I remember him from my time living at the Griffin's country estate." I put forth.

"He has always latched onto anyone he believed he could use to gain power." Hawthorne cut in, "Pinus, being the brother to the king at that time was the closest he could get to the throne."

"Did he not try to ingratiate himself to Magnus Quercus?" I interjected.

"He did, but my father saw right through his scheme and banished him from the capital." Hawthorne frowned, "My father was no one's fool, most especially someone such as Orson. It saddens me to think that Lucian has been under his influence in any way."

"It didn't seem as if Lucian listened to Orson near as much as Orson believed he did." Nikolas fell into a troubled silence for a moment before adding. "I do worry about Serafina though. Lucian left her in charge as his proxy with Orson at her side."

Now I had to laugh at that image and laugh I did. Nikolas and Cassandra stared at me as if I had sprouted horns. Tears streamed down my cheeks as I pictured my old friend facing off against Orson.

"I am sorry," I rubbed my palms across my cheeks drying the wetness there. "Serafina is no weak child that would allow Orson to gain any control over her. I am sure she is holding her own against him. Plus, you said she and Arlien mated which means she has a strong and fair supporter should she need to remain the queen."

"Has Lucian been made aware of his sister's vision?" Hawthorne inquired with a look of deep concern on his face. Joviality crushed, we returned to our more vital topic.

"No, Sera insisted he not be told until he met his mate." Cassandra responded. "She said in all her searching of the future, any time he was told before he met her, he remained in his own world causing the fae to win."

"Hmm, perhaps it is best he is not told yet then." Hawthorne added. Each of us reacted with various levels of concern. "He has met his mate but as of yet it does not seem as if he has been overly successful in mating with her. Perhaps it would be best not to muddy the waters, so to speak, until they have fully accepted each other. They already have enough to contend with considering each of their temperaments."

188

We sat in pondering silence. My eyes roamed the forest around us. The cacophony of the wolves training, breaking through the sound of the surf from the sea. The moon was just peeking over the horizon, the sky was clear, the air crisp with the scent of burning hemlock. For a few minutes, I basked in the feeling of contentment.

Our future was uncertain, but I had my son back, his mate at his side. I did not know what would happen, prophecies and visions were not always one hundred percent accurate. I hoped for Lucian and Aisling's sake that there was more to it than what Sera had seen. I had to agree with Hawthorne though; they needed time to accept each other before being told of Sera's vision.

As if our thoughts had joined, Cassandra broke the silence, echoing my opinion. "Knowing both of them I agree. I know Aisling better than Lucian, but with what I do know of each of them, their mating is not going to be a quick and easy affair."

Chapter Twenty-Seven

Aisling

L eaving Cassandra, I returned to the house allotted to my family. A quick internal check told me Lucian was no longer inside. My stomach growled like a pissed-off lynx. I made a quick detour to the kitchen. Not in the mood to cook anything, I grabbed the plate of left-over baked ham from last night's meal out of the fridge.

I plopped the plate on the table we had brought from home and dug into the cold meat with gusto. I was hungrier than I had realized. I polished off the last of the ham and was debating on getting something else when I heard the front door open. Once again, I checked my mate bond and was happy to realize it was not my mate. A twinge of disappointment reared its ugly head which I quickly tamped down.

Jasmine and Cormac entered the kitchen; hands laced together, eyes gazing at each other with love. Gods, could they be any more sickening. (Okay, fine. I was jealous.) It almost didn't happen though.

Jasmine is a very powerful witch, and she had foreseen her mate. She believed, based on one stupid vision, that he would be a horrible brute. Having seen only one side of him, she placed a spell that would repel her mate that would only lift if he proved to not be evil.

Luckily, the scene she had divined happened right in front of her. She had viewed his killing of Nikolas' sister, Penelope. Something that needed to happen. I was a bit busy myself when this all played out. They told me she helped kill the dragon bitch. Then apparently, they were so overcome with lust that even though we were still in the middle of fighting Luis and his minions they lip locked right then and there.

Her repelling spell lifted; they professed their undying love for each other and have been by each other's side since. Jasmine even left Almerinda's side and came to the west coast to live with Cormac. That was something we were all a little shocked by. Jasmine and Almerinda have worked together for over a hundred years. Ever since Jasmine came of age and began working for the Council.

"Hey, Ash," Cormac ruffled my hair as he passed by me on the way to the fridge. He eyed the empty plate in front of me. "Hold up, did you eat all the ham?"

His growl would have scared lesser people, but I knew that for the most part, Cormac was all bark and no bite. When pushed he could be ferocious, but it took quite a lot to push him to that point. He was the best tracker in our family, but everyone knew I was the best fighter.

"Yep." I shrugged, motioning toward the fridge. "There's still some salad in there."

"Salad? Do I look like I need a salad?" Jasmine laughed while taking a step back as Cormac lunged playfully for me. "I oughtta string you up for trying to make me eat salad."

I laughed as I dodged his grasp, slipping under the table to come up on the other side. A quick snap of my knee knocked his left foot out from under him. Jasmine guffawed as Cormac, the largest and youngest member of our family, crashed to the floor. Jasmine launched her tiny body to land on top of his chest. "Run, Aisling, I shall subdue the savage beast." Their passionate laughter chased me from the kitchen.

My senses must have been dulled by the frivolity in the kitchen because I faceplanted into a wall of dragon. Lucian's chest, to be exact. Solid as a damn boulder, and unmoving like one too.

I tried to push away but his steely arms wrapped around my shoulders. His scent enveloped me, and I felt my arms snake around his narrow hips of their own volition. Gods, his body was perfection. If only his personality was more to my liking. Reason reasserted itself, and I yanked my arms back to my sides.

"Release me." I demanded. I could feel a rush of desire sneaking through my body as I inhaled his burnt amber aroma. Lucian did as I insisted, placing his hands to either side of my shoulders, he slowly moved me away from his body. The brief spark of desire soon turned to disappointment.

A sinewy hand cupped my chin, lifting my face to meet his. Laughter danced in his odd colored eyes. I felt my mind drawn into his through the swirling reds, yellows and oranges of his long-lashed eyes. Gods, please help me, I thought, only to hear his voice distinctly in my head. *You have no need of assistance from the Gods, you have me.* What an ass I yelled in my mind. Lucian merely chuckled as his lips descended on mine.

The second our lips touched, fire exploded in my gut. Since when did kissing feel like being struck by lightning. I stepped into Lucian's space, returning to his arms felt natural in ways that I had never believed possible. My hands wandered up his chest to wrap around his neck. Twining my fingers through his hair I pulled my body closer to his. I could feel his arousal pushing against my abdomen. My body, seeming to have a mind of its own, pressed closer to his quite ample girth.

Lucian moved ever so slightly, sending a frisson of longing to my core. *Gods, Aisling.* He pleaded as he pushed me back, pinning my body firmly between him and the wall. His hands roamed slowly down to my hips, to pull me firmer against his thick erection. I squirmed in anticipation with each caress of his hands upon my backside. *Submit to me, Aisling.*

His commanding words felt like a slap in the face as I wrenched my mouth from his. My knee jerked toward his groin on instinct. I managed to stop it; I considered that progress. My breathing came in ragged gasps as I fought every impulse to step back into his arms. He reached for me again, but my common sense was returning. I brushed his hand aside and stepped from within his orbit.

"I will not submit to you like some subservient woman." I inhaled through my mouth; his scent of amber and sage would be my undoing. "I may be attracted to you physically but you, King Lucian," I spat derisively, "still have a lot to learn about how to win me over."

"You are my mate." He roared back in anger. "I do not have to win you over. The Fates have decreed you are mine."

"I belong to no one but myself." I yelled back at him, pivoting on my feet I stomped down the hall. His hand grabbed my arm, spinning me to face him again.

"Aisling whether you want to accept it or not we are mated. It would be best that you accept that fact now." He sneered down at me, his back ramrod straight.

I stared down at his hand holding my arm hostage. A rage I had not felt since Cillian was killed came over me. Partially shifting my arms into my lynx form, I twisted my arm free and grabbed his arm in my hand. Using his surprise at my sudden transformation, I wheeled his body away from me, slamming him into the wall opposite us.

I pushed him hard against the wall, pulling his arm hard behind his back. The scent of blood hit the air as my grip tightened, my claws puncturing the skin on his arm. Whispering in his ear, I professed, anger heating my breath. "Hear me now,

Lucian. I will accept that we are mated but there is nothing in this world that will make me submit to any man." I shoved my elbow into his back, enunciating my proclamation. "It would be best if you accepted that fact now."

I released his arm and shoved myself away from him to continue down the hall to the front door. Pulling the door open, I turned back to gaze longingly at the beautiful body of the asinine man that was my mate.

"You are not a king here, Lucian, and probably the most important part, you are not my king. You might want to come to terms with that fact before you come near me again."

I walked through the door, head held high. I kept my back firm until I was out of sight of the house. Once I was sure no one could see me, my courage and my body crumpled to the ground in a heap of unresolved anger, desire, and fear.

Gods, that was close. I could still feel his hands running over my body. And that kiss, how was I ever going to keep my sanity when his velvety lips sent sparks of lust and warmth through my core. Damn him. Oh, who am I kidding, damn me more.

Anger, that's what I needed to feel to banish the craving my body had for him. How dare he demand that I submit to him? Gods, he was so controlled by the mating that he didn't even want to get to know me. "The Fates have decreed," I growled. Really, the Fates? Who cares if you actually like the person, as long as the fates say it is so.

The cool evening air cleared my head of his intoxicating scent. It also helped to erase the anger I was feeling, replacing it with uncertainty. What am I going to do? Where was the man Cassandra had described? Did that man even exist?

I was not one to run from my problems. I just needed to treat my mate like a problem that needed to be solved. Much like in battle, you needed cunning and strategy to defeat your foe. I probably shouldn't think of my mate as my foe though.

I gazed at the rising moon, allowing the scent of the hemlock fires to flow over me. Damn, damn, and double Gods damn. I needed to face him again. This time without all the kissing and touching. We needed to learn more about each other if we had any hope of having a happy future.

Purpose firming my mind and my back, I stood up and brushed the dirt and leaves from my clothing. Following the same path I had taken in my frenzied flight; I returned to my house. I could sense Lucian was still inside, so I walked quietly up the front steps and opened the door. Lucian was in the kitchen talking to Jasmine and Cormac. Unsure how to proceed I stood in the hallway listening to their conversation.

"Your brother, Evan, told me much about Aisling earlier." Lucian's tone was subdued. "I must admit, I have made a bit of a bungle out of my interactions with your sister thus far."

Bit of a bungle? I assume that must means fucked up completely in dragon speak. Cormac responded to Lucian, "Well I am sure you will unbungle the situation immediately."

Well, that's not a word in the English language at all Cormac. I thought while shaking my head in exasperation. Gods, I love Cormac, but he can be a little silly sometimes. Probably because he was our mum's last child and was coddled by us all growing up.

"I am not sure I know how." Was that sadness I heard in Lucian's voice? "I fear that I was expecting things to be more like they are in my home world. When dragons mate, we do not wait to get to know each other before consummating the bond. We submit to our mates knowing that the fates have a plan for why we were kluvened to each other." Cormac and Jasmine must have looked confused because Lucian added, "Uh, kluvened is when your souls are bound together."

"Yeah, that's not really how it always works here." Cormac chuckled. "Aisling can be stubborn, but I promise you she is one of the best people you could ever meet."

Jasmine agreed with Cormac. "Absolutely. I have known Aisling for years. Like all of us, she has her faults, but her good traits outweigh any of her faults." Thank you, Jasmine for having my back. "Like Cormac said she can be stubborn, she also has a bit of a temper and can be rather sarcastic at times."

"I believe I have experienced that temper." Lucian interjected.

"Well, yes, we did hear a bit of a scuffle in the hallway." Jasmine replied. "On the other hand, Aisling is faithful and loving, if she cares about you, there's nothing she wouldn't do to help you. She also has a bit of a comical side. Wait until you see all the O'Briens together. They love to joke around and have fun."

"I would love to see the comical side. I fear all I have seen so far is the temper." Lucian replied.

"Well, I am sure you'll get to see it." Cormac answered him. "You just had a bit of a rough start. Keep in mind that although she is fighting you it is not because she does not want to be mated to you. I think, and I could be wrong, that she feels as if you are trying to force her to become less than you."

"I swear that is not what I am doing." Lucian explained. "In Fabeldyrverden mates are equals. Neither one is above the other. When a dragon meets their mate, they submit to each other becoming one and therefore stronger."

"That sounds wonderful." Jasmine stated. "The whole submitting then getting to know each other thing might work in your world but here you will need to actually have conversations with her before she'll as you put it submit to you."

"I believe I have much to learn. Cassandra and Nikolas both tried to tell me how different things were here in Gaia. I just did not think those differences would matter when it came to mating." Lucian paused and I could hear them moving around the kitchen. It sounded like they were moving closer to the backdoor. "Thank you for taking the time to help me."

"No biggie." Cormac answered. The back door opened, and their voices moved further away. "We're glad to help. We all want what's best for Aisling." The door snicked close, and I waited in the hallway for a few more minutes. I could still feel Lucian close but there was no sound coming from within the kitchen. He must still be near the house.

I counted to ten then when I still hadn't heard anything from the kitchen, pushed my way through the swinging door. I came face to face with my nemesis. Oops, I mean my mate. Gods how did he stay so quiet. I wasn't quite ready to face him. I was really hoping to get to the bottle of Ali's vodka from the fridge. I needed a little liquid courage before I confronted the devilishly sexy man standing in front of me.

Our eyes met and his smirk faded at my raised eyebrow. A slightly less smug look replaced it. He walked over to the fridge and pulled out the bottle of vodka. After opening a couple cabinet doors, he located two glasses. Sitting at the table, he poured two generous glassfuls of vodka. With one eyebrow raised in challenge, he gestured toward the chair opposite him.

I harrumphed then gracelessly sat at the table. He handed me the second glass of vodka, and we both took long swallows of the burning alcohol. It would seem we both needed a little bit of that liquid courage. He choked a little on the taste then gulped another large swallow before placing the glass on the table.

"What is this drink?" He raised his glass, peering at the clear liquid inside. The peppery citrus scent of the alcohol wafted up from my half full glass.

"It's vodka, a kind of alcohol." Amused, I watched as he downed the rest of his drink then poured more from the bottle. "You might want to slow it down; it can make you intoxicated in large amounts."

"It is much like our vitae except no taste of the grape in it." He replied with a boyish smile. Now that smile could be my undoing. His smile widened as he picked that thought off the surface of my brain. "I believe I need a little intoxication. It has not been an entirely pleasant experience coming to Gaia."

Well, that was a kick in the teeth. Apparently, he wasn't entirely happy with our mating.

"Stop putting words into my thoughts." He stumbled a little over his pronouncement. "I am happy with our mating. I am just not used to bungling through things so ineptly."

His words were slurring even more, causing me to realize that while we were sitting here, he had finished off the entire bottle of vodka. Gods, he was going to regret that in the morning.

"You're so beautiful and you got fire in your blood that's for sure." It took me a minute to decipher his sentence through the slurring, his so sounded like show and beautiful sounded more like bue full. King Lucian was a little drunk. How splendid.

"Alright, big man let's get you somewhere you can sleep it off. Maybe next time you want a drink, don't consume the whole bottle at once."

"I am fine." He slurred some more at me. "Not drunk, kings don't get drunk."

"Well, good thing you're not a king here then, because you are definitely drunk." I hauled him to his feet. I dragged him out of the kitchen and up to my room. I didn't want to take anyone else's sleeping area, so I plopped him down on my pile of pillows and blankets. I lifted one of my blankets to toss over him, but something pulled me closer. I knelt to tuck the blanket around him.

196

His eyes popped open, and I felt myself caught in his gaze. He seemed to be staring straight through me. Then speech clear as a bell he said, "Sera, you were right, she is a spitfire but she's my spitfire."

With that his eyes closed, and a low snore emitted from his throat. I sat down with a thump. His hand reached out and grasped mine. A warm happy feeling came over my body as I gaped at this enigma of a man before me.

Each time I tried to pry my hand from his, he gripped tighter. I probably could have forced our hands apart but for once I felt truly at peace. Instead, I sat there staring at him in wonder. I lay my head back on the wall, all the while keeping my eyes on Lucian. My tense muscles unwound, and my breathing slowed. My eyes had just begun to drift close when I heard a heavy sigh from Lucian.

"Aisling." His possessive whisper had me leaning closer to those perfect lips. "Aisling." He murmured again. My heart sped up, my mouth dried, I searched his face for any indication he was awake. His eyes snapped open, meeting my startled ones. That self-satisfied smirk crossed his face again, then his head slumped forward as he passed out.

My mate. Gods, this man was my mate. If his conversation with Cormac and Jasmine was anything to go on, there was hope for us. We just needed to have our own conversation in which he was not ordering me about and I managed to control my temper.

Chapter Twenty-Eight

Cassandra

Nikolas and I talked with his mother and uncle for a while longer before heading down to the beach where Aisling and I had walked earlier. We strolled along the pebbled beach, hand in hand. The sounds of birds cawing and screeching combined with the mild surf was peaceful. Both of us seemed content to walk in silence, listening to nature.

About two hundred feet down the beach, we came to a small creek. Deciding to do a little exploring we left the beach and followed the path of the water to a deep pool fed by a small waterfall. After several months in Fabeldyrverden, seeing the greens and browns of the forest was still a little jarring. Some small birds twittered and tweeted in the trees around us, but we heard no other sounds of life near us.

Nikolas pulled me to stand in front of him. Our eyes met and I knew he had the same idea that I had. Slowly we undressed each other, lingering touches, and quick kisses to exposed flesh, slowing the process even more. I whispered a quick spell, warming the water just a bit to take the chill off. Nikolas held me away from him and perused my body, causing heat and tingling to erupt everywhere his eyes landed.

"Gods, woman, you are a vision of perfection." He pulled me closer. Then with a quick dip of his knees he swept me into his arms and carried me into the warm water. We spent many hours exploring each other's bodies in and out of the water. Fully sated, we dressed and slumped by the side of the water, skin still humming.

"We need to come up with a plan to save Lucian and Aisling." Nikolas broke the silence first.

"I know. We need more information." I answered, slowly lifting my head from the cradle of his arm. "Sera did not give us enough to go on." I pulled a blade of thick grass from the ground, slowly twirling it in my fingers. "I wish seers would just spell out what needs to be done instead of giving cryptic information."

"Have you had a lot of experience with seers?" One eyebrow raised, Nikolas poked me in my side. "I have only met the one."

"There were a few at the Council headquarters." I giggled from his poking. Nikolas seemed to find it fascinating that I was ticklish and proceeded to tickle me in earnest. Needless to say, our conversation came to a halt as our clothes came back off. A while later we surfaced from yet another bout of splendid lovemaking.

"I suppose we might want to sit a bit apart." Nikolas grinned cheerfully at me, scooting a few feet away from me. "You are just too damned tempting."

I gave him a rather lascivious smile and a wink. "You aren't so bad yourself, big fella."

Nikolas threw his head back and laughed, a full belly deep sound. at my clumsy flirting. Thank Gods he was already my mate; I was never particularly good at flirting or even talking to men. The sounds of the forest changed, as full night set in. An owl hooted behind us somewhere and an image of Delilah, all browns and non-descript looking popped into my head.

"Wait." I gasped through my laughter. "There's a seer on the island." Nikolas stopped laughing too. "Maybe she'll have some ideas without being super cryptic."

"I think I need to know more about everyone on the island." Nikolas advised me. "I know you told me a little about those we saw in the viewing pools, but there are more people here then we had seen."

"Alright, well let me think on the best way to describe each one." I sat back, leaning against the trunk of a large spruce tree.

"There is a lot of people here. I don't need to know who everyone is." Nikolas interrupted my thoughts. "Maybe just the highlights, for example there are over fifty wolf shifters."

"That would probably be easier." I answered. "Since you brought up the wolves first...they are from the Collier Pack. Michael Collier is not here but his brother and cousin are. Brian Collier is the brother. He is an elite guard for the Community and part of Almerinda's personal team. James is the cousin. He also is an elite guard and was on Almerinda's team, but fun fact, he recently mated with Davina so probably not going to be a guard any longer."

"So, we can count them as a definite on our side." Nikolas mused before adding. "What of this Almerinda, is she trustworthy?"

"I would trust her with my life. She is a very old vampire, close to thirteen or fourteen hundred years old. She is strong, and her sire was Luis." I stopped speaking at Nikolas' indrawn breath.

"Luis?" He growled. "I know of only one Luis who would be old enough to sire someone of her age. He worked with the Fontaines and my father."

"That is the Luis I am talking about. Around the same time that you and I mated and disappeared into Fabeldyrverden, Almerinda and a few others killed Luis."

"How? He was one of first vampires made by dragons." Shock and maybe a little bit of worry creased his face.

"I do not know the whole story." I plucked another blade of grass from the ground, twirling it. "I overheard Evan and Jace speaking about it but when they saw me near them, they changed the subject."

"You still trust her after she killed her own sire?" His eyes narrowed, skepticism laced his tone of voice.

"I know I can trust Almerinda because she's been by my side since my mother," my words stuttered a little, hands shaking I dropped the grass, "I mean, well since you know, since what happened with her all those years ago."

Moving closer, Nikolas pulled me into a hug. He rubbed my back soothing my fretfulness. When I finally had my emotions under control, he released me and moved away, putting distance between us again. He gave me a small smile and a shrug as if to say sorry. I get it, his scent and nearness were too heady if we wanted to be able to finish our conversation.

"I forgot that you mentioned her before. Okay so we have the wolves and Almerinda. Who else?" I noticed that while he looked calm his fists had pulled large clumps of the thick grass from the ground.

"Evan and Jace." I answered. "Evan is head of the O'Brien family now. They are shifter vampire hybrids. His father is vampire, and his mother was a cat shifter. I heard that she died not long before they came to the island and his father has remained in Oregon. There are nine O'Brien siblings still alive, the eldest died a while back. All but Saoirse are great fighters. They are a fiercely loyal family. Five of them have also mated and produced offspring. Evan, Cormac, and Aisling are the most recent to find their mates. I think there are about twenty O'Briens on the island of fighting age."

"Then they will be loyal to Lucian since he is Aisling's mate?" Nikolas mumbled to himself.

"Exactly." I replied to his low spoken question. "Now onto Jace. Jace McFadden and his brother Jaxson. Both former elite guards with mates and a small group of friends that all live in Pennsylvania. Jace's mate is Cat, she brought decent fighting skills from her human life. An interesting addition to their family is a vampire named Gabriel. He was once of the Fontaines. Turned by Marcel Fontaine, he left the family hundreds of years ago and until recently lived with a group in Cleveland. He mated with Cat's best friend and moved to Pennsylvania, taking a witch named Tina with him."

I paused for a moment to take a few breaths of the fresh air around me. It was clearer than what I was used to having lived in Philadelphia for most of my life. Although, the air in Fabeldyrverden was sweeter and I really hoped we could return there someday. "Following me so far?" I asked my handsome mate.

"Yes. Do you know why Gabriel left the Fontaines?"

"No and to be honest, until the fight between Marcel and Jace occurred, I had no idea Gabriel came from that family. Almerinda told me about it before she left to search for Evan. Some kind of bad blood between him and his maker." I shrugged, as far as I was concerned it wasn't that important. He mated with Cat's best friend so I knew he would stand with them.

Nikolas sat silently for a few minutes, taking in all the information I had given him. I gave him time to think and listened to the owl hooting in the trees. Nikolas broke our quiet contemplation with another question. "Who is the very large black vampire with the entourage of mostly men?"

I giggled at his description. He could only be referring to Jonesie. "He is an unusual vampire. His name is Jonesie. He is one of the few I have ever heard of to have killed his own mate and survived. He says fate led him to kill his maker. Since then, he has languished in Cleveland, Ohio with his ever-changing harem of men and women. Gabriel once lived with him too. He is good friends with Jace and Jaxson. His group currently has one witch; Delilah and she is the seer I mentioned. I have dealt with her a few times, but she prefers Jonesie's, as Almerinda puts it, den of inequity."

"The last group is Almerinda's personal elite guards and the vampires she inherited when Luis died. Her mate is Damian, the one who got in Lucian's face.

And there is a witch named William with her. Another one of her members is Twyla, she comes from the northern reaches of Canada. Sera's vision was of Lucian and Aisling in a frozen landscape."

"Could our battle be somewhere near her family?" Nikolas mused. His eyes wandered around the clearing. That is a good possibility, I thought, my hands twisting circles in the grass. Canada does have a lot of snow. I spent a minute going through the list of people in my head.

"Oh, I forgot to mention Jasmine before. She intersects with a majority of the groups. Until recently she was Almerinda's right-hand woman. Not long ago she helped Jace when she defeated Delphine, the Fontaine's top witch. She is William's older sister and has mated with Cormac, the youngest O'Brien.

"There are others on the island, mostly stragglers that were sent to us by the O'Brien's father. I even think some may be bear shifters, which will be quite helpful in a fight against the fae."

"We have a formidable force on our side. We may just stand a chance at winning this." Nikolas conceded with a pleased look on his face.

"Especially with the bear shifters." I grinned, "wolves get all the hype, but bears are really the strongest shifter race."

"Aside from dragons." Nikolas murmured in my ear. My heart jumped, how had he moved so silently. "Once we are done here, I think we need to find this Delilah witch and pick her brains."

"That would be my suggestion too. Hopefully, she can help us figure out how to win and not lose too many people in the process." I glanced at Nikolas in confusion. "What else do we need to do here?"

With a seductive grin he yanked me onto his hard chest. "I can think of a few things." His fingers traced my hip, and for a heartbeat, I forgot about seers and battles. Images of all the things he wanted to do to me ran through my head. I must admit, every single one piqued my curiosity.

The heat in his gaze was a distraction I craved. When his hands slid higher, logic drowned in a wave of want. Shifting ever so slightly, I rubbed against his growing erection. As we tugged off our clothes again, I thought that we really needed to invest in robes so we could get naked quicker.

"Now that is an amazing idea." Nikolas murmured as he nuzzled my neck, pushing me onto my back.

202

Chapter Twenty-Nine

Arianna

The crackling fire and bright moon were our only companions after Cassandra and Nikolas disappeared down the beach. Just me and Hawthorne, two lonely old souls with too many ghosts between us. We talked about Fabeldyrverden.

Our paths had not crossed while I was living with the Griffins. I first encountered him the day I found Fraxinus dying on the battlefield. At the time I had thought he was a heartless bastard. I believed much of what Fraxinus said about him until I learned the truth about my mate.

The more we talked, the more my chest ached with all the what ifs. The man sitting across the fire from me was kind and compassionate. The losses he had endured over the years could have turned him into something more like my mate. My intuition told me he had not. The only anger I sensed in him was directed at his brother. Gods, why couldn't it have been Hawthorne, anyone but Fraxinus.

Fraxinus was cold, calculating, and vengeful, nothing like Hawthorne. Fraxinus had an insidious vileness to him that seeped through our bond like poison. Even with Serafina's warning not to allow my mate to gain his full powers, I still held out hope that he was redeemable. He'd hidden his madness well from me, right up until after our children were born.

The fire shot embers into the night sky, "How?" The word almost stuck in my throat. "How did he hide his true self from me for so long?" I asked Hawthorne.

"From a young age, we were taught how to guard our thoughts, even from our mates." Hawthorne's sorrow filled gaze met mine. "Those who are in charge need to be able to have secrets. Most of us open our minds fully to our mates since that is supposed to be the one person you should trust above all else."

I considered my mate, Fraxinus only opened his mind to me fully when he let his guard down after sex. The few times I was able to see fully into his mind made me cringe with disgust. I did my best to keep my deepest thoughts closed off from him. I must have succeeded since he did not realize I had been working against him for centuries until right before we fled our warm Greek island for this cold Alaskan one.

My hand flinched when Hawthorne's calloused hand covered mine. He knelt in front of me, his stern face, grave. "What are you willing to do to stop my brother?"

"Anything." I insisted vehemently, I clutched his rough hand to my chest. "Anything I must."

"Can you kill him, knowing the consequences that will befall you?" He looked at me with sorrow in his eyes. I was a dragon's mate, not a full dragon, I knew exactly where his sorrow stemmed from.

I recoiled as if slapped. I searched through my deepest feelings. He had stolen everything from me, my happiness, my chance for love, my children. The sun had set, and the fire was burning low but the hatred I felt for my mate was stronger than ever. My blood warmed as I felt my vow settle over me. "I can kill him." I answered, my voice forceful.

"Good," Hawthorne replied, a forlorn expression on his face. "I hope it does not come to that but no matter how, he must be stopped."

We fell into an uncomfortable silence, both of us lost in our thoughts. Me staring at the smoldering embers of the campfire. Hawthorne gazing dejectedly at the dark clouds above the grey expanse of sea around our little refuge.

Chapter Thirty

Aisling

My body jolted awake, disoriented. Steel bands held me immobile. I shifted just enough to pull my face out of the pillow it was mashed in. The most amazing set of arms enfolded me against a solid chest. I glanced over my shoulder to find Lucian curled around me in sleep.

"Must've fell asleep." I mumbled to myself.

Stretching my body to give me some space, I rolled in his arms, facing him. His breathing didn't change. The vodka must have really knocked him out. His burnt amber scent had a mildly alcoholic tinge to it. The peppery smell of the vodka hung between us. Not entirely unpleasant but also not a smell I would like to wake up to every day.

The light in the room was dim; we must have slept most of the day away. Not that it mattered much, it's not as if we were supposed to be anywhere. The leaders of our little army were still hashing out plans, then rehashing those plans, then discussing more plans.

Nothing had been decided in days, and no one seemed to have a definite idea as to what to do. So, those of us who were more of a foot soldier than leader, spent the days twiddling our thumbs or training for a fight that we weren't sure when would happen.

A slight hitch in his breathing and a stiffening of his body alerted me that Lucian was waking up. His eyes slowly opened meeting mine. The initial glimpse of happiness was replaced with weariness as realization clouded his face. I understood his reticence. We hadn't exactly had the best of encounters since his arrival. I was determined to start this one off on a better foot though.

"Good evening, or maybe afternoon. I'm not exactly sure what time it is." I gave him a timid smile; my heart missed a beat when he brought one hand up to my cheek. Our eyes held for what felt like an eternity.

Whatever he saw in my face must have reassured him since I felt his tense muscles relax a little. "Good evening." He looked around the room we were in with confusion. "Where are we?"

205

"In my room." Startled he lifted the blanket covering him and looked at our closely lying fully clothed bodies. "We only slept here. You got drunk and I brought you here to sleep it off."

"Kings don't get drunk." He mumbled to himself then he asked louder. "Why are you still here?"

My shoulders hunched, anger simmering in my veins. I shoved back and put my hands on the floor to stand up. This was not going to work.

"I am happy that you are by my side." He rushed out as he grabbed my arm, holding me in place. "I am just trying to understand what is happening."

I settled myself back beside him, sitting with my back against a pillow. Damnit, I needed to control my temper. Better foot, remember.

"You downed an entire bottle of vodka, got very drunk, so I brought you here to sleep it off." *Kings don't get drunk,* murmured into my head. "I know, I know." I held my hand up to stop him from speaking. "Kings don't get drunk. I hate to tell you this, King Lucian," I poked him in the shoulder, "but you did get drunk."

He shook his head as if to argue or maybe to clear the fuzziness from it. "How abhorrent were my actions when I was intoxicated?" He hung his head in embarrassment.

"You were fine, you slurred your words, told me I was beautiful then passed out. All in all, not that bad." When he continued to not meet my eyes, I placed one finger under his chin to lift his head. "Did you mean everything you said to my brother and Jasmine?"

Now where did that come from? I wasn't ready to start that conversation. Not with him looking so vulnerable and delicious lying next to me on my pile of pillows and blankets.

His swirling eyes sparkled intensely at me. "I meant every word of everything I said to them. I also meant every word of my drunken declarations too."

The swirling colors solidified into a deep crimson, his gaze lowered to my lips. Unbidden, my tongue snaked out to lick my suddenly dry lips. His sharp inhale sent a stab of fire into my stomach. His breathing sped up, his eyes remained locked on my lips.

His hand touched my arm in a blaze of heat, pushing me over the edge. Gods, I know I shouldn't, but I can't stop myself. My arm snaked out clamping around his neck, and I dragged his mouth to meet my own.

Our lips came together in a clash of desire, all teeth and desperation and too many days of pent-up need. Reason tried to assert itself, his tongue dipping into my mouth, pushed it far away to the back of my mind. Gods, his mouth was magic. Imagining all the things he could do to me with it sent shivers down my spine.

Lucian moaned loudly as he caught glimpses of those images in my mind. His arms wrapped around me, jerking me against his chest. Gods, he is so…no wait, Gods, damnit, we need to stop, I thought. This is not how I want our mating to happen. Lucian growled deep in his throat, but he pulled away, taking his wonderful lips and tongue away. I groaned unhappily but knew this was for the best.

"I'm so sorry." I blurted just as he said, "I apologize."

We chuckled for a second, adjusting our clothing and bodies. Then we both became serious. "Perhaps, I should sit over there." He motioned to a spot a few feet from me.

I had no furniture so he would remain on my pile of pillows and blankets just far enough away that we weren't touching. I nodded to indicate that he was right. Lucian moved over to his new seat. I felt the lessening of our connection as a drain on my soul.

"Thank you."

"For what?" Lucian asked.

"Just thank you." I responded. "You could have not stopped kissing me and I probably would have gone along with anything you wanted."

"I heard your refusal." Lucian replied while pointing at his head. "I would never force a woman, especially my mate, to have intercourse with me."

A giggle escaped me at his use of the word intercourse rather than just saying sex. I really do find the most inopportune things funny. His only response was one raised eyebrow. "Will you tell me about yourself?"

"What do you want to know?" His eyes lowered while he fidgeted with the large ring he wore on his left ring finger. It was beautiful, what looked like rubies and diamonds surrounding a dark gem with a red dragon embossed in the center.

"Everything." I replied.

"We have forever for everything." I felt a warm glow at his words. He was correct we did have forever for everything. "Maybe we should start with something more specific. Is there anything you need to know to help you be more accepting of me as your mate?"

I thought for a few minutes, really trying to decide what fact would help me accept him. My soul searching must have stretched to an uncomfortable silence because Lucian cleared his throat a few times.

"The more I think about it the more I realize that I do accept you as my mate. My vampire and shifter sides accepted you almost immediately." His elated smile faded almost immediately with my next words. "I just need more time to get to know you. That may not make much sense to you but that's how I feel."

"We were raised in different worlds. We can take the time you need to learn more about me." His words rang true, my apprehension lifted some. "Where I come from, we do not question the fates decisions. A dragon is born knowing they will meet their other half someday. We live in anticipation of that day for many reasons."

"We also believe that we are all fated to meet our mate." I cut in, "We just don't expect them to fall at our feet when we do."

I see." Lucian twisted the ring on his finger again. Seeing my gaze fixed on it, he held it up before him. "A symbol of my position, passed from ruler to ruler, it conforms to the wearer." I craned my head to get a closer look as he continued to explain how it works. "It changes size and colors based on who the current king or queen is."

A cold chill snaked down my back. Gods, why do I keep forgetting that he is the king of the dragons? Yet another adjustment I would have to come to terms with. Me, a queen? Seems so unlikely.

"Is that why you want me to submit to you?" My voice trembled, I sat on my hands, hiding their shaking.

"In a roundabout way, yes." His answer seemed more like a non-answer to me, but I chose not to call him out on it for now.

For now, I want to keep the peace between us. Later I would revisit the whole submitting to him thing. "I get wanting to meet your mate," I changed the subject back to being mated. "but you make it sound as if it the only thing worth living for."

"A king or queen cannot rule without a mate." Lucian answered, once again pounding his king status into my head. "However, there is also the feeling that you are not complete until you meet your other half. Our full powers come from mating and completing the Sanguis Draconis ceremony. I have been alive for more than a thousand years and have spent all those years feeling incomplete because I knew my mate was still out there somewhere."

Wow, my mouth dropped open. That is different than how any of my siblings or friends ever described their mating. It was so much more intense sounding.

"I had no idea that she was in Gaia." Lucian nudged my small foot with his larger one. "If I had known, you were here waiting for me I would have moved the heavens and hell to find a way to you. Serafina, my sister, probably knew that the portals would open one day but she is always very tight-lipped about the futures she has seen. She only shares relevant knowledge when it is relevant and not a moment sooner."

"How did she get you to come here?" I asked then rushed to ask another important question. "Did you know I was your mate before you came through the portal?"

"I hoped you were." His reply was said so quietly that had I been human I doubt I would have heard it.

"You didn't know me before you stepped through that portal. Why would you hope it was me?"

"Sera told me I needed to come to Gaia to meet my mate." His brows drew together in irritation. "She did not tell me who my mate was only that I would find her here on this island amongst allies. After Nikolas and Cassandra broke through the spell, our high priestess was able to open the viewing pools back into Gaia."

I held my hand up, "Viewing pools?" I sat up. "Like scrying mirrors?"

"Similar," he admitted, uncrossing and recrossing his long legs. "They use water from both worlds. You cannot travel through them, only see things in each world. Also, before the spell was broken, they were not working."

He shifted a little closer to me but remained just out of reach, two large floor pillows separated us. "The first time I saw you through the pool I could not take my eyes from you. Cassandra was describing what we were seeing but I could barely focus on her words. Your face held me captivated. I found myself drawn repeatedly to the pool in hopes of catching a glimpse of you."

"Did you know I was your mate at that time?" The hope that laced my whispered question brought a smile to his face.

"I did not know for certain, but I believed you had to be. I felt that I would not have been so entranced by anyone I was seeing unless they were my mate." The heat in his gaze had my toes curling. "When my sister confirmed that my mate was with Arianna, I was even more certain than ever. I still needed to come through the portal to feel the pull of you but by then I had already convinced myself you were my other half."

He closed the space between us and pulled my hand into his. "I watched you for weeks. You always looked so carefree, even when you were training. I thought that anyone who could laugh and show happiness even when training to fight the fae would be the perfect mate for me." He lowered his head, then with a hushed voice, added, "I need more laughter in my life."

His thumb drew little circles in the palm of my hand. I could see myself falling in love with this version of Lucian. My skin flushed, warming to the idea of being in love. The jackass that walked through the portal and laid claim to me like I was an object however was not to my liking. That thought cooled my ardor, I needed to know which version was the real Lucian?

"When I stepped through the portal my one and only thought was getting to you and returning to Fabeldyrverden. I just wanted to keep you safe from the fae. You are part vampire and the fae are notorious for their treatment of vampires as food rather than actual people." A small derisive chuckle escaped him, "I am also the king of my land and therefore quite used to just issuing orders and having them obeyed. I must admit that I have not handled our situation very well, but I promise to try to do better."

"I will hold you to that promise." I scooted a little away from him. I needed some distance. His scent was just a little too intoxicating even with the underlying alcohol odor. Lucian rested his head back on a pillow to stare quietly at the ceiling. While his gaze remained fixed on the pale white expanse above him, my eyes perused his delicious form.

He was tall, had to be close to seven feet. He seemed strong, physically, and lucky for me, he was not a bulky mass like his cousin Nikolas. His height and muscle mass made him a formidable specimen. Thank the Gods. since I had always worried, I would mate with a human who was smaller than me. At my five foot seven inches, Lucian dwarfed me and actually made me feel petite.

210

Like me, he had red hair but his was a much darker shade. I noticed as I looked closer at the colors that he had several shades of red, brown and black running through his long strands. His hair hung a little longer than mine. I had been in the habit of just chopping my hair short and letting it fall any which way. Since we had been on the island the length was almost to my shoulders now. The same red, brown, black shades colored his close-cropped beard that hugged his strong jaw line.

All in all, with the dazzling color changing eyes, I could not complain one tiny bit about my mate's physical attributes. Lucian smiled happily at the ceiling, making me realize I had either thought that idea quite loudly or possibly spoke the actual words. He nodded his head but maintained his reclined position on the bedding. Will I never have a private thought again? *You will learn with practice how to shield your thoughts from me.* Well, that's a relief.

"Why am I only picking up your thoughts when you send them to me?" I complained. I thought mates would share all their thoughts.

With barely a glance in my direction, Lucian explained, "I was taught at a very young age how to close my mind to others. It is common for rulers in my world. They need to have more control over who could peek into their minds."

"That makes sense." I scooted closer to Lucian and pulled his hand off his chest and back into mine. "It just wouldn't do for anyone to have access to state secrets." I joked, trying to lighten the mood again.

A slight squeeze of my hand was his only reply. We lay awake, side by side, holding hands for hours. We talked about his sister, my many siblings, his parents and mine. He told me more about Fabeldyrverden and I told him more about Gaia.

As the night wore on, we eventually grew tired. His breath evened out first, his arms tightening about me instinctually. Somewhere between his heartbeat and mine, I followed.

Chapter Thirty-One

Cassandra

We crawled from our tent, the following morning, and went in search of Delilah. Nikolas' mother had offered us her room, but we felt that Nikolas' chances of being accepted increased if he interacted with everyone. Yesterday had been a great day to relax but now it was time to start planning. We had no clue when the Fontaines, Fraxinus and the fae would attack. We planned to be ready first.

We wandered amongst the different groups, unsure where to find the seer. We stopped when we heard loud music blaring from a small clearing surrounded by tall cedars. The pine scent evoked a memory of the binding ritual. Nikolas yanked me into his arms and kissed me thoroughly. I stood there with a bemused expression on my face, my heart racing, my toes curling.

"Why did you stop?" I pouted at my mate, who was clenching his hands spasmodically.

"We have a mission to fulfill," his voice gravelly with want. "Focus, my heart." With a tap of his finger on my nose, I nodded. He was right, of course, we needed to talk to Delilah.

Parting the branches with his large arms, Nikolas beckoned for me to follow. The scene we came upon was unexpected to say the least. Cat, looking almost like she was dancing, was fighting three of the wolf shifters. Jace and Jaxson stood on one side watching. On the other end of the field, several shifters, Gabriel and his mate Robert, and Tanya were lying about as if at a garden party, complete with snacks.

Upon seeing us enter, Cat called a halt to the action. One wolf didn't stop fast enough and barreled into her, tackling her to the ground. Jace reacted instantly, snatching the shifter by his neck, he tossed him almost twenty feet away then went to check on his mate. For a moment I thought she was actually injured, but then her laughter howled across the earth.

"You shoulda seen your face." She gasped, doubled over she held her stomach while she tried to get her giggling fits under control.

"Ha ha." Jace got to his feet then went to check on the shifter he had thrown.

I could hear him apologize to the uninjured shifter as he held his hand out to help the shifter stand. Robert clicked off the music, suddenly I felt very exposed. We needed to get people to trust us though, so I stiffened my spine and walked over to Cat.

"That was impressive." I said rather than hello. "Why were you fighting the shifters?"

"Training." Her curt reply made me jumpy, I took a small step back, bumping into Nikolas.

"We're looking for Delilah." I pressed on, meeting her gaze, with what I hoped was kindness.

"They're over that way." She pointed in the direction we had been heading when their music caught our attention. Her eyebrows raised in curiosity, but she didn't volunteer anything else.

Robert, on the other hand, had plenty to say. "Cat, stop being such a bitch." He bellowed, his colorful scarf flaring behind him as he tromped across the field to us. Gabriel walked by his side, whether to protect or just because his hand was gripped in Robert's, I couldn't say for sure.

They came to stand in front of us and Robert held his hand out to me. I took his hand and gave it a quick shake. "Hello there. I'm Robert, you probably know Gabriel, that brat over there is Cat." He stuck his tongue out at her when she flipped him her middle finger. "And, if rumors are true, you're the feared Cassandra and her savage mate Nikolas, right?"

His smile was infectious, and I found myself grinning back at him. "You nailed it." I responded, trying to keep the mood light.

Jace and Jaxson had come to stand on either side of Robert and Gabriel, Jace dragging Cat to his side. "Forgive my mate, she is," his voice cut off when she elbowed him in the side.

"You don't need to apologize for me." Cat smiled sheepishly at us. "I can do that on my own. Sorry, you just kinda surprised us." She held her hand out to me too. I shook it as did Nikolas.

"Nothing to feel sorry for." Nikolas assured them. "I do wonder, would I be able to join your training sessions? I have not been able to train with a group for a very long time."

I could feel the concern wafting off them in waves and once again Robert came to the rescue. Well, he at least broke the silence. "Of course, we meet here every day around this time."

My shoulders sagged with relief; I had worried his request would be met with a resounding no. We talked with them for a few more minutes before taking our leave. The music clicked back on, and I glanced over my shoulder to see Cat readying to battle the three shifters again.

We found Delilah by following Jonesie's booming voice. Delilah was of average height and size with light brown hair, what my mother called dishwater blonde. She had a pretty face, but she dressed in a manner that screamed 'don't look at me', wearing bulky sweaters and loose pants with sensible shoes.

Our approach brought everyone to attention. Jonesie materialized in our path like a living blockade. Not overtly threatening, but his crossed arms said 'give me a reason' clear enough. We knew it was going to be hard to overcome people's fears. Hopefully this type of behavior will taper off the more everyone got to know us. I include myself in that since all most people know about me is that I have been the Council's savage interrogator for years.

"Hello, Jonesie. It's been a while." I gave him a timid smile then turned to introduce Nikolas. "This is my mate Nikolas." Nikolas reached his hand out and left it hanging to see if the large vampire would shake it or spit on it, or worse.

Jonesie eyed me and Nikolas for a few seconds then must have come to a favorable conclusion as he took Nikolas' hand in his to shake it. "Cassandra," his deep voice boomed at me. "It is wonderful to see you out from under the Council's paws. Nikolas, pleasure to meet you let us hope it remains so."

"I was hoping we could speak with Delilah." I stated looking at the witch in question.

"Well, now I suppose that all depends on whether she wants to speak with you." Jonesie glanced over his shoulder at the bland witch, raising one eyebrow.

Delilah walked over to join us. "I do wish to speak with them. Jonesie, please come too. We need to go somewhere private for this conversation."

The four of us walked down to the beach together. There were very few people about since the sun was hiding behind a bank of dark clouds. Fifty or so feet down from us a few wolf shifters were fishing but otherwise we had the beach to ourselves.

Jonesie stood with his back to the ocean feet spread apart. His cold gaze never strayed far from Nikolas. I bristled a little at the treatment of my mate, but I knew there was nothing to be done about it.

"I was wondering how long it would take you to search me out." Delilah began in a strong and confident voice that was mildly surprising coming out of such a bland person. "I know what you want to talk to me about." Jonesie's left eyebrow shot up at her statement. "Seer, remember?" She tapped the side of her forehead with a finger.

"I know damned good and well what you are. I'm wondering why it is that I am now just hearing about this." Jonesie admonished her.

"Because you didn't need to know until now." Delilah jumped back in his face, well at least the general direction of his face seeing that he is close to seven feet and she is just barely five and a half feet.

"I decide what is important and what isn't." Jonesie rebuked her.

"Since when?" Delilah stomped her foot, sending pebbles flying. She jabbed Jonesie's chest so hard, I thought she might actually knock him down.

"Ahem!" I loudly cleared my throat, bringing both sets of eyes swiveling toward me. "Can this argument wait for another time?" Dipping my head in the direction of the wolf shifters who were now watching us with interest, "I thought we came down here for privacy."

"Yes, of course." Delilah replied while Jonesie looked on with chagrin. "Sorry, but ever since we learned about the fae, Jonesie here has been a bit of a control freak. Constantly asking if I have any information and nagging everyone in our group to be ready for a battle."

"We do need to be prepared." Nikolas grumbled. "If even half the stories my father told me are true, the fae are very formidable fighters."

"I am not arguing against being ready," scrunching her face in a grimace at Jonesie, Delilah added, "however there comes a point when the continuous barrage of questions can get annoying as all get out."

215

"Unfortunately, that is what we are here for." I redirected the conversation back to why we had sought her out. "We are hoping you have seen something that will help us all survive this."

"What you really mean is you're hoping to save Aisling and the dragon king." Delilah announced.

Nikolas and I shared a quick look before nodding with desperation. "Do you know what happens to them?" My voice cracked, I had finally found people willing to be a family to me, I wasn't ready to lose two of them so quickly.

"I am sorry, but I do not." She answered her voice just as quiet as mine. "I have seen the same vision many times over the past several months. Aisling and the dragon king standing in a snow- and ice-covered landscape. I did not know who the man was until he came through the portal yesterday. I figured he must be her mate though since they are always holding hands and staring down an army of what I believe are fae."

Should we tell her about Sera's prophecy? Nikolas asked me through our mate link. Yes, I believe we should, I answered. I kept my eye on the sea; it looked like a storm was brewing to the south of us.

"Lucian, the man you call the dragon king, has a sister who is also a seer." Nikolas informed Delilah, his grip tightened on mine. "She told us of a vision she had seen of the two of them. She described the same vision you have seen. She also said that if they do not go to that field that the fae will win, overrunning our world and hers."

"I can't see beyond that field for the two of them." Sadness-tinged Delilah's voice. "Normally I can see different futures based on different actions or decisions, but this future is the only one I see for them. I wish I had better news for you."

"Do you ever see them joined by any of us in their standoff?" I asked hopefully, the wind whipped my hair, lashing my cheeks.

"They are always alone." Her gaze wandered to stare out at the crashing waves.

My eyes streamed tears, I was not giving up, I vowed. We would find a way to save them. Nikolas wrapped his arm around me, giving me support. *I won't give up either.* He promised, and I felt a shiver at his words. A streak of lightning lit the sky, followed by the roar of thunder so close my teeth rattled.

216

The dark clouds were moving closer to our island. We're about to get wet, I thought just as Delilah stated with a delighted lift to her voice. "Don't worry; the rain will go around us. Whatever protections Arianna put on this island also prevents extreme weather from touching it. There is a witch with her that can control all the elements."

The storm hit Arianna's barrier with an audible crack, forking around our island like rivers diverted by a boulder. The rain and lightning continued to thrash the water around us, never touching the land we stood on. The power of Nikolas' mother was astounding to me. I now understood how she battled a fae general on her own and prevailed.

"Quite impressive, isn't it?" Delilah asked seeing our astonished faces. "We have had cooler temps since arriving here as would be expected for this time of year, but no storms have reached land."

"We may not be able to change Aisling and Lucian's fate, but I have been looking at the best chances for the rest of us." Delilah dragged our attention back from the storm raging out in the ocean. "I have some ideas but did not want to mention them until we were all on the island."

"So, you have been keeping stuff from me?" Jonesie demanded, his feet getting wet from the surf.

"Don't start again." I begged. "We need to focus on the future not the past." The large man gave a brusque grunt while motioning with his hands for us to continue. "Now, what can you tell us that will help?"

Delilah laid out many of the different visions she had seen for us. We would all be fighting in a snow-covered landscape. She was unsure exactly where but believed she knew the correct person to ask. "We should meet with Twyla; she is a witch on Almerinda's personal guard. I think she may know the place I am seeing."

We moved away from the edge of the sea, Jonesie shaking his wet feet. Delilah stumbled on a slick stone. Jonesie caught her and instead of setting her down, carried her to the grassy area. With a fatherly pat on her head, he looked along the beach with an admiring gleam at the fishing shifters.

"Sounds like a good place to start." Nikolas agreed. "For now, we must keep Aisling and Lucian's fate to ourselves. I would like my cousin to have some happiness with his mate if he is not going to survive the war."

I grinned at my own mate. "That is if he can stop being such a pompous ass and actually win her over."

Chapter Thirty-two

Arianna

Fourteen days since my son stepped through the portal. My Nikolas, no longer caught in his sister's spells, had been returned to me. I had Cassandra to thank for that, at least partly. Thank the Gods and Fates that he was mated to someone for love. Once I knew my mate's true self, I worried that the same unhappy circumstances would befall my son.

I've spent the morning tending to the fruit trees we're growing. Magic and a hastily built greenhouse have allowed us to supplement our diets with fresh fruits and vegetables. I could use magic for all the upkeep of our garden, but having my hands in the soil can be very therapeutic for me. As my mind wandered back to my son and his mate, I saw them crawl out of their tent.

I dip my head, covering my happy grin, as I watch the two of them crossing the clearing. Hand in hand, leaning into each other. The kisses they think no one sees. I truly don't think I've ever seen my son this happy and carefree. Even with the pending war looming over everyone and everything, he and Cassandra always have blissful smiles plastered on their faces.

On the other hand, watching Lucian and Aisling dance around each other has provided hours of entertainment. Evan had let it slip that the two of them hadn't left her room for two nights, leading us all to believe they had accepted each other. We all expected they would emerge happier or at least not in the manner they had. Their return to the outside world treated us to a deafening disagreement that to be honest none of us could quite understand.

It is obvious to anyone that the two are at least attracted to each other. Neither one can take their eyes off the other. However, they seem to be so determined to take shots at each other. Hawthorne has expressed his worry that they will never join together properly. The visions seen by both Serafina and Delilah show them united in the face of the fae. If their courtship continues as it has been, they're more likely to kill each other than face the fae.

Just this morning, Aisling was sparring with the large wolf shifter Brian. They grappled with each other, both partially shifted. Aisling had the claws and teeth of her lynx form extended as she swiped at Brian's wolf hind legs. She flung her head to the side, spraying sweat. That split second gave Brian the advantage and he pounced. Grabbing her arm, he spun her to the ground, pinning her beneath has massive size.

Lucian's dragon took over, and before either Aisling or Brian could react, he had yanked the wolf shifter off his mate. Aisling wedged her body between her mate and Brian who was hanging by his throat at the end of Lucian's outstretched claws. For one heartbreaking moment, Lucian looked like a scolded toddler, then the dragon king mask slammed back into place. With an apology to Brian, she tromped off the practice field, Lucian following, all the while arguing with each other.

I have seen encouraging moments between them as well. She always saves him a plate, even if they argue right before the meal. Lucian, upon learning that Aisling loves pears, brings her one from my tree every day. Plus, according to Evan, they sleep in the same room every night, no matter what disagreement occurred before bedtime. They are just too stubborn to get out of their own way. Lucian keeps forgetting he is not the ruler of all around him, and Aisling seems to revel on pushing every button he has.

As fascinating as their two-step around each other has been, the rest of us have been working on a different type of dance. Ours will decide the fate of the worlds as we devise the best way to fight my mate and his allies. Based on Delilah's visions, we are certain that Andre and Marcel Fontaine will assist Fraxinus with at least twenty to thirty of their best fighters.

They have also seen several other vampire and witch groups from Europe joining them. Jace mentioned that the Fontaines were looking to make the Americas more like Europe.

"The Community's rules keep our numbers low." Jace explained, tapping the map. "No feeding from humans. No turning new vamps unless it's your mate. They see our region as choice hunting grounds."

We have also determined that the fight will be in the frozen tundra of Canada. Thanks to a witch named Twyla that hails from Canada we have a well mapped area that we plan to lure our enemies to. Her magic prickles along my skin like a magical 'keep away' sign that puts many of us on edge when we're near her.

Twyla says it is a common trait amongst many in her community. They have used this power for many generations to keep people from coming near their settlement. By incorporating this power into the spells used to hide their village, they have warded off oil and logging companies that have come to their area in hopes of raping the land of its resources.

A couple days ago, we convened in my living room. I, along with Evan, Jace and Almerinda spoke with Twyla's future mother-in-law. We invited Jonesie and Brian, both declined with very similar responses. 'Just point us where we need to fight'. After the typical pleasantries, Twyla introduced Maria, then turned the call over to us.

"Aelwyd, will fight with you." Maria's serious voice echoed a bit due to a bad connection."

"Um, who is Aelwyd?" Evan scooched closer to the phone.

Twyla giggled, "Not a who. Aelwyd is my home, it literally means heart of the home."

"We currently have seven witches at Aelwyd with the same power as Twyla who are trained fighters as well." Maria's tinny voice brought our attention back to the phone. "We can deploy them to the front of our forces to push our attackers in the directions we want them to go."

"That should help." Almerinda smiled, she had firsthand experience with Twyla's powers. "Have you noticed any unusual activity near your settlement?"

"Not as of yet." Maria assured us. "I have increased our patrols. But you say the fighting takes place in winter, right?"

We all agreed that is what we have been told by two different seers. Hopefully their visions are accurate, except the part where two of us won't make it. We weren't so naïve that we thought none of our side would die, but we would do everything in our power to prevent any deaths, if possible.

"Then we have some time." Maria informed us. "The snow will not start for another twenty days."

"How sure are you of this timeframe? Jace's hands twitched at his sides. Until he moved, I had almost forgotten he was there. He had posted himself near the door, behind me. I suppose once a guard, always a guard.

"I can say with one hundred percent accuracy." Maria's smug voice warbled at the end, damn electronics, I thought. The sound steadied out as she continued speaking, "My weather witch has never been wrong."

221

We discussed a few other concerns then ended the call with a promise to keep her informed of any and all plans we had. Twyla agreed to call her at least once a day to check in.

The one thing we don't seem to be able to determine is how many fae will join my mate's forces. We also don't know who has been able to open a portal to Alfheimer. There must be someone within our enemy's group that has a large enough amount of fae blood. Without fae blood, no portal can be opened to Alfheimer.

Delilah, the witch seer, believes she is blocked from seeing the fae properly. She has also seen the same vision of my friend Serafina, but she is unable to see the force that Aisling and Lucian will face. She says her vision shows an advancing army, but the actual soldiers are blurry, and their size, numbers and forms are difficult to discern.

Malina has not had any new visions since arriving on the island. Her greatest powers lie with the four elements, but she has had visions in the past. Most often when she has one it is sudden and needs to be acted upon immediately, such as when she learned that my mate had found out about us working against him. Malina has promised to inform me at once if she has a vision but thus far has not had anything to report.

Delilah's indistinct visions have led us to believe that Fraxinus and the Fontaines are probably also joined by fae that she is just unable to visualize. With this knowledge, or should I say lack of knowledge, we are going in partially blinded.

Fortunately, we have several former Elite Guards that have been in different forms of war in the past. While we plan and alter our plans of attack and defense, we have Delilah and Malina constantly searching for different outcomes. We had seers and plans, what we didn't have is exact numbers and time and that scared me most of all.

Chapter Thirty-Three

Aisling

I don't know what in the hell is wrong with me. A month has passed since Lucian walked through the swirling silver portal from his world and we can't seem to get out of our own way. Every damn morning, I swear, today is the day I will stop being such a bitch, it always backfires. Even when we have spent several hours together with no incident something always pushes me to blow up. I really don't understand what is causing me to act like this.

I tried talking to Ali, Evan's mate, since she is new to this whole mating thing too, but she was not much help. When she and my brother mated, other than her shooting him, they didn't have many issues accepting each other. Cat said the same thing. She just knew Jace was her soul mate even before she knew anything about our world.

Everyone I have spoken to about their mating process has pretty much responded the same way. Cassandra, Jasmine, Almerinda, all of them. I even went so far as to talk to my sister Fiona who has two mates thinking perhaps, she had some insight.

No one seems to be able to help me. This morning, I snuck out of the house before anyone else was awake. I needed to get free of everyone and everything for a little bit. I have been wandering the island since dawn and have found myself on the opposite side from our settlement.

The shoreline on this side is more rocks and cliffs with a couple of small alcoves of sandy beach. My wandering feet have led me to a small cove where I have sat my ass down and have not moved for over an hour.

The cawing of the seabirds was interrupted by unusual noises that sounded almost like a frog croaking. I tracked its source and saw that it was small black and white birds with orange beaks. Perhaps I would look up what kind of birds lived in this area when I had access to our satellite signal again. For now, I was going to enjoy their odd sound mixed in with the screeches and caws of the larger sea birds.

I need to examine my feelings for my mate. I can admit that I am at least very attracted to him. Physically he is perfect, tall, muscular, and his hands are calloused from the use of a sword. When he runs them over my skin my body immediately ignites.

We definitely do not have a problem in that area. I mean I don't think we will since we haven't managed to complete the dirty deed as such. But when he touches me or all the times we've kissed my body reacts instantly to him.

So, my issue is not physical. He has improved as he promised he would that first night. He tries to not be too overbearing, but I can't seem to stop myself from provoking him to turn back into the pompous ass he was when he first arrived. I'm the problem.

Gods, two days ago at breakfast, I blew up at him for no reason. It was a nice moment, no fighting or arguing, totally ruined by me. He always wears red or black, stupid, right, that's what set me off. He explained that it is the way it is in his world, which pissed me off even more. He turned stiff and arrogant towards me then just got up and walked away. Of course, I got more mad and hurled insults at his retreating back.

Looking back, I know I was in the wrong for how I reacted. I just can't seem to stop myself. Gods, I need some guidance here. I really don't know why I keep pushing him away. I dig my hands in the pebbled sand, enjoying the feel of the grit on my calloused hands.

My hands burrowed deeper, pulling clumps of sand, stones, and shells from the earth. Letting the detritus sift through my fingers, I find a small chunk of malachite. Perhaps my luck is about to change.

My heart thumped loudly in my ears, as my mother's face swam before my eyes. I remember my mother showing me different stones and telling me all about how they affected our lives. Malachite is supposed to help with personal growth and emotional healing; two things I could use a lot of right now.

"Damnit, I could also use a little personal space." I grumbled under my breath when I noticed the woman striding across the beach like she's on a mission. I glare at Arianna as she stalks towards me. My facial expression wasn't having the desired effect.

"You know, I came all the way to the other side of the island to be alone." I shouted at her advancing form.

She waited until she was next to me to answer. "I am quite aware of that, but I don't care." She sat next to me, uninvited, ruining my perfectly good sulk. "Now, I think it is time for us to have a conversation about you and Lucian."

I started to stand up but found I was unable to lift myself off the ground. "What are you doing to me?" I gasped, the veins popping in my arms and neck as I struggle against her power.

"I told you we needed to talk." Her innocent smile did nothing to relieve the pressure on my body. "We can't do that if you go stomping off, now can we?"

"Fine," I spat letting my straining muscles relax. I knew when I was beaten. "What do we need to talk about?"

"Now that we have that settled," Arianna gave me a sweet smile, "perhaps you can tell me why you are fighting so hard against your mating."

I stewed in silence for several minutes, the salty breeze pushing my hair off my shoulders. That is the question I came out here to figure out. I wish I knew the answer to it. "I don't know.", my voice shakes, my head hung low in defeat, I stare morosely at the gray waters.

"Hmm," Arianna hummed to herself for a moment. I lift my head for a second, she is staring out at the waters too, as if the answer is right there. "I am not sure if this will help but maybe it will. I think you are purposely putting up roadblocks because you are afraid that submitting to Lucian will erase who you are."

"Why would you think that?" My stomach dropped like I had fallen off the edge of the cliff behind us. Was she right? A small part of me sort of agreed with her. What if I was no longer me? He is a king, and I am a fighter. He is such a proper ass while I am more relaxed. I don't know how to fit into his world.

"I have watched the two of you for over a month. I see the feelings you both try to hide. I can also see the lust in both of your eyes when you watch each other." Arianna gave me a sympathetic yet knowing look. "I see Lucian trying to bend to your will, but he has difficulty not being in charge. You on the other hand seem to take great pleasure in needling him at every opportunity. At first, I believed you were brought together by the fates much as Fraxinus and I were. I no longer maintain that opinion."

"Why did you believe that?" I asked sheepishly, my hands covered my eyes. I don't know if I'll like the answer, but I need it. "And what made you change your mind?"

"I have been watching the two of you quite closely." She turned her head to stare out to sea again. "I worried that your mating was just another means of fighting the fae. The Fates can be quite cruel when they are trying to meet an objective. Whether that objective is for the good of the world or not, we can only guess. They are the only beings who truly have future sight."

"So, you thought we might be stuck in a mating with no love?" The wind picked up, sending my hair into my face. When I swiped it to the side, I saw some of those weird sounding birds had moved closer to Arianna.

"When they brought Fraxinus and me together it was with the sole purpose of our producing Nikolas and Penelope." She spoke quietly, watching the birds with keen interest. "My daughter has served her purpose and now my son will serve his. I hope that he survives but I learned many centuries ago that when the Fates intervene, we have no choice but to follow their edict."

"That doesn't exactly answer my question." I grumbled while continuing to glare at the intruder of my sulking marathon.

"I am working up to that." She sniped at me. "My mate and I were ill-suited in so many ways that I knew the only reason we were brought together was to do the Fates bidding. I may hate their tampering, but I have faith in the Fates decisions. I worried that they would intervene with my son's mate as well, but I have watched him and Cassandra just as closely as I have watched you and Lucian. Your future may be uncertain at this time, nevertheless your mating is a love match, just as Cassandra and my son's mating is. So, again I ask what are you afraid of?"

Gods, what am I afraid of? Arianna is correct. I do feel that we are drawn together by more than just our blood calling to each other. My emotions are so tangled up and confused. On the one hand, I see a man I can fall in love with quite easily in Lucian. However, on the other hand he is the king of his world and I do not see how I could ever be a queen. I can't see myself ever being prim and proper and wearing gowns and crowns. That's it, a lightbulb literally turned on in my mind.

"I can't be a queen." I squawked in a very unqueenlike manner.

"Ah, that is why you are scared." She replied solemnly. "Have you considered that now that he has tasted freedom from being a king that maybe he no longer wishes to be one?"

My mouth dropped open as I gaped at her in bewilderment. Could he really not want to be king anymore? No, he was raised to be king. I can't imagine he would walk away from all that power. "I doubt he would want to leave his kingdom. He told me as much when he got here. His only thought was taking me back to his world."

"Are you sure that was his only thought?" she asked. "What were his exact words?"

I searched through my memories back to our conversation. "No, he wanted to protect me from the fae. He never said anything about needing to return to his kingdom, only that he needed to keep me safe." I hung my head, shame staining my cheeks red. I shoved my hands into my hair on either side of my face. "Gods, why am I so stupid?" I wailed to the cloudy sky above.

"I don't think you are stupid." Arianna reassured me with a few small pats to my shoulders. "I do however think you are very stubborn. You focused on the one thing that worried you the most above everything else. Clearly you have no wish to be a ruler, so it is in your best interest to talk to your mate about how you feel before you push him too far."

My head snapped up to meet her caring eyes. "What?" I moaned in fear. "Do you think I've ruined our chances?"

"No, I don't believe so." More of those aloof pats to my shoulder, I don't think Arianna had much experience giving comfort to people. She didn't seem to be very good at it. "You are mated. Nothing can tear apart that bond. But if you want a happy future with your mate, it might be in your best interest to stop being such a bitch."

Arianna's arrival interrupting my peace had upset me at first, but I must agree, even if I do so grudgingly, that she gave me sound advice. For whatever reason, Arianna looked quite sad when she mentioned our future. There must be something she is not telling me. Maybe Delilah has seen something about my future that goes wrong if I don't change my course quickly. I would have to puzzle that out later though.

Now, I have more important things to deal with. I needed to find Lucian so we could resolve things. Hopefully I can keep my temper in check so we can talk. Knowing me, that was a big 'hopefully'.

Chapter Thirty-Four

Arianna

Aisling gave me a quick hug then bolted from the sandy little cove like Cerberus himself was chasing her. I decided to stay here a little longer, finding the peace of not having so many people milling about wonderful. The sound of the tufted puffins chirruping in the brush around me added to the calm.

The birds were one of the reasons I chose this island all those centuries ago. Many moons ago, puffins were known to have prophetic powers and offered protection to sailors. Believed at one time to be enchanted Manxmen which are reincarnated monks who were devoted to Manannan Mac Lir, our sea god.

I sat in silence waiting, hoping that I would find solace in the sounds around me. The crashing of the sea lulled me into a tranquil trance. Resting my head on a log behind me, I stared at the cloudy sky in contemplation. The future of my son and those who have gathered for battle may rest on one simple act. Could I kill my mate?

I had assured Hawthorne that I could. My hands shook; I took a deep calming breath to center myself. But could I really? The doubt invaded my peace, when the moment came, would I hesitate? If I hoped to succeed, I could not. Fraxinus may not have all his powers, but he has surrounded himself with powerful allies.

One ally is Martine, a powerful witch with the ability to shield herself and anyone near her. She can also place someone under her control simply by skin-to-skin contact. That is how she was able to subdue Nikolas so easily. I will have my work cut out for me, when I face my mate since he never allows Martine to be very far from him. I vanquished Morbicus, I can face Fraxinus and whoever he has with him.

My little pep talk to myself cut off as the silence descended on my surroundings causing me to raise my head in concern. The wind had cut off abruptly, the waves not reaching the shore. The salty aroma of the sea intensified. I rose to my feet, preparing for whichever deity had come to find me.

The world had stopped moving except for the bearded man currently striding from the water. Only the puffins moved, gathered around him in greeting, all chirping and bouncing in happiness. Manannan Mac Lir, seawater streaming from his beard, marched toward me with long, purposeful strides.

I had not seen him in many centuries and honestly had thought he was dead. The old gods lived for many centuries but since I had not heard any tales of him or many of the other gods and goddesses of old, I believed most of them had moved on. I stood hastily to meet him, slowly lowering my head in reverence.

"Arianna of the Danu line." His deep voice boomed across the frozen beach. The words vibrated in my bones, older than the stones. "It is time for you to come home."

"With great respect, I disagree." I replied, falling to my knees. I knew that even the smallest bit of rebellion could be cause for my death. I also knew that my death would not stop Fraxinus, it would not stop the plan he set in motion. I needed to remain in this world a while longer to ensure my son's survival if possible.

"You would dare to oppose my decree." The sea god bellowed, his hand touching the hilt of Fragarach, his sword. "You have walked this world longer than any caster, even one of your heritage, should have. It is time for you to come home to Sidhes."

"I cannot. I have unfinished business here." I peeked at Manannan Mac Lir while keeping my head lowered in a deferential manner. One bushy red eyebrow lifted in question. I proceeded to explain why I was on this island and all of what had transpired. At the mention of the fae, anger raged across the sea god's face.

"Those abominations from Alfheimer?" He growled menacingly; lightning streaked across the sky as he raised his fist into the air. The scent of burnt ozone tickled my nose.

I finished my explanation as to why I would defy him at this time. His hand released the sword, coming to rest on my hair. He lifted tipped my head back, "I grant you permission to remain to complete your quest." His voice rang with finality. Whether I died or not, I believed I would be going home to Sidhes soon.

I bowed my head and expressed gratitude for his leniency. I gestured to the rocky beach, inviting him to sit with me. His grinning acceptance sent a shiver of anticipation into my groin. We sat on the side of the stopped ocean with only the puffins for company. We talked for many hours about past experiences and mutual acquaintances.

When he left me, it was with the promise that he would see me soon and welcome me home to Sidhes, I finally felt at peace with my decision. Fraxinus would die by my hand if it was the last thing I did. Which in a way it would be, considering that my life was tied irrevocably to his.

Chapter Thirty-Five

Aisling

Leaving Arianna, I felt lighter than I had in weeks, maybe since the moment Lucian's leather clad leg had emerged from the portal. I finally knew why I had been throwing up roadblock after roadblock to completing my mating with him. Who would have thought that the woman less than a year ago we believed was our enemy would be the one to help me?

So much had changed since my oldest brother Cillian died. Evan disappeared then reappeared and found his mate. Ali was great and the perfect match for my brother. She was fitting into our family so well that it was hard to believe she hadn't been with us for years. Her sense of humor was just as twisted as mine so we got along better than I could have hoped for. Evan is my best friend and I always worried that I would not like his mate.

I also worried he would not like mine when I finally met him. I have seen Evan and Lucian talking to each other quite frequently. I think if I hadn't been so determined to cause problems I would have noticed sooner that my brother and Lucian were becoming friends as well.

Just about everyone in our camp showed signs of trust and respect. I was the only one who was pushing others away. Well, just Lucian. I had welcomed Nikolas with more gusto than I had my own mate, and he had tortured my brother.

It was time to face the music. I tromped through the scraggly trees determined to have that heart to heart with Lucian as soon as possible. I couldn't keep pushing him away if I hoped to have a happy future with him. I finally knew what was causing me to act out so now I needed to find out if I even had a reason to fear being a queen.

My walk back to our encampment took less time than my meandering had this morning. I entered the open field where we had our campfire and chairs to find Lucian waiting for me. No one else was around, which caused me to wonder if he knew I was coming. His infuriating, knowing smile told me he'd been waiting. Damn mate bond.

Once I was in front of him, my tongue became stuck to the roof of my mouth. I didn't know how to get the words out. What if he told me what I didn't want to hear? Gods, why was I so afraid? I could face down a bear shifter with no qualms but asking my mate one simple question caused me to freeze up.

Lucian took my hand in his and pulled me into his steely arms. I relaxed but could still not bring myself to ask the question. Fear kept my mouth sealed shut.

"I don't know what it is that you are keeping locked in your head," Lucian whispered into my ear, "whatever it is I promise I will listen with great care."

Gods, why is he so perfect? No sooner had that thought entered my brain than he had heard it through our bond. *I would not say I was perfect, but it heartens me to hear you think it.*

Suddenly I could not control myself and I burst out laughing. Sometimes his way of speaking reminded me so much of Ali's romance novels. I needed that release of the pressure building in me.

"Can we go somewhere private?" I murmured.

"Of course." He responded matching my serious tone. He must have sensed something in my demeanor. "Perhaps we should go up to your room."

Even though he slept there every night, he still called it my room. I stepped from the circle of his arms and took his hand in mine. We walked to the house in silence.

I shut the door to my room behind me, leaning my back on it for support. My knees had suddenly turned to jelly. I motioned for him to take a seat on my pile of pillows and blankets. He sat far enough away from me that we were not touching, back leaned against the wall opposite me.

Nervousness began to creep back in now that I was no longer holding his hand. My hands fidgeted, twisting my fingers around each other. I took a moment to center myself, allowing calm to settle over my body with each slow deep breath I took. Once my knees stopped knocking together, I sat on one of the pillows facing him.

"I don't want to be a queen." I blurted; I hadn't meant to say it quite so abruptly but now that it was out, I couldn't take it back. I closed my eyes, fearing his reaction. When no sound came from him for several minutes, I peeked one eye open and stole a glance at him.

232

Relief showed on his features, and oh Gods, his smile. Not exactly what I was expecting. "Is that why you have fought me tooth and nail?" His flat tone was not helping me figure out if he was angry or not.

"I think so." My hesitant answer caused him to lift one eyebrow at me. "Okay, I am sure that is it. Arianna helped me figure it out." I rushed on to explain about my conversation with her.

"I had wondered where you had taken yourself off to this morning." He rubbed one hand down his face and scratched his beard. "I sensed your emotional turbulence this morning and thought I would give you some space."

"Thank you. I needed it." Smiling, I scooted a little closer to him. "I have been trying to come to terms with so much since we met but what bothered me the most is that I really don't think I would be a good queen. I really can't see myself in that role."

Lucian shifted closer to me. Close enough to touch me but he kept his hands to himself. My body yearned to run my hands up his arms and across his chest, but I needed to know how he would respond to my declaration.

"When my sister saw that I would travel here to meet my mate," Lucian began soberly. "She put forth that I may not return to Fabeldyrverden. I made my peace with that thought the minute the portal closed behind me. My kingdom was left in her care. She is strong and has a stalwart mate to help her. If we survive this war with the fae, I will go wherever you go."

I inched closer to him and grabbed his hand, holding it tight. A month of fighting him and all I had to do was ask the one question I was afraid to even acknowledge to myself. He squeezed my hand but held me away from him.

"I want you to know that I think you would be the most beautiful and electrifying queen to ever rule Fabeldyrverden." I dropped his hand, did I misunderstand? At my look of concern he added, "I also want you to know that I don't need a queen. I need my mate. I need the exasperating, stubborn, comical, beautiful, sensuous woman sitting in front of me."

I froze; can I believe his words? He held his left hand out to me, palm up. It took a full minute for my mind to comprehend what he was showing me. My breath whistled through my lips, oh Gods. The evidence was right before my eyes. He had renounced the throne.

I brought my hand up to meet his, caressing the bare ring finger. His king ring, as I had started to call it in my head, was gone. His hand turned in mine, gripping it tight and yanking me across the pillows.

A tear escaped me to run down my cheek. Lucian brought one finger up to capture it. My heart stuttered when he brought that same finger to his mouth, sucking my tear from it. His swirling-colored eyes turned crimson, a clear sign of his arousal. I climbed onto his lap; his eyes devoured me as his lips crashed into mine.

Weeks of pent-up passion exploded sending heat coursing through my veins. Lucian pushed me off his lap long enough to pull my shirt and pants off. Pulling me back into his arms he ran his calloused hands down my bared back to cup my lace covered ass in them. His breath harsh, he nipped his teeth along my neck.

Gods, I wanted him naked above me not fully clothed under me. Hearing my need he pushed himself away from the wall, laying my mostly naked form on the blankets. His deft fingers unbuttoned his, as usual, red shirt and stripped it off baring his hard muscled chest to my roving eyes.

My mouth watered at the thought of running my teeth and tongue along the hard planes of his chest and abdomen. The fire in his molten eyes increased while they followed the trail of my hand across my stomach. His growl, when I dipped my finger under the edge of my panties, sent a jolt through my core.

My mouth went dry as he shoved his pants down, revealing… Oh Gods, you must really love me. My thoughts jumbled as I stared at this man, this splendid specimen of manhood. Lucian lay beside me, pulling me close, his rough hands caressing my soft skin. One hand snaked around to my nape dragging my mouth to his while the other grazed and fondled my breasts.

We melded together in blissful harmony. When his tongue thrust between my lips, an electric pulse shot through my center making my hips jerk off the blanketed floor. Lucian's hand jittered across my stomach, following my arm to rest on my hand inside my frilly panties. I guided his searching finger to probe into my moist center. Each of his tentative touches elicited a moan of pleasure from me and soon his rhythm intensified.

I turned slightly in his arms, brushing my palm along his hard length. His sharp indrawn breath emboldened me to clasp his cock firmer in my hand. I stroked and massaged his shaft feeling him buck harder against my palm the faster I went. I could feel the tension building in him when he suddenly removed his fingers and pulled my hand away from his thick staff.

He moved so quickly, covering my sweat slicked body with his, fire jolted through me when I felt his throbbing member prodding my wet entrance. He held himself immobile, meeting my earnest gaze with yearning. "Aisling, I submit myself to be yours forever."

A feeling of love and acceptance poured into me, and I felt a sense of correctness settle over my body at his declaration.

I finally understood what he meant when he asked that I submit to him. He was not asking me to be subservient but to become one with him. I was not losing myself but gaining my other half. Our joining together was a form of submission to each other but neither of us lost anything.

"Lucian, I submit myself to be yours forever too."

His crimson eyes bore into mine, as our minds merged. I felt his happiness combine with mine. I experienced his fears and desires. I saw his past and present. When I saw me through his eyes, I saw what he considered his future. At his indrawn breath, I knew he was making the same connection with me.

Sharing our minds increased our passion for each other. My body became more inflamed, as Lucian drove his hard cock into me. I wrapped my legs around his narrow thighs, opening myself wider to his thrusts. The pressure built and I urged him to go faster.

My nails raked down his back, drawing blood. The burnt amber scent of his blood ignited my hunger even more. I brought my fingers to my mouth, sucking the blood from the tips. His eyes tracked my every movement. His rough hands dug into my ass, lifting me up to meet his thrusts.

Take from me what you need. Still, I hesitated. *Bite me, Aisling, bite me now.* Lucian commanded, his imperious voice sending shivers through my body.

At your command, I thought. Running my tongue along his throat I found his rapidly pounding pulse. A low moan escaped his lips when my teeth nipped the skin over his artery. My fierce growl ripped through my throat a second before my teeth tore into him. Blood erupted into my mouth. The euphoria I felt at the first taste of his fiery blood cascaded into an orgasm like no other I had ever had.

My body convulsed and trembled beneath Lucian. I drew my mouth away from his neck, meeting his lips in a scorching kiss. His body shuddered and bucked above me, and he lifted his head arching his back.

I watched in amazement as his skin fluctuated between human and orange, red and yellow dragon scales. I ran my hands along his side enjoying the feel of the scales beneath my fingertips. Lucian let out a roar, piercing my body with a final thrust. Warmth cocooned my body and fire blazed inside me.

Lucian's spent body collapsed on top of me. He pulled me close then rolled us to lie on our sides. I snuggled into his chest and for the first time ever, I felt content. I trailed my fingers along his sweat soaked chest, twirling around one nipple.

His hand clamped over mine, halting its wandering. *Not yet.* Before I could ask why he stopped me, the flame our lovemaking had lit, suddenly engulfed my body in a scorching inferno. Gods, what the fuck is this? My body convulsed, darts of pain shooting through my arms and legs. Lucian held me close, soothing me, but I could see the fire was burning him too.

An eternity later, or at least that's what it felt like, our bodies cooled, and the pain abated. The subtle heat continued to simmer inside me, but the white-hot flame was gone.

"That was the searing of our souls." The reverence in his voice had me lifting my head from his chest. "Something only true mates experience."

A tear leaked from his eye, and I found myself repeating his earlier action. I caught it on my fingertip, bringing it to my lips. Our eyes met, my heart spluttered at the significance of his words. Was I ready to say that word? Lucian tucked my head under his chin, my cheek resting near his heart.

The steady rhythm beating beneath his sternum, softened my racing heart and mind. His rough hands caressed my back, calming me even more. Content and drowsy, I pushed that word to the back of my thoughts.

My eyes grew heavy, and I wondered how long this feeling of contentment would last. Lucian placed a soft kiss on the top of my head. *Forever.* He murmured sleepily in my head. The drowsiness in his voice was contagious, and I felt myself succumbing to sleep too.

Chapter Thirty-Six

Cassandra

At last, Aisling had accepted Lucian, the whole damn island knew before the sun set. The two in question were currently sleeping off their adventurous afternoon. The rest of us had decided to meet to discuss plans. First being when we should inform them of Serafina's full vision.

"They should be told immediately," Arianna insisted, she waved the stick she held at everyone. "They need to prepare."

"I want my sister to be prepared too," Evan's knuckles whitened on his chair as he interjected, "but I also want her to have a little bit of happiness."

"Have we heard anything about Fraxinus or any of the other bad guys we're going to be fighting?" Ali asked from her place at Evan's side. The smoke of the fire wafted toward the couple.

"No." Davina responded. "James checked in with his alpha and as of this morning no one has seen or heard of anything to do with Fraxinus, the Fontaines or the fae."

"I also talked to my father yesterday and he has not heard anything." Evan and Ali shared a look that told me there was more to his conversation with his father than he was sharing. More than likely a family thing that was not pertinent to our current problems.

Nikolas remained quiet through all the arguments for and against telling them. At this point we had been going in circles for almost an hour. We could not come to a consensus of whether they should be told or not. We all seemed to agree that they needed to be told and also that they deserved some happiness before their probable death at the hands of the fae.

Delilah continued to scour the future for any glimpse that they survive. The best she can guess is that if they do it is blocked from her the same way the fae seem to be. The fae are never clear in her visions. She can see that they will be aiding Fraxinus in the battle, but she is unable to get a count of their numbers. They are just a blur in the picture she is seeing.

"I agree with Evan." Out of nowhere, Nikolas spoke interrupting the revolving argument. "Until we have more concrete information on my father's movements, I think we should let them have some time together. For all we know it will be the only time they get."

I'm not sure why, but Nikolas' pronouncement seemed to end the debate. Everyone still deferred to Evan, Almerinda and Arianna on most decisions but recently I had noticed more were also seeking his opinions. There was a quiet strength to my mate that seemed to instill confidence in those around him. Our worries that he would not be accepted due to his past seemed to be unfounded.

"Then it is settled." Arianna announced. "I do have one suggestion though." She looked at Davina hopefully. "Have you and Hawthorne completed the calculations for the Sanguis Draconis ceremony yet?"

Davina's radiant smile could have powered the entire island. Just about everyone else, looked on with confusion. "I have. The alignment will be in twelve days. If we are to perform the ceremony it will need to be done at two o'clock in the morning. Hawthorne has agreed to perform our ceremony. As you are the only other person who knows how to do it, might I suggest that you perform the ceremony for Lucian and Aisling."

Arianna gave a small nod of acceptance. "I would be honored, but ultimately it is their choice." Her hand traced a symbol that looked like a sword in the dirt at her feet.

"Exactly what is this ceremony you are talking about performing on my sister?" Evan sat up straighter in his chair. His protectiveness of his sister was heartwarming to me.

I never had that growing up and anytime I encountered a close family like the O'Briens I always felt a small stab of jealousy but an abundance of hope that someday my children would have the same closeness.

"It is a ritual that must be performed for Aisling and Lucian to gain access to their full powers." Arianna explained to Evan and everyone else present who did not know about the ceremony. "When dragons mate their powers combine, the oil binds them. Without it, the power transfer is like trying to mix fire and ice."

"I am curious," Ali asked, "did you perform this ritual with your mate?"

238

"I did not." Arianna replied. "I knew of the ritual, but I was also warned to keep him from gaining his full powers. I assume he knew of the ritual but for whatever reason never forced me to complete it."

"That is because he never believed in the properties of alsklingberry oil." Hawthorne snorted, providing the answer I am sure Arianna had wondered about for centuries. "He always viewed the spirit dragons as less than all the others. He ridiculed their practices and looked down his nose at them. If he hadn't been so full of himself, he might have figured out how wrong he was and forced the ceremony on you. Then you would have had no choice but to give him his full powers."

"Well, I guess we're lucky he was such an arrogant ass then." Ali laughed. The rest of us chuckled at her comment. I shuddered a little at the thought of Fraxinus with more power. If not for his arrogance and sense of self-importance, who knows where we would be right now.

"I am sure Lucian is aware of the ceremony though since he kept Profitis Magda close to him." I assured them. "Do you think he has told Aisling about it yet?"

We all looked at Aisling's window. Considering how much they had fought with each other over the past month; it was doubtful that he had been able to tell her much of anything. Hopefully some of that anger will turn to other emotions. I shared a knowing look with Nikolas as I thought about what other emotions tied so closely to anger.

"You have become closer to her since we arrived." Nikolas spoke, bringing my thoughts back to more appropriate topics. "Maybe you should speak with her about it."

"When she comes up for air I will talk to her." I grinned at Nikolas.

The ritual talk wound down and more practical concerns surfaced, mainly our dwindling resources. Arianna had not anticipated so many people living on the island for so long. We had fish from the wolves, and fruits and vegetables from Arianna's garden. But everything else, including blood for the vampires, was gone.

Jace and Cat agreed to take a small group to the Alaskan mainland for a supply run. They would bring back more food, blood and some much-needed building materials. Roughing it for a few weeks was all well and good but those who did not have shelter were beginning to grumble a bit. We would not be able to build full houses but figured we could at least build some smaller cabins or lean-tos.

Once it was settled who would go for supplies our meeting broke up. Nikolas and I were heading toward our tent when we noticed Aisling and Lucian emerging from their house. It was good to see them holding hands and smiling at each other. I pulled on Nikolas' arm, and we changed direction, moving to intercept the love-struck couple.

Lucian saw us before Aisling did and came to a stop to wait for us. "Good evening." He always sounded so formal compared to the average way Americans tended to greet each other. "Was there something you needed?" He asked us, a small amount of annoyance creeping into his voice.

Aisling glanced at him then turned to us. "We were going to go for a walk together." She explained smoothing over his tone.

"It is nothing of great importance." Nikolas began, pulling on my arm. "Cassandra needs to speak with Aisling when she has a moment. However, it can wait until you are less distracted."

They need a little more time alone. Nikolas reminded me of how we were when we had first consummated our mating. Hell, we were still like that a couple months later. We watched until they disappeared between the pines, their laughter floating back to us in the crisp evening air.

Chapter Thirty-Seven

Arianna

Thank the gods, Aisling and Lucian had finally figured out their issues. Now I could stop fretting about them for a moment. Now I could focus on the other mystery that I had yet to solve. When Aisling first arrived, she mentioned some concern about a vampire named Derik. With everything else going on I had not taken the time to investigate.

My first stop was to speak with Almerinda. She seemed to know just about everything about everyone gathered on my island. After our impromptu meeting, she and her mate had strolled toward the beach. Luckily, they were not in the middle of anything too personal. There were an awful lot of newly mated couples on my island. You just never knew what situation you might interrupt.

"Almerinda," I called out as I approached them, "do you have a minute to talk?"

The tiny vampire tore her gaze from her mate. "Of course, Arianna. What is it you wish to discuss?"

I took a seat on the pebbled beach beside her, close enough to keep our conversation between us while also not crowding her. "What do you know of Derik? The tall blonde vampire with Jonesie's group?"

Almerinda took a moment to think. "He joined Jonesie and his little menagerie a few hundred years ago. He was one of the original members of the Community when we formed it. He has always kept himself separate from others all while seeming to be a part of everything. Is there a problem I should be aware of?"

"When Aisling first arrived on the island she mentioned some concerns about him. She could not put her finger on what exactly was bothering her but thought I should be aware." I drew small circles in the sand beside me needing to feel the cool sand to help center my thoughts. "I have been so focused on making sure my son settles in safely and the issues between Lucian and Aisling that it slipped my mind."

Almerinda turned to Damian. "Have you picked up on anything off about him?"

"Not exactly." Damian answered. "He reminds me of a captain I once served with in the Seals. Very slick but not totally trustworthy. How he made it through the selection process always baffled me. Captain Andrews was the first to boast about his exploits but always seemed to be the last into a fight and first to retreat. Not exactly a normal seal team soldier. The few interactions I have had with this Derik person makes me think of Captain Andrews."

I really tried to understand everything that Damian was saying but I truly had no idea what most of what he said meant. "I'm sorry but what is a seal team?"

He looked slightly taken aback at my question but quickly recovered. "I'm sorry. I keep forgetting that I am dealing with so many people that have not had much contact with the human world. In the United States one of the military branches, the navy, has a subdivision called Navy Seals. They are trained more intensely than average military personnel. We are an elite fighting force, but we are also a family to each other. Our teams are taught to support each other through anything and everything. Captain Andrews seemed to miss that training and caused many issues within our unit. He didn't last long and was transferred through three different units before he was finally demoted and no longer a Navy Seal."

"Oh, I see." Interesting, I thought to myself. So, Almerinda mated with someone with fighting skills that were probably much like the Elite Guards of the Community. "What is it about Derik that reminds you of this Captain person?"

"Nothing specific but there is just something unworthy about the vampire." Damian shrugged, his gaze fixed on Almerinda. "He has a shiftiness to him that, like I said, reminds me of Captain Andrews."

Almerinda quickly rose to her feet. "Well, no time than the present to go figure out what set off Aisling and Damian's alarm bells." She reached down and grabbed Damian's hand, pulling the tall sinewy man to his feet. "We need to find either Jasmine or William."

"I saw Jasmine strolling off into the trees with the large O'Brien hybrid." I really had a hard time remembering all their names. "Who is William?"

"He was near the tents, about an hour ago." Damian told Almerinda then answered me. "He is Jasmine's brother. One of their family traits is ferreting out lies, not sure how they do it, but they can always tell."

I picked myself up off the ground and followed them to find William. We found him in a hammock outside his tent reading a book. When he saw Almerinda approaching, he snapped the book closed and came to his feet. "Is something wrong?"

"I am unsure," Almerinda explained the situation then added, "So we are in need of your skills."

"Before we approach this vampire, I think we should talk to Jonesie." William suggested. "I think it would be in our best interest to have him on our side just in case things don't go well."

"That is very good thinking." I agreed with the witch.

Jonesie was a rather formidable vampire and while I had ample powers I would rather not have to use any of them on an ally. Our little group headed towards where Jonesie and his crew had made camp. Thankfully we found Jonesie sitting alone at his campfire.

He welcomed us with open arms until we shared our concerns. His jovial smile slid away leaving a less welcoming visage. "So, you mean to accuse one of my oldest friends on a feeling that something is off?" He growled with ire at me.

"If he is innocent then I will apologize. However, if he is here under false pretenses and somehow got past my wards, we need to know now before he learns of any of our plans." I growled right back. "I invited all of you here as friends, but I do not know any of you all well enough yet to know if you can all be trusted."

"I can understand that, but Derik has been with me for a very long time." Jonesie's massive form rose to tower over me. "I was led to believe no one could pass through your spells if they were not faithful to you and your cause. So, how would he have made it here if he were not on your side?"

I thought about his question for a long time. There are ways to circumvent different spells. Many of which are known by different witches. My spells are quite powerful but there are a few witches out there that could probably make a counter-spell. Two of those witches are Delphine and Martine who have worked closely with my husband and the Fontaine family for many years.

If Martine had a spell that could get past my wards, Fraxinus would have learned of my duplicity much sooner. That leaves Delphine as the possible culprit.

According to Almerinda, Delphine had aided an old enemy of Jace McFadden's named Amanda a little over a year ago. Amanda had teamed up with Marcel, although neither one had been entirely upfront with each other on their true goals.

Amanda was just trying to get back at her maker and his brother, while Marcel was trying to capture his sister. Everyone was very tight-lipped about Marcel's sister. There was something different about her, but no one would say what. According to Almerinda, Delphine was spelled by Jasmine to keep her from coming back to this continent.

Distance would not prohibit a spell she cast from working though. There is a chance she was able to place a spell on someone that would allow them to infiltrate our ranks. The big question is whether she did and why him? I explained my theory to Jonesie, Almerinda and Damian.

"I have no reason personally to suspect this man; however, two of your people are having misgivings about him." I finished as gently as I could. "Has he been acting differently than he normally would recently?"

Jonesie continued to glare down at me from his great height. I could see the wheels in his brain turning though. Good, I thought, he is at least thinking about our concerns rather than just dismissing them out of hand. A crestfallen look came over his face as he slumped back into his chair.

"I can't argue one way of the other for my friend." He began slowly in a low voice. "Ever since we aided Jace against Amanda, Derik has not been at our home as much. I have had him checking in with our allies up and down the east coast. We have had centuries of peace, and I worried that all the unusual unrest was brewing to be something more."

"What kind of unrest?" I asked. I tried to keep up with new human technologies and changing political tides of both human and supernatural states and countries. But day to day life, often slipped by me unnoticed.

"There have been more rogues created in the past five to ten years. They have been raiding our hidden communities all over the northern and southern continents." The large vampire explained. "The rogues have also been causing some issues within the human world. Luckily the Community has been able to capture and stop them before humans were able to figure out what has caused their problems."

Almerinda cut in adding, "There is also the incident with Amanda and the backing she received from the Fontaine family. Then what your daughter did to Evan. Plus, Alonzo, the Central American region leader told me that not long after Evan was found all the rogues in his region suddenly left."

At my look of confusion, she revealed the significance of that. "Alonzo has always allowed the rogues to live in peace so long as they are circumspect. We are sure that he allows them to feed from humans. If none of the deaths can be chalked up to something supernatural, he leaves them alone. In that area of the world there is a high incidence of deaths from drug cartels, so dead bodies are often not looked at too closely."

"And you're telling me," I fixed Jonesie with my hardest gaze, "that Derik has been patrolling all over the eastern side of the country on your behalf?" He gave me a terse nod. "So, at any time he could have been turned against us." I chose to say this more as a statement than a question.

"I can see where you are going with this," Jonesie grumbled under his breath. "But I know Derik; he has been my friend and sometimes lover for a very long time."

"Do you defend him because you are certain in his faithfulness or because he is your family?" Damian stooped down, placing himself at eye level to the bereft vampire. "There is nothing wrong with loyalty if it isn't unfounded. If you can say with one hundred percent certainty that Derik is the same as he has always been, we will believe you." Damian looked up to us for confirmation. We all nodded in agreement.

Jonesie's shoulders dropped in defeat. "I don't know." He moaned in a hushed tone. "I don't want my friend to be my enemy."

"We don't either." I reassured him. "We just need to be sure. Fortunately, we have not made any specific plans yet. If he does turn out to be a turncoat, then at this point nothing has been said in front of him that can't be easily changed."

Resignation settled on his face, and he dragged his large body back to standing. "Alright, let's get this over with."

We followed Jonesie to the fifth tent from the campfire. Derik must have sensed our approach because just as we arrived outside his tent, he stepped out to face us. A raised eyebrow in curiosity greeted us. "Jonesie, is something amiss?" Derik looked from his leader to each of us questioningly.

"I hope not." Jonesie responded, sorrow clouding his voice. "Can you come down to the beach with us?"

Derik agreed; the only emotion I was picking up from him was confusion. Perhaps Aisling and Damian's concerns were wrong. I glanced at William to gauge

245

his response. If he was a lie detector then surely, he would pick up on something. Distress creased his brow but whether it was because he sensed something from Derik or something else, I could not say.

We walked back to the beach where I had found Almerinda and Damian. Derik came to a stop not far from where I had sat to voice my concerns to the two vampires who now stood on either side of him. Jonesie remained at my side and William stood behind him, effectively flanking the blonde vampire.

"Is there something you need to tell me?" Jonesie's voice tinged with sadness and resolve.

"I don't know." Derik replied helplessly. "Could you be more specific about what exactly it is you want to know?" Either he was an excellent actor, or he really was innocent. I still could only pick up confusion and mild unease. The unease could be simply because of Jonesie's manner towards him.

Something must have rang untrue with Jonesie though. He stared long and hard at his friend. Derik began to squirm under Jonesie's scrutiny. Just as I opened my mouth to intercede, Jonesie's beefy hand shot out, clasping Derik's neck in a death grip. "Tell me!" He bellowed in the pale vampire's face. "What did you do?"

Derik's gaze darted around looking for an escape. He stepped back, bumping into William. Jonesie moved with him, keeping his hand wrapped around Derik's neck. Almerinda and Damian moved closer, cutting off his escape should he try to bolt to the left or right. Derik pushed against William, who must have used a spell to keep the trapped vampire from being able to overpower him. One moment fear showed in Derik's eyes then was morphed into cold calculation.

"So, you found my mole?" I high pitched feminine voice with a French accent squealed from between the caught vampire's lips. His gaze turned to meet mine. "You are just as weak as your mate said you were. I am surprised, considering your rumored lineage."

"Delphine, I presume?" I stepped closer to Derik. His eyes had changed to a purple hue more common to witches. Whatever he had done had not been of his choice. Much like my son, he was controlled by a powerful spell.

"You would presume correctly." The witch spoke through Derik. "I had hoped to utilize this body for longer but as he has been found out there is no reason to keep him in play any longer." For a mere second the real Derik stared at Jonesie

246

with fear and love in his eyes only to be replaced by the cold gaze of Delphine once again. "Dissolve!" The witch spoke and within moments, Derik's body turned to ash.

Jonesie's massive form crashed to the ground and an anguished keening issued from deep in his throat. Delilah, the seer witch from his group came running down the beach. She shooed us away and wrapped her arms around the giant man. We watched as more of his group came to envelope him in a cocoon of friends. As one, William, Almerinda, Damian and I turned to leave them to their sorrow.

The four us ascended the hillock and convened around the main campfire. Dispirited, we sat in silence, broken only by the lone hoot a snowy owl from the tree behind me. After about ten minutes, Almerinda broke the silence. "How can we be sure he was the only one?"

"We can't." My morose reply seemed to surprise them. "I did not know that man, but he did not deserve that ending. I really thought my wards would keep an enemy from getting through."

The ever-pragmatic Almerinda patted my arm twice then announced, "Well we need to be sure. We're going to have to question everyone. William you and Jasmine will need to meet with every single person on this island."

"So, you expect me to just ask everyone if they've been taken over by Delphine?" William scoffed.

"Yes." Almerinda snapped. "Word will travel around that we have ferreted out a traitor. Since that will be on everyone's minds, I expect it shouldn't be too difficult for the two of you to determine if there are any other moles amongst us."

"I propose that we order everyone to meet with Jasmine or William to be screened." Damian announced. "If there are other moles, we will find them quicker when we see who resists the screening process."

"That is an excellent suggestion." I agreed with Almerinda and Damian. "We need to know who we can trust before we finalize our plans."

We gave Jonesie and his group the rest of the night to mourn the loss of Derik. The next morning, we announced that everyone would need to meet with us to ensure there were no more traitors. By that time the news of Derik's death had spread sending ripples or shock and anger throughout our little community.

We learned of another vampire and two shifters. The vampire had been spelled by Delphine and came alone to the island. We assumed she had been sent by the O'Brien's father but when we called him, he said he had never seen her.

One wolf shifter had not been spelled but hated Michael Collier and hoped by joining the Fontaines he would be killed. He had made it through by knocking himself unconscious right before the crossing. Brian, the de facto leader of the wolves on the island dispatched him. The other shifter had been taken over by Delphine and when confronted she used the same spell to turn him to ash as she had on Derik.

As soon as we finished interrogating everyone, I set to reinforcing my wards. I never thought to guard against unconsciousness and added that into my spell. Now, anyone trying to come through the wards would not be able to pass if they were unconscious. It was also decided if any new people showed up, they would be met by either Jasmine or William before being allowed full access to the island. Although now that Delphine had been found out we didn't expect any more of her puppets.

Chapter Thirty-Eight

Aisling

One week. Seven whole days before they ripped our world apart. Lucian and I are destined to die. And apparently it would seem that everybody else knew except for us. If I'd known, I wouldn't have squandered that whole month away. I wasted our time together by being fearful and angry at the Fates for sending me a king for a mate.

Cassandra cornered me this morning to share the details of our impending doom. Lucian and I are expected to meet a horde of Fae in some kind of snow-covered field where we will meet our certain deaths. Cassandra and Nikolas both try to argue that it's not an absolute certainty that we will die but our prospects don't look good. We are both trying to remain optimistic, but I can see in his eyes that he knows more than he is telling me.

After Cassandra clued me in on the closely guarded secret, Lucian and I retreated to our room. I could not take all the pitying glances people kept giving us. I am sure he was getting a little bothered as well, however he was much better at hiding his discontent than I am.

"Spill it," I demanded once the door to our room closed behind me. I leaned back on the door, keeping my distance from his wonderful scent and devilishly talented hands.

"Spill what?" His casual innocence brought me to full attention. In the little over a month of time I had known him, I realized the only time Lucian spoke with such feigned nonchalance was when he knew something he really didn't want to share.

"Lucian, darling, I know you are keeping something from me." Lacing my voice with a saccharin sweet tone, I added, "now be a dear boy and just tell me."

His left eyebrow shot up at the word boy, but he kept his stance relaxed. "I have no idea whatsoever of what you could be speaking of."

Yet another clue he was hiding something. Lucian only stumbled over words or mixed his way of speech with the more modern speech whenever he was trying to keep something from me. The last time he tried to keep me in the dark about something was when he had a surprise for me. Nikolas had told him about a beautiful waterfall with a pool beneath it that would be the perfect setting for a bit of carnal activity.

All day while he was planning our little excursion he kept slipping in his way of speaking. I even heard a couple of thee's and thou's out of him that day. For the most part he had assimilated rather quickly into this new modern world. I often had to remind myself that he had not been in Gaia, what he calls our realm, for over a thousand years.

Technology was the one area he still could not completely grasp. He was slowly becoming less wary of the cell phones that most of us carried but would not go anywhere near the satellite dishes.

I held my ground, not budging from the door I was leaning against. Raising my own eyebrow back at him, I counted to ten in my head. I know there is something he is not telling me.

More than likely something he believes I need protection from. Even though in his realm mates work together equally, no gender held higher than the other, he has admitted that he can't seem to help himself when it comes to trying to protect me.

Keeping his eyes locked on mine, he pivoted away from the window he had been gazing through. *It is of no importance.* He spoke into my mind. He stalked toward me, eyes swirling closer to that deep crimson.

I shook my head at him and placed my hand on his chest keeping him from moving any closer to me. I was not going to let him distract me with his body.

"If that were true, you wouldn't be hiding it from me." I stamped one foot in frustration. "Now, spill it!"

With a heavy sigh, he retreated away from me to stand at the window once more. His back stiff, he stared at the yard below. "Serafina said she couldn't see if I ever returned to Fabeldyrverden." His shoulders sagged and he rested his forehead on the windowpane.

His pain radiated off him in waves, dragging me to his side. I wrapped my arms around his waist and rested my cheek on his back. "Maybe she just couldn't see past the battle we will face." I whispered hopefully. "Delilah says that futures change based on so many different variables. She also said she can't see the fae clearly, maybe your sister has the same blockage."

He wrapped his arm around me, crushing me to his chest. "Gods, dear one, I hope we find a way through this. I just can't see it yet."

I gripped him tightly. How cruel the Fates were to send me my mate only to lose him so quickly. Our comforting of each other smoldered into a more animalistic emotion and we lost ourselves in each other's bodies for a long while. Our lips met like crashing waves, our fear pouring out until we were just two bodies finding comfort in each other's heat.

Our sweat slicked bodies finally collapsed, limbs tangled with each other and the blankets. Lucian's hand drew small circles on the back of my hand. My mind wandered, bringing me back to the rest of my conversation with Cassandra. After telling me about the visions, she made a one hundred eighty-degree pivot. She gushed, pink tingeing her cheeks, about some type of ceremony that Lucian and I would need to complete.

Evidently, it's some kind of highly sexual dragon ceremony. Cassandra's description makes me think I'll love it. The Sanguis Draconis ceremony will bring the two of us closer together and allow us to share our different powers. I will be able to transform into a dragon, which I must admit sounds freaking awesome.

Maybe we will have a chance against the fae if we are both large dragons that can breathe fire. Lucian is a fire dragon which is the only type that can shoot fire from their mouth. The fire comes from the throat as Lucian likes to tell me but since it shoots out of the mouth I just keep going with that description.

"Davina and Hawthorne worked out the exact timing for the ceremony. Lucian murmured beside me; sleepiness slowing his words. "Plus, Cassandra brought back some alsklingberry oil from Fabeldyrverden. We just need to find someone to perform the rites."

"We can ask someone tomorrow." I yawned, snuggling deeper into my mate's strong arms.

Sleep overtook both of us quickly. I slipped peacefully into what at first, I believed was a dream then realized I was wondering through my mate's memories. His sister featured prominently in most of his memories. Occasionally, I would see an older couple who I assumed were his parents. They were most often dour and stern looking.

A younger Arianna also featured in many of the memories causing me to realize how close they once were. That is who we should ask; Arianna has been a

251

part of Lucian's life for thousands of years. She may not be full dragon, but she is the closest thing to family aside from Hawthorne. I just don't feel like having Hawthorne oversee what sounds like a rather erotic ceremony.

The next morning, I jostled him awake just as dawn broke. Lucian is going to show me his dragon form today. I rushed him through breakfast then dragged him to one of the empty fields. I hope Lucian is as majestic as Cassandra's descriptions of some of the ones that she had seen in the dragon realm.

Our hands clasp each other as we walk across the mist covered field. It is a wonderful feeling holding the hand of my mate. The news we received yesterday still fills me with dread, but I have decided to face each day as if I have hundreds of years to be with him.

We reach the middle of the field and Lucian pulls me to a stop. Looking deep into my eyes, the connection I had tried to deny pulls me deeper into his soul. His slow seductive smile brings a quivering to my legs. He leans down slanting his mouth across mine with a kiss that leaves me breathless and wanting more. Pulling away, his satisfied smirk tells me he can feel how much his kiss has affected me.

Stepping back, he points to the edge of the field, "you will want to stay about 20 ft away from me. I am much larger in my dragon form."

I nodded and turned to move far enough away. My mischievous side took over, turning back around, I threw myself into his arms. I kissed him full on the mouth delving my tongue through his lips with a passionate kiss. Lucian meets my passion with his own and we spend many long moments in each other's arms.

Gods, why did I waste that month in fear of being a queen? A knife twists in my gut over my regret. I would accept that title if that's what it took to stay alive and keep this man with me forever.

Our lust for each other slaked for the moment, we return to the reason for the trip to this field. As I turn to walk away to give Lucian space, I feel a playful slap on my buttocks. It would seem I am bringing out the playful side of my mate that Cassandra told me existed.

Lucian waits until I am far enough away, then he closes his eyes. I can't help but marvel at the beautiful male specimen in front of me. But playtime is over, and it is now time to see my mate in his dragon form.

A fiery red and smoky shimmer encases my mate as he pulls his dragon form from his core. A wave of heat washes over me, I shut my eyes to shield them

252

from the wind. When I open them again, standing in front of me is the most amazing sight I have ever seen. Where the man once stood, now stands a twenty-five feet tall red and black dragon.

His scales are predominantly red with some yellows and oranges mixed in and a black underbelly. A black fringe runs along his elongated neck. I stare into his eyes which no longer swirl and have settled on a deep crimson with orange and yellow catlike slits.

I step closer to my mate holding out my hand to rub it along the scales of his neck. They are soft and smooth while also having a very firm texture which more than likely helps protect him in battle. He nods his enormous head, answering my thoughts. Gods, this man is beautiful no matter what form he takes.

Most men prefer to be called handsome. echoes through my mind. Laughter bubbles up my throat as I throw my arms around his neck. His burnt amber scent permeates the air around me. I dig my toes into the rough grass to keep my mind focused on the dragon.

My arms barely span the front of his neck, and I marvel once again at his beauty and size. I take a few steps back and begin to pace around the length of Lucian. His forelegs, or maybe arms, are thinner and shorter than the hind legs and have hands that easily span my height. Each finger is tipped with a claw about twelve inches long.

His hind legs are large with feet the size of a small car and have long talons on the ends of each toe. I bend to peer closer at a talon, Lucian lifts one from the ground and I realize each one is almost as long as I am tall.

I continue my perusal of the massive dragon before me, arriving at his barbed tail. The barb at the end has eight or nine lethal looking spikes protruding from it. Lucian thumps his tail causing me to jump in surprise.

"Not funny!" I yell over my shoulder although my giggling betrayed that sentiment.

A loud grumble issues from his throat, and I realize my dragon is laughing at me. I finish my inspection, returning to stand in front of him. My jaw drops open when Lucian spreads his wings. Each wing must be at least twenty feet long. He rustles them causing a strong wind to buffet me. I have to take a few steps back to catch my balance. He lets out another of those grumbling laughs.

Have you seen enough? He asks me through our mind link. I nodded with a happy grin on my face. Fire and smoke surround Lucian's form again. Once more, my mate stands in front of me, naked, glorious and human.

Lucian winks at me as he bends over to grab his clothing. Unable to hold myself in check any longer, I rush forward tackling him to the grass covered ground. His arms immediately wrap around me, pulling me in closer for a scorching kiss. All thoughts of anything but the feel of his lips on mine run from my brain.

Calloused hands reach under my t-shirt, drifting across my stomach. One hand cupping my breast while the other travels further south to work the button open on my jeans. Relinquishing my breast, he uses both hands to yank my jeans free from my hips. I rip my t-shirt off, tossing it away onto the grass beside us. This movement places my nipple in perfect alignment with Lucian's mouth, which he takes full advantage of.

His tongue swirled around my erect nipple sending jolts of desire through my core. Gods, I want him so bad. I moaned deep in my throat when I felt his finger dip into my wet center. His rhythmic probing sent shudders through my body. Just as I thought I was going to cum he removed his finger and placed his hands on my hips. He lifted his mouth to meet mine and slowly lowered my quivering sheath onto his hard shaft.

"Gods, yes!" I screamed and howled to the heavens above us with each thrust from his pulsing cock. I rode him with wild abandon. He rammed his rod harder and faster into my core. My climax cascaded over me as I collapsed onto his firm chest, his seed pulsing hot into me filling me with magnificent warmth. His muscular arms gripped me close to his heart. Our contented sighs mingled together in the morning mist.

Chapter Thirty-Nine

Cassandra

Aisling's voice cracked across the lawn like a whip. Her eyes shone with that particular O'Brien determination. While I waited for her, Lucian pulled her in for a thoroughly steamy kiss before heading off to the practice fields. I chuckled at their state of dress, grass stains and leaves caught in their hair.

"Hey Cass, it's alright if I call you that, right?" Words tumbled from her mouth like marbles from a burst bag. "Do you think Arianna would be willing to perform that ceremony for us? I mean I don't know who else to ask besides Hawthorne and I'm just not really sure that I want Hawthorne to do it because you know it's kind of one of those crazy sex things that we supernaturals seem to like to do but..." She trailed off upon noticing Lucian and Nikolas crossing on the opposite side of the yard from us. "Uh, sorry, what was I saying?"

Her infatuation with her mate was gratifying to see. I also really liked being called Cass rather than my full name Cassandra. Having a nickname made me feel more accepted by her and those around us.

"We actually already discussed this, and Arianna is more than willing to perform the ceremony for you." I answered her, dragging her attention away from our delicious mates. Nikolas and Lucian took the path to the beach and were gone from view. With her mate no longer in her line of site, Aisling was able to give me her full attention.

"You guys talked about that ceremony without me there, about me, I mean geez now I kind of understand why Ali is always so bothered about how we just talk about sex as if it's nothing big." I don't think I've ever seen Aisling O'Brien quite so tongue tied in all the years I've known her.

"Slow down. Take a breath." I took her arm, propelling her along to sit on one of the chairs near the fire pit. "What has you so worked up?"

Aisling sat motionlessly for a few moments as she brought her breath and mind under control. "I think Lucian and I can beat the fae if we are both dragons." She mumbled under her breath. Then louder, "I know all the seers can't truly see the outcome, I'm just not ready to lose him. I mean I just found him for Fates sake."

255

The unfairness of her situation reminded me of how dire all our situations are. No matter what Delilah and any other seers have portended, things are never completely set in stone. I grabbed her hand and held it in mine, lending my strength to her. I didn't have a good response considering that we all believed they had such a slim chance of surviving.

We sat in silence, holding each other's hands for a long time. I glanced out of the corner of my eye to see a tear stream down her cheek. A few more minutes passed, then she pulled her hand from mine and stood up. Fingers trembling, she swiped at her wet cheeks angrily as if she was ashamed of showing any weakness. I got to my feet and yanked her into my arms. Hugging her seemed more natural now.

"I know our mates are merely cousins," I spoke quietly, "but I think of you as a sister. I wish we'd been closer before all this."

Aisling sniffled then gave me a tight squeeze before stepping out of my embrace. "Me too. I always liked you." She smiled sadly. "Okay enough of the maudlin crap. I need to learn how to become a dragon."

I followed her as she tromped through the grass to Arianna's house. Annie and Matthew were sitting at the kitchen table when we barged in looking for Arianna. Annie told us she was out for a wander communing with the flora and fauna. I took that to mean that she had gone for a walk in the woods.

We left the two vampires with their glasses of blood and headed out in search of Arianna in the trees. Aisling marched along the trails with purposeful strides. I was glad to see her trying to be proactive about her upcoming meeting with the fae.

None of us knew if or how she and Lucian would be able to defeat them. Perhaps mastering her dragon form is the impetus that brings about the fae's downfall. Honestly at this point I would take anything that would keep the two of them alive past our upcoming battle.

After almost an hour of traipsing through the trees, Aisling came to an abrupt halt then pivoted towards the opposite side of the island. "I think I know where she is" She called over her shoulder in explanation of her sudden direction change.

I had no idea where we were headed but followed her anyway. We came to a barely there trail that she turned onto as if she had come this way before. A little over a mile passed when we emerged at the top of a sheared off cliff. She veered to the left then disappeared.

I rushed to the edge of the cliff, unsure what to expect. A spike of fear raced down my spine only to be replaced by a nervous giggle when I saw her lithe form jogging along a steep path. The bottom of the path met up with a small sandy cove.

Arianna sat motionless on the sand, staring out at the churning sea. As we approached her still form, the world seemed to stutter for a moment. I swear Arianna looked like she was a statue for a few minutes right up until she turned her head to face us. Her body shimmered then settled as if it had come a long distance to meet us. A gull shrieked nearby, clearing the unusual image from my mind.

"Hello, ladies. What brings you to see me?" Her voice had a strange echoing quality when she began to speak. It was almost as if it was catching up to her mouth from a great distance. Her movements were jerky and stiff as she rose to greet us.

I must have made a weird face because she added, "Sorry, I was communing with the Gods" Her voice clear, no longer echoing. She gave us a serene smile.

"Hey Arianna," Aisling said by way of greeting then rushed headlong into her request. "So, Lucian and I need to do that dragon ceremony. And I know we haven't known each other for that long but I feel like you helped me quite a lot recently and maybe you would be willing to perform the ceremony for us. Plus, I know that you and Lucian were once close whenever you were back in his realm thousands of years ago. I mean I would understand if you wouldn't want to, but I was really hoping you would."

My mouth dropped open in surprise. This babbling woman was much different than the Aisling I had interacted with at Council headquarters. Whether it was her mating, her possible imminent death or a combination of both that had caused her to be less in control, I couldn't say. It was a little disconcerting to me to witness it though.

Arianna dusted sand and was that dark mud, from her pants. Where did she find mud on this island of sand and rock? The salty air felt thicker on this side of the island. My hands had a sticky feeling to them making me want to wash them.

Arianna gave Aisling a quick once over then took Aisling's hands in hers. "I would be honored to perform the ceremony for the two of you." Linking her arms through each of ours she walked us towards the cliff face. "We will need to prepare. The proper alignment is in two days."

We reached the face of the cliff where Arianna released our arms. "I will return to our little village within the hour. Find Lucian and meet me at my house at that time."

With a little push to our backs, Arianna dismissed us and returned to the beach. She must not have been done communing with the Gods. I laughed under my breath then followed Aisling back up to the top of the small cliff.

When we returned to the field near her house, she gave me a quick hug and left me to go in search of her mate. Thank the gods she finally fully accepted him. Speaking of mates, mine had just emerged from one of the trails that descended to the beach. I met him halfway to be immediately pulled into a close embrace. I must say I was starting to enjoy all the hugs I was getting.

Nikolas leaned back, raising one eyebrow. "Who all have you been getting hugs from?"

Giggling I pulled him closer, "Just you and Aisling. Your hugs are better than hers though." I sighed as I inhaled his burnt woodsy scent.

"They better be." He chided me gently.

We walked over to sit at the campfire. Temperance, one of Arianna's witches had spelled all the fires in the camp to remain lit and always contained. Although I had been born part witch, the Council had kept me apart from other witches. I knew there were different powers but had not seen many of them in action. Simple spells still caused some amazement on my part.

"I was thinking," Nikolas interrupted my musing. "When this war is over, how would you feel about living in Fabeldyrverden?"

"I would love it." I blurted.

I didn't even have to think about it. I could just be Cassandra, and he could just be Nikolas. No more worries that someone one of us had been used against would come back after us. His sister had used him to inflict pain and torture on many people over the years. Much like the Council had used me. The dragon realm was also very beautiful and the people I had met were all wonderful.

"Do you think Serafina would allow it?" My heart raced, worried his answer would dash my hopes.

"I know she would. I spoke with her about it before we came back to Gaia." Nikolas reassured me. "She offered her family's estate to us."

"What about their parents? Don't they live there?" I didn't want to make enemies of her mother and father. I also was not overly fond of them. If we survived the fight with Nikolas' father and the fae, I wanted my days to be carefree and happy going forward.

"They are moving to a different estate in the South. The ruling family has several estates all over the world. Sera offered the northern estate because it has a similar climate to what you would be used to. Just wait till you see the pink snow."

We were joined by Evan and his new mate Ali. "Pink snow?" Ali questioned. "Does it look like cotton candy?"

"More like rose quartz." Nikolas grinned as he described Fabeldyrverden to Evan and Ali. While he regaled them with stories of our time in the other world, I let my mind wander. Perhaps Aisling is correct, she just needs to master her dragon form. Something I need to do too.

Since returning to this realm, Nikolas and I hadn't even tried to merge our powers. Aisling told me Lucian transformed in front of her already and I have yet to see Nikolas as a dragon. *Whenever you are ready, just say the word.* Nikolas whispered into my head. *When we finish talking to Evan and Ali.* I responded back.

"So, you plan to live there when this war ends?" Ali asked. "Man, I would love to see another world."

"Maybe we can find a way to reopen the permanent portals so we can travel between the worlds easily like they used to." I suggested, eyeing Nikolas to gage his reaction.

He seemed open to the idea, especially when he stated, "We'll need to talk to my mother about it. She was part of a coven that helped close them."

"For fucking real?" Ali blurted.

"Yes." Nikolas detailed the events his mother had told him about as a young boy. Although she was redirected by the Fates to find his father on a field of battle, she was one of the original casters of the spell used to close the portals.

There once were designated areas around the globe that remained open to visitors. The portals were under the control of whomever held dominion of the land being traveled to. Much like the modern world with the use of passports and travel visas, you had to receive permission to enter different realms.

259

"What if the permanent portals can't be reopened?" Evan asked. "Would you be able to take people through like you brought Lucian here?"

"I am sure we could." Nikolas answered. "Plus, Lucian and Aisling should be able to once they..." Nikolas stopped short, realizing his blunder.

Evan's hands turned to fists and a vein popped out across his forehead. Ali leaned in closer, massaging his shoulder. He quickly slapped on a grin, but we had both seen his fury at the mention of his sister and her mate.

"I am sure," Nikolas coughed nervously, "we can figure out a way to bring the two of you to Fabeldyrverden so you can see its majesty all for yourselves."

The pall of their possible deaths hung over everyone but probably Evan more so than anyone else. He and Aisling were not just siblings but best friends. I have wondered a few times since learning of Aisling's fate whether Evan would succumb to his darker side if he lost her.

If he had not met Ali and mated, I think he would return to his old ravager ways. The tales of his exploits as an Elite Guard were astounding and occasionally horrifying. At one time Evan had some real anger management issues that the Council used to their benefit.

Ali continued soothing, with slow caresses to his arm. Clearly, she knew what he was capable of as well. She must have felt his tension build up and was using their bond to help calm him. Finally, his strain and agitation seemed to leave him, and we were able to return to normal conversation for a while.

We talked about less stressful topics for almost an hour. Arianna appeared across the field from us and Nikolas shifted, intending to greet her. I placed a hand on his arm, keeping him by my side. "Leave her be for now. She is going to meet with Aisling and Lucian to discuss the ceremony." Nikolas settled back into his seat with a satisfied sigh.

"So, this ceremony will allow my sister to become a dragon, right?" At our nods he continued, "How else will it change her? Will she still be my sister or something different?"

"She will still be Aisling." I assured him. "Her personality won't change. She'll still be a hybrid like you. She'll just gain a few powers."

"Not sure that's a good thing." Evan grumbled. "If she has more powers, her already overinflated ego will just be worse." Ali poked him in his ribs, but she was smiling too. "You know she tells everyone she's the best fighter of our family, right?"

"That's because she is." Ali needled him a little. "Remember, I've seen you both fight. She definitely has more skills than you."

"Oh, really?" Evan teased, turning his head, his eyes bore into Ali's. "You think my sister has more skills than me."

Nikolas and I looked at each other as we both realized the two hybrids were no longer talking about fighting skills if the fiery looks, they were sending each other was any indication. As if they suddenly realized they had an audience, the two jumped up and hastily excused themselves. Nikolas and I watched them rush to their house with bemused expressions on our faces.

Turning to my mate, I asked, "Are we like that?"

"Most definitely." He growled low in his throat, sending shivers down my spine. "Up for a little swim?"

He asked, a vision of me lying naked beneath him beside the pool of water in the forest broke into my mind. The shivers melted as heat stabbed through my nether region causing me to wiggle in my chair. The tension between us snapped like a rubber band. Different realms, Ali and Evan, even Lucian and Aisling, completely forgotten. In half a second, I was airborne over his shoulder.

Once we entered the trees and he found the trail that led to our favorite place on this island, his hands began roaming over my backside. He sprinted through the trees, and we arrived at the water within seconds. Nikolas placed my feet on the ground and reached for my shirt. We quickly wrenched our clothing off, falling to the ground in each other's arms. We didn't surface for air until the moon rose, tangled in each other, no realm between us.

Chapter Forty

Arianna

My solitude had been interrupted by Aisling and Cassandra. I didn't begrudge their intrusion, but I still craved a few more minutes before diving back into battle preparations.

It was gratifying that Aisling asked me to perform the ceremony herself. She really didn't have many options, but I appreciated her asking rather than me dictating. I worried she would be uncomfortable with me leading what is a rather sexual experience.

Once Aisling and Lucian told me where they wanted to complete the ceremony, I would need a full day to prepare it. I rose from my place on the sandy beach and brushed myself off. It was time to get back to work.

The two of them were waiting for me in my kitchen when I arrived back at my house. Annie and Matthew kept them company. Judging by the looks on their faces, my two vampires were prattling on about something rather unexciting.

I loved the two of them but sometimes they could blather on about very uninteresting topics. Once, I got sucked into a three-hour dissertation on the properties of different types of wood. I guess I should be thankful that with all the different woods out there, the lecture only lasted three hours, though by the end, I could've built a coffin from sheer boredom.

"I'll take it from here." I announced as I walked through the door. "Thank you for keeping my guests amused while they waited for me." Annie and Matthew could hear the dismissal in my voice and immediately rose to leave.

The pair I needed to speak to smiled at their retreating backs before slumping into their chairs. "Your coven is quite, uh, interesting." Aisling seemed to be searching for the correct word before settling on interesting.

"Oh." With a smirk, I took the seat Annie had vacated across from Aisling and Lucian. "I suppose they can be. I am also quite certain that they probably bored you to tears with random information about something you have no interest in."

Aisling grinned at me while Lucian looked a mildly abashed. "They did. I had no idea that a group of porcupines has a specific name. It's a prickle. Who knew?

Apparently, Annie and Mathew knew that, plus many more facts about porcupines." Aisling's knee hadn't stopped jittering since I sat down. Her words tumbled out like stones down a hill. Lucian placed his hand over hers, quieting her with his touch.

Their good humor faded, and I noticed Lucian's grip tightening on Aisling's hand. The burden of the prophecy had turned her into a chatterbox and him silent. No longer abrupt and succinct, she now seemed almost to be manic. Lucian, who was usually more congenial, had withdrawn into a shell. Gods, we need a solution that will save them.

"We must plan your ceremony." I began now that Aisling had relaxed into Lucian's side. "I need to know where you plan to complete it."

As one they looked at each other than back at me and stated, "The pool."

"What pool?" I asked, we didn't have a swimming pool on the island.

"Cassandra and Nikolas showed us a pool of water that has a small waterfall that feeds it. It's in the forest about two miles from here." Lucian answered, a secretive smile hovered over his mouth.

I vaguely remember a pool of that description being on the island when I first scouted it a few centuries ago. It should be quite perfect for their ceremony. Beautiful and secluded, with springy moss surrounding it. Yes, it should work.

"Just so I am certain, I will need you to show it to me."

"It might be a good idea to wait a bit." Aisling giggled with a slightly hysterical glint in her eyes. Lucian once again squeezed her hands, calming her. "I just saw Cassandra being carried off into the trees by Nikolas a few minutes ago. Pretty sure they were heading in that direction."

"Oh, well, then probably not a good time to interrupt them." I glanced out of the window as if I expected to still be able to see my son dragging his mate off for a little love tryst. "How is the plumbing in your house?" I asked receiving quizzical looks from them. "You will need to bathe in alsklingberry oil before the ceremony." I explained.

"That may be a problem then." Aisling replied. "We only have one working shower, no bathtubs."

"You will have to prepare here then." I advised them. "The ceremony will need to begin tomorrow at two in the morning. Davina has done the calculations to ensure alignment is correct. How long will it take to walk to the pool from here?"

"If we hurry, we can get there in a minute or two." Lucian replied.

263

"But how long at a normal pace?" I asked.

They looked at each other for a few seconds, then Lucian answered. "I'd say ten maybe fifteen minutes."

"When my son and Cassandra reemerge, we will need to walk it out. The timing needs to be precise."

"Why can we not just run there?" Lucian asked, bringing a small smile to Aisling's lips.

"The oil must remain damp on your bodies. Moving too quickly could cause it to dry." I responded. "Tomorrow night you will bathe in the oiled water for an hour"

"So, we're supposed to just lie around in some kind of oily water for an hour?" Aisling bit out, her nose wrinkled.

"What you do in that hour is completely up to you. You just need to keep your body submerged in the alsklingberry oil for an hour." Based on the pleasurable looks that passed between them, I believe they had just silently communicated with each other exactly what they would do to pass the time.

I snapped my fingers, bringing their attention back to my instructions. "At the end of the hour, wrap yourselves in a couple of sheets and walk to the pool. I will be waiting there for you. I will complete my part, then once I depart you will complete your part."

I handed a piece of paper to each of them. "You must memorize these lines for the ritual." They each took their respective papers and read them.

"When Cassandra and Nikolas return, let me know and we will pace out the distance to the pool. After you have shown it to me, I will need to be left alone so I can prepare the area." I shooed them out of the house with instructions to come back here once my son and his mate had returned.

After they left, I checked my supplies. Jace and Cat had picked up everything I needed on the supply run. This ceremony had to be perfect. I counted the vials of oil again. Three, still three. Good. I don't know if combining their powers would help them defeat the fae, but I wanted every arsenal at their disposal available.

Chapter Forty-One

Aisling

"It's time." My ominous voice filled the room. "The ceremony looms."

Lucian's withering look was enough to stop my nervous joking. But, in all seriousness, it is time to complete the ceremony.

We'd been ordered to meet Arianna at her house at midnight. Now, here we stood in her kitchen, my pulse pounding like a jackhammer. Lucian's grip on my hand like a steel trap. His tension seeping through our bond, snaking down my spine to pool in my stomach.

Arianna pulls a small red vial from her pocket, holding it like a sacred relic. The alsklingberry oil, a tiny titter creeps up my throat. Lucian's grip tightens, warning me to be serious.

"The walk from tub to pool takes exactly thirteen minutes, no faster or the oil will dry. The tub is filled and bespelled to stay at the correct temperature. Pour the entire bottle into the water then get in. Be sure to make sure you keep your body under the oiled water for the entire hour. At the end of the hour, come straight to the pool to complete the ceremony. Any questions?"

Neither one of us had any questions. Arianna then asked, "Have you memorized the lines I gave you?"

We both nodded, our throats tight, making it difficult to speak. Gods, I hope I don't freeze up when I need to speak during the ritual. Lucian's grip on my hand tightened for a second, calming me. Arianna pushed us towards the stairs. "I will see you in the forest. Don't be late." She left with a smile on her face.

We climbed the steps and entered the candlelit bathroom. Someone, likely Arianna, had decorated the room. Flower petals of all types were strewn across the floor. Incense very similar to Lucian's scent had been lit. Ten candles cast a warm glow around the room. Warm mist rose from the bespelled bathtub.

With shaking hands, Lucian held the bottle of oil over the water. I reached my hand out to help steady him. The two of us upended the oil into the steaming water.

A scent I couldn't quite place enveloped us. It had a hint of juniper and oranges, but different. The heady scent pulled at my body, filling me with an arousal so powerful that when Lucian's hand brushed my arm, I whirled toward him, lips crashing against his before I could think.

His hands gripped my simple dress, shredding it as he ripped it from my body. Then he stripped off his own clothing, letting it fall to the petal strewn floor in pieces. His practical side surfaced long enough to check the time on the clock. His rough hands yanked my naked form to his chest. Then he swept me off my feet and stepped into the scented hot water.

Our bodies sunk into the delicious wetness. My skin tingled and heated as the water lapped over my breasts. Lucian's eyes caught on my erect nipples and his hand snaked through the water to cup my breast in it.

I don't know what was in this oil, but I loved what it did to my body. When he rubbed his calloused palm across my hardened nipple I shuddered in climax. Every nerve ending was oversensitive, every movement Lucian made brought my body to fruition. When I reached out to skim down his abdomen and grasp his cock in my hand, his shaft bounded in release. Gods, this was amazing.

Lucian brought his mouth up to capture my lips in his. Our tongues dueled with each other sending more electrifying spasms through our bodies. Lucian pulled me lower into the water, making sure to keep both of us submerged. I cried out when his hard shaft penetrated my already pulsating center. "Oh, Gods, Lucian!" I screamed to the ceiling.

His arms wrapped around me, holding me close as he pounded harder and faster into me. A low growl built in the back of his throat. I could feel him stiffening in readiness for release. My legs clung to his hips, prodding him deeper with each thrust. The orgasm, when it ripped through my body, sent me to new heights of pleasure.

Lucian drove deep, burying himself inside me ripping a moan from me. A loud bellow of ecstasy roared from him while my body shuddered and convulsed beneath him. I stared, mesmerized at his changing skin as dragon scales rippled up and down his chest and back.

We held each other as the rippling water settled around us. Holy shit. I thought to myself. That was absolutely insane. *I agree.* Lucian's murmur in my head was accompanied by a small chuckle. We moved as one, keeping our bodies below the surface of the water. Lucian lay back on the rear of the bathtub, keeping me between his legs. I rested my back on his chest.

"What in the world just happened?" I finally asked mild confusion with a lot of happiness in my voice.

"I do not know." Lucian responded. "I never asked anyone about the ceremony. I always felt it was a private moment that should not be shared." His arms encased me on either side, keeping me close.

"Cassandra said it would be mind-blowing but Gods, she totally undersold it." I snuggled into his chest, sending shooting pulses of desire through my body again. Could I really be ready for more already? Lucian must be feeling it too as his rod was stabbing me in the back.

Round two was just as quick and intense as our first bout of lovemaking except that it took longer to recover from. Spent I lay in my mate's arms, gripping his forearms to keep my head from slipping under the water. I felt my head begin to nod with sleepiness causing me to jerk in Lucian's arms.

The sudden movement shot bolts of pleasure through me. Our third round left us both panting and gasping for air. Partly because of the orgasm but also because we lost our leverage and both of us ended up underwater completely.

Laughing, we clung to each other. For the first time since entering this oiled water I didn't feel an immediate reaction to touching him. I'm not saying I no longer lusted after my mate simply that our third time must have satiated me enough that I could cuddle into his chest without needing to have sex again.

We lounged back in the tub, Lucian against the back of the tub with me between his legs again. "Aisling?" Lucian began with a questioning tone. Whatever he was about to ask or say must be important. I could feel his heart speed up and he had locked his mind up tight. Rather than rushing him, I simply murmured hmm.

Almost five minutes passed before I felt him move a little behind me. "Aisling." His voice was more confident this time.

I craned my neck so I could look him in the eyes. He looked so serious that I began to get nervous. Our eyes locked, Lucian leaned in placing the sweetest most loving kiss on my swollen lips. My heart melted when he turned me fully to face him, cupping my head with his hand.

"I love you." Lucian whispered. A tear ran down my lips the second I heard his words. "You have my heart forever. I will do everything I can to be with you forever."

Full tears were streaming down my cheeks now. Gods thank you for sending this man as my mate. "I love you too." My voice squeaked.

I guess the oil doesn't just bring out the horny side of a relationship. Lucian's laughter echoed through the room as he picked up that thought. I loved to hear this man laugh. From the stories he had shared with me, I don't think he had enough laughter in his life before meeting me.

"And I will do everything I can to bring more joy to your life." I promised him.

"It's time." Lucian announced as he checked the clock on the wall.

We climbed from the tub and wrapped the cool sheets loosely around our bodies. When the night air hit my damp body a slight chill caused goose bumps to erupt all over my skin. We walked hand in hand to the pool in the forest and found Arianna waiting for us. Clothed in a long fuchsia colored ceremonial robe, her black hair tied back in a long braid, she watched us walk across the clearing.

She stood in front of an altar that held ten candles. One of each color of the dragons lined the back of the altar. Two red ones in front on the side Lucian stood and one black and one silver candle on my side. A small pewter bowl with an athame lying beside it sat in the middle.

The mossy ground was covered with more flower petals and large white candles with three wicks were placed around the clearing beside the pool of water. Twinkling multi-hued lights flickered in the trees around us and the pool of water had a luminescence to it that had not been there before.

Arianna motioned for us to move closer to the altar. We stood side by side his left hand gripped tightly in my right one. Arianna moved around us in a clockwise direction chanting low in a language I didn't recognize. After her third time around us, she came to a halt and turned her back to us, facing the altar.

Hands raised in the air, Arianna called out. "Aine hear my plea and place your blessings of love upon these two who stand before you. Danu hear my plea and place your blessings of fruitfulness upon these two who stand before you. Ostara hear my plea and place your blessings of fertility upon these two who stand before you. Cernunnos hear my plea and place your blessings of life upon these two who stand before you."

The wind picked up and swirled around us, pulling the flower petals from the ground. We stood in a whirlwind of beautifully scented petals. A feeling of warmth and acceptance encased me. The wind slowly died down, and the flower petals fluttered back to the moss-covered ground. Arianna turned to face us, holding the athame in her hand.

"Step forward." She ordered and we both took two steps closer to the altar. "Give me your hands. We stretched our clasped hands out and lay them in her palm. With a quick jab of the athame she pierced each of our palms then cut long ways causing blood to well. Quickly she set the athame down and grabbed the pewter bowl to hold beneath our hands capturing the blood as it dripped from the cuts.

She moved to the other side of the altar and placed the bowl in the center again. Then she motioned for us to step closer to the altar. She pulled a small bottle from a pocket in her cloak. When she pulled the stopper, I smelled the same scent from it that I had come from our bottle.

The alsklingberry oil's potency was already giving me chills. She dropped two small drops of the oil into the pewter bowl with our blood. She once again spoke in a language I did not know. The blood and the oil swirled around the bowl together then came to a stop.

"Drink." She held the bowl to Lucian first.

He took a long swallow then passed it back to Arianna. She then held the bowl out to me, and I finished what was left in the bowl. Euphoria spread through my body at the taste of our blood and the oil combined. My knees almost buckled from the feeling and if it weren't for Lucian I probably would have hit the ground. We clung to each other while Arianna continued the ceremony.

"Time turns, life becomes, death repelled, future held. Combine into one. Bring them together, a dragon and his mate, united forever." The candles representing Lucian and I erupted into tall flames at least five feet in the air. "Now, Lucian, recite your oath." Arianna commanded.

His deep velvety voice responded sure and strong, "I, Lucian Rowan Griffin, pledge my life and submit my will to be yours forever, abstaining from all others. I promise to follow where you lead in life and death. Your soul shall be entwined with mine for all time."

The moment Lucian finished speaking, my world tilted on its axis causing a weight to lift from my body. The candle flames froze mid-flicker, even as the wind howled around us. Lucian's skin rippled with metallic red and orange scales. His eyes swirled their marvelous three toned color, then settled into a deep crimson. I stared, mesmerized by the beauty of my mate.

A full minute passed before I dragged my gaze back to Arianna. At her nod, I recited my own oath, my voice ringing loud and clear. "I, Aisling Sinead O'Brien, pledge my life and submit my will to be yours forever, abstaining from all others. I promise to follow where you lead in life and death. Your soul shall be entwined with mine for all time."

The wind slowed, cocooning the two of us in warmth, the tall flames flickering to life again. My skin shimmered where it met his. Small red scales flared across my skin, bleeding into deep bluish-purple scales. Lucian's triumphant smile sent my heart fluttering.

Arianna pulled two small objects from the pewter bowl. I recognized them as two of the items we had recovered from Cillian's hidden cabin. They were relics from the dragon world used in ceremonies to help a dragon pair become pregnant. I wanted to have Lucian's child so badly, but I wasn't sure now was the right time.

We were going to war soon and who knew if we would survive. I pushed that thought out of my head, deciding again to live each day as if I had forever with my mate. Lucian raised my hand to his mouth, placing a loving kiss on the back of it then turning it over to kiss the palm.

Arianna stood between us and whisked the sheets away from our bodies. The oil, surprisingly, was still wet on our skin. We stood, naked, in the cool night air. Arianna circled us three times clockwise again then stopped in between us. She held the small dragon relics in each hand.

"Goddesses and Gods bless these two. Lucian and Aisling may the goddesses and gods shine upon you in all their glory." A bright light shone from the dark night sky. Arianna reached between us and placed the relics on our abdomens just below the navel. Much to my shock, it disappeared into my body, as did Lucian's.

I whipped my head up to ask Arianna only to find she had disappeared too. It was now just Lucian and I in the clearing. The candles flickered in the light breeze casting interesting patterns across Lucian's taut abdomen. I lifted my eyes to meet his smoldering ones, and my mind came undone. Gods this man was beautiful.

"Handsome." Lucian corrected, laughing.

"Handsome." I agreed. "Also delicious, scrumptious and gorgeous."

I stepped closer to my mate and ran my hands across his chest, then down his abdomen. My hand went lower still to clutch his already erect member eliciting a deep moan from him. I stroked his long shaft from base to tip in a slow smooth motion. His swirling eyes solidified into the deep crimson that told me he was thoroughly aroused.

"Lie down." I commanded. I followed him to the ground, keeping a firm grip on his throbbing cock.

Lying on his back, he reached for me, but I swatted his hands away with a playful grin. One eyebrow raised, he watched my hands continue their ministrations of his shaft. I stroked and squeezed until a small bead of precum formed on the tip. Running my finger through the pearlescent liquid, I rubbed it down the length of him.

His hips jerked when I lowered my mouth to take in his engorged cock. I licked and sucked from base to tip, while massaging his balls with one hand. He bucked and pulsed with each stroke of my tongue.

"Gods, Aisling." He roared up at the black night sky.

I knew he was close to finishing. I could feel him tightening more with each caress from my fingers. Just when I believed he would cum I felt myself being propelled through the air. I landed on my back with Lucian coming down on top of me.

Prodding my legs open with one knee, his shaft slammed into me. Within minutes, my body tensed, clenching tightly around him, sending us both to our finish. His hot seed filled me, leaving a contented warmth all over. He collapsed on top of me, panting, our gasps mingling in the cool night air.

We lay there in a pile of sweat-soaked body parts for several minutes while we caught our breaths. "That was amazing." Lucian whispered in my ear.

The awe in his voice had me looking at him closer. He was acting as if no one had ever done that before. He lowered his eyes from mine and, for the first time in over a week, his mind slammed shut to me.

"Don't hide from me." With two fingers under his chin, I tilted his face to mine. "There's no shame in it if you haven't." I wonder if that is why every time,

271

we've had sex it's always been face to face. Him on top or me on top but no other positions.

"Disappointed?" Lucian responded to my internal monologue.

"Gods, no." I assured him. "Have I complained once?" He still didn't look entirely convinced. "I figured in all your years of life you would have tried other things than just typical sex."

"It is not kingly." He mumbled, his voice low, his eyes shrouded.

"I'm sorry, what?" I had to hold back the laugh that was building. This was not funny but so incredulous to me that I couldn't help myself.

"My father instilled decorum and propriety in me from a young age. It was not considered king like to perform, well, you know, to do what you just did."

"Okay, so let me see if I have this right. You have lots of experience when it comes to the type of sex we have had but that's it?" His shoulders slumped and he nodded his head dejectedly. My whoop of happiness made him look at me like I was crazy. "That is perfect."

"Why is it perfect?" He asked suspiciously.

"Are you willing to be more adventurous, you know now that you're not a king anymore?" I grinned seductively and waggled my eyebrows a little. A small smile began to form on his face, and he asked me what I had in mind. "Well, I love to do all kinds of things, like what I did tonight. I'd love to teach you." His smile broadened into a wide grin. "For example, you liked it when I licked your cock."

"Correction," he interrupted, "I loved it when you had my cock in your mouth."

"Oh, believe me, I could tell." I pulled his mouth down to mine. "Just imagine how much I would enjoy the same treatment."

His eyes widened in surprise as I used my tongue to pry open his lips. We kissed for several minutes then Lucian pushed me onto my back. He ran his tongue along my jaw line then down my neck. My nipples hardened in anticipation of his next move.

He massaged my breasts scraping his tongue and teeth across each nipple. Sparks of desire shot through my body. He lathed his way down my abdomen to the top of my moistening curls. He hesitated, looking up at me. I gave him an encouraging smile.

His hand lowered to probe my clitoris with a finger. He always knew exactly where to hit. I shuddered at every tweak from his finger. Yet, still he paused, his mouth just inches from where I wanted it.

I imagined what I wanted him to do to me. Following my mind's eye, he brought his mouth to my nether lips. The anticipation was driving me mad, and I think he knew it because he carefully placed a chaste kiss on my labia then looked at me with a sheepish grin.

"Lucian, please." I begged.

Using two fingers he spread me wide to his view; his breath blew softly across my clit. I moaned quietly then let out a cry of pleasure when his tongue swept along my sensitive nub. His beard tickled the insides of my legs. I reached down, twining my fingers in his long locks. Using my grip, I guided his mouth to exactly where I wanted it.

Once again, I pictured what I wanted from him and he readily obliged. One hand kept me bared to his mouth while the other probed my core with his fingers. His tongue was like a magician causing sparkles to erupt all through my body. I lifted my hips in tune with each thrust of his tongue and fingers.

My climax was building; Lucian seemed to sense exactly what I needed as he increased the tempo of his thrusts. My body began to clench around his fingers when he replaced them with his tongue sending me over the edge. Heat burst through my body pulling a groan from deep within me. Lucian held me close with a satisfied smirk as I lay in his arms panting.

My breathing finally began to slow, and my heart rate returned to normal. "Gods, Luc." I sighed into the cool night air.

"I assume that was acceptable." His breath tickled the hair behind my ear, self-satisfaction ringing in his tone.

I turned in his arms, placing my head over his heart. "Darling, that was more than acceptable. You're a quick study." I smiled content just to be held by this man.

"I think I'm going to love not being king, so long as you keep teaching me all the new things I've missed out on." Lucian grinned, a ravenous gleam in his eye.

We spent the rest of the night frolicking in and out of the water. I taught Lucian many new things, not all of them sexual. For tonight we would pretend that the world wasn't closing in on us. Tomorrow we will begin preparing for war.

Hopefully we can find a way to beat the fae and survive. But for tonight, I was content to fall asleep in the arms of the man I loved who also loved me.

Chapter Forty-Two

Arianna

I have found myself pulled to this side of the island almost daily. I knew I was neglecting my responsibilities but after more than a thousand years I was tired. Years of worrying about everyone else and never giving much care for myself.

Most days I found Manannan Mac Lir there as well. Our talks did nothing for our cause, but they soothed me. Helped me come to terms with the end of my existence in this realm.

Today we discussed Sidhes' beauty, and I could not wait to go there. I had to complete my purpose in this realm, ending Fraxinus. Once that was done, I would get to rest. Manannan Mac Lir also turned out to be quite adept in more carnal exploits.

After so many years, I delighted in the feeling of a man's hands and mouth on my body. Sex with my mate had lacked the passion I felt in the sea god's arms. I had never once considered finding pleasure with any other man. I could not risk Fraxinus knowing. My next meeting with him would be to end his life so my faithlessness would be the least of my worries.

The sea god bid me farewell, returning to Sidhes. My mind back on my duties, I retraced my path back to my house. Cassandra and Nikolas wanted me to see her dragon form. After several days of hard work, yesterday, Cassandra had managed to complete the change.

Nikolas had also partially channeled Cassandra's power of pain. Diana said it felt like she was being stabbed in the arm. However, the pain was not as severe as what Cassandra could inflict. It was a good start and as they worked together, I expected he would improve.

Lucian and Aisling had been working tirelessly since the ceremony five days ago. I saw them exit her house every morning before dawn broke and they often did not return until well after dark. If what I know of shifters is true, I expect Aisling may have a little more difficulty. Shifters tended to have a specific type of animal

275

they were most comfortable with. Being a large cat shifter, Aisling will need to convince her mind that a dragon's form is better.

The cool morning grass was covered with sparkling dew as I rounded the corner of my house to find Cassandra sitting on my front steps. Her nervous energy seemed to be vibrating the entire front porch. Her already pale skin glowed like moonlight. Her left foot jiggled on the bottom step. The instant she saw me, she jumped up, rushing to meet me.

"Arianna, I need to speak to you before Nikolas comes down from his shower." She grabbed my arm, propelling me away from the house.

I glanced at her out of the side of my eyes. Her eyes darted every which way, and she tugged at a strand of hair. She guided me down a path that led to a small clearing that a few of the wolf shifters had turned into an area to relax and play games.

There was some kind of game set up with boards that had a hole in each one. The people who played this game tossed some kind of bean or corn filled bag at the holes. I really didn't understand the excitement behind it but since it helped those who played it unwind, I saw no reason to judge.

Cassandra flopped into one of the canvas chairs that were placed around the clearing. She yanked me down beside her to sit in another chair. "Is something wrong?" Her jittery movements were beginning to ruffle my post lovemaking sedateness.

"N-not really." Cassandra stuttered. A branch snapped behind us. She jumped so hard the chair legs buckled. A small ermine poked its head out of the brush then scurried off when it laid eyes on us. "Actually, something might be wrong. I mean, Gods, I don't know."

"Slow down and take a breath." I patted her shaking hand trying to soothe her. "Has something bad happened?" I asked after she had stopped fidgeting and darting glances around the clearing. She looked as if she expected to be attacked at any moment.

"No, nothing bad." She inhaled deeply and closed her eyes. Her lips moved in a quiet chant; she must be centering herself.

I relaxed back in my chair and waited for her to speak. The ermine had snuck back out of the brush and sat watching the two of us with curious eyes. After a few minutes it darted back into the brush leaving us alone.

"I think, no I know I'm pregnant." Cassandra gulped the air that had caught in her throat. She looked at me with both elation and fear in her eyes. "What am I going to do?"

This was the greatest news I could have heard from my son's mate. She was rightfully nervous considering all that was going on right now. "Have you told Nikolas yet?"

"No, not yet." She bit her upper lip and could not meet my eyes. "It's still early; I'm at most three or four weeks along. But I have felt the awareness nudging at me."

"Cassandra, your body knows. That awareness you feel is your magic recognizing new life." My reassurances fell on deaf ears. If things hadn't been so hectic recently, Cassandra would have probably known within one to two days that she was pregnant.

"This is wonderful news." I exclaimed. "So, what has you so worried?"

"We are training to go to war." She yelled.

"Oh." Gods, no one had taught her anything. "Cassandra dear, I feel as if you have led a very sheltered life. Has no one ever explained how things work for your different species?"

"Obviously not if I am freaking out and you are looking at me like I'm crazy." She glared at me, defiance burning in her eyes. "Clearly you have not been paying attention to any of the stories I have told of my life." Venom laced her voice, and she shot to her feet.

I placed a calming hand on her arm. "Forgive me." I pulled her back to the chair beside me. "I have been listening. I just did not expect that they would leave you woefully ignorant about something as important as this."

She resumed sitting, her posture held rigid. "I don't think they ever expected me to find my mate." She sniffled, wiping her hand across her leaking eyes. "I didn't have a mother to tell me what to expect."

My heart went out to this poor girl. She had not had the easiest life. Used by the Council to inflict pain on people as either punishment or for interrogation, or both. Nikolas had told me about her mother. Gods, if I didn't already hate the Council for other reasons, I would surely hate it just knowing how they had treated this girl.

"Cassandra, if you would allow me, I will tell you what you need to know." I kept my voice low, hoping to ease her anxiety.

The tension released from her shoulders and she slumped into the chair. Her cheeks flamed with color and she released the breath she had been holding. Turning her hope filled eyes my way, "Thank you," she whispered.

"You are part vampire and part witch. Also, you carry a dragon's child. As a hybrid you can conceive a child where a vampire cannot. Your child is protected in so many ways at this time that there are few things that could bring actual harm to it. If you were to die, that would obviously be a problem but not many other things will."

"But what if I get hit really hard in the stomach or stabbed." Cassandra cried, her breaths coming fast again. She scanned the trail as if looking for danger to come barreling around the corner.

"Your baby will be protected." I reached my hand out, gripping her twisting fingers tightly. "A witch's body forms a magical shield around the womb when it senses the awareness as you described it. Also, your vampire side has already made your body impervious to so many forms of harm that it would be almost impossible to harm the child. Finally, a dragon fetus will develop a hard casing around its body by the tenth week. The only issue you will have is once you have reached the tenth week, and I promise you your body will let you know; you will not be able to change forms again until you give birth."

"So, as long I manage to survive this battle, my child will be safe inside my body?" She asked, the fear slowly leeching from her eyes.

"Yes. Survive the fight and your child does too." I'd never hold this child. Another loss to lie at Fraxinus' feet. Devastation crept into my voice evoking an odd look from Cassandra. "It is nothing dear, don't worry." I reassured her with a wave of my hand.

"I am sure it is not nothing." She responded. "But I have also learned that sometimes a person has a right to their secrets." I gave her a grateful smile, squeezing her trembling hand.

I could see her mind was still racing with all the possibilities of a child. As well as all the problems a child presented. Her excitement seemed to be a mixture of happiness and fear. As my information settled in her mind, I noticed a lightening to her body as if I had lifted a great weight from her shoulders.

278

Sensing she was no longer frantic over her pregnancy, I suggested, "Now, how about you show me the dragon who will protect my grandchild." I stood up and she followed.

We walked back along the path to our house and found Nikolas standing on the front porch. His posture was tense, until he saw us walking across the yard. Pleasure erupted across his face, when his eyes landed on our linked arms. Gods, if only I could have a little more time with my son.

Nikolas bounded down the steps and swept his mate up in his arms as if he hadn't seen her in months instead of just a few short minutes. I smiled at their open display of affection with each other. He held her away from him, giving her a questioning look. She shook her head and mouthed later at him.

A small stab of jealousy hit me, and I quickly pushed it down. The Fates had chosen my path, but I would go to my next life content with the knowledge that my son would have a brighter, happier future than his past had been. I let their happiness fill me, warm and inviting. It would have to be enough.

"Mother, are you ready?" He asked, nearly dancing with excitement. I nodded and he grabbed my hand to pull me to stand beside him. He gripped our hands as he led us along a small path that opened into a large clearing. Aisling and Lucian stood in the middle of the field and waved a greeting as we entered.

"Are you doing it now?" Aisling hollered out. She and Lucian walked over to join us. Cassandra gave a sharp nod of her head; she shifted from foot to foot. Determination blazed from her eyes though.

"Thank you for being here for this." Cassandra embraced Aisling in a warm hug; then faced me. "I am so glad we were able to talk this morning."

Nikolas pulled her away from us to the center of the field. They stared into each other's eyes for several long minutes. Whatever silent communication they had put the steel back into Cassandra's back and her anxiety fled. With one last rather tempestuous kiss to her mate she shooed him off the field.

Her lips moved in a quiet chant while she disrobed, her movements now purposeful. My eyes widened as her body became enshrouded in purple and green smoky haze. When the smoke dissipated, a dazzlingly radiant dragon stood there, head held high. Her amethyst and emerald scales twinkled in the bright sun. Her deep walnut colored underbelly matched the brown in Nikolas' eyes.

A blood red fringe runs along her neck and down her back converging into a red spike at the end of her tail. She must be a little over twenty feet in height. Nikolas' dragon form is close to thirty feet, but as a human he is also a mammoth of a man. Cassandra is quite tall, especially for a woman, but few dragons reach the size of the Quercus line.

We all walk around her form, admiring the beauty of her scales. Amethyst and emerald are the dominant colors, but we can see lighter shades of greens and purple mixed in. The ground trembled as her tail flexed. We all took a step back, all but Nikolas I should amend. His grin told me he knew she planned to do that.

I returned to stand in front of her, and she lowered her head to my height. Blazing eyes of violet with crimson catlike slits meet mine. With a small chuff at me she unfurls her wings to their full width. I step back clapping; a wide grin stretches my face. She is astonishing.

Nikolas comes to stand beside me, his pride puffing his chest out. Love shines from his eyes as he gazes in wonder at his mate in her dragon form. She lowers her chin into his outstretched palm. I glance at Lucian and Aisling and give them a knowing look. It's time for us to leave.

Chapter Forty-Three

Cassandra

Nikolas stands before me, palm outstretched. I rest my scaled chin in his hand. *Perfection.* His voice sends shivers through my body. A pleased rumble vibrates through me eliciting a smirk from my mate.

I tell him to change through our mind link. I want to test my wings. Nikolas grins, then walks several feet away from me. He takes his clothes off and piles them on the ground beside mine.

His eyes close, and his body is encased in the smoky green and purple haze, which clears within seconds. The dragon beside me, a towering blend of amethyst and emerald, looms ten feet above my height. His fringe along his back is dark brown and his tail ends in a point with no spike on it.

"Why don't you have a spike?" My eyes are drawn to the other differences we have.

"The red fringe with a spike is from your vampire blood." He lumbers around the field, pointing out each difference. *"Every dragon has different defense mechanisms built into their forms. Earth dragons, like me, do not have extra tools to fight since I can control the earth and make weapons from it."*

He walks me through the basics of flying; turns out it isn't just flapping my huge wings. After several failed attempts I am finally able to rise from the ground. We ascend about thirty feet into the air, and I think I've mastered it. Oh, how wrong I was.

A strong gust of wind slammed into me like a wall of brick. My wings buckled and the ground rushed at me. I barely landed on my feet, but the force of impact jarred my teeth, and I bit down hard. A blast of energy lashed out, ripping a nearby tree from the soil. Damnit!

Nikolas touches down beside me, much more graceful than my landing. After inspecting the fallen tree, he lets out a low huff. He plucks the tree from the ground and shoves it back into the gaping hole. Energy gathers around me, and I feel a small drain on my own reserves. Within moments, the hole around the tree is sealed as if I never even touched it.

"Thank you." I smile as Nikolas spends several minutes checking me for injuries.

"So, other than being a lumberjack, how do you feel about flying?" His mammoth body shoots into the sky just before my tail could connect with his hind leg. My laughter cuts off when he does a fancy triple spin in the air then alights beside me again.

Wow, that was impressive. *"I need more practice but there is something we need to talk about."* His large head nods letting me know he heard me. Back in our human forms and clothes, I pull him to the edge of the field to a few logs that we can lean against while we talk.

My fidgeting starts again. I think he'll be happy but there is also the fact that we are getting ready to fight a war. Maybe it's too soon to think about having a child. Not that we can do much about it now.

"Gods, Cass, whatever it is please just tell me. Your anxiety is starting to worry me." Nikolas pulls me closer to his side while rubbing his hand down my arm. "No matter what you need to tell me just know that I love you and nothing will ever change that."

"I think it is good news, but with the war coming the timing may not be best." I pulled away from his side so I could meet him eye to eye. I needed to see his immediate reaction. "Nik, I'm pregnant."

As I stare at his face, a wide grin spread across his face as he yanks me to him. The passionate kiss that followed had my toes curling. *I guess that means you're happy.* A roar of giddy laughter filled my head as he deepened our kiss. That kiss led to much more intimate actions.

Sometime later, our mutual affection slaked, we lay in each other's embrace. The deep afternoon sun warmed our naked skin. I curled tight against his chest. "How far along are you?" his deep voice reverberated through my cheek.

"Three to four weeks, I think." I explained my lack of knowledge about pregnancy in my different species. "I noticed something different about a month ago but had no idea what it was. Yesterday I overheard Fiona, one of the O'Briens talking to Jasmine about how she knew each time she was pregnant, and it clicked. The sense that something was new and building in my body was a child, our child."

"You're right, the timing is not the best." Nikolas agreed with my earlier worries. "But I've never wanted anything more than to have a child with you."

A small frown puckered my forehead, "Even with our upbringing?" I leaned away from him, placing my hands on his cheeks. "Do you think we'll be good parents?"

"We know what not to do." He punctuated his reassurance with a peck on my nose. "We'll give this child, and any other children we have the best life we can."

His certainty lifted a weight I hadn't realized was bearing me down. As I stared into his eyes, I could almost picture the future he was envisioning. The unknown outcome of a war we hadn't fought still loomed, but our future looked brighter on the other side. A long sigh bled through my teeth, releasing the last ounce of concern I had.

I lay my head back on his chest, snuggling into his warmth. "We can do this." I whispered.

"Cass, you have given me the most amazing news." Nikolas cradled me in his arms; bliss radiated from him.

His face lit up like a bright star. He was as joyful as a witch flying under a full moon. Before I could blink, he crushed me against him, lifting me up and spinning me until the world became a hazy, twisting mess.

"A child,' he breathed, voice rough with reverence. He stopped our swirling, letting my feet return to the grass. His eyes twinkled with unshed tears, "Our child."

Chapter Forty-Four

Aisling

Ali and I were having breakfast when the news destroyed our morning. Lately, I'd been clinging to every moment with my family, especially her. If I did not make it Evan would need someone like Ali, smart, sensible and a weird sense of humor like me. His serious side needed a bit of quirkiness every now and again

Yesterday Cass successfully transformed into her dragon form. She was such an impressive sight to behold. Lucian and I were working hard every day to get me to change but I was having a lot of difficulty. Every time I reached for my dragon, my bones twisted wrong, fur sprouted instead of scales, and there I sat a pissed-off hissing lynx.

"I'd spent my whole life as just a human." Ali explained while sipping her coffee. "And changing that deep belief was next to impossible. Evan told me I needed to connect with my animal self and get her to accept me. Maybe that's what you need to do."

"That's how we all learn to bring out our shifter." I grumbled around the sausage link I was munching on. "I just can't seem to find her."

"Have you asked Lucian to help you find her?" She placed her cup down on the table and reached for some bacon on her plate. "Maybe your dragon is hiding deeper in your mind, and you just keep getting sidetracked by your cat form."

I inhaled more sausage and eggs while I thought about that. She might just have a point. I was so used to being a cat shifter that maybe I was putting up a block in my mind. Lucian might be able to sense my dragon and then be able to guide me to her.

I opened my mouth to thank her for her good advice only to be cut short by a commotion outside. Evan came rushing through the back door, face crumpled with grief. His hands gripped several envelopes as he rushed into Ali's waiting arms. My stomach rolled, I wasn't sure how much more bad news I could handle this year.

A small group of the vampires, shifters and hybrids that had been living at our compound in Oregon arrived by boat this morning. Gerard, one of my father's oldest friends, and his maker gave Evan the bad news. Last night my father had taken his own life. With shaking hands Evan passed me one of the envelopes into my trembling hands, my letter from our father.

My father's scent, leathery with a touch of evergreen, wafted out as I opened the letter. Dread pooled in my belly, I knew what it would say having recently mated myself. If Lucian was to die in our upcoming fight and I survived I know I would not live for long after.

Aisling Sinead, I go to your mother content, knowing you've found your mate. Everything you and your brother have told me about him brings peace to my mind that you will be safe and sound in your future. Evan has also informed me of the future multiple seers have seen. I have no way of knowing with any certainty, but I truly believe the Fates would not have brought a man such as Lucian to you if they meant to take you from this world so soon. Have faith my darling stubborn spirited daughter. You are very resourceful and if anyone can find a way to thwart fate, I believe that person is you. I will see you in the next life many, many centuries from now. Know that I go to be with your mother in the next world and I face my death with a firm belief that she will welcome me with open arms. With all my love to the end of days, your loving Father. PS Don't let Cormac wallow in grief and keep bringing your sarcastic sunshine into the world. Da.

The letter flutters to the floor, tears streaming down my face. The front door slams open, just as my knees give out. Lucian barrels through the door, scooping me into his arms before my ass can hit the floor. He must have felt my heart rupture through our bond.

"What is it?" He asked the room, knowing I was unable to answer at this time.

Ali handed him my father's letter and exited the room with my brother. She would provide the much-needed solace that he needed. As I am sure Lucian will do for me. Lucian clutches me to his side as he reads my father's letter.

"Oh, my darling." are his only words as he sweeps my legs out from under me and carries me up to our room. We lay down on our bed of pillows and blankets. No words are spoken as he holds me allowing me to cry woeful tears wetting his blue shirt.

Why is he wearing a blue shirt? He always wears red or black. And why in the hell am I thinking about this right now when my father is dead. My father's words reverberate throughout my brain. I must believe he's right; the Fates would never have brought Lucian and I together just to tear us apart so quickly. We will find a way through this war together.

Lucian has wrapped me in one of the blankets and is cradling me like a small child. Since he carried me up here, he hasn't spoken a word. He knew empty words couldn't fix this. All I really needed was his presence and he wisely gave me just that.

My crying jag has tapered to hiccups and sniffling, and I am finally ready to talk. "Thank you for coming so fast."

"Of course," his simple response brought a small smile to my face. Just two words, and I knew he would be by my side for anything and everything. It is an awe-inspiring feeling to know that he truly means it.

"My mother died not too long before we came here to meet Arianna" I stumble over my words, the pain of losing my father so soon after my mother clogging my throat with emotion. Lucian silently holds me close, allowing me time to compose myself again. "I've told you some of my past but never talked about my ma and da."

"I knew of your mother's passing from Evan and Ali. I believed you would talk to me about it when you were ready." His hand presses me closer, his fingers twining through my hair.

Gods, how did I get so lucky and unlucky at the same time. Lucian was everything I could ever want or need in a mate. Mind you, sometimes I wanted to strangle the shit out of him but for the most part he was perfect. Well at least perfect for me.

Our stubbornness gave us a rough start. Now that we've gotten to know each other, many of his traits that used to bother me I can see as pluses. Like knowing when I need to be treated like a breakable little girl. I felt like one now and being curled up on his lap with a blanket and his body keeping me warm I truly felt cherished.

"You are more than cherished by me." He whispered into my hair.

A small hiccup escapes me as I stifle my tears. "My ma was only a shifter so we knew she wouldn't be with us forever. We knew da wouldn't last long without her. I guess I just hoped he would be able to overcome the mate bond."

"Ah, Aisling, I wish the same for you." Lucian tilted his head so he could see my face. "Your parents were true mates and that helped them know how to show love and affection for each other and their children."

His regret mixed with my grief, and it dawned on me that his parents must not be true mates. No wonder he could often seem standoffish with people. His parents raised him without love. Gods, how lonely that must have been for him.

"I had Sera" He replied to my unspoken thoughts. "She was light and carefree no matter how much our parents tried to make her not be."

"So, she's who I need to thank for the side of you I actually like?" I nudged his stomach to show him I was joking.

"Yes." He grinned with the devil in his eyes and stated with his most imperious voice. "Who should I reprimand for the little imp in you?"

I pouted as if I was really upset but he could hear the giggling in my mind, so my petulant look was wasted on him. "Gods, I love you." I growled just as he kissed away my pout. A loud knock sounded on the door before our kiss could become too heated

"What?" Barked Lucian, clearly, he was a bit irritated by the interruption. I was too if I was being honest.

Saoirse opened the door a small crack, "Evan needs you two to come to the meeting. Gerard brought more news than just our father's death." She was dry eyed; her knuckles were white as she clutched her tablet like a lifeline. Grief looked different on her, less showy tears, more frantic coding.

"We're coming." I grumbled, not enjoying being interrupted like we were. I also knew it was unlike Evan to summon us if it wasn't important. He was never one to abuse his power as head of the family. With one last lingering kiss, Lucian and I headed downstairs and out to the large campfire we all seemed to like to gather around.

Chapter Forty-Five

Arianna

The commotion died down, leaving an uneasy silence across the island. Everyone returned to their tasks, except me. Gerard introduced himself, his mate and the rest of the group, his eyes never straying from the O'Brien's home.

Gerard exhaled, launching into Ronan's past like he rehearsed it. "Irish born, English by force. His mother was dragged to Southampton as a servant when he was three. I came across him in the early 1600's. His human life of crime landed him on a prison ship with a free trip to the American colonies."

"Is that where you met him?" My curiosity was peaked; I loved people's backstories.

"It is." Gerard leaned back in his chair; a happy reminiscent look wiped the gloom from his face. "We became friends, and I guided him away from a life of crime. The Community was already forming in America, so I broke one law when I changed Ronan into a vampire."

I shrugged with a brush of my hands, "Considering our current situation, I thank you for that little transgression."

He chuckled and reached over to grab his mate's hand. "When I met my Kaitlyn, we stopped traveling together but remained friends. After Ronan met his mate and moved to Oregon to raise his family, we visited often but we loved our nomadic life.

"What brought you to Oregon now?" I asked, he had passed Jasmine's inquisition, but I still needed to confirm he was not another spy.

"I heard that Ronan had lost his Bridget and came to offer comfort to my old friend." The thin blonde vampire stated.

Gerard was just shy of six feet and thin as a whip. His mate, Kaitlyn, a buxom brunette was at most an inch over five feet, confirmed his statement with a nod of her head. "We arrived three days ago to find Ronan wallowing in his grief. I knew he would not be with us much longer, so I took it upon myself to make sure he left this world in a proper manner."

"What do you mean by that?" Gerard's stare burned into the O'Brien's house like a man bracing for a storm.

"I helped him complete his task while remaining faithful to our upbringing." I must have looked confused because he then stated. "We were raised Catholic. Taking one's own life is a sin. Christianity may be just a made-up fairy tale but why take the chance. Ronan wanted to see Bridget in heaven, so I helped." His voice rose an octave on helped.

"Are you saying you killed him?" My voice quiet as I stared into the fire.

"In a manner of speaking, yes." Gerard replied also in a low tone. "He planned to take his life regardless of whether I was there or not. We talked and he agreed to let me do the actual deed, again, hedging our bets. What if suicide kept him from seeing his Bridget again?"

In my long life I have dealt with many different religious groups. They all had many similarities to each other. Follow these specific rules and you will get to whatever form of heaven they espouse. Don't follow the rules and you go to their version of hell. For all I know each of us ends up in the place we believe in.

I will go to Sidhes when I complete my final task. Maybe Ronan, a lapsed Catholic of sorts will end up in the Christian heaven with his Bridget. Who was I to judge, I had regular conversations with a god, and my mate was a murderous dragon.

"I appreciate your candidness. Do you worry his children will hold it against you?"

Gerard's stare remained fixed on their house, "I told Evan when I gave him the letters. What he does with that information is his choice. I felt you, as the leader of this ragtag army, should be aware. If you learned of my act, I didn't want you to think I betrayed them."

"I shall keep this conversation between us." I assured him.

We congregated around the large central campfire. On the day my son arrived there had only been about ten chairs. Now the pit itself had grown to almost ten feet across and there were at least forty or so seating places spaced around it.

Temperence, Malina and Diana, the three witches in my coven joined us. They were having a lively conversation about their most recent sexual exploits with several of the wolf shifters. Upon seeing the newcomers their entertaining discussion came to an abrupt halt.

"Don't stop on my account." Kaitlyn joked, "I love a good ribald story."

They dragged her into their stories leaving Gerard and I to our more serious discussion. "I sense you have more than just conveying the details of Ronan's death to impart." I opined.

"You would be correct." Gerard confirmed while shaking his head at one of Kaitlyn's outrageous comments. "However, I wish to give Ronan's children some time to grieve."

I understood his desire, so we enjoyed a few hours getting to know each other. While we waited for anyone to come from their house we spent a pleasant afternoon together. Gerard was the more serious one, Kaitlyn enjoyed more frivolous pursuits. They seemed well matched though as he did not seem disturbed by anything she said, and she liked to chide him about his stalwart nature.

Matthew and Annie joined our little group with more news that brought a girlish grin to Diana's face. Tygus, the ship captain who had aided us in our journey to our current home had been spotted about fifty miles south of us. A few minutes ago, a missive had arrived through the fire in the kitchen. Jacky, his young errand boy had set this up with Temperence before we left their ship. Missives allowed communication without using modern technology, a thing Tygus abhorred and avoided at all costs.

"He is requesting directions to our island." Matthew remained standing. "He has almost fifty people with him who wish to join our cause. Do you wish for me to give him instructions on how to reach us?"

"Soon, but first we must call a meeting." I answered Matthew. "Gerard has some information for us but wants to wait for Evan and his family to grieve their father's death." I looked at Gerard kindly, "I am sorry, but we cannot wait any longer. As much as I would like to give them time, I feel an urgency to our situation."

"I understand," he answered rising to his feet. "I will go tell Evan."

"Bring Aisling and Lucian as well. The others may be left in peace for now unless Evan deems otherwise." I advised Gerard and he walked off to their house. Turning back to Matthew, "You may inform Tygus that instructions will be forthcoming then return here."

Matthew strode across the lawn to my house to send the message leaving Annie behind. The gaiety of my witch friend's conversation had come to an end. "Will the three of you go around the island and gather the following people?" I listed off the de facto leaders of the smaller groups that had joined us. Annie, Kaitlyn and

I fell into silence, each of us lost in our own thoughts, while we waited for everyone to gather.

Jace and Cat were the first to arrive, a quick hello as they took seats across from me. They sat quietly, holding hands and if their expressions were anything to go by, having an internal conversation with each other. Davina, James and Brian arrived next. They also said little before taking seats around the fire. Within twenty minutes my three witches had gathered everyone from around the island. Oddly though, very few were talking as if they all felt the same sense of urgency that I was feeling.

Gathered around the fire now were Almerinda and Damian, Jace and Cat, Jonesie, who still looked dejected after the death of Derik, Gabriel sans Robert, Jaxson also without his mate, Cassandra and Nikolas, Davina and James, Brian the massive wolf shifter who represented the wolves as well as Almerinda's elite squad. Temperence, Malina and Diana returned with William, the witch and they all took their seats.

Matthew came back a few seconds after William sat down. "The missive is sent, Tygus says he will await our decision." I nodded and Matthew sat next to Annie, taking her hand in his. Silence resumed as we watched for Gerard to return with the O'Briens. A few minutes passed when the front door opened on their house.

Cormac stepped out first, followed closely by Jasmine then Evan and Ali. They started across the field with Gerard following. A few seconds later, Aisling and Lucian emerged followed by the younger O'Brien, Saoirse. They all had red-rimmed eyes from crying; holding themselves stiffly they each took a seat around the fire. Gerard remained standing and looked to me for guidance.

Rising to my feet, everyone's attention fell on me. "I called you all here because Gerard has information he needs to impart." Looking at the O'Briens gathered. "I wish I could have given you more time, but I feel as if we are running out of it now." Without any further preamble I turned the floor over to Gerard.

"I have news but first I feel I must tell you how I came by my information, so you do not dismiss it out of hand." He looked pointedly at Cassandra and Almerinda with that statement. "For the past two hundred years, I have roamed the world, passing myself off as nothing more than an avid traveler enjoying life with my mate. People tend to open up to someone they view as a fop or popinjay." A few people smirked while others looked a little perplexed at his choice of words. "I showed no interest in anything aside from gaining pleasure from my mate and the world around me. My true purpose though had been set forth by Almerinda."

All eyes spun to look at the pixy like vampire. She motioned for Gerard to continue with an imperious wave of her hand. "She set me on a mission to ferret out traitors within the Council. I am happy to say that for the first hundred years or so, I found none. She however believed there had to be someone due to different incidents that had occurred."

Gerard paused for a moment before turning sympathetic eyes on Cassandra. She squirmed under his gaze, anxiety evident in her fidgeting. My son pulled her into his side, calming her with his touch.

"A little over a hundred years ago, not long before Cassandra was born, a plot to overthrow the Council was hatched. A vampire from Europe named Desmond was sent to America by the Fontaine family. He was dispatched here to perform one task then return to the family."

"I know Desmond." Gabriel announced in a loud voice. "He had been with the Fontaines before I was turned. He was especially fond of children, and I don't mean caring for them."

"So, you know what he is capable of. However, his horrid acts are not why he was sent here." Gerard resumed his tale. "Desmond arrived in America with the sole purpose of impregnating a witch. He has one power that no other vampires seem to have. He can inflict pain upon someone with his mind."

Cassandra flinched as if she had been slapped. "Tell me I didn't hear you correctly." Her nails dug into Nikolas' arm and her skin shimmered with her newfound dragon scales. "Tell me my father isn't a Fontaine."

"Yes and no. He has lived and worked with the Fontaine family for as long as anyone can remember but he is not of their blood. He was changed by Luis, Almerinda's maker many years before then." Gerard answered her question then looked at Almerinda. "Do you wish me to tell this part?"

"No, I will tell it." She answered blithely. "Desmond and Luis had a falling out over me. Desmond was created first, but Luis favored me. Desmond demanded Luis kill me, but Luis refused. Desmond tried to use his powers against me, but they didn't affect me. To this day I don't know why. Having seen what Cassandra can do, I am quite happy that they failed."

Almerinda rose from her seat, moving in front of Cassandra. "When your powers manifested, I knew you had to be Desmond's child. You see it is such an uncommon power. As far as I know you and your father are the only ones ever to have it."

Tears coursed down Cassandra's face, but she held her back stiff, as if refusing to give into the despair she must be feeling.

Almerinda softened her voice, "I couldn't understand why Desmond would come all the way here just to father a child on a witch. I tasked Gerard to search for answers, while at the same time I watched over you. I kept you close, so I could guide you along the right path."

Cassandra kept her gaze averted from Almerinda's. My heart broke for my son's mate once again. She deserved so much more than she had been given in this life. I prayed to the Gods and Fates that she would get the chance for a better life.

Almerinda took her seat by Damian, turning the tale back over to Gerard. "I kept up my vagabond ways, letting people believe that I had no interest in politics or anything serious." Tired of standing in front of everyone, he took a seat next to Kaitlyn. "About four months ago, I finally had the information I needed but by then you all had mostly disappeared. When Ronan reached out to me a couple weeks ago, I knew I could return to aid my friend as well as report back to Almerinda on my findings."

Gerard dumped a tidal wave of secrets on us. The biggest shock of all was the fact that a Council member named Alistair Michaels was still alive. We had all believed he had perished almost twenty years ago. Gerard had found him quite by accident.

Tatiana, a vampire who was one of the top five Council members sent him to hide out in Peru. Almerinda had intercepted a missive between Tatiana and an unnamed person speaking about their safe transportation. She sent Gerard in search of someone although she did not know who it was.

On a so-called wander about South America, which was in fact a spying mission, Gerard had located him near some ancient ruins. Several years passed before Gerard could gain his trust. Once he had though, Gerard had learned quite a large amount of information.

Tatiana had been working with Luis; they shared the same sire. She wanted to reopen the portals to Fabeldyrverden, although for different reasons.

"Tatiana's mate is trapped in Fabeldyrverden." Gerard said. The fire spat sparks in the air, no one spoke. "She'll burn the world to the ground to get him back."

Gerard kicked a small rock away from his foot, then looked at the O'Brien's, a mask of anger on his face. "I also learned Alistair had restarted his experiments. The people he kidnaps are well cared for as far as I could tell. I left him to his work since I needed to get back to Almerinda to report all I had learned."

"We have fewer dragons finding their mates in Fabeldyrverden." Lucian said, his arm gripping Aisling as if he were holding her up. "I doubt this Alistair knows that though. He must not be aware that the portals may open again."

"He must be hoping to breed a mate." I added, my hand gripped the arm of my chair. Gerard shared Alistair's location, and we swore to rescue the captives once we finished the fight against my mate and his allies.

"I initially went to Council headquarters," Gerard resumed his report looking at Almerinda. "You weren't there, so I snooped for a couple days then headed to Oregon when Ronan called me. But I learned Andre and Marcel Fontaine are both in Quebec, Canada."

Jasmine's face clouded over with rage but with the object of her anger not here she had only Gerard to vent it on. "How?" She howled at Gerard, her eyes blazing with fury. Cormac held her in her seat as if he expected her to attack his father's best friend.

"Tatiana told Marcel about your tracking device." Gerard answered with a grimace. "He gave his ring to one of his soldiers. There was also a large man with them who looks a lot like you." Gerard pointed at Nikolas.

"My father," my son hung his head. Cassandra caressed his cheek, bolstering her mate. "Fraxinus." Nikolas raised his voice. "They are closer than we thought."

That chilling statement brought a deafening silence over the group. The fire crackled, but the warmth didn't reach my chilled heart. I truly would not see my grandchild. Almost as if he heard me, my son placed his hand over Cassandra's still flat abdomen.

"Wait," Ali's voice rang across the quiet meeting. "I'm missing something." Ali, ever the inquisitive one, stared at Almerinda. "Why was Desmond sent to father a child?"

294

"I believe," Almerinda stated, "that they hoped to have her be raised by one of their allies. If Cassandra had been molded by them rather than me, she may have turned out differently."

Almerinda knelt in front of Cassandra taking her hand she forced her to look up, "Your mother did not choose to live away from the coven. She was exiled. I allowed you to believe that she was a kind and innocent witch. I wanted you to grow up without the evil shadow of your parentage hanging over your head."

"So, you left me be to be raised by the Council?" Condemnation tainted Cassandra's speech as she yanked her hand from Almerinda's.

"I tried to take you to raise you myself, but I was overruled by the Council. I did the next best thing by remaining a constant figure in your life trying to instill as much goodness in you as I could." Almerinda placed her hand under Cassandra's chin and lifted her bowed head. "I knew I had succeeded many years ago when you omitted to report the fact that you allowed a prisoner to go free."

Cassandra's eyes narrowed, her head swung back and forth in denial "Yes," Almerinda confirmed, "Melissa was innocent, and you knew it, but you also knew that the Council still intended to put her to death. You just didn't know why."

Almerinda pivoted to face all of us again. "Melissa was a wolf shifter that had worked for me, much like Gerard has done. Someone found out and turned her in for violating the rules of the Community. Trumped up evidence was presented and she was sentenced to death." She looked at Cassandra again, "Melissa is safely living in Australia now thanks to you."

"If Cassandra had not accidentally turned her mother into a blithering idiot, she would have been raised by her. I am sure her mother was carefully chosen by Desmond due to her proclivity for violence and the darker side of witchcraft." Almerinda explained. "Alistair and I both tried to gain custody. We were both outvoted and she was raised at Council headquarters. The Fontaines probably hoped to use her to bring down the Council, effectively ending the rule of the Community."

"Other than Tatiana, do we know of any other traitors within the Council?" Evan asked once Almerinda returned to her seat.

"I only learned the names of her and Alistair." Gerard responded. "There may be more, but I could not learn them without seeming too interested and thus blowing my cover."

"Tatiana is bad enough." Jonesie growled, the muscles on his neck taut. "I am sure there are many more since the vile woman has many friends within the Community."

"Why do you call her vile?" Cat looked at the ebony skinned vampire.

"I had a little altercation with her a few years ago. She was also quite close to your mate's recently departed enemy, Amanda." Jonesie gave his succinct answer then seemed to decide that was enough and said no more. Judging by Cat's reaction to the name Amanda, I could assume that she needed no further reason to dislike this Tatiana vampire.

"Gerard," I asked, "is there anything else you need to share?" He shook his head no. "Then I think we may need to start considering moving our encampment closer to our hoped-for battleground."

Everyone seemed to agree, so I added. "Currently a friend of ours is anchored about fifty miles from here. His ship is impervious to spying from witchcraft and human technology. Matthew, please send instructions to Tygus to bring the ship as close as he can."

Matthew rose to do my bidding; I held up a hand stopping him for more instructions. Before I could say more, Delilah, Jonesie's seer, rushed down a path from their encampment.

Delilah staggered into the firelight, blood dripping from her nose. "Seventeen days," she gasped. Everyone froze. "The battle will be in seventeen days. If we leave too early, we die at sea. Too late, and we're slaughtered on our way to Aelwyd."

She shoved a piece of paper into my hands before collapsing into a chair. "Your friend needs to be here. They'll find him tomorrow night if he stays where he is." Matthew snatched the paper from my hand and sped off to our house to send the coordinates to Tygus.

Jonesie bent over her in concern. "Child, have you not been taking proper care of yourself?" He asked worry creasing his brow.

"We needed answers." Delilah whispered in response, her voice shaking now that she had delivered her news. "Malina hasn't been able to see anything, and I knew we needed answers." She looked sadly at Aisling and Lucian. "I am sorry I don't have any for you."

Aisling and Lucian shared a look that I could not read. "We will survive, or we won't, we have made our peace with it either way." Lucian's strong voice echoed into the night air. Backs stiff in defiance of our pitying looks, they marched into the dark forest.

Chapter Forty-Six

Aisling

Seventeen days. The number echoed in my skull like a death knell. How were we going to win in just, Gods, seventeen days? Gods, Fates, whoever is controlling my future, I need more time.

"Aisling, stop." Lucian pulled my body to a stop at the same time. We were in the small clearing near the waterfall. Fond memories of our Sanguis Draconis ceremony flitted through my head for a moment only to be replaced by Delilah's shout of seventeen days. "My love, stop. We will figure something out, I promise you."

"Don't." I pleaded with him. "Don't promise something you may not be able to honor." Sadness fell over his features, and he pulled me in for a tight hug.

"Alright, then I'll promise this." he murmured, his lips brushing my ear, "I will make you a promise I can definitely keep then." I sniffled into his blue shirt. Once again, the inane thought struck me that he was wearing the wrong color. "Every second we have left; I'll love and cherish you to my last breath."

His words wrought the tears I had been holding back from me. My knees buckled, only Lucian's grip kept me from crumpling to the moss like a discarded tissue. Lucian lowered our bodies to the springy ground, holding me close to his heart.

I sobbed relentlessly; it was too much. I was normally a very strong person, but the last few months had just been too much. The losses were piling up. My mother. My father. I wasn't ready to lose us too.

When my tears dried, I lifted my head to meet my mate's solemn eyes. "I love you too. I am not giving up on us. I'll stand by you, and we will face the horde of fae together."

His lips twitched but his eyes stayed grim. We both knew our days were numbered. His tender kiss brought a pool of tears to my eyes again. He dipped my head, tucking it back under his chin. We lay on the mossy ground, listening to the sounds of nature all around us. The rush of the small waterfall provided the perfect background noise to fall asleep to.

The rising sun greeted me when I opened my eyes again. Lucian's body was curled around mine. We lay on our sides by the pool of water. I felt him stir behind me and felt his warm kiss on the nape of my neck.

"My dearest heart." His breath in my ear, sending a tingling down my spine. I rolled onto my back so I could gaze upon his beautiful face. *Handsome,* rustled through my thoughts bringing a small smile to my lips.

I rubbed my hand up his bare arm to rest on his blue shirt. "Why are you wearing blue?" I blurted.

One eyebrow cocked up as he tried not to laugh. "I have always had to wear some variation of red or black. As king, as heir to the kingdom and as a fire dragon, I had no choice in my home world but to conform. Here, I can be and wear anything I want."

I opened my mouth to ask another question, but he shushed me with a quick peck. "Also," he added with a wicked grin, "I overheard you once think how sexy you thought I would look in blue."

"You do look sexy in blue." I ran my hand down his abdomen to rest at the top of his pants. "You look even sexier wearing nothing at all."

Licking my lips, I unbuttoned his jeans and pulled the zipper down. Lucian watched my hand as it dipped into the front of his pants to grasp his hardening shaft. We spent the next hour or so showing each other how much we enjoyed each other's bodies.

Later, tangled in each other and sated, Lucian traced his finger down my hip, "Ready to try finding your dragon?" I murmured a drowsy positive reply, trailing my fingers through the clear water of the plunge pool beside us.

I told him about my conversation with Ali yesterday morning. We agreed that her idea had merit, we rose up from our positions on the ground to sit opposite each other. Facing him while holding his hands in mine, I asked him what I needed to do now.

"Just open your mind to me. Allow me into your innermost thoughts." My steel grey eyes met his swirling ones, and I found myself pulled into his mind first. His inner being grasped my hand and I led him out of his mind and into mine.

Now, give me control. The hazy form of Lucian spoke to me.

I hesitated for about a second before relinquishing my control. We stood in a dark empty space for several minutes, our corporeal forms the only objects visible.

There she is. He said, pulling me toward a faint glow off to my left, the opposite direction of where my lynx lived. I followed my mate along the quiet pathways of my mind.

We rounded a sharp corner in my consciousness; to enter an area I had never seen in my mind before. Standing in the center of a swirling sky of reds, blacks, and blues was a magnificent dragon.

Her scales shone, rippling as if under a spotlight. Garnet and indigo like a storm at sunset, she was Lucian's twin but fiercer, her barbed tail lashing. Her black underbelly absorbed the light, like a black hole. She was not as large as Lucian's dragon, but she was no less impressive.

I stood in front of her; her eyes opened to gaze upon me. My own grey eyes with red catlike slits stared back at me. My consciousness got drawn into her and a sense of oneness enveloped me as we combined into one being. My mate's mirage stands below me. His smile is one of satisfaction and excitement. Apparently, he likes my dragon form. His grin widens confirming my suspicions.

I pull myself out of her mind to return to Lucian's side in the swirling room. With his hand in mine, I guided us back to the velvety jade clearing. "You're going to be stunning." Lucian grips my hands tightly; the crash of the waterfall soothes my jumbled nerves.

"I'm ready." My palms sweat, this should be easy, but a dragon is so much bigger than a lynx. I could do this, repeated like a mantra in my head.

We stand up together. With a gentle squeeze of my hand, he moves away from me. I remove my clothes, folding them slowly. Stop procrastinating, I chide myself. The lust in his eyes at my naked form tries to drag me to his side. No, I growl, stay on task.

I centered my mind, taking slow deep breaths. I need a little more concentration than I would to bring out my lynx, but I can feel the change coming over my body. A smoky haze of red and blue surrounds my body and then I suddenly find myself towering over my almost seven-foot-tall mate. He runs his hands along my shimmering scales with admiration. He sheds his own clothing, and within seconds his dragon form towers over me.

300

Lucian spreads his wings wide and launches himself into the sky. I watch his movements for a few minutes then follow his motions. My first attempt had me crashing into the treetops. Lucian's laughter boomed in my head. *Again!* He growled.

After a few more failed attempts, I soared to his height. Flying is so freeing. We soar along the coastline, and I point out where Arianna strays to every morning. I felt rather than heard Lucian sigh. Our connection felt deeper in these forms.

His larger dragon swooped next to me, forcing me into a dive. *What the hell!* My mind shrieked at him.

He kept pace with me, showing me how to spin and defend myself while diving. *We need to train.* The setting sun brought out a bright moon that shined in the clear sky, lighting our way as we practiced flying and diving, attacking and defending.

Gliding over the crashing waves of the ocean, our bodies cast strange rippling shadows in the moonlight. My mind wandered, as we headed back to the island. Seventeen days, screeched through my concentration, and suddenly my stomach dropped as I plunged toward the ocean. Lucian's fear filled roar snapped me back. Righting myself, I hurled myself back to land.

Lucian gave me no time to recover, attacking me as soon as my clawed feet hit the ground. We battled each other for hours. I transformed back and forth from dragon to human to lynx and worked on different ways of attack. I needed to speed up my transformation times if I hoped to use this form in battle.

Lucian also tried to turn into a large cat but was not yet successful. We used the same mind trick on him. And even though we found his cat form, it refused to acknowledge our presence. Typical cat, I thought, bringing a loud guffaw from Lucian. It wasn't necessary for him to master his cat form anyway since his dragon form was much more lethal.

Dawn crept up on us, like a thief in the night stealing our bright moon. Clouds were rolling in, and even though the island had protection, the sky above would not be safe.

One day we'll fly through a storm. Lucian promised, *it is one of the most awe-inspiring moments you'll ever experience.*

We decided we would get some sleep, then resume our practice later. We returned to our room just as the sun poked its head over the eastern horizon. Our spent bodies were good for nothing but sleep at this time. Curled against his chest, I fell asleep in my favorite position, the little spoon to his big spoon.

301

Chapter Forty-Seven

Cassandra

After the meeting finished, Nikolas and I took a stroll along the beach. In ten days, we would sail into frozen hell, also known as Canada. Twyla's family lived in the northern part of the Northwest Territories.

Twyla reassured us that her family's arctic homestead would shield us, from both the cold and prying human eyes. Their two centuries in the frozen landscape had taught them spells to cheat death by frostbite.

Twyla had shared the ingredients and invocation needed to perform the spells that would protect our bodies from the elements. Several of the witches amongst us, with far better skills than I, had been working non-stop to mass produce the potions. Since I had not had a typical witch's education; and the Council only cared about my gift of pain, I was banned from potion making.

We came to the end of the beach and took a seat on the rocky outcropping leaning back against a tree that seemed to grow right out of the rocks. The crash of the surf on the shore was comforting to me. I never knew how peaceful just sitting on the side of an ocean could be.

The sun crawled across the sky as we watched gulls dive bomb the waves. Their shrieks cut through the surf's rhythm. The briny scent of the sea mixed with the pine of the land unlocked my subconscious distress. Nikolas stayed quiet at my side, giving me time to brood.

Almerinda's confession that my mother was not a good witch had rocked me. My entire life I had believed that my actions had hurt an innocent woman. Gods, both my parents were monsters. Their blood runs through my veins, I shuddered and felt Nikolas' mind reach out to me. Does that make me evil too?

"Cass?" Nikolas' voice broke into my turbulent thoughts. I shook my legs, stretching them in front of me. Pins and needles shot through the foot I had been sitting on, and I realized we had been sitting here for almost two hours. "Are you alright?"

I dragged my eyes away from the ocean to look at him. My cheeks were wet and gritty, tears, salt and sand mixed. "Yes." I replied, but was I really?

"My heart, then why are you crying?" He turned me to face him, keeping my hands in his. His forehead wrinkled with concern.

"I didn't realize I was." I pulled my hands from him, scrubbing the tears from my cheeks. I tried to smile, I wanted to erase those wrinkles, wipe away his worry. Instead of reassuring him, I asked, "Do you think I could turn evil like my parents?"

"No." He responded with no equivocation. "If I were to think that about you, should you not worry about me then? My father is the reason we are all preparing for a fight."

"Some do blame you." I argued.

"Do you blame me?" His face darkened as he turned away from me.

Shame flamed my cheeks red, "No, I don't" the words raced out of me. "Gods, Nik, I am so sorry. I don't know what's wrong with me."

His gaze softened, but his frown remained. "You got blindsided by Almerinda."

"True, but that's no excuse for attacking you like that." I shifted forward, so I could see his turned away face. "I swear I don't hold any of your past against you."

"Then don't hold your past against yourself either." His growl demanded that I obey his words.

"But what of all the people I tortured for the Council." I cried. "How many of them were innocent and didn't deserve what I did to them?"

"Cass, you can't blame yourself for the Council's use of you." Nikolas reassured me. "I've walked through your mind. Regret and determination, but not an ounce of rot."

"I see how some people still look at us." People still avoided me, a few, not many, steered clear of Nikolas too. He was more open with others than I was. His daily training with Jace, Cat and Gabriel also improved their perception of him

"Fear thrives in ignorance. The power you wield has been used for many years as a warning to them. I don't think it's you as much as the ingrained fear of your power." He brought my hand to his lips to place a soft kiss on my palm. "I do not fear you or your power as I know you would never use it against me or anyone I care about."

303

"Aren't we a pair?" I lean into his side. His reasoning was sound; I shoved my parentage back into my subconscious where it would hopefully stay forever. "When this is all over, I am looking forward to returning to Fabeldyrverden."

"I am too." He chose that moment to stand, dragging me to my feet with him. "We should get back. Now that we know the when and where, we need to be planning the how."

I stole one last pining look at the horizon. Ten days. Maybe our last calm before the storm.

Chapter Forty-Eight

Arianna

We sail in two days. The last eight days had been a blur. Our plans were falling into place; but there was one gaping hole. No one had figured out a way to save Aisling and Lucian. I kept my secret that I didn't expect to survive the war either. I think Cassandra suspected something, but she had not revealed her suspicions to anyone, not even Nikolas.

Damn the Fates, my teeth ground together. Over a thousand years of misery, and now that I have a modicum of happiness in front of me my time was being cut short. It was unfair, but life never is. I would do everything in my power to make sure my son and his mate get the future I never had.

Smoothing my face, I unclenched my teeth and began my daily duties. Most of my days were spent answering everyone's questions and checking in on their progress.

Cassandra's dragon form still emerged clumsily, scales rippling like disturbed water. But when her pain power exploded from her, trees fell, and boulders shifted. After Nikolas replanted the fifth tree, they decided her talents would be better used in her human form.

Aisling took to her dragon form like she was born to it. She and Lucian were often spotted in the sky practicing together. I noticed that she spent each morning with different members of her family before the two of them headed off into the trees to practice.

They usually returned late into the night for a few hours of sleep then repeated the process the next day. My heart went out to them, and I prayed to the Fates daily to spare them. However, if there is one thing I have learned in all my years it's that the Fates don't actually listen to our prayers.

Lucian came to see me yesterday to discuss the problem his home world was having finding mates. He knew that I was one of the witches tasked with closing the portals. He needed to know if I could reopen them. I told him I knew the reversal spell but would only share it with everyone if we won.

I had already given it to the three witches that were part of my coven with the express orders to use it when and if we were triumphant. Lucian thanked me then left me to return to his mate with a little lift to his steps. He may not survive the upcoming fight but at least he felt like his world would.

Tygus' ship brought fifty more fighters to our ranks, only one turned out to be a traitor. Tygus and Jacky took care of the witch who had managed to fool them. The two of them had become constant figures in my home as they had been spending each night in the arms of two of my witches.

Diana had resumed her affair with Tygus and much to my surprise Jacky and Temperence had started their own torrid affair. Malina, being the odd one out, had been spending all her nights at the wolf compound.

Hawthorne, who had not been around much for a few weeks, started joining in the planning again. He had told me he needed some time alone to center his thoughts then wandered off into the center of the island. When he returned the day after Gerard's arrival, he seemed happier as if he had learned something wonderful while he was alone.

I chose to let him keep his private thoughts private and simply welcomed him back. I knew he missed his Marlena and had only fought the pull of his mate bond so he could one day face his brother. With that day looming ever closer, I believe he was feeling relief that soon his years of suffering would be over.

Davina told me James was also improving his skills as a dragon. They had started practicing immediately after performing their Sanguis Draconis ceremony. Since her mating, I've seen very little of my oldest friend. I missed her but was thankful for her absence. If anyone could figure out my plan to sacrifice myself, it was her.

Our plan relied on James being able to fight in his dragon form alongside his mate. Davina was a spirit dragon and would be able to swoop in to steal life from our enemies. If James was able to master that power too, we would have two deadly dragons on our side.

It was stupid of Fraxinus to dismiss spirit dragons as less than the others. In some ways they were more powerful as they could command life and death. Much like fire dragons spewed fire from their throats, spirit dragons could send a stream of a misty substance at their foes. When the mist settled on the skin it would sap the life from that person.

What made their power dangerous to their own body was how close they needed to be to hit their targets. A fire dragon could spray a large area from a distance with flames and continue its journey. The spirit dragon could only hit one target at a time and needed to be within ten feet of it. James needed to be adept at sudden twists and turns while in the air if he wanted to hit his targets while also being missed by any attacks from the ground.

Very few of us were around during the first fae dragon wars. With so few of us having experience fighting the fae, those of us who had were also spending much of our time training everyone. I wandered through the training fields. Sweat and ozone filled the air as the shifters and witches practiced tirelessly.

I took a moment to watch Jace and Cat spar. They grappled with each other, neither one able to overpower the other. Just as Cat seemed to get the upper hand, Jaxson moved in to attack from behind. She didn't even flinch, spinning she propelled Jace into his brother's advancing body, knocking them both off their feet. Then with a high kick, knocked Gabriel back as well.

"That's my girl!" Robert yelled from the sidelines.

After she helped Jace to his feet, the four of them regrouped. Cat called out a challenge. I watched twelve rise to take that challenge. The four vampires turned as one to meet the challengers. Within minutes, only Jace, Cat, Gabriel and Jaxson remained standing. I knew exactly where to place these four in the battle.

Even in exhaustion, people were finding comfort in the arms of willing partners each night. I could not begrudge them, even if it meant they were not acquiring enough sleep. Once we moved to Canada, I would try to put a stop to it. We needed a well-rested army if we had any hope of beating our enemy.

I let it be known that tomorrow there will be a full meeting with everyone on the island. Then, the next day we'll sail to the port town of Kugluktuk. Diana would guide the ship through the fastest waters while Malina would help propel it. Cassandra and Nikolas would take Twyla through a portal to prepare for our arrival.

The fact that each mated pair could only pull one or two people through at a time, crushed our plans to simply portal to Aelwyd. James and Davina were focusing solely on fight training. No one knew if Aisling and Lucian could open portals, as they had been keeping to themselves. Cassandra and Nikolas would not have the time or strength to transport over four hundred people on the island.

Once we arrived at Kugluktuk, we would then have a two-day overland trek to get to Twyla's home. The witches amongst us would fare the worse since they did not have extra strength and stamina. Twyla would send help to us from her base but did not elaborate further on what that help might be. If the twinkle in her eye was any indication, it would be something interesting.

I was stopped by a couple witches on my way back to my house. While describing some of the magical abilities of the fae to them, Saoirse came running out of the O'Brien's house. She went to Evan first but the manic way she clutched her computer, pulled me closer.

Aisling and Lucian left? What? How? Eavesdropping just wasn't going to work so I pushed through the mass of O'Briens that had formed around Evan and Saoirse. "She sent a timed email." Saoirse was explaining when I made it through everyone. "They probably left hours ago." She pointed at her computer tablet that she carried everywhere with her. "She wrote the email early this morning."

"What exactly does it say?" I needed to know if they would fulfill their destiny or if I should just try to remove Fraxinus before the battle and hope for the best.

Chapter Forty-Nine

Aisling

I spent the morning with Fiona and her family. This would be the last time I could say with any certainty that I would see them. Fiona's shifter mate was out practicing with everyone else. Her vampire mate was with us and their children. Normally her kids would be driving me crazy but today I was just happy to have them near.

Lucian had gone to say goodbye to his cousin Nikolas, without actually saying goodbye. We were leaving today but hadn't told anyone. Once he returned, we would go out into the trees as we did every day but today would be different.

The intoxicating thrill I had felt when the portal snapped into perfect symmetry still coursed through my veins. It has taken us six of the last seven days to perfect it. Grit and determination, plus impending doom, were great motivators.

The day after Delilah delivered our end date I had discussed my plan with Lucian. It had taken some convincing, but I was determined, and he loves me enough to trust me.

"I want to see your world." I had announced once we were out of earshot of anyone else. "I want to show you my world too."

"Gods, my love, I want nothing more than that too. But we don't have time." Lucian's crestfallen expression and response did not deter me. I laid out my plan, I felt like I had worked out what we needed to do and how we could do it and still make it to the field of snow to face the fae.

Lucian had taken it all into consideration. His only argument against it was that his sister had seen that he never returned to his home world. I corrected that statement, "no she said she didn't know if she would ever see you again."

We decided we would visit uninhabited areas of his world just to be safe. We didn't want to mess with the prophecy and possibly be the cause for Fraxinus and his allies to win. I'd composed the email at dawn, timing it to deliver after we'd gone, no tearful goodbyes, no arguments. Just slipping away like ghosts.

Family, I write this knowing I may never see any of you again. Lucian and I have kept a small secret from everyone. We have successfully opened many portals and have decided that before our end comes that we want to see the world together. We promise to be on that field before the sun rises in nine days. But for now, we are going to be a bit selfish and take some time for ourselves. I love you all and hope that I see you again someday, if not in this life than the next. Please take care of each other. Love Aisling and Lucian.

Lucian came through the door about twenty minutes later and I said goodbye to my sister and her brood. We walked out of the house for the last time and down the trail to the waterfall. We stood at the side of the plunge pool, the falling water sending sprays of mist our way.

This was my favorite place on the island. We joined our souls together in this spot. A tear ran down my cheek, mixing with the mist. Lucian kissed my tear-streaked cheeks, then placed a tender kiss on my trembling lips.

"Where to first?" He asked when he pulled his lips from mine.

"Fabeldyrverden." I answered, bringing a radiant smile to his face.

Using our combined power, Lucian concentrated on a place he said was his favorite in his entire world. The shimmering multi-hued silvery orb hung in the air in front of us. I felt a tug on my power and the orb expanded to a size big enough for the two of us to walk through comfortably. We stepped through, stepping out into a clearing much like the one we had left, only on a grander scale.

Thick purple moss covered the ground around a large pool of pink hued water fed by a waterfall that had to be at least a hundred feet high. Trees with black bark and bluish-purple leaves surrounded us on all sides. I looked up at a bright orange sun in a dark blue sky. Off in the distance, hung a second planet with rings around it. Cassandra's description of this place did not do it justice at all.

We spent the rest of the day lounging at the side of the pool of water created by the waterfall. The citrus scented air, soothing and clear. Lucian's voice as he played tour guide for me was more relaxed then I had ever heard before.

"There's an underground river that drains the lake into a larger above ground river about five miles away." His voice caught in his throat, the tiniest hint of sadness penetrating it. "Eventually the river snakes its way out of the mountains to travel past the capital city."

When night fell, I got to be amazed again by the splendor of this world. The sky darkened to a deeper blue almost black. Twinkling orange and yellow stars filled the sky. The planet of rings shone brighter much like the moon in Earth's sky glowed at night. Small, winged creatures flitted through the trees around us, their wings bioluminescence sparkling in multihued beauty.

"Fairies." Lucian explained. "When the portals were sealed the fairies remained in Fabeldyrverden. Before they traveled between all the worlds trading their honey for other items they needed. Their honey has healing properties that rival any potion a spellcaster could brew."

We decided we would spend the night by the rose-colored lake then move onto a different location here. I lay curled next to him, the happiest and saddest I had ever been. Lucian must have sensed that I didn't want to talk so just held me close until we both fell asleep.

My dreams were fitful, past present and future all vying for attention. I woke several times through the night, cocooned in my mate's arms, silent tears streaming down my cheeks. If Lucian was aware of my turmoil, he chose to remain quiet, focusing only on our stolen happy moments for now.

The next morning dawned, a blazing orange sun above us and thankfully, dry cheeks for me. We woke up to find a gaggle of fairies snuggled up next to us. I jumped a little, but Lucian reassured me that they were just enjoying our body heat and nothing else.

When we moved to sit up, the fairies scattered into the thick leaves of the trees around us. Sitting on the ground near us were several small bottles of amber colored liquid. We picked them up and stowed them in the packs we had brought with us. Healing honey just might come in handy.

We ate a quick breakfast of berries and smoked jerky then prepared for our next jump. Lucian seemed very excited about where we were off to next but wouldn't tell me anything. I lent him my power, and the shimmering orb of our portal began to form. This time he needed less from me, and the transition was much smoother.

"Going between worlds takes a bit more effort." He explained as we stepped out of our portal and into a field full of enormous horses with horns. Unicorns? Although much larger than any horse I had ever seen.

"Another species that chose to remain in Fabeldyrverden when the portals closed." Lucian held me back when I moved to approach a pearlescent horse with a pale-yellow horn. "You must wait for them to come to you. They are very territorial."

My mouth hung open, amazement robbing my voice. There had to be at least forty unicorns all at least eight feet tall, a few were taller. Their chests spanned on average six to seven feet across. And, as everything in this realm seemed to be, they were very colorful. Pale gold coats with different colored single horns on their heads. They were magnificent to behold and even if I didn't get to touch one just seeing them was awe inspiring.

We sat on the edge of the field of unicorns and watched them frolic. I use that word because there was no other way to explain it. The gigantic horses were jumping and running around in what looked like a game of tag. My mind started to wander while watching the cheerful site.

I worried my family wouldn't understand why we left the way we did. It was just something I felt I deserved. A week of happiness with my mate seemed like a small ask when no one could be sure we would survive. I think everyone should have found a way to find some happiness before the battle. We really didn't know if any of us would make it. None of the seers could pin down anything definitive.

Delilah told me the reason for that is because any slight deviation from what a seer has seen can and most often will change the outcome. Everyone saw us on that field, but no one could see us leaving the field. Maybe our selfish trip is the change we needed to turn the tides in our favor.

Lucian nudges my side dragging me out of my reverie. A lone unicorn approached us. If unicorn anatomy is the same as a regular horse, this one is male. Lucian pulls me to my feet, bowing his head in honor to the magnificent beast before us. I bow my head too, not wanting to cause offense.

The unicorn's horn glowed faintly. Lucian's grip on my hand tightened in warning a second before the voice boomed in my head. *King Lucian and his mate.* The voice echoes as the unicorn sniffs me.

Lucian responds back out loud, "Hello, Abraxus. This is Aisling."

"Nice to meet you." I bowed while also doing a sort of curtsy without a dress. Lucian smirks at me but manages not to laugh. Abraxus on the other hand does not and his booming laugh bounces through my skull.

There is no need to curtsy, I am not a king like your mate. Abraxus lowered his large head to make eye contact with me.

"I have given up the throne." Lucian advised, drawing Abraxus' eyes away from me.

Is that so? Serafina now rules?

312

I moved closer to Lucian, something about the unicorn's eyes made me feel a little unsettled.

"When I traveled from our realm to Gaia, I left her in charge as my proxy. But I have decided that I will not return to Fabeldyrverden as king regardless of the outcome of the upcoming fight with the fae."

Abraxus turned his odd eyes on me again, but no voice boomed through my head. A few minutes passed and I started to think it might be time to move on when a second unicorn joined us.

Lucian must have picked up on something that I didn't because he gripped my hand tighter and pulled me closer to his side. I looked at him about to ask what was wrong. An almost imperceptible shake of his head held my tongue.

The two unicorns stared at each other for several minutes before bringing their attention back to us. *So, the seer was correct.* Abraxus murmured then more succinct, *take them.*

We had no time to react when the second unicorn stepped closer to us lowering her head to bring her horn to rest on Lucian's head. I suddenly felt a sucking feeling and the world started to spin. An eternity passed, well at least it felt like an eternity; and then we were spat out in front of a house made of silver bricks.

We landed in a thump on the ground, a loud oof bursting out of me. Lucian helped me to my feet then turned to the female unicorn that had dumped us here.

"Why did you bring us here?" Lucian demanded from the unicorn.

We were told to watch for your arrival and deliver you here at once. The unicorn raised her head in the air then without saying anything else vanished.

Lucian looked warily at the house in front of us. He obviously knew who lived in it. "I did not expect this," he began just as the large black door banged open. A woman with silver-streaked red hair and lined skin emerged with a grin on her face.

"Ah, Lucian and his new mate." The woman embraced him then pulled me into a tight hug as well. "Just as Janita predicted. Although, you are actually late." The woman turned on her heel, heading back inside the house, "Come now, we must not dottle."

Profitis Magda Lucian explained. *She is our most powerful spirit dragon. The powers she wields generates a great burden on her body. She is also very old, some say at least eight thousand years, but no one knows for certain.*

Well, that explains why she is the first immortal being I have seen with deep lines in her skin. We follow her inside. Clearly Lucian knows and trusts this woman, so I see no reason not to as well.

Profitis Magda ushers us into a room with a blue glowing fire and comfy looking chairs. We take a seat, and a tray of drinks appears beside Lucian. He removes one for each of us and the tray disappears. The mug has some kind of steaming liquid in it.

I take a small sip to be polite and find that it tastes very similar to hot cocoa. We sit quietly while the woman bustles around the room pulling things out of the air. I grew up with all different types of people and still I am impressed by how easily she conjures items.

We are sitting in a room surrounded by a hidden different room that only she can see. Lucian tells me to explain how she can seem so powerful.

Her bustling stops and she carries her load of items to the fire. She throws them on the fire and mutters something in the dragon language. The blue fire leaps high toward the ceiling, rapidly changing through all the colors of the rainbow.

I watch the fire change colors then as if on a television with no sound, we watch scenes from the last few months play out. Some last a few minutes, others just quick seconds of a glimpse. We finally arrive at a scene that is more recent, we are standing in the field back in Gaia readying to open the portal to Fabeldyrverden. Magda waves her hand in front of the flames, bringing the play by play to a stop.

"As you can see, Janita has been closely watching you. Three days ago, she informed me you would be here soon. I began preparing for your arrival immediately."

"What exactly did you need to prepare for?" Lucian asks, his foot tapping an irritated rhythm on the stone floor.

"I sent out word amongst a few of those I trust, such as Abraxus, that I needed to speak to you both." Magda replied. "Janita has looked for your futures."

"We already know our future." I was getting so tired of being reminded that our time was limited. We left Gaia on our trip so we could have some stress-free time before the fight.

"You know you face an army of fae, but you don't know everything." Magda spat out angrily then realized she was speaking to the former king. "I apologize, sire."

"No need, I am no longer king." Lucian answered causing Magda to raise an eyebrow although she said nothing further on the subject.

"Be that as it may, I should have tempered my response." She waved her hand and the images before us began to crawl along as if on super slo-mo speed. "As you can see, Janita has foreseen your arrival here. She has also divined that you will have assistance in your battle although who assists you is hidden from her."

A small sliver of hope snaked into my mind. Maybe we would survive. My hand trembled in Lucian's hand.

Then Magda stated, "Unfortunately, sire, I mean Lucian, she is unable to see the outcome. She believes the fae are using their magic to block us from seeing them clearly."

"It would seem that you interrupted our reverie to tell us very little more than we already knew." Lucian's dry rejoinder had no effect on Magda's calm expression.

"Perhaps that is the case," she replied mildly, "however I thought it was imperative that you know you will not be abandoned entirely on that field of battle. We also believe that for the others who shall fight that day to be triumphant, you need to face the fae."

"Again, that is something we were aware of and have every intention of doing." Lucian growled, my mate was clearly becoming vexed with her.

"I think what Lucian is trying to say," I placed a hand on his tensed arm, "is that while we appreciate the information it is not exactly new to us. Well other than the part about thinking we'll have help. But essentially you pulled us from a lovely day to tell us we still needed to do what we already planned to do."

"I suppose that is how you would see it." Magda answered without even the tiniest bit of chagrin in her voice. "I, however, believe differently. If there is no hope of success one is more likely to fail or not even try."

"Don't worry; I plan to fight like hell." My fierce answer brought a smile to Lucian's lips and a happy nod from Magda. "I will do everything in my power to keep my mate beside me for a very long time."

Lucian embraced me tightly and whispered, heatedly in my ear. "I shall do the same for you."

With a very unladylike snort, Magda clapped her hands loudly and the scene before us changed to one of horror. All our friends lay dead or dying at the feet of

Fraxinus and his army of fae and other supporters. We stared, aghast and disgusted at the vision in front of us.

"Janita saw two paths before you, one where you fight, one where you don't. Only one ends in deaths of everyone." Magda gazed at us, with an expectant look on her face.

We looked at each other then back at Magda. Our minds were opened fully to each other, so we didn't need long to decide. What could ever keep us from fulfilling our destiny?

"What is your recommendation?" Lucian bowed his head; our hands shaking in his lap.

"Return immediately to Gaia. Go directly to this location," an image of a snow-covered field appeared in the flames. "Remain there until the fae army marches upon you." Magda walked across the room and knocked on a part of the wall. A door appeared in the wall and a young woman with pale blonde hair and silver eyes stepped into the room carrying two packs.

"We have provided shelter and provisions for you that shall keep you safe and fed for seven days." Janita held out the packs for us to take.

Lucian takes them from the woman who I assume is Janita. He hands one to me, it feels overly light to be able to carry a week's worth of supplies. I peak inside; it looks empty as well.

Seeing my confusion, Lucian reaches his hand inside and roots around for a second then pulls out a yellow fruit or vegetable. I really am not sure what it is other than it looks like something we could eat, and it came out of my empty bag.

"The bags are spelled to carry large amounts of items while not appearing to have anything inside them." He pulls a pillow from my bag next then puts it back in. "I will teach you how to use it but when we first arrive, I'll get us set up."

Just like Hermione's bag from Harry Potter, I think to myself. Lucian looks at me with a question on his face. *I'll explain wizards in train stations later.* He nods then gives his attention back to Magda.

"We don't know what could have prevented us from making it to that field, but nothing will now. We will go there at once and remain until the day of the battle." He promises her, I nod my head with fervent agreement. I may not be happy about the chance that I may not survive, but I would never turn my back on a fight, especially one to save my friends and family.

316

Chapter Fifty

Cassandra

The ship made Kugluktuk in two brutal days, exactly as promised, though no less miserable for it. They disembarked in scattered small groups since the ship was magically hidden from the human population.

Nikolas and I greeted each group, providing directions to the rendezvous point. Once the ship was empty, Jacky used a spell to send it further into the Arctic Ocean far from nosy humans.

On our arrival two days ago, we met Twyla's future mother-in-law and the leader of her coven, Maria. She was a tall, thin and somewhat imposing woman with dark brown hair and piercing blue eyes. My impression of her based on Twyla's comments and how well Aelwyd operated was of a capable and fair witch.

Twyla gave her our numbers and explained the need to assist the witches within our group with transportation. Maria yelled an order to 'gather the herd' much to Twyla's glee.

My jaw gaped when I saw what the herd was. I was expecting heavy furred horses or some type of beast of burden able to withstand the cold. What we got was something altogether different.

Twyla told us they are called calygreyhounds. They seem to be many animals combined. They have the head of a tiger; their bodies looked like some form of deer, front paws ending in the claws of an eagle, the hind legs and tail of a lion, and a few of them even have antlers. They are fed the same concoction we would all be imbibing daily to withstand the cold.

We joined our large group a few miles outside of Kugluktuk and prepared for the two-day journey to Aelwyd. Everyone drank their daily cold repellent potion, most of us making a face at the bitter taste. The witches climbed on the backs of the calygreyhounds.

We planned to eat and drink as we walked, taking no breaks. Nikolas squeezed my hand as we marched, his palm unusually clammy. Even dragon kings fear what's coming. Our breaths steamed white in the freezing air, but the potions kept us warm.

Twyla assured us the calygreyhounds could withstand the pace and the cold too. This is the only reason they have bred them for so many years. "They taste horrible, and their milk isn't safe for witch consumption. They are however great pack animals." Her cheeky grin brought a smile to my face.

We reached Aelwyd a few hours earlier than we expected. Maria and a few of their strongest witches greeted us at the border of their lands. She had news from one of her scouts.

An army of what she believed was fae based on the descriptions was gathering about three hundred miles southeast of us. Her scout said it looked like close to fifteen hundred fae as well as a few hundred vampires and witches. We only had five days left to prepare.

"Lucian and Aisling will be expecting a fae army on their front." Arianna told Maria, providing the best coordinates we had to the witch leader.

On Maria's orders, one of the witches with the power to repel an attacker, took a small group to begin the process of separating the forces. Anger had my fingers twitching in Nikolas' hands; our actions could cause the end of my friends' lives. But we knew for any chance of success we needed to stick to the prophecies we had been sent.

Maria walked and talked, giving us her information while also guiding us towards makeshift tents and lean-tos. We were all exhausted and once her report finished, we fell into the provided quarters, promptly falling asleep.

Well rested after a few hours of sleep we all rose and began the final preparations for the battle to come. We organized our fighters into groups that we hoped had the best chance against the fae.

"We'll take Twyla and head to the northeastern edge." Evan pointed out on the map. The entire O'Brien clan sans Saoirse would march with them.

Almerinda and Damian would take the rest of her squad, who all had rather interesting skills and powers to the south. They would join up with the group already in place helping to divert part of the army toward Lucian and Aisling.

"Will you lead a group up the middle?" Arianna asked Jace and Jaxson, two former Elite Guards.

They scanned the map of the battlefield. Gabriel and Cat shifted in beside them, and after a few minutes of discussion they agreed. They would lead a frontal attack that would work to distract our enemies so Nikolas, Arianna, Hawthorne and

I could sneak through to get to Fraxinus and the Fontaines. We would take Jonesie and a few wolf shifters with us.

James and Davina would take to the sky while Brian and the wolves would run their own ground game. The dragon's powers over life and death were the only sure way we knew the fae would die. The plan was to have them swoop in on distracted fae and coat them with their life sapping mist.

"We'll cause as much havoc as we can." Brian assured us, a gleeful grin on his face, his teeth bared. They would work as berserker fighters, attacking and withdrawing, keeping the enemy confused. Thus, hopefully providing the distractions that Davina and James needed to get close enough without being brought down themselves.

We would integrate the Aelwyd witches into our forces over the next three days and be in position on the fourth. Most of them were not skilled fighters, rather armed with lethal spells.

On our third night, curled in my mate's arms, my mind was ill at ease. What if we're placing too much faith in the visions and prophecies? One prophecy sat in my gut like bad meat. What if we'd misread it? What if 'pain at his side' meant I'd betray him?

'Our savior sprung from the root of a sickened tree, with pain at his side they will stave off the impending hordes.' Everyone, Nik and I included, believed this referred to the two of us.

One thing I did not know at first was that Fraxinus and Hawthorne were both types of trees and their father, Magnus Quercus, was the Mighty Oak. So, we all believe Nikolas is the savior from a sickened tree. I must be the pain at his side since my power is to inflict pain with just my mind. Now we just need to figure out exactly how we stave off impending hordes.

Chapter Fifty-One

Arianna

Dawn breached the horizon, cruel bright and knife cold. The temps had dropped below freezing, without the potion to keep us warm we'd be dead.

Our chosen battlefield was perfect for fighting. It was mostly flat and surrounded by trees. Once we met in battle there would be little places for our enemy to hide without retreating. That was also the same for our side, but we'd fight to the death to protect this and all other worlds from being overrun by the fae.

The fae were not always the evil beings they had morphed into. I continue to hope that those that are joining my mate in his quest for power are the minority within the larger population of Alfheimer. If the entire fae populace is set on ruling this realm then I fear our efforts will be in vain. Either way, we will meet them in a matter of hours to determine the future of our three worlds.

Our plans had been made, and everyone was in their appointed positions. Now we wait. Yesterday we received word from Almerinda's group that at least a quarter of the advancing army had split from the main body. Sadness tried to overcome me when I thought of the two waiting to face that smaller, yet still formidable army. I hope that their stolen time alone was a happy time.

My force stood behind and off to the left of the main fighting force that would lead the charge up the middle. Davina and James were already in their dragon forms just waiting for the bulk of the fae warriors to enter the field before they would start their attack runs. The wolves were spread amongst us, about half already changed into their animal forms.

Jonesie met my eyes in silent communication as if asking if I was ready. I nodded and steeled my back readying for battle. Over a century ago, I had faced Morbicus in battle and came out triumphant. This time I knew I would not survive since to win I needed to kill that which has kept me alive long past my normal lifespan.

The army finally broke through the tree line, and we readied ourselves for attack. The fae had been joined by several hundred vampires and witches. I did not see any shifters, but it was hard to tell from this distance especially if they were in their human forms. The potions bitter aftertaste clung to my tongue as I adjusted my grip on the dagger at my hip. Nearby a wolf whimpered, not from fear, but eagerness.

Brian's massive form came to stand beside me for a moment, "No shifters, just as I expected. My kind would never be so foolish as to join with that scum."

I acknowledged his comment with a slight smile, and he moved on to rally his wolves. I continued to scan the numbers on the field. Fraxinus and the Fontaine brothers were nowhere to be seen. We had expected them to stay in the back, so would bring the fight to them. I was done hiding, now was the time to end Fraxinus and the Fontaines once and for all.

I stamped my feet; the cold was seeping through the potion's effects. A strong wind blew ice crystals into my face. The ozone scent of building magic told me the witches were ready.

The signal to begin echoed down the lines once the army had filled a large part of the field with their numbers. Jace led his crew in a charge across the field. His mate at his side made it easy to track them as her red hair shone brightly in the morning sun. Jaxson and Gabriel were close behind the two of them and I watched in awe as the four of them worked in unison together as if they had been fighting side by side for many years.

I knew Catriona had not been a vampire for long but clearly, she had brought some skills from her human life into her new one. They had about sixty people fighting with them and within a few minutes had a swath of bodies cut through the front lines. Jace let out a shrill whistle, signaling for the wolves to begin harrying the edges of the oncoming army.

James and Davina took to the sky and the wolves moved in and out of the ground forces. More of the fae fell with each swoop from the two spirit dragons. They had to be exact with their deadly mist to only hit our enemy as well as be able to move quickly out of the way of any weapons or spells from our opponents on the ground.

Temperence appeared dressed for battle in full leather gear. As a warlock she wore the bespelled leathers that covered her body from head to toe. She marched onto the field and pulled a long sword from the air. Following closely behind her were Annie and Matthew, each with a shorter sword of their own. The three of them attacked the enemy ranks severing body parts in a flurry of motion.

321

Malina and Diana stood off to one side, waiting to attack any enemy that made it across the front line. Their powers were better suited for one-to-one combat rather than against a large group. Anyone who made it through the front would be met with fire from Malina and whatever element Diana chose to throw at them.

Jonesie nudged me reminding me it was time to move. The chaos on the field should hopefully hide our activity. Cassandra and Nikolas were opening a portal so we could get to a predetermined spot in the trees. Last night four shifters had taken up position there. We hoped they had managed to remain undetected and that we weren't opening a portal directly into the hands of Fraxinus.

The portal shimmered like disturbed water. Hawthorne stepped through first, always the sacrificial lamb, with Jonesie and I breathing down his neck. Once we were through Cassandra and Nikolas followed us, the portal slamming shut behind them. Thankfully the four men were all that were waiting for us.

We crept through the dense undergrowth, the sound of the battle behind us, masking our sound. Every snapped twig sounded like a gun blast. My heartbeat thundered louder than the distant battle.

A tracker from Jonesie's group led us through the trees, occasionally stopping then changing directions slightly. He assured us he could lead us to Marcel Fontaine, which is where we should find Fraxinus. If the tracker was wrong about Marcel's location…I stopped that thought in its tracks.

Chapter Fifty-two

Aisling

Our frozen fingers intertwined, an unbreakable knot, we would stand together. The tundra stretched endlessly, our tombstone of ice and snow. Where was the aid Magda said we would have? Fate had decreed this day; we would face it as one.

We arrived here a week ago, crazy Harry Potter bags on our backs and trust in each other's determination to see this through. Lucian pulled items from our sacks and set up a tent. There better be some magic involved in its fabric or we were going to get real cold real fast.

Yep, there was some magic juju in them, our magical tents kept us warm. Over dinner, I told Lucian the story of Harry Potter and his friends. He enjoyed it, loving the idea of a small group of kids prevailing against so many enemies. I couldn't help but see the parallels he was making to our situation.

We spent our time learning more about each other. The more I found out about my mate the more I loved him. The more I loved him the more I cursed the Fates for giving him to me only to take him away from me so quickly. Now that the mantle of being a king had been removed, Lucian had become less stiff, and he was much quicker to laugh and relax than when he first walked through the portal.

Our week of learning and lovemaking had come to an end and now we stand at the edge of a frost-bitten field staring down our enemy as it advances slowly toward us. Their shapes were still mostly a blur, but we estimated there was anywhere from four to five hundred.

Snow whipped around us as Lucian gazed at me with all the love in the world shining through his swirling eyes. Gods, why ever did you send me my mate if we were going to have such a short time together?

"I love you Aisling O'Brien." Lucian declared. "I don't care if our time was short, I only care that we had any time at all."

Tears pool in the corners of my eyes. I would not cry. If for no other reason than the tears would probably freeze my eyes closed. We knew our fate was to meet this legion of fae. Serafina had seen us being overcome on this field of battle. She

323

knew the chances of her brother returning to their world were almost non-existent. She also knew that if he failed to meet his mate and face this army that all the worlds would be lost to the fae.

"Lucian, you are my world and if it is to come to an end, I am forever grateful that I get to meet that end with you by my side." Our breaths mingled in the frosted air.

Lucian pulled me into his arms, kissing me so tenderly that the tears did start to flow. Our tender kiss held an underlying desperation, and I damned the fae even more for the loss of my future with my mate.

Reality tore open, the pressure making my ears pop. Elodie emerged, a vision of golden hair and questionable fashion choices, her stilettos sinking into snow that should have swallowed her whole.

"What in the hell do you think you are doing?" her exasperated French accented voice cut through our tender moment like a knife.

I spun to face her, almost tripping, yanking Lucian with me. "Elodie!" I gasped. "Well, it sure took you long enough to show up."

"I had not realized I was expected." She replied blandly cinching her fur stole closer to her shoulders.

"You actually weren't." I could not help but feel a little hope that Lucian and I may actually make it out of this alive. "You just seem to like to swoop in and save the day." I noticed Lucian eyeing Elodie suspiciously. "This is my mate, Lucian. And this is Elodie, ah, well; I'm not really sure how to describe you."

"She is fae." He growled, red and orange scales undulating across his skin. My muscles coiled, ready to spring between them. Her powers slapped him back, holding him in place, his feet slipping on the icy snow.

"You would do well to stand down King Lucian Griffin." At his look of surprise, she added. "Yes, I know who you are." Dismissing him, she turned her gaze back to me. "I came to offer assistance, however if the menace I feel from your mate continues, I shall withdraw it."

"Lucian she is an ally. Please relax." I held his cheeks in my hands. His multi-colored eyes turned black with blood red slits. My mind screams 'Danger!' at me, but I knew he would never hurt me. My fingers dug into his skin, "Lucian, please."

His gaze softens, but his posture remained rigid. *How do you know her?* He asked through our bond. *She has helped us before; I will explain all later if we get out of this.* Trusting me, Lucian stood back and released the tension in his posture.

"Good, now do not be alarmed but some of my friends will be joining us in a minute. I don't have much time to explain so let me get through it quickly." Elodie proceeded to lay out her plan and since we had no choice but to either go along with it or meet our certain death we obviously agreed.

A line appeared over Elodie's shoulder, the pressure in my ears built again. Then with a final whistling, my ears popped and a fae thin as a whip and taller than Lucian with pitch black hair and porcelain skin stood in front of Elodie. "Ah, Aengus I see you were able to follow my thread."

"Elodie," He bowed his head in respect then turned to face us. "Lucian Griffin, how many years has it been?" The unusual looking man asked my mate.

"Well over a thousand my old friend." Lucian stepped toward the newcomer. "That is if we are still friends." Lucian held his arm out to the fae named Aengus.

I held my breath in fear that we were dealing with a double cross. The fae stepped forward and reached his hand out to grasp Lucian's elbow. Lucian also gripped the fae's elbow as they gave three quick pumps of the arms and then released them.

"There was a time when the fae and the dragon were friends." Elodie explained quietly to me. "Aengus and Lucian were great friends before the war came to a head. As I tell everyone, not all fae are bad. Just like not all dragons are good."

"If not for Casius' inability to control himself," Aengus's raspy voice made the hairs on my neck stand up, and my lynx hissed, "our friendship would have continued unabated."

Aengus and Elodie crouched behind us. Due to our position on a small hillock, they were able to hide their presence from the oncoming fae. "Now when the moment is right, we shall spring our trap."

The army of fae continued its slow advancement towards our position. I hopped from foot to foot, my lynx roaring, ready to attack. I looked for weaknesses in their line and found none. The front line all carried long spears with deadly blades on the tip. They blocked any view of what awaited us behind them.

I did not know how this would end but for the first time since learning of Serafina's vision, I felt hope. Elodie's plan gave us an edge we didn't have before, but there were still so many things that could go wrong.

Our beginning was not the easiest and yet we found our way to the love that we now shared. We would prevail or fall as one on this field of battle. Neither of us saw a future without the other. Gods, Fates, whoever might answer my prayers, please let us come through this together.

Snow continued to drift down around us, but I no longer felt the cold. Lucian's grip on my hand tightened and I leaned into his body. Our energies combined, readying to spring Elodie's trap.

Chapter Fifty-three

Cassandra

The portal's magic clung to my skin as we emerged into a winter wonderland. If not for the battle raging behind us, I could almost find it peaceful. We followed the tracker, hopefully to Fraxinus and not our deaths.

The tracker came to an abrupt halt, his fist in the air. The attack came from everywhere at once. A fae soldier stepped out of one of the trees along our path. One moment he was not there and the next he had literally stepped out of the tree, not from behind the tree but from within the tree. Seven more fae materialized out of trees, bark peeled back like skin, revealing glistening muscle before reforming behind them.

The morning sky turned dark, and icy snow began to pelt us. The fae surrounded our small group and looked closely at each of us as if they were searching for something specific. Apparently finding what they wanted, the first fae said something in their language that prompted the others to attack.

Within a matter of seconds, the four shifters fell to the ground. Their dead eyes stared at the once clear sky. Jonesie massive hands ripped the head from the skinny body of the fae nearest to him. He hurled the body at the next fae that was moving into attack.

Suddenly, Jonesie's body stiffened, his eyes met mine. The same scent of cloves that preceded the shifters death assailed my sinuses. I realized if I didn't do something quickly, he would meet the same fate as his friends. Rage detonated in my chest, and I let it consume me.

A supernova of pain tore out of me and ripped through the fae like shrapnel. Fury fueled me as I poured more of my power of pain into the seven remaining fae warriors. Drool began to form at the corner of their mouths. Their eyes rolled into the back of their sockets and each of them began gibbering.

Flashbacks of my mother pulled a wail of anguish from my body. Nikolas yanked me into his arms. Pushing his thoughts through the discord within my mind, he dragged me back from the brink of pain and madness for myself.

I collapsed into his arms, staring around at the devastation I had wrought. I felt no guilt at the deaths of those who would do harm to me and my friends. Jonesie lumbered back to his feet, his mind free from the fae's control. His grateful grin was all the thanks I needed.

We regrouped, with the loss of the tracker, finding Fraxinus would be more difficult. We headed in the direction the shifter had been leading us, praying this was the right direction. The snow thickened, cutting our visibility to only a few inches. If I hadn't been holding Nikolas' hand I would not have been able to locate him.

Nikolas and I moved as one trying to find a break in the unusual weather. The storm was clearly the work of a witch. Without knowing if our enemies were close, we kept silent. We just had to hope that the others would find their way through.

We walked for at least a mile before the snow cleared enough that our visibility returned. Our feet had led us to a small field. In that small field stood Fraxinus, a witch I assumed was Martine, Andre and Marcel Fontaine. Hawthorne emerged from the tree line behind our foes. There was no sight of Jonesie or Arianna.

My hand tightened on my mate's as we walked toward his father, Nikolas called out. "Hello father, I would say I am happy to see you but that would be a lie."

Fraxinus' face darkened, then smoothed out to a placid expression. "Nikolas, how wonderful it is to see you. Thank you for bringing your mate directly to me so I would not need to search you out." He surveyed the dense forest behind us. "Where is your mother?"

"She was never with us." Nikolas answered.

"You lie." Martine screeched from her perch behind Fraxinus. "We saw her, she was standing beside that large black vampire."

Hawthorne chose that moment to march across the snowy field, "Fraxinus, you must stop this at once. You bring shame on our family with your actions." Fraxinus moved to meet his brother in the center of the field. The large identical forms crashed into each other and if not for the different clothing I would have had difficulty telling them apart.

Blow after blow fell, while the rest of us watched to see who would prevail over the other. Hawthorne overpowered his brother and held him in a tight grip, one arm around his throat and the other wrenching Fraxinus' arm behind his back. "Give up this foolish war and come back to Fabeldyrverden to face judgment."

"I will never return there in defeat. Once I have wiped you and all others who oppose me from this land I will return as the triumphant conqueror." Fraxinus smiled wickedly and I knew he had planned this.

"Hawthorne!" My warning shout came too late. Martine snuck up behind Hawthorne, plunging an iron infused sword into his back. Agony rushed across his face as he flailed his arms trying to grab the sword handle.

Once Fraxinus was free from his brother's grip he stood up and pulled a dagger from his waist. He thrust forward, seating the dagger to the hilt in his twin brother's chest. Hawthorne's blood steamed in the snow. The coppery scent flooded my nose as Nikolas' grip turned crushing.

As one Nikolas and I attacked. The Fontaine brothers moved to intercept us, and ten more vampires and witches materialized out of the surrounding trees. We fought with our backs braced against each other. My anger over the death of Hawthorne fueled a power in me I did not know I had.

Nikolas's fury poured from him as he grabbed enemy after enemy, ripping them limb from limb. Andre Fontaine managed to break through and grabbed my arm trying to pull me away from my mate. Nikolas spun toward him and with the strength of twenty men removed the vampire's head from his body, catapulting it into the trees.

Marcel, at seeing his brother killed, rushed by the four remaining vampires. His hand clamped down on my arm, pulling me hard against his chest. "Ma Cherie, you will pay for my brother's death. I will despoil you for many, many years before I allow you to die." He placed a dagger at my throat when Nikolas turned to confront him. "No, no, I will slice her throat before you can make it two steps."

My eyes met my mate's; agony shone through his as he looked at my face then glanced at my abdomen where our child was growing. Disgust filled me when I felt Marcel's obvious excitement over despoiling me prod my back. I tried to move away but he pulled me closer, grinding his insubstantial member against me.

"Ah, I see you feel my desire for your body. Once you have performed your duty for Fraxinus, you will spend your days performing for me."

There was no way Nikolas could get to me before Marcel could kill me. "Don't think of using your power on me, I am immune from witch's spells." Marcel whispered into my ear giddily.

Martine used Nikolas' distraction with me to her advantage. Stepping out from behind Fraxinus, she placed a hand on Nikolas' arm. His body became docile, all the rage leaving it at once. *I am still here.* He informed me through our link. His mind was still his own, but his body was now under the control of Martine. She forced him to kneel in front of his father.

"Marcel, bring the hybrid bitch." Fraxinus ordered, pointing to the cold ground beside Nikolas. Marcel dragged me to Nikolas' side, forcing me to my knees. "You will now open a portal to Fabeldyrverden."

"Never." I yelled, spitting at the ground in front of him. "We will never allow you back into that peaceful realm." Fraxinus backhanded me, sending my body to the ground. I pulled myself back to my kneeling position defiant in the face of this evil man.

"Nikolas, convince your mate to serve me, or you will both spend the rest of your lives locked within your bodies by Martine being despoiled by Marcel." Fraxinus threatened us. Marcel's dreamy grin as he gazed at Nikolas was all the evidence I needed to know that he probably lusted after my mate more than me.

Use your power. Nikolas spoke into my mind. I can't, I wailed. Marcel says he is immune to a witch's power. *You power is not from a witch; it comes from a vampire.* He was right, my vampire father gave it to me.

"Pay attention, son." Fraxinus smacked Nikolas across the face. "You have no choice but to obey me." His father looked at Martine, "loosen his tongue; I need him to be able to talk." Martine made a small gesture towards Nikolas' mouth freeing it from the spell. "Will you do my bidding or do you prefer to be rutted upon for centuries by that depraved vampire."

You must take out Marcel! Revulsion coated his words in my head. "I will not let you back into Fabeldyrverden." He vowed to his father.

Marcel's erection pressed against me like a tumor. Nausea boiled up my throat at the thought of this man touching me or Nikolas. I couldn't allow him to have dominion over our bodies. His hand fondled the side of my breast; my disgust stoked my anger. I let it build.

My power felt heavy, almost like a solid weight sitting on my chest. I dug deeper, pulling every last ounce of energy I had into my center. Heat coursed through my veins, and I knew I couldn't take anymore. I inclined my head, meeting the unsuspecting vampire's vile gaze. A small mile quirked my lips as I unleashed my power on him.

Marcel's grip loosened but didn't release me. I pushed more pain into his body. "How are you doing this?" His anguished wail howled to the trees around us. "I am immune, how are you doing this?"

His hands fell completely away from me, and I was free from his grip. I rose to my feet and faced him and the four vampires standing behind him. Pain erupted on all their faces as I emptied everything, I had into them.

The four vampires fell to the ground, grabbing their heads as blood began running from their eyes, nose and ears. Their bodies jerked and convulsed on the ground until one by one they fell silent, dead.

Marcel writhed on the ground; apparently, he had some immunity to my pain. His 'I told you so' smile ignited something in the depths of my soul. More power than I ever had in my life flooded my veins. I pushed all of it out of me and into him.

His eyes widened and he clutched his head. His eyes glazed over, and drool began to run from his constricted mouth. The world shattered into white noise as Marcel's scream followed me into darkness.

Chapter Fifty-Four

Aisling

Twenty feet. That's all that separated us from five hundred fae warriors. The army began to fan out, surrounding us with their numbers. My fingers twitched, every instinct screamed to attack or flee, but we held our position.

"Now!" Shrieked Elodie and we sprang into action.

Lucian transformed into his dragon form, and I vaulted onto his back pulling my swords from their sheaths. I partially shifted my arms, giving me greater strength and long talons. I have fought many times with my swords in this manner and knew I would have a better chance against the superior strength of the fae in this form.

With a quick sweep of his long-barbed tail, he decimated close to fifty of the fae nearest us. If any fae managed to get by his tail, I was quick to cut them down with my iron infused blades. A roar of fire spewed from Lucian's throat taking out more fae. Within the first minute, we had killed almost one hundred of their forces.

We knew this would not be enough though. A shrill whistle from Elodie alerted us to the second prong of her plan. Pressure built in my ears, cutting sound off for a few seconds. Loud pops released the pressure as reality itself seemed to tear a hole in the air around us. One hundred fae warriors materialized from nowhere, their burgundy armor glinting against the snow.

We were still outnumbered four to one but with a fire dragon on our side, we had more than a fighting chance of succeeding. The surprise we saw on the face of the army surrounding us was also welcome. Being confronted by their brethren seemed to give them pause and their attack slowed.

Lucian took to the sky, causing me to screech as I clung to his neck. *Warn me next time!* A low chuckle in my mind was his only response. Lucian flew to the rear of the attacking army as planned and set to fight. Fire belched from his mouth and his dangerous tail swung menacingly. My swords brought death to any fae that broke past his fire and tail.

Lucian's sharp claws ripped the head from the body of a fae warrior, tossing it into the next one to advance. The spurting blood was cut off by a blast of fire that incinerated the headless body as well as several other fae in the area. Ash filled the air, and the acrid taste of burnt flesh filled my mouth.

"Ugh!" I spat the taste from my mouth. "That's nasty!

A tall blonde fae managed to get past Lucian's tail, jumping onto his back. I quickly spun, bringing the sword in my left hand around to parry the thrust of his sword. My right hand swung deftly through the air at the same time.

The fae knocked my right sword from my hand. I watched it sail over the side of Lucian's back, ducking as the fae brought his blade around again. I parried with my left, blocking his swing, then swiped my right arm toward him. With the added strength from my partially shifted arm my extended claws cut clean through the fae's torso. His body fell to the ground landing on either side of Lucian's barbed tail.

We fought like this for what felt like hours but it was in fact only about fifteen minutes. The pristine white ground turned red from all the spilled blood. The once serene landscape was now flooded with dead bodies, many in several pieces. Smoke and ash filled the air. No enemies stood before us, Lucian swung around ready to engage in more battle. I gripped his black scaled fringe, ready for anything.

We turned at the sound of Elodie's voice calling for us to stop. There were still about fifty or sixty enemy fae standing but they had all laid down their weapons and had their long arms in the air. We flew the couple hundred yards to our tent, and I climbed off Lucian's back.

We reverted to our human forms and grabbed the clothes we had left in the entrance. My body shook, whether from gratitude or just the adrenaline fading. Lucian wrapped his arms around me, pulling my naked, blood crusted body against his. With my back to his chest, he kissed my neck.

"We're alright." His deep voice stirred the hair on my nape, giving me a different kind of shakes. I rested my head on his chest, taking a small moment just to feel his heartbeat against my back. He's right, we're alright.

I pivoted, facing him now and placed my hand on his cheek. His strange eyes swirled as he lowered his mouth to brush my lips with his. Gods, I could get lost in this man forever. Then it hit me, we did have forever.

"We should check in with Elodie." I said, forcing myself to move out of the arms of my mate. "Plus, as much as I love you, no way are we having sex covered in blood and guts."

333

Lucian's laughter filled the tent. We used the last of our water stores to clean off, then donned fresh clothing. With a final yearning glance at our unmade bedding, we left the tent. We walked through the carnage to stand at Aengus and Elodie's side. A little more than fifty fae knelt on the ground, surrounded by the burgundy armored fae.

"All you who have opposed the will of Ríonmháthair shall be returned to Alfheimer for breithiúnas." Aengus called out to the defeated fae.

A blonde fae stepped forward, "Why do you side with the dragons?" he demanded. "They mean to lay siege to our world."

"I do not side with the dragons. I side with the fae." Aengus responded, glaring at the prisoners. "You have all been lied to. The dragons had no plans to attack Alfheimer. The seals are still intact." Aengus stared down the blonde fae until he knelt back with the rest of the fallen fae. "You were all so blinded by bloodlust that you believed a family of vampires not known for their truthfulness. And you disobeyed Ríonmháthair." His raspy voice echoed across the bloody battlefield.

Aengus turned to the other fae that had joined our side in the fight. After giving them orders he turned his attention back to us. "Lucian, it has been a pleasure to see you again. I do hope that we can rekindle our friendship once the furor of yet another battle between our kinds has died down."

"I look forward to it, Aengus." Lucian gave the fae a quick hug. "I shall send word when the portals are open. You may come to Fabeldyrverden again so long as you honor our laws."

"Perhaps we can begin to trade with one another again. I do so miss the vitae of your world." Aengus licked his lips at the thought of the liquor Lucian had described to me. "Ah, and fairy honey, I have long missed its soothing healing."

"I am sure we can scrounge up a few bottles of vitae for you." Lucian grinned at the taller fae. "Possibly we could share one of those bottles for old time's sake."

I scrounged around in my pack and pulled several bottles of the fairy honey we had received in Fabeldyrverden and showed them to Lucian. He took all but two of them and handed them to Aengus who whooped with pleasure at the sight of one of the items he had been missing for centuries.

"I would enjoy that very much. Let us hope the other battle that is raging further north of here ends justly as well." He swept the bottles of honey from Lucian's outstretched hands. "Thank you, my friend."

With a small bow of his head toward Lucian than me, Aengus popped out of our world and into Alfheimer. The rest of the fae had slowly departed while Aengus and Lucian were speaking.

Now it was just the three of us. Lucian eyed Elodie with concern. "So, Elodie?" I looked at her with a question in my voice. "Do you want to tell my mate about yourself or shall I?"

With a serene smile Elodie walked across the field of blood and snow. "Mon enfant, you may tell him anything you wish." She came to a sudden stop; dread seeped into her eyes, her face paled. "I feel my progeny calling." And then she was gone, moving faster than even vampires could track.

Lucian pulled me into his arms. "Should we try to follow?" He asked while at the same time making no movement to do so.

"I don't think so." I snuggled closer to his broad chest. "Your sister's vision did not show us leaving this field. It may be best if we stay out of the rest of the battle so as not to mess with any positive outcomes she and Delilah foresaw."

"You have a point." His strong hands massaged my back and shoulders. "Why did you not change as we had planned?"

I stiffened at his question. I knew he was going to ask it since we had planned to fight side by side in our dragon forms. I should say he planned for us to do so. I on the other hand felt I would be better suited half shifted to my lynx form to use its power but still have control of my swords. "I didn't feel like I had practiced enough in my dragon form. I know how to fight without having to think too hard on it as a lynx or partially shifted as I did today."

"I noticed." His look of possessive pride warmed my heart. "Why didn't you just say so then? I never would have forced the issue."

"When I changed into my dragon for the first time, you looked so satisfied and excited. All the times we practiced on the island, I could feel your pride in my dragon." I tucked my chin into his chest. "We were doing so well, not fighting near as much, especially after Cassandra and Nikolas told us about Serafina's vision; that I just wanted to keep the peace going." His arms tightened around me, pulling me even closer. "I guess I just wanted to savor our happy times."

"Oh, Aisling, my darling, now that we have a future," Lucian tipped my face up to his with a finger under my chin, "you must promise to fight with me over anything you don't agree with me on."

"Now, that is a promise I can make." Laughing I pulled his mouth to mine.

We broke off our kiss before it could get too heated. Making love on a bloody snowy ground was not on my to-do list, ever. We walked hand in hand back to the tent. Our celebration of life was going to start in the warm confines of the spelled tent and each other's arms.

Chapter Fifty-Five

Arianna

Ice and snow swirled around me, the sounds of the distant battle my only guide. I angled away from the battle, heading into Gods knew where. Somewhere in this frozen hell, my son fought for his life, and I couldn't find him.

A young vampire emerged from the snow, and I cursed myself for not taking more time to meet everyone that had come to my island. I did not want to attack if he was an ally.

When the young man launched himself at me, he took away all doubt that he was on my side. I parried to the left, his teeth just skimming my neck. The cold brush of dread spread down my spine, even as my sword found its mark. "Disintegrate." I spoke over his prone body, evoking the spell to finish him off.

Advancing through the snow I eventually found my mate. The scene froze my blood worse than any arctic wind. Cassandra lay at his feet, motionless. Nikolas kneeling. Fraxinus triumphant. Martine stood behind and to the left of Fraxinus. The witch must have spelled Nikolas. There is no chance he would not have attacked his father otherwise.

"You will open a portal, son, or I will kill your mate." Fraxinus roared at Nikolas.

I surveyed the field around my son and his father. Marcel Fontaine lay crumpled on the ground, gibbering with drool running from the corner of his mouth. There were also several dead bodies of vampires and witches.

"I will not allow you to gain entry to Fabeldyrverden." Nikolas seethed.

Fraxinus prodded Cassandra's body with his boot. I could see the strain on my son's face as he fought the bonds holding him in place. Cassandra's chest rose and fell as she breathed. She must have been knocked unconscious somehow.

Fraxinus kicked her harder in the side, "I won't ask again. Open the portal or the next kick will be her death."

"If you kill her, I will lose the ability to open a portal." Nikolas reasoned. "We are at a stalemate, it would seem. You need us both and I promise I will die before I allow you back into Fabeldyrverden."

Wrath took over Fraxinus as he attacked his son. Nikolas was unable to defend himself due to Martine's spell. "Disintegrate." I whispered as my gaze was locked on Martine. My spell was blocked by a shield spell. Damn, I needed to be closer to Martine to be able to knock her out. I was going to have to face Fraxinus if I had any hope of saving my son.

"Fraxinus, hold!" I hollered, marching to the middle of the empty field. I stepped over a headless vampire. My nose twitched at the coppery scent of blood pooling where his head should be. "Have you no shame, beating your son like that?" I reprimanded my mate as if he were a small child.

"Ah, Arianna, I wondered when you would arrive." Fraxinus ceased pummeling Nikolas. "You can stop there, my love. No reason for you to come any closer to our little party."

Standing still, I took in the scene around me. Cassandra was still immobile. Nikolas was bloodied and bruised. Martine moved closer to Fraxinus, using him as a shield. The Fontaine vampire was still gibbering and drooling. I had no idea what caused that but whatever it was, it made him insubstantial to our current situation.

I gripped my sword in my hand, contemplating whether I could make it to Martine or Fraxinus. "Frax, you must stop this madness." I implored still searching for anyway out of this.

My son stared forlornly at his mate. She had still not moved and based on his look her mind must be locked away from him. "If you made it home, they would not welcome you. They know of your plans and will be prepared to fight you."

"I am the rightful ruler of that world. My brother should never have been given that title." His hand waved off to the left and I followed its path to see Hawthorne lying dead. Pain stabbed my chest; my hand flexed on the hilt of my sword.

"Hawthorne was no longer ruler there. Lucian Griffin is the current king." I could barely pull my eyes off Hawthorne's body. I shuddered at the look of pain etched on his still face. His suffering at the hands of his brother was finally at an end.

"Bah, how dare the Griffin line attempt to hold the throne. They are weak of will, mind and body. When I return the lad Lucian will be killed for his insolence." Fraxinus proclaimed. "You will return with me to live in the dungeons. Gods, why did the fates saddle me with such a feeble mate that I can't even rid myself of?"

An idea for how to end this begins to form in my mind. I must shield my thoughts. "I am not a feeble mate, Fraxinus." I step closer, but he is too busy ranting at me to notice my movements.

"Of course you are." He scoffed. "I should have gained more powers with our mating, but I didn't. If not for how impotent your powers were I would have returned home centuries ago. We could have returned together and raised our children where they belonged. Instead, we were stuck in this hellish world because you couldn't even lend me enough power to open a portal."

"Had you paid any attention to anyone but yourself before you left our home in anger you would know that your words are untrue." I moved closer to him, mumbling under my breath to lift the spells that had held back the joining of our powers. I could feel the rush of his powers melding with mine. Even without performing the Sanguis Draconis ceremony, we are stronger than before.

"What are you doing?" He roared, his focus finally returning to my advancing form.

"I am giving you what you wanted. I am joining our powers." The intensity increased as I opened the pathways wider and pulled more of his power into me. "You always believed I was a weak and ineffective witch. But you were dead wrong." The power rushed around my body like a mini tornado. My hair whipped around in the maelstrom and a faint glow emitted from my skin.

"Mother!" Nikolas howled. "Don't do it. Please do not do it."

My son must have figured out my plan. His father on the other hand still had not. 'I love you', I mouthed at my son.

Tears streamed down his cheeks. We had just found each other again and now I was going to leave him. I knew of no other way to be absolutely certain that Fraxinus would never cause problems again.

"Fraxinus, I'm going to let you in on a little secret." I spoke softly knowing full well he would hear me through our mate link. "I have never been a feeble witch. I am Arianna of the Danu line. My ancestors were the strongest spell casters to ever walk in any world. For more than a thousand years I have held your powers in check. I sensed the evil in you and vowed to never allow you to obtain your full strength." As I spoke, I moved closer to my mate. My eyes held him transfixed, keeping him from moving.

339

Arriving to stand directly in front of my mate, I gave my son one last wistful look. Meeting Fraxinus eyes again I brought the tip of my sword to rest on his abdomen.

Martine moved as if to attack but I sent a surge of our combined powers into her body. She fell back, clutching her chest then collapsed to the ground. Pain creased her forehead as she took her last breath. Over my mate's shoulder, my eyes met the smiling image of Manannan Mac Lir. I would be welcomed home to Sidhes with open arms.

"What do you think you're doing?" He glared down at the blade I held. "If you kill me, you kill yourself, you foolish woman."

A feeling of serenity enveloped my body. This is what I was meant to do. I reached my free hand up to stroke the hard line of my mate's jaw. "I really did want to love you, but you made it impossible. You turned my daughter into a murdering psychopath, and you enslaved my son. I wanted so much for you to be the man I deserved."

With one last loving glance at my son, I thrust the blade deep into his father's abdomen. Fraxinus' eyes widened, fear and surprise boiling within them. A quick flash of Fraxinus, smiling, holding Penelope and Nikolas in both arms, clamped my jaw shut. Fraxinus' maniacal grin at my hesitation, washed that happy memory away.

Resolve renewed, I summoned all the power at my disposal and screamed, "Disintegrate!" Our combined powers rammed the powerful spell into the wound. His eyes burned with hatred, then widened; pain, confusion, anger and was that regret?

My mate's body had turned to ash, its swirling mass frozen in the air in front of me. My world came to a standstill, no wind, no smell of blood. When I had called out my spell, I expected to meet the same fate as him.

"No, my child." The sea god came to stand beside me, resting his large hand on my shoulder. "You have given your entire life in service to good. It is only right that you spend your afterlife in rest. Sidhes awaits you."

Manannan Mac Lir waved his free hand towards the horizon. The smoke and ash cleared, the air redolent with summer sunshine and the sweet scent of primrose and honeysuckle. A warm breeze caressed my cheeks as the icy cold fell away. Reality unraveled like a frayed tapestry. The battlefield dissolved into golden light and suddenly, impossibly, I stood before paradise.

Before me was the most beautiful field of green grass and shamrock surrounding a clear blue pool of water. A small stone cottage sat on the opposite side of the pond, smoke wafting from the chimney.

The sea god curled his hand around mine, guiding me toward the next world. I spared one final look over my shoulder and said goodbye to my son and followed the god to my final rest.

Chapter Fifty-Six

Cassandra

I clawed my way out of darkness to find Nikolas crying over my body. Reaching up I wiped the tears from his cheeks. *I'm here, my love. I'm here.* He roughly pulled me into his arms, raining kisses on my cheeks and lips.

Nikolas told me what happened to his mother. She sacrificed herself to save us. I would forever be grateful to her for that and many other reasons. If not for her, I never would have met the man currently cradling my body close to his chest. When Arianna plunged the sword into Fraxinus' body and cast the disintegration spell she caused both of their bodies to turn to ash and blow away on the wind.

Nikolas crumbled into me, his despair mixing with my own. Ash and snow coated our clothing; remorse seeped into our bodies. I had suspected Arianna had a plan that would probably take her from us. Our sobs slowly tapered off, we pulled ourselves together. We needed to get back to the rest of the battle. There would be time for mourning later.

He helped me to stand, and we surveyed the land around us. Bodies littered the ground, the metallic tang of blood mixed with the crisp arctic air, making each breath like swallowing knives. The snow had stopped, and a spear of sunlight struck the ground near me.

My breath hitched, Gods, why? Hawthorne, innocent and caring, I wished he could have seen Fabeldyrverden one last time. His face was a contorted grimace of pain from the iron sword that still protruded from his back. I reached down to lay my fingers across his eyes, smoothing them closed. I wish I had gotten to know him better. *Me too.* Nikolas fell to his knees beside his uncle.

A loud crashing noise came from across the clearing. I turned to face whatever new enemy was coming. Nikolas began to pull himself up when the large form of Jonesie clamored into the clearing.

"Gods, what a fucking shit show that was." He bellowed upon seeing our startled faces. "We were all together and then the snow came, and I couldn't see a gods damned thing. No matter which way I turned I kept finding myself back in the trees with all the dead fae."

He came to a stop and looked around at the carnage on the ground. When he saw Hawthorne's body, a look of deep sympathy clouded over his confused expression. Jonesie came to stand beside me and placed his hand on my shoulder.

We stood in silent commiseration for several minutes. The sun was out, but I feared I'd never be warm again. Jonesie pulled Nikolas to his feet then yanked the sword from Hawthorne's back. Tossing the sword into the trees, he bent over and lifted his body into his arms, cradling him like a child.

The three of us walked out of that clearing, heads high but hearts low without a look back. We could no longer hear sounds of battle and hoped that our side had won. With nowhere else to go though, we made our way back to the battlefield.

The scene that greeted us was one of subdued relief. We had won but at a heavy price. Of the over four hundred people that had assembled to fight; only about half had survived. The survivors had rounded up the remaining fae, vampires and witches that had backed Fraxinus and the Fontaines in a circle in the center of the field.

Jace McFadden saw us first and walked away from the group with his mate Catriona at his side. "Fraxinus?" With only one word, he was really asking whether the fight was over or just beginning.

I nodded while Nikolas described what happened. "The Fontaine brothers are no longer a problem. Andre is dead and Marcel is a blithering idiot wandering the forest somewhere. My mother killed Fraxinus."

A small gasp escaped Catriona's lips. "But doesn't that mean she would die too?"

Despair threatened to overcome my mate. I placed my hand over his heart, sending love through our bond.

"She sacrificed herself to save us." I yelled out to the gathering the crowd. "Arianna has moved onto the next life; let us all hope it is a happier one than this one had been for her." A tiny uplift at the corner of Nikolas' mouth was the only indication he gave that he heard my words. "Does anyone know Lucian and Aisling's fate?"

"Aye," Jaxson stepped forward. "Not long after the battle began, my maker appeared out of nowhere. I was battling the fae feachd. To be fair, they were close to taking me out. She cut them down as if they were nothing. We fought until the captives over there gave up. She told me Aisling and Lucian lived and that she would return soon. Then walked into thin air and disappeared."

"How is she able to open portals?" Nikolas perked up a bit at this information. "Is she a dragon?"

By this time, I was happy to see Evan and Ali come to stand next to several other O'Briens. Evan, Jaxson and Jace all shared a look but none of them seemed to want to share the secret. Ali and Cat were whispering something to each other. "Don't you think it's time for the secrets to end?" I yelled.

"Normally we would agree with you." Ali answered for everyone who was looking everywhere but in my direction. "But this is not our secret to share. Elodie has kept this hidden for centuries."

"So, no one is willing to explain," my shout cut off as a sudden pressure built in my ears followed by a resounding pop. What in the world? A tall blonde-haired blue-eyed vampire in a satin evening gown and fur stole had just appeared out of thin air. However, she accomplished this was nothing like the portals we used.

Blood speckled her stilettos, yet she glided forward like the battlefield was a glamorous ballroom. She swept toward us, prancing daintily through the blood and gore.

Her melodic voice interrupted our argument. "They could not tell you my secret because they are true and faithful friends and family." She stepped between the McFadden brothers, taking their hands in hers. "Now that the prophesied war has come and gone, my secret can come to light. I am part fae, part vampire. Long story that I will not go into except to say I was changed as a child by the fae, and they failed to collect me before I was bitten by a vampire."

She walked over to stand in front of the captives. "Ríonmháthair arrives soon, and you shall all face breithiúnas." Fear and dread spread through the fae captives. The few vampires and witches just looked confused by her statement as were the rest of us.

"Breithiúnas?" Ali asked. "What the hell does that mean?"

"Who or what is Ríonmháthair?" Evan asked at the same time.

"Ríonmháthair is the ruler of the fae and breithiúnas means judgment." Elodie explained in a tone that seemed to imply we should have known that.

"Are we sure it is a good idea for the fae ruler to come here?" Nikolas growled low in his throat. "Did we not just battle an army of them?"

"Nikolas, my dear," Nikolas looked confused that this vampire fae woman knew who he was, "one thing you must understand is that she will be coming whether you will it or not. She forbade her people from participating in this battle and must come to pass judgment on them all. We have already sent about fifty back to meet their fates, but I am unable to send such a large group back on my own."

Pressure built and a much louder rending sound erupted behind us. The most dazzling woman I had ever seen stood where Elodie had first arrived. She was tall with pale red hair, large black eyes, and porcelain skin stretched over sharp cheekbones. Her gown, like Elodie's but with more gems on the edges, clung to her voluptuous form. Standing on either side of her was a tall thin black haired fae. The three fae moved in synchrony as if one being. It was a bit disconcerting to watch.

Ríonmháthair approached Nikolas and me. With a slight bow of her head she stated. "I apologize for my subject's actions and thank you for sparing some of them to allow for breithiúnas to occur. I fear if I cannot make an example of them to their peers then my kingdom will not learn that disobedience is dealt with swiftly and justly."

"Why didn't you stop them before they came here?" I asked.

"They had not broken any laws and therefore I could not prevent them from coming. I also did not know who all the traitors were. Punishment for thought is against our laws." The fae queen responded. "The fealltóirí have now acted on their thoughts therefore they can be punished."

"But I thought the fae hated us," Ali stammered when the fae queen turned to look at her. "Isn't that why the portals were sealed all those years ago?"

"No, the portals were sealed to protect the humans." Ríonmháthair replied patiently. "The ruler of our world was unreasonable, so I and a few others supplied the final ingredients for the spell that closed the portals. An uprising happened in Alfheimer, and I came to power. For the last thousand years we have been fighting to maintain control. Within our ranks there are still some that believe they should be allowed to hunt vampires for sport."

She looked pointedly at the fae captives who all cowered as she walked closer to them. "I forbade my people from joining this useless fight. The radicals you have captured did not follow my edict." The captured fae shrunk back at the fae queen's approach. She spoke loudly in a language I did not understand but the captives' reactions were proof it wasn't good.

345

While the fae queen spoke the two male fae that had arrived with her stood quietly at her side with their arms raised in the air, palms facing the captives. The queen's voice rose in volume and I felt a strange tingling in the air around me. I looked at my friends to see if anyone else was feeling anything.

Several were rubbing their arms as if they were chilled. As the queen continued speaking, I noticed a repetition of the words she was saying. Even if I couldn't understand the words, I recognized she was chanting a few phrases over and over again.

The tingling feeling became heated, and pressure was building in the air. Small sparks of blue and white were forming in the outstretched palms of the two male fae. The captives became more agitated as the chanting accelerated. The sparks were now lightning bolts jumping between their palms. My friends shuffled and hopped in agitation. The pressure in the air was starting to feel suffocating. Whatever the fae queen was doing, I wished she would get it over with.

Suddenly, streaks of blue and white electricity shot from the fae's palms. The streaks from each of the fae met, converging into one powerful bolt of energy. I watched in horror as the lightning rushed toward the captured fae, piercing each one through the forehead. It raced from fae to fae, shooting into the heads causing them to disintegrate into charred piles of ash. Within a few minutes every fae that had been captured lay in ash heaps at our feet.

Ríonmháthair ceased her chanting, and her two companions lowered the hands to their sides. When she turned to face us, she noticed our looks of repulsion, "Harsh, but necessary. They knew the consequences of their actions. Their madness would have festered, infecting my kingdom, and in all likelihood spread to all the realms."

Nikolas, the first to recover his voice, stepped forward. With a slight dip in his chin, he acknowledged her words. "Once the shock goes away, I am sure everyone here will agree with your actions. They were your subjects; you dealt with as you saw fit. What about the fae already sent back? Did they meet the same fate?"

The queen's cunning smile did not match the wrath in her eyes. "They did not. Their punishment will not be so quick. I promise they will suffer for many years before I allow them to travel to their next life."

Ríonmháthair tilted her head towards the two males with her. A few minutes of silent communication passed between the three. A sharp nod of her head

346

had the two stepping back from her. "My mates have requested that I ask. Would you be opposed to re-opening the portals?"

We all looked at each other but no one answered. The silence stretched uncomfortably, before I spoke up, "I believe we need to have a discussion about that idea before we can say yes or no."

"I understand perfectly. As it stands right now, we can only come if someone with strengths such as our dear Elodie here, calls us." The beautiful queen assessed Elodie appraisingly. "Perhaps we could meet in a fortnight. We very much wish to restart trade with Gaia and Fabeldyrverden."

I looked around to gauge everyone's thoughts. No one appeared overly for or against reopening the portal between Alfheimer and Gaia. "A fortnight is an acceptable time frame." I searched the crowd for Maria, the leader of Aelwyd but was only able to locate Twyla and a man that looked very similar to Maria. "Twyla, where is your future mother-in-law?"

Twyla, holding hands with the man, came forward. "She fell in battle." She pulled the man forward. "This is her son, Andrew. He is now leader of Aelwyd." The tall dark-haired man stepped closer to Twyla. He seemed uncomfortable with everyone's eyes on him. If I were to come back here in a few years, I expect it would be Twyla leading this commune, not Andrew.

"Would you grant us permission to return here in two weeks to meet the fae queen?" Nikolas asked the timid man.

I thought we would be gone from Gaia by then. *We will be shortly after; we must make sure everything is settled before we disappear into our happily ever after.* I suppose he was right. If we hoped to have a peaceful future, we needed to make sure the present was in good order first.

Andrew looked at his mate and future wife before answering. "That will be fine. You may meet at Aelwyd if you would prefer to have some amenities available."

Nikolas glanced at our friends before speaking to the fae queen. "Will that be acceptable to you?" She agreed then drew Elodie to the side.

I assume to plan for her return since she would not be able to come to Gaia without Elodie working as an anchor for her. Once she finished speaking to Elodie, she and her two mates promptly popped out of our world.

"I suppose we need to decide what to do with the rest of our prisoners." Evan mumbled. Even with Elodie's assurances, his fear for his sister kept his eyes glued to the southwestern sky.

"We need to all be here to make that decision." Nikolas answered him. "Someone should go retrieve your sister and my cousin." James and Davina volunteered to go.

As James and Davina took to the sky, I leaned into Nikolas. No matter how this ended, we would face it together.

Chapter Fifty-Seven

Aisling

Who knew fairy honey would renew our energies and lust for life so quickly. The thunderclap of dragon's wings had us scrambling into our clothes. We emerged from our tent to find Davina, in human form. The war was over, and we were needed back at Aelwyd to discuss a few matters.

"We'll be there soon." Lucian promised. "We just need to gather our supplies." Davina took her dragon form again and the two returned the way they had come.

We tore down and repacked the tent in the bottomless bag. Removing our clothes, we stowed them in the bag as well. I pulled my dragon from around me, my garnet and indigo scales undulated along my skin, seconds later my dragon burst from me.

Lucian, in all his beauty and splendor, took to the sky first. *Handsome!* He blasted into my head. I pushed myself into the air, laughing and happy, I followed my mate. We flew low over the land, scanning for anything of concern. The bloodied battlefield gave way to clean snow covered trees. The sky was clear, and we had an unimpeded view for miles.

About ten minutes into our flight, Lucian's warning broke my revery. He had seen something moving in the snow that was not an animal. He wanted to circle back to investigate. He turned left and I went right, taking ourselves closer to the ground.

There! I had spotted something too. Whoever it was wasn't being very stealthy. The man was stumbling around in the snow and small trees.

We flew closer and to my surprise we found Marcel Fontaine bumbling around the white hillside. Lucian snatched the man up in his left claw. We returned to our original flight path. The man gibbered and giggled the entire way. I had no idea what the hell had happened to the man. My twisted humor found it quite entertaining though. I heard Lucian's laughter in my head; he apparently was enjoying the man's downfall just as much as me.

When we arrived at the field of battle outside Aelwyd, Lucian deposited the insane vampire at his cousin's feet then we flew to a copse of trees to transform and get dressed. Evan reached me first, Ali at his side. His arms were like a vise around me; I am pretty sure I squeezed just as hard back. He finally released me, then to Lucian's surprise engulfed him in a bear hug too.

Ali and I stood with our arms around each other, watching our mates hug. Lucian's initial discomfort bled into a hearty hug back. *Better get used to it,* I grinned at him, *we're huggers.* His brilliant smile sent my heart tripping in my chest.

Evan gave my mate back to me, and Lucian pulled me into his side. Ali kept one of my hands in hers as she wrapped the other arm around Evan. We joined with our friends and family with many more hugs and smiles. Our reunion tapered off, now we need to take stock of our situation.

We learned of the fae queen's arrival and how she meted out justice to the fae here. *Kinda glad we missed that.* Lucian grumbled agreement in my head. I was happy to see Elodie was still here. I made my way closer to her side so I could thank her again for her aid.

"It was all as foretold." Her somber and succinct response effectively closed the subject. She marched over to her blathering brother and yanked him to his feet. She held his face close to hers, staring deep into his eyes.

"Whatever you did to him," she spoke to Cassandra, "has sent his mind far away. He is mostly harmless now, but I prefer not to worry that he will recover." With no fanfare at all, she reached up and separated his head from his body. She dropped each piece like discarded trash. "I shall return in fourteen days." Elodie sped south, barely a blur across the white fields.

"We have two weeks to decide if we want to reopen the portal to Alfheimer." Nikolas tore my attention away from the headless Marcel. "My mother shared the ritual with Diana, Malina and Temperence."

"I think we're all in agreement," Almerinda moved to the center, kicking Marcel's head to the side. "Fabeldyrverden should be opened."

No one spoke out against that idea. "But what of Alfheimer?" I asked, my voice rang loud across the field. "Lucian and I were aided by the fae." I pointed at the clumps of ash, all that remained of the enemy fae. "But if not for them, we wouldn't have needed that aid in the first place."

"The queen said she dealt with the traitors." A vampire I didn't recognize argued.

"We lost thirty of our brothers!" Brian's thundering voice ruptured the air like a bomb. "Look around, how many of us died because of them?"

"I agree," Damian interjected. I didn't know Almerinda's mate well, but it would seem he had a following as fifteen or so vampires had formed behind him. "From a strategic standpoint though, keeping them locked away is not the best idea."

"Really?" Brian growled back. "I would think them not having access would minimize any damage they could do."

"I suppose but look what happened here." Damian swept his hands, showcasing the blood and bodies that still littered the field. "If there were a way to safely give them limited access, we would be able to keep an eye on them, maybe not get blindsided again."

Nikolas held his hand up for silence. Nikolas must have had a solution that he was not quite ready to share with the rest of us. "We'll be right back." Then he and Cassandra opened a portal to Fabeldyrverden and walked through it.

About five minutes passed when a new portal opened, ending our continued arguing. Nikolas stepped through with Cassandra and two other people. Judging by how similar the woman looked to Lucian, I assumed the two newcomers were Serafina and her mate Arlien. My assumption was confirmed when she rushed to embrace her brother, sobbing, tears streaming down her cheeks.

"I thought you died." Serafina whispered quietly to Lucian. She held her left hand up and I saw the ring that once adorned Lucian's hand on hers. The colors were the same, but it had conformed to fit her smaller hand.

"It was close," Lucian's voice was muffled by Serafina's long hair.

Arlien pulled her from Lucian's arms after almost ten minutes. He tucked her into his side, whether to give her support or keep her from running back into her brother's arms, I couldn't say.

Nikolas cleared his throat, "I assume we're still deadlocked." At our nods he added, "That is why I retrieved Sera and Arlien." He focused intently on Lucian and me. "Am I correct in the knowledge that you will not be returning to Fabeldyrverden as king?"

His question made me squirm. Now that Lucian could return, I worried would he still choose me over his kingdom. "You are correct." The breath I was holding rushed out of me at the same time Sera gasped with shock at the same moment.

"What do you mean?" She marched up to stare at him, her eyes flashing red and orange. "Why?" She poked him in the chest.

"Many reasons." He grabbed her hand, twining her fingers with his. "The biggest one is standing next to me. Sera, this is Aisling." Serafina smiled at me kindly. I saw no evidence that she was angry with me over her brother's decision. "When you saw me come here and possibly never come back to Fabeldyrverden it did not mean that I died. The ring you wear, I gave up freely with no coercion."

"Are you certain, brother?" Serafina held her hand out to him.

"I have never been more certain of anything in my life." He gripped her hand in his, smiling as he used his free hand to grab mine. "I have spent my entire life either preparing to be king or being king. The past few months, even though the shadow of death hung over us, have been the happiest I have ever been." He pulled me closer, "Aisling is the reason I feel that way. I will return long enough to officially abdicate the thrown to you but after that I go wherever Aisling goes."

"I honor your choice, brother." Serafina replied to her brother with a small grin then turned to me. "Please tell me you will visit us in Fabeldyrverden often."

"Absolutely, I want to explore the worlds." I promised my new family.

"Now that we have that settled." Nikolas interrupted our little love fest. "We have a proposal from the fae queen to reopen the portals permanently. We can't come to a consensus on whether we should or not. Everyone wants to reopen the portal to the dragon's realm. My proposal to you," Nikolas indicated Serafina and Arlien with a chin tilt, "is whether you would allow the Alfheimer portal to be placed in Fabeldyrverden rather than Gaia."

"Who is the queen of the fae now?" Arlien asked, speaking for the first time since they arrived.

"Ríonmháthair." Nikolas answered.

"What happened to Braetlin?"

"Ríonmháthair said there was a revolution about a thousand years ago." Cassandra answered. "She didn't elaborate much further than that."

"Aengus is still with her." Lucian told his sister and Arlien. "He helped us in our battle."

Serafina paced for a minute with Arlien at her side. Occasionally they would stop and stare at each other, communicating soundlessly, then resume their pacing. They came to a stop, apparently coming to a decision.

"I propose that the portal to Fabeldyrverden be placed somewhere near here. We shall allow the portal to Alfheimer to be placed in our realm in an out-of-the-way location. Thus, anyone wanting to use the portals will not be able to just wander across them."

Nikolas addressed Andrew and Twyla to ensure they would take responsibility for the dragon portal on this side. Twyla squeezed Andrew's hand as he stammered agreement, his Adam's apple bobbing.

Once that decision was made, we turned our attention to the prisoners. I would love to say that we all voted in favor of letting them go to live their lives in peace. We knew that was unrealistic and therefore our more pragmatic natures won. The captives had already demonstrated that they would rise against us and if given the chance would do so again.

We had lost so many friends and family that the decision was unanimous. A few of them tried to argue that they were just following orders but that did not sway us. Once they knew what we had decided many of them tried to either flee or fight. To the last, they were all put to death. The snow drank their blood hungrily, crimson spreading like blooming roses.

The next two weeks were spent in Aelwyd. We all worked together to clean the fields of body parts, restoring them to their former pristine beauty. A little more than half our forces did not survive.

My family did not come through unscathed. I crumpled to the ground, Lucian rushing to my side, when I found their bodies. Ciaran and Ciara, the twins, my fun-loving brother and sister. Gods, if I could bring the ones we killed back, just to kill them again, I would. I trembled in Lucian's arms, wailing sobs to the dark sky above us.

Brian and the remaining wolves left the day after the fight. Michael had ordered them all home. James remained, no longer part of the pack. A service would be held for the fallen wolves. We all plan to attend. I hoped that Michael's mate would be more welcoming to me now that I had found my own mate. I suppose I'll find out once Brian gives us the date.

Almerinda and Damian planned to set things right at Council headquarters. Gerard would be traveling with them. Almerinda's team was splintered now due to life changes. She was working on meshing the guard she inherited from Luis and the remaining members of her personal squad.

Her guard would now consist of William, the witch, Samantha and Frederic, mated vampires, Kalinda a vampire witch hybrid and the vampires who had served Luis prior to his death. Alicea, Arthur, Daniel, Heather and Andrea had all come to fight at our side. Daniel and Heather had not survived. Brian also planned to return to her team as soon as Michael released him from pack duties.

James and Davina volunteered to go to South America and find Alistair Reynolds so they could free the different people he had kidnapped. He would be brought back for trial. They would leave after the portals were opened and planned to travel to Fabeldyrverden once Alistair was captured. Serafina requested that Alistair face judgment for his crimes in the dragon realm. Almerinda gave it some thought and decided that it was a grand idea.

Cleaning completed, the fields around Aelwyd glistened white with fresh fallen snow. The portal to Fabeldyrverden was opened in the center of Aelwyd. Arianna's three witches performed the ritual while borrowing power from Cassandra, Kalinda, Twyla and about twenty other witches amongst us.

Word would be spread to the different species around the world that travel to the dragon realm would be open. Anyone wishing to travel would have to make the trip to northern Canada to do so. Serafina and Arlien, the soon to be crowned queen and king of said realm, promised to send dragons to live in Aelwyd to help protect the portal.

The fae queen, Ríonmháthair, would arrive tomorrow. Elodie returned this evening in her usual style. To this day I will never understand why she was always dressed as if she were going to a fancy ball. What was more impressive was that she never damaged any of her clothing even when she butchered her enemies.

She warned us that Ríonmháthair may not be entirely happy with the Alfheimer portal being placed in the dragon realm rather than Gaia. I suppose we will find out tomorrow when the fae queen arrived.

For tonight, I would spend it wrapped in the arms of my mate.

Chapter Fifty-Eight

Cassandra

Grief and joy walked hand in hand through Aelwyd. We all mourned the loss of so many lives at the hands of Fraxinus and his allies. Delilah had come to see me a couple days ago to share a vision she had seen that didn't make much sense to her.

She told me she saw Arianna in a small cottage having tea with a rather large man with red hair. The couple were smiling and laughing, clearly enjoying each other's company as more than just friends if their scant attire was any indication. The man's booming laugh shook the teacups as Arianna's toes curled against his thigh.

She didn't know if Nikolas should be told or not since he said he saw her die. I thought about it for a while then decided I would tell him. Delilah's vision probably didn't mean anything, there would be no secrets between us.

His face lit up like a child who just got their favorite toy as a gift. For as long as he can remember his mother has always told him when she died, she would hopefully enter Sidhes. If she was true and faithful to good, she would travel to Sidhes, or the Otherworld. She always joked that it was her retirement plan.

When he was younger, this made little sense to him since dragons lived forever unless they were killed. After his sister took control of him, he began to understand her mindset better. She knew someday she would die since she also knew someday her mate would need to be stopped. Delilah must have seen her in Sidhes. Perhaps one day we would go there too, but not for many years to come.

The fae queen was due to arrive at any moment. We all gathered in the center of Aelwyd near the portal to Fabeldyrverden, our breaths puffing in the cold air. The entire camp was present. We meant to show we were united in our decision and, if necessary, would fight to enforce that decision.

Elodie pushed by us, stepping into the open area in front of us. She held a small dagger in her hand. She sliced it across her palm then flung the pooling blood into the wind. A line, more like a crack, appeared in front of her.

The queen emerged through the crack with a loud pop, followed closely by her two mates. Three fae in burgundy rounded out the group. Ríonmháthair showed no surprise at the amount of people surrounding her.

"Have you decided against reopening the portal?" Her melodic voice asked.

Serafina and Arlien moved to greet the queen. "Ríonmháthair," Serafina inclined her chin in greeting. "How wonderful it is to see you again after all these years." The fae queen smiled at Sera's greeting but her eyes remained distrustful. Sera continued with deliberate slowness. "We have decided no such thing. Alfheimer will be reopened just not directly into Gaia."

"Why not to Gaia?" Aengus asked. He and his brothers, Brogan and Eoghan had come in support of their queen. "Elodie, what deceit is this?"

"Do not worry, brother dear." Elodie replied. "I swear on our family's bloodline that there is no deception."

"Ríonmháthair, Aengus," Serafina's voice cut like honey in whiskey, sweet but with bite. "The people of Gaia need time to become accustomed to the new reality they have been thrust into. I proposed reopening the portal to Alfheimer in Fabeldyrverden. Our friendship can be renewed and passage to Gaia can be granted to those who wish it so long as they prove true in that rekindled friendship."

Elodie moved closer to Jace and Jaxson, taking a protective stance as if she expected the fae to reject this proposal and attack. Ríonmháthair met Serafina's steady gaze with a hard stare. I shifted closer to Nikolas, pulling power from him. After a few moments of tense silence, a smile spread across the fae queen's face.

"Well stated, young Queen Serafina. Fabeldyrverden will be in sure and steady hands with you at the helm. We accept the proposal with the hope that someday we will prove true to that friendship and be able to travel to Gaia directly."

As one we all relaxed, the crisis we worried would come had been averted with some pretty words from Serafina. She would make an amazing queen. The pride on Lucian's face told me that he felt the same. Sera then announced where the portal would be placed, causing everyone to turn their focus to Nikolas and me.

"We have decided the portal will be placed at our summer residence. Nikolas and Cassandra will be living there. With a small contingent of palace guards they will protect the portal." Serafina stated. The inquisitive stares from those around us made me squirm a little. Nikolas held my hand in his, sending me comfort through our bond.

356

Now that the war was over, I couldn't wait to leave this realm and retire to our country estate in Fabeldyrverden. I didn't think I would ever be truly accepted by the Community here since I had been used by the Council for so long as their torturer. Nikolas had ingratiated himself with more of the people than I had, but he was looking forward to no longer being under their scrutiny.

Serafina and Arlien escorted the fae queen and her guards through the portal to Fabeldyrverden. Malina, Diana and Temperence followed behind. They would work the spell to reopen the portal to Alfheimer. Serafina assured them that Profitis Magda and her acolytes would be able to aid them so no more witches were needed at this time. With the departure of the fae queen and her entourage, everyone resumed their previous duties.

Aisling pulls me aside, "Why didn't you tell me you were going to live in the dragon realm?"

"We decided a few weeks ago." I answered, pulling my arm from her tight grip. "No one knows me in Fabeldyrverden like they do here. I just want some peace with my mate and our children."

"Your children?" Aisling sputtered. "Are you pregnant already?" She stares at my belly as if expecting something to burst out of it any second now.

"I am." I answer and her eyes flash to my face for a few seconds then return to searching my abdomen. "I am not going to give birth any second now. I am just about nine weeks along; in another week I won't be able to change into a dragon until after giving birth."

"I am so happy for you." Aisling blurted happily then turned more serious. "Are you scared?"

"Of what?" I asked, matching her solemnity but not sure where it stemmed from.

"I don't know how dragon babies work. I mean do you lay an egg or give birth to a human? I studied every damn type of being I could possibly mate with and now I've mated with one I never even knew existed." The normally calm and collected Aisling was close to hyperventilating.

"I talked to Arianna a little about it before she died." I pulled Aisling to sit beside me on a wooden bench with a heavy heart. I miss Arianna daily. "Serafina was also able to shed some light on the subject. Don't worry; when you get pregnant you will not lay an egg."

I laughed when she released her pent-up breath. "Whew, that's a relief."

"What I have learned so far is that a hard shell, like an egg I suppose, forms around the baby at the tenth week. The normal length of pregnancy for a woman carrying a dragon baby is eleven months. Once the shell forms, I'll have thirty-eight more weeks. When the baby is ready to come, the shell breaks apart and is expelled from the body. I guess that is kind of like when a human woman's water breaks. Once the shell comes out, labor begins and from what has been described it sounds just like any other species in labor."

Her look of relief was almost laughable; then I remembered how scared I was when I first realized I was pregnant. Aisling at least had women in her life that would have prepared her for most of it. She thanked me for the information and our conversation segued into other concerns she had.

"Okay, so, nine months of not being able to change into a dragon or cat. I can handle that." She nudged my shoulder almost knocking me off the bench then pulled me in for a side arm hug. "I am a little upset that you're going to another world though."

I poked her playfully in the ribs. "It's not as if you and Lucian can't just open a portal to visit us at any time from wherever you happen to be."

"True, true." She mumbled. "You will have to let me know when the kiddo will be born and we will come to visit then."

"I would like that." My throat tightened. This woman who'd fought beside me would now be a portal away. "Please don't wait that long to visit though."

"We will visit so often you'll get sick of seeing our faces." Aisling promised.

Chapter Fifty-Nine

Aisling

Ten years have passed, that's how long it took for the nightmares to loosen their grip on me. For the first time in all those years Lucian and I have come back to the little Alaskan island where we met. I still refuse to return to Aelwyd or Canada.

The island has changed in a lot of ways since I first came here all those years ago. The death of Arianna lifted all her spells, and the island became visible to humans for a short time. Twyla and Andrew shared the spells they used on Aelwyd and hid the island before it was noticed. My family and Arianna's coven have turned it into a small village.

There is now a small port for visitors to land at as well as a bustling little town with several shops and a small inn. Travelers wanting to use the portal to Fabeldyrverden come through the island for screening before being given access to Aelwyd and the permanent portal.

Tygus stays on the island now and with the use of his magical ship, anyone who is approved to travel is taken to the port of Kugluktuk. Twyla has also set up a meeting point where anyone who wishes can use the calygreyhounds to traverse the terrain between the port and Aelwyd quickly.

Jace, Cat, Gabriel and Robert all returned to Pennsylvania after the fight. Jonesie and Delilah went with them. Jonesie decided to sell his block of brownstones in Cleveland due to the loss of all but Delilah and two vampires from his den of iniquity, as Almerinda liked to call it.

He bought a house near Jace and Cat. They plan to buy out any humans living near them and turn their neighborhood into a sanctuary of sorts for wayward supernaturals. At last count they owned eleven out of the twelve houses on their street, leaving only one human holdout.

Evan and Ali had their first child two years ago, a boy. They named him Cillian after our oldest brother. He even looked a lot like Cillian, which was both wonderful and sad at the same time. Ali is pregnant again and expects to give birth around the same time as me. I think if she is able, she'll try to have more children than my mum and da did.

Our travels have taken us all around both our worlds. We even went to Alfheimer to visit Aengus. Old wounds have healed especially after the fae queen wiped out all the rebellious fae. Lucian was happy to have his old friend back after more than a thousand years. I even confirmed the suspicion I had when talking with Aengus and his brothers, Brogan and Eoghan. Something Elodie had said once made me wonder.

She referred to Aengus as brother and mentioned their family's bloodline. It was his parents that had stolen Elodie as a child and tinkered with her DNA, making her part fae. He would not go into details about how the fae performed the tinkering he mentioned. He did say however that without the occasional integration of fresh blood into their families, the fae would eventually begin to die out.

Before the portals were re-opened, like the dragons, the fae were beginning to have problems with fertility and mating. I took that to mean they had started stealing children again but decided it was not a hill I was willing to die on. From what I understood, the children were returned to their parents unaware of what had happened until they started to gain their powers. Almerinda was aware of the practice and would deal with it, however she saw fit.

The Council has been re-imagined under Almerinda's rule. With her mate, Damian, at her side and his military training things were changing drastically for the Council and the Community in general. For centuries she had resisted being the one in charge. After the traitors within the ranks were found out she felt she had no choice.

Tatiana, a high-ranking Council member and a traitor, was given a choice, give up all her co-conspirators and in exchange Serafina and Arlien would grant permission for her to return to Fabeldyrverden. Tatiana's mate had been sealed away when the portals were closed. She had only worked with Fraxinus and the Fontaines because she was desperate to get back to her mate.

Tatiana agreed to the ultimatum and named everyone that had supported Fraxinus and the Fontaines in their bid for domination. With a long list of traitors, Almerinda wielded her new powers like a scalpel, cutting away rot while preserving what still lived.

Almerinda was now the head of the Council and had handpicked a few advisors. The Council still had the regional leaders in place but now there would be a panel of ten who would have final say over any changes.

Almerinda had asked Lucian and I to be two of the ten advisors, we politely declined. Neither one of us wanted anything to do with politics. Lucian was basking in his newfound freedom from being the king of his land. I was just enjoying not having to be responsible for anyone else.

Jaxson and Tanya agreed, which was rather surprising to me since Jaxson had retreated from the Community when they failed to deal with Amanda properly for so long. Evan and Ali would also be two of the ten but only if they could perform their duties from the Alaskan island, they called home.

The reshaping of the Council and Community took some time but any time someone put up a fuss or grumbled, Almerinda simply reminded them that if not for those of us who stood against the fae there wouldn't be a Council or Community.

While we traveled the worlds, Cormac built us a small cottage near my favorite waterfall. We would be settling down for a bit. Our first child is due in a few months, and we want her to be raised around family.

Cassandra and Nikolas will be coming to visit closer to my due date. The two of them have been busy monitoring the portal to Alfheimer as well as single handedly trying to increase the dragon population.

They are on their fourth pregnancy now. They have seven children; the first-born was a single girl named Arianna after Nikolas' mother. They had three sets of twins after that. Cassandra says this will be her last one, but I'll believe it when I see it.

Lucian and I sit on the mossy ground beside the pool of water formed by the waterfall. My back leans against a tree, legs stretched in front of me with my favorite person's head lying in my lap. I run my fingers through his thick hair and marvel at the beautiful man before me.

Handsome. I hear through our mind link and chuckle under my breath. One of his hands rests on my swollen abdomen as he communes with our daughter. *She is content.* His swirling eyes open to meet my slate grey eyes.

Every day, I thank the Fates, Gods and anyone else who will listen for sending this man to be my mate. A satisfied grin spreads across his mouth as he reaches up to pull my lips down to his in a scorching kiss that has me panting for more. Soon I'll be too far along for this kind of play but not yet.

I pull back and yank his blue shirt over his head. My hands run down his smooth skin, his chest muscles bunching, scales of red and orange ripple under my touch. His hands reach under my shirt, cupping my breasts he tweaks my nipples, pulling a gasp of pleasure from me. Lowering me to the ground, our kiss intensifies as the sun sets behind us.

Thank you to everyone who took the time to read these books. I have more stories to share and hope when I publish them you consider reading them as well. Jace, Cat, Evan, Ali, Nikolas, Cassandra, Aisling and Lucian live on and may show their faces again someday.

Please leave a review on whichever platform you purchased or borrowed them from.

Did you know that very few readers leave a rating but for every new review (good or bad) an author squeals their delight? Reviews help your favorite authors gain visibility. Please do your part to help make them successful.

If you are interested in learning about upcoming books feel free to reach out to me at katiescarletedwards@gmail.com

www.ingramcontent.com/pod-product-compliance
Lightning Source LLC
Chambersburg PA
CBHW070733180626
46818CB00007B/2825